CATHEDRAL CITY

CATHEDRAL CITY

Gregory Hinton

KENSINGTON BOOKS
http://www.kensingtonbooks.com

KENSINGTON BOOKS are published by

Kensington Publishing Corp.
850 Third Avenue
New York, NY 10022

Copyright © 2001 by Gregory Hinton

All Kensington titles, imprints, and distributed lines are available at special quantity discounts for bulk purchases for sales promotion, premiums, fund-raising, educational or institutional use.

Special book excerpts or customized printings can also be created to fit specific needs. For details, write or phone the office of the Kensington Special Sales Manager: Kensington Publishing Corp., 850 Third Avenue, New York, NY 10022, Attn. Special Sales Department. Phone: 1-800-221-2647.

Kensington and the K logo Reg. U.S. Pat. & TM Off.

Library of Congress Card Catalogue Number: 00-109712
ISBN 1-57566-849-1

First Printing: June, 2001
10 9 8 7 6 5 4 3 2 1

Printed in the United States of America

For my brother and Ron

"We've razed downtown rather than rehabili-
tated it," said city spokeswoman Julie Baumer
of the [Cathedral City] real estate makeover.
—Los Angeles Times, April 13, 1998

ACKNOWLEDGMENTS

I would like to express my love and gratitude to Tom Ferris, Christine Dziadecki, Dirk Shafer, Randal Kleiser, Susan Fine Moore, Niki Marvin, David Groff, Greg Sarris, and Fred Ebb; my parents, Jeanne and Kip Hinton; my agent Fred Morris and my editor John Scognamiglio.

Thank you to Lupe Ontiveros for introducing me to Thelma Garcia, Alva Moreno, Sylvia Tzoc, and Sylvia Valerio at the East Los Angeles Center for Women; Matt Lopez of the Imperial County Film Commission; Officer Henry Rolon of The United States Border Patrol; the staff and volunteers at The Desert AIDS Project. While writing my book I hung out at The Hollywood Hills Coffee Shop, Espresso Mi Cultura, Musso-Frank, The Kings Road Café, and Orso.

For support, patience, and encouragement my deepest thanks to Donna and David Alvarez, Dianne Ardourel, Carol Assa, Monica Avila, Diane Baker, Kerry Barden, Bess Barrows, Linda Blazy, Brandon and Cara Campanella, Lynette Cimini, Martin Curland, Barbara DeWitt, Tom De Simone, John Dziadecki, Carmen Flores, Santiago Flores, Patricia Glatfelter, Scott Golden, Marjorie Graham, Sara Hammerman, Skip and Victoria Harris, Gilbert Hernandez, Ann Johnson, Nancy Kelley, Kathy Kennedy, Marylin Kent, Gene and Harriet Kevorkian, Michael Kohn, Christina Lehr, Christopher and Linda Lewis, Jorge Ivan Lopez, Jose Lopez, Jack Lorenz, Dessie Markovsky, Paul McKibbins, Virginia McDowall, Elfriede Morrissey, Phylis and Yasha Nicolayevsky, Edward Nachtriebe, Pat Oygar, Karl Romaine, Michael Roth, Peter Rudy, Pablo Santiago, Diane Schnitzer, Charlotte Sheedy, Sam Smith, Jose de la Torre, Simon Tukc, David Van Houten, Mike Vayne, Venus Ventura, Steven Wolfe, and Stewart Weiner.

Remembering, particularly, Steve Rutberg and his wonderful family . . .

PART ONE

Retablo of
Maria Lourdes Castillo
August 1997

1

A Marriage

To the priest, he resembled a factory worker in an American Realist painting. All tendon, angle, and angst. Father Gene had noticed him at morning Mass, humbly handsome, entering the cool sanctuary at half past seven, sitting near the back alone, the only Anglo in a sea of Latino faces.

Outside the entrance to St. Louis Catholic Church stood a statue of St. Anthony, donated by the Frank Sinatra family. At the base of the pedestal the words *Pray For Us* were engraved, but it actually looked like it read *Pray For Us, Mr. Sinatra*, because the Sinatra name was ten times the size of St. Anthony's.

Mr. Sinatra had been very generous with the residents of Cathedral City. Instead of attending Christmas Eve midnight Mass in the more upscale cities of nearby Palm Springs or Rancho Mirage, the Sinatra family often came to Cathedral City's St. Louis Parish, where parishioners were mostly poor Latinos from the local desert barrio of stucco and tar paper shacks.

As others filed forward to receive Holy Communion, the Anglo man remained on his knees, powerfully built, sensual, a shock of thick black hair crowning his lowered head. He looked to be in his late thirties. He wore a white T-shirt, blue jeans, and a pair of well-worn work boots. His face and arms were the color of light bronze.

By the time Mass was concluded, he was about to disappear, but the curious priest managed to catch his eye and indicated that he wanted to speak with him after the service. The man nodded briefly, suggesting that he would stay, but to Father Gene he seemed vastly uncomfortable with the idea. To prevent him from sneaking away, the priest shot down the aisle and trapped him by standing at the end of his pew while he wished the other parishioners good day.

Father Gene spoke fluent Spanish and patted several hands. Some of them seemed to know his prisoner fidgeting nervously behind him. If they didn't greet him, their eyes widened in recognition, even surprise. Finally a tiny woman nodded and spoke his name in acknowledgment. Her name was Inez Quintero.

"Hello, Mister Kenny." More of a statement of disapproving fact than a greeting. She kept walking.

"Hello, Inez," Kenny replied. Finally the priest and Kenny were standing alone. He motioned for Kenny to follow him.

"I used to want to be a priest."

"So did I," the priest laughed, thinking himself rather droll. It occurred to him that he wanted to impress the younger man, for Father Gene was older by three decades. To calm himself down, he clasped his hands, took a deep breath, and traced a life line with his thumb. "So what made you reconsider?"

"I guess I wasn't really cut out for it."

They were sitting in the parish office, and after inspecting its appointments—the plain table, a cluttered bookshelf, a simple wooden crucifix—Kenny fixed his eyes on the priest as if maybe still considering the idea. He was framed in the office window, and behind him the priest could see clouds gathering over the softly listing desert foothills of the Little San Bernardino Mountain Range. An August storm was gathering. Even with the air conditioning, the room would soon be wet with humidity.

"Maybe I should explain why I wanted to talk with you." Father Gene cleared his throat. "Why don't you partake of the host?"

Kenny stared at him blankly.

"Why don't you take Holy Communion?"

"I haven't been to confession."

"How long has it been?"

"Over twenty years, Father . . ."

"Care to elaborate?"

Kenny shrugged. He smiled apologetically. "Lately I find myself missing the church. I always liked weekday Masses. Especially the mornings. You have a daily morning Mass."

"So we do," said the priest. Then he pressed on. "I think you'd benefit greatly by partaking of the host. The body and blood of Christ."

"And to do so would require my confession."

"Well, yes."

"I'm not prepared to do that just yet. I haven't made up my mind to come back."

"If you don't mind me being blunt, son, what seems to be the problem here?"

Another long silence.

"I was told I didn't deserve a relationship with God."

"By *who?*"

"I think you know what I'm talking about here."

"I think I do." Father Gene leaned forward and clasped his hands over his knee. "But you should understand that the church's position on this issue has much, for lack of a better way of putting it, *matured.* The church's official position is as follows. We recognize and welcome—"

Kenny looked at him wearily.

"You are not by your nature in conflict with the Catholic Church. Look, I know who you are. You have a restaurant down on the highway. I've been in it many times. Not dressed like this, of course. I've known Nick for years. What brings you here?"

"What brings you to our bar?"

Loneliness, thought the priest, but he said nothing.

"I get lonely, too." Kenny read his thoughts, only the priest knew he was referring to more spiritual matters.

"Abstinence from sex outside of marriage. This in no way persecutes your minority group from any other."

"I've been committed to the same person for eighteen years."

"But you can't *marry,* son."

Kenny's fingers grasped the arm of his chair. They were thick and expressive. Outside, the light changed. Somewhere over Cathedral City, high above the desert floor, a cloud formation muted the harsh rays of morning sunlight. Now they were sitting in shadowy darkness.

"Maybe I should take off . . ."

"It wasn't my goal to be so confrontational," Father Gene began to apologize.

"You weren't being confrontational."

"Then what's the problem?"

"I just won't turn my back on Nick for anything," and Kenny stood up.

"Let's take a deep breath here," said Father Gene. "Please, sit back down."

Secretly he was hoping he hadn't chased him away for good. He had begun to look forward to seeing him every morning. Now Kenny was staring at him uncomfortably, really wanting to escape. "Just tell me one thing before you go. Why did you want to be a priest?"

Kenny spoke plainly. "I liked the ritual. I liked the silence. I liked the humility. And I like prayer. I still like prayer."

"I like prayer, too, son. You don't need to be a priest to pray a lot."

"I know. I'm no priest and I pray a lot."

"I hope you'll continue to do some of it here at St. Louis." The priest stood, feeling as if he had been detaining Kenny against his will and should release him. To his surprise, Kenny remained seated. Father Gene hesitated, not knowing what to do.

Suddenly he wanted this perplexing man to leave. He had no business calling him in here in the first place. He was still self-deceiving, even as he was about to retire. Kenny finally stood up.

"Someday I'll come back and tell you about it. Why I thought I didn't belong."

Oh *good,* the priest said to himself. Just great. He pressed his fingers to his temples as though he had a throbbing headache.

"I've upset you," Kenny murmured.

"No, it's just been a frustrating several weeks. A number of my parishioners are getting eviction notices. Many of them are very poor. They have no place to move. They're very distraught."

"Why are they getting evicted?"

"The city renewal plan. Surely you know."

Kenny looked at him blankly.

"They're tearing down most of the old construction in Cathedral City. A lot of houses around the church. All the way to the highway. Do you own your property?"

"We live up in the cove."

"The nice houses won't be touched. It's the barrio. From Grove to H Street. That's where your bar is. Are you relocating?"

"Our bar isn't getting torn down."

"You own your own land then."

"No. We rent. But we aren't being torn down."

"You're lucky then." The priest stood up. "I'm glad. Nick's has been in the desert forever. It wouldn't be Cathedral City without it."

Father Gene hesitated, then nodded for Kenny to leave. Before Kenny left, he cleared his throat and asked, "Father, do you believe in miracles?"

"I wouldn't be much of a priest if I didn't," he chided.

"Then maybe you can explain what they're *for.*"

"It's been my experience that when God is gracious enough to perform a miracle, it typically gets explained away as an obscure scientific phenomenon, superstition, or coincidence. I never saw any specific miracles and frankly I'm glad. I prefer to rely on my faith, the belief in things without seeing . . ."

"Never mind, then," Kenny said sadly, and Father Gene felt bad. Finally Kenny ambled into the hallway, and maddeningly the priest felt compelled to follow him out to the parking lot.

"If you've experienced a miracle, I'd certainly be open to discussing it with you."

"Sorry I took your time," Kenny muttered, and began the long walk across the pavement to an older four-wheel drive with the top sawed off. Alone against the backdrop of Cathedral City's cloudy desert vista, staccato bursts of sunbeams scorched the priest's black robe. He felt like the last rag tag crow in a traveling circus shooting gallery. Occasionally rays of sunlight would pierce through, bouncing on the pavement as Kenny continued walking. They had the effect of lightning bolts being fired from the heavens.

At who? the priest wondered. Him or me? The vision of the troubled man maneuvering the open truck out of the church parking lot on its huge rubber tires caused an involuntary outburst of emotion from the priest. After Kenny waved goodbye, and long after the truck roared down Glenn Avenue toward the highway, Father Gene stayed rooted to his spot. "God Bless," he was crying. "God bless, God bless . . ."

Soon raindrops began splatting on the pavement at his feet. A hot wind came up, and a burst of wet sage perfumed the air. Moments later a nun appeared in the door of the rectory. He saw her look up at the threatening sky.

"Father Gene! Come inside before you get washed away."

Reluctantly he trudged slowly up the steaming black pavement to the church rectory.

Sometimes when it rains, the old colors of the stucco walls of the bar bleed through, a pentimento homage to past establishments. In one instance it might shimmer the color of desert sage. Then a sud-

den cloud change might deepen it to a pale, earthy umber, under-
scoring the fact that the structure had a long history before Kenny
and Nick painted it a soft, muted pink.

A restaurant location can have many themes, many facades, but
few could boast such historically disparate clienteles as Nick's out in
Cathedral City, the tiny desert community situated on a lonely
stretch of highway somewhere between Palm Springs and Rancho
Mirage.

The local residents of Cathedral City were often confused by the
antics of the men who owned the bar. Today Nick lined the entire
street with pairs of red shoes—red shoes of all shapes and sizes to
commemorate the death of *After Dark* photographer Kenn Duncan.
When a shapely but heavyset El Salvadoran woman discovered a
pair of red platform high heels, she left her own espadrilles in exchange, hoping to wear her new shoes dancing.

"Who's Kenn Duncan?" she asked her friend as they scurried
away. A banner flapped in the breeze above them. KENN DUNCAN
DAY—2 FOR 1 IF YOU WEAR RED SHOES!

"Maybe the shoes were his!" the friend observed, and they both
dissolved into gales of laughter. They ducked behind the bar into the
alley.

Another successful desert rat promotion.

"This bar has been here since the *thirties*. Al Capone used to gam-
ble in the basement. Joan *Crawford* and John Garfield drank martinis unnoticed in this very booth!"

Today a desert restaurant critic walked in and asked Nick if he
might be willing to answer a few questions for her weekly column.
Nick's seven-year campaign to be reviewed in the local desert newspaper had finally borne fruit. Nick spun around, a tall handsome
blond man of indeterminate age with perfect teeth, tan and gregarious; a happy fool who liked to drink.

"Why did you name the bar after yourself?" The critic fumbled
with her tape recorder. She was a golf blonde—slender with dry
bleached hair, tan freckled arms—a first wife with tiny lines draining
into her upper lip. She noted the restaurant's decor. Broadway show
posters. Framed photographs of old movie stars. A wall dedicated to
the career of Frank Sinatra. A wall dedicated to Nick himself.

"The bar was me and vice versa," he replied. "If Palm Springs is
Zsa Zsa and Eva is Rancho Mirage, Cathedral City is surely the

Magda of all the Gabors. This bar represents what Cathedral City had always stood for. The outsider. A church for the loner. The individual who wants a little privacy. The desert rat. A place where you go not to be seen."

"You think of yourself as an outsider?"

"I was raised in a Catholic orphanage. Orphans never feel like they have a home. But it gave me a love of people. A desire to make others comfortable. To nurture."

"So what happens to this church under Cathedral City's proposed renewal plan? Will you relocate or just close down?" She referred to a massive facelift planned for the area which would displace current business owners and residents to make way for a huge city hall and shopping complex, complete with Imax theaters, department stores, an ice-skating rink, and food courts.

Nick paused to take a swill of his drink. "Luckily, Sam Singer, our landlord, has a keen sense of history. He won't tell you but I will. He won the bar in a poker game from a Chicago mob boss. Later he passed it on to me. He was here. He saw it all. We aren't going anywhere."

"Do you think the previous patrons would be disappointed by what it's come to?"

"I don't understand what you mean." He signaled his bartender, Marcella, to fix him another drink. Marcella was a sexy, hard-looking black woman who'd been eavesdropping on the interview.

"She's asking if you mostly serve homosexuals," Marcella interrupted, imperious from her position behind the bar.

"Well, not exactly," the critic sniffed, looking at her with annoyance. Then she looked back at Nick. "But do you? I'd have to alert my readers."

"No, our menu is continental. Mostly steaks and chops." He grinned extravagantly. "Everyone is welcome at Nick's. Look around for yourself."

The Happy Hour crowd was starting to arrive, a snappy mixture of straight desert retirees, men, women; some singles, some in pairs. A smattering of gay men lined the bar, joking with Marcella. Men in white mesh tank tops or Hawaiian shirts. Old men swathed in gold chains and tennis bracelets buying rounds of drinks for drifting, muscular, sun-beaten younger guys. They all seemed to know each other. Seemed like they got on great. Glad to escape the heat. The white-hot light of those August desert days.

"That said, what do your customers most like to eat?"

"Let me start by saying this," he grinned. "We don't eat at Nick's . . .
We *dine.*"

Later that afternoon after Nick wandered down the alley to the
corner liquor store to buy cigarettes, he found himself surrounded in
the alley by three blonde teenagers—one willowy girl and two
angelic-looking boys. They looked like Ralph Lauren models, only
creepy and malevolent. Kenny always told Nick if he had to be
mugged by any ethnic gang in a dark alley, the group he'd fear most
would be middle-class Anglo teenagers.

The girl, Misty, spoke first. "Will you buy us some beer?"

"*No,*" Nick said authoritatively. He was still flying from his interview. His confidence was at an all-time high.

"We *have* the money."

Nick surveyed their faces and sighed.

"Judging by your new SUV, you probably own a condo, too, but
you're underage and I won't buy you any alcohol."

"It's just a fucking six-pack of Budweiser, *maaaan.*"

"Case," the other boy corrected her. Misty looked at him and
laughed really, really hard.

"A *case* of Budweiser."

"The answer is still no, but I'll give you a hint."

"Whatzat?" She smirked at her two companions, one obviously
her twin brother. They now had Nick backed against a wall and both
boys flanked either side of her, blocking Nick's exit.

"You're too young to wear so much eyeliner. It's clumping and it
makes you look cheap. I'm surprised your friends here haven't already told you."

"You can't tell Misty *sheeit,*" her brother grinned.

"Fuck you, Drew." And she turned to smack him.

Nick saw an opening and stepped out of the circle.

"Hey!" The third of the trio spoke up. His name was Logan, and
his demeanor was far less lighthearted. He seemed the oldest of the
three and looked like he needed a beer. Lots of them. "Not so fast."

"Not so *fast?*" Nick replied incredulously and drew himself to
full height. He leered into Logan's face. Logan reacted to the fumes.
"Am I being detained against my will here? In broad daylight? I have
a business two doors down. See that bar? That's *mine.* It's full of customers and employees. You think they won't come if I yell? I have
neighbors in the houses across the alley. They're all Latinos. You

think we all aren't being watched right this very minute? You think they don't know you're here to make trouble? They probably have your license number written down. In an hour they'll have your address. Tonight they'll be tagging your house, stripping your new car."

"Fucking faggot," said Drew, surreptitiously scanning the fences.

"Lemme tell you this, sweetheart," Nick grinned at Misty. "Whose idea was it to come out to Cathedral City and make a little trouble? That guy, he's the one you wanna watch. In five years, maybe ten, he'll come to you crying, tell you something's on his mind. And then he'll confess he's homosexual. The worst homophobe is *always* gay. And that guy, of the three of you, is the closet case." He studied them seriously. Then he contemplated Misty.

"Unless you happen to be a dyke."

"She's no dyke." Logan shoved him. Nick fell back against the brick wall, hitting the back of his head. "Take it fucking back!"

With that, a nearby gate creaked open and a young girl, maybe fourteen, peered into the alley. Nick recognized her. Her name was Soila Quintero. She was very pretty, but the right side of her face was disfigured with an enormous birthmark. She stepped boldly into the alley.

"You okay, Mr. Nick?" She stared brazenly at Nick's three captors.

"Yes, sweetheart. They just wanted directions." Nick smiled at her sweetly. Kenny had noticed Soila's schoolgirl crush on Nick and liked to tease him about it. They both felt sorry for her, and Nick, after a few drinks in him, often promised that one day they'd have enough money to send her to a good plastic surgeon. Whenever Soila saw him her almond eyes blazed with love. He always treated her like the most beautiful girl in Cathedral City.

"I can get my father," Soila offered. She smiled at Nick. "And my cousins."

Misty, Logan, and Drew all looked at each other. The serenity in her voice, combined with the horror of her birthmark, made them all uneasy. With exaggerated nonchalance, they ambled back to their white Chevy Blazer. Soon they were peeling away.

"Thank you, honey." Nick smiled at Soila.

"You're welcome, Mr. Nick. But now I have to go to confession."

"Why, sweetheart?"

"I lied to them. Lying is a terrible sin. My father's really at work and I don't have any cousins except in Mexico." She grinned and crossed herself. She slipped inside her fence and closed the gate.

*   *   *

In Sam Singer's alley two subcultures converged, gay and Hispanic, and sometimes pressure built up, causing the fault line to constrict; like men having sex in full view of the windows of the barrio houses with no thought as to whether neighbors in such a shabby neighborhood deserved more respect.

The residents of the alley had seen a hundred sexual acts in the nine years since the bar opened. Shadowy and dark, the alley fences ran crazily, jutting in and out to create small, enclosed, semiprivate cavities, very inviting for anyone seeking quick sexual ecstasy.

These same pockets could also conceal an occasional thief wanting to steal a car radio, or maybe gay-hating vandals wanting to slash tires or roll a sunburned drunk, staggering late at night from Nick's to the alley with wallet, keys, and sport watch in hand.

How many times have the residents of the Cathedral City barrio witnessed such activity in an alley which by day was benign with white hot sunlight, shimmering palm trees, and the vista of the soft pink mountains on the opposite side of the California desert's sun-drenched Coachella Valley?

What else might they see from their hidden viewpoint in Sam Singer's alley? Of sex, violence, compassion, forgiveness, melodrama, murder, and redemption—luckily they had yet to witness murder.

Watching Kenny and his crew through the open door of the restaurant kitchen always provided great entertainment on hot summer nights. The smells of cooking floated into the alley and mixed with the perfume of sage and creosote. Deeper into the bar music could be heard—jazz, show tunes, and the sound of erupting laughter.

And then occasionally, later in the evening, Kenny might step into the alley for a cigarette, dropping to his haunches not so much to escape the heat of his cramped kitchen but simply to enjoy a star-filled desert evening, a sweet black night.

"Hey Nicky," Marcella whispered. "It's slow. Sing 'New York, New York' . . ."

When the bar was quiet and Nick got drunk, Marcella liked to have her fun, which Kenny got wind of because inside the kitchen they could hear him swearing and throwing pots and pans. Now Nick was already commandeering the poor lounge singer's microphone.

"Start spreadin' the news, I'm leaving today, I wanna be a part of it, New York, New York!"

Nick's imitation of Ol' Blue Eyes was so unflattering that when he used to devote entire advertised evenings to his Frank Sinatra impersonations, Sinatra's bodyguard Jilly Rizzo came in personally to order him to stop it. Mr. Sinatra drove through Cathedral City every day and didn't appreciate seeing his name on the marquee for Happy Hour.

So now Nick usually attempted it unadvertised and impromptu, and the only ones who objected were Kenny and the customers because it was such a painful thing to watch.

"My little town blues, are melting away, I'll make a brand new start of it in old New York . . ."

And then the audience would reluctantly oblige him by singing along.

"If I can make it there, I'd make it anywhere, Come on, come through, New York, NEW YORK!!!"

The kitchen door flew open revealing an outraged Kenny brandishing a meat cleaver in one hand, looking for all the world like Sweeney Todd. To add to the effect, a bun warmer expunged a cloud of steam behind him as Kenny stomped into the dining room to try to get him to stop.

"He tells everybody he's Frank Sinatra's illegitimate son."

Marcella gleefully clapped her hands as she and Pablo, a sexy new waiter Nick had hired earlier that afternoon, stood behind the bar and watched Nick bump and grind out the number while Kenny watched helplessly nearby. During the finale, if he was really drunk, Nick liked to sit atop the baby grand piano, but tonight as he was scrambling up to it, he lost his footing and fell headfirst into the front row of customers.

A pall fell over the room.

The lounge singer began to pack up her music. "I'm sorry, Kenny," she shook her head, "but an owner who wants to sing is a lounge act's worst nightmare! I quit."

Most of the other customers nervously called for their checks, and within five minutes of Nick's Frank Sinatra imitation, the entire house was cleared of paying customers.

"What happened?" Nick slurred as Kenny pulled him to his feet. "Where'd everybody go? I was just having a laff. Whatsa big deal?"

"Jesus, Nick. You promised me," Kenny said quietly.

"I thought you were pretty good." Pablo smiled good-naturedly. He was a sweet kid, a college student on hiatus from a university in Mexico City.

And behind the bar Marcella laughed.

Kenny and Marcella were old enemies, but Nick and Kenny had a deal. Nick didn't interfere with the kitchen, and Kenny laid off the crew in the bar. But this was different and Marcella knew it.

"Fuck you, Marcella," he said. "Set him up again and you'll find *rat tails* in your black linguini."

Tonight when Kenny emptied his trash, he encountered Pablo having sex with an older customer against the side of the abandoned garage, the side facing the bedrooms of the small house rented by the family of Thomas and Inez Quintero. It was clearly sex for hire. Kenny didn't want to believe it largely because he liked Pablo and he also knew he was from a very wealthy family in Mexico.

Kenny didn't know what to do. He was too embarrassed to intervene. Inside one of the windows Kenny could see Soila Quintero reading by the light of a small bedside lamp. She could hear noise and stood to go to her window to inspect. Suddenly her mother entered her room. Inez could plainly see the two men, rutting in the alley. She yanked Soila back away from the window, and pulled down the shade.

The customer was kneeling and giving Pablo a blow job. Partially clothed, his shirt unbuttoned, Pablo's jeans had fallen down around his ankles. Kenny was about to break them up when Inez charged into the alley and began prodding and beating the men with her broom, swearing at them in a mixture of Spanish and English.

"What do you think you're doing? My daughter can see you! Get away!" she cried. Inez continued her assault and finally managed to run them off, Pablo still with his pants down around his ankles. Then, to his embarrassment, he saw Kenny standing in the shadows watching the whole thing. Pablo yanked up his pants and shrugged apologetically.

Inez whirled on Kenny, brandishing her broom.

"People live here!"

"I'm sorry, Inez . . ." Kenny threw his hands up. He looked over at Pablo. "She's right, you know. I've got to let you go."

Pablo studied Kenny in amazement. He didn't think he had it in him.

"You're the boss," he shrugged. Then he ambled down the alley into the darkness.

Inez glared after him. If she was surprised Kenny had acted on her complaint, she wasn't about to give him any credit for it. Instead she continued her barrage.

"My little girl was in there! You think she needs to see something like that?" She spat on the pavement to show her disgust.

"We warn them about the alley but they just don't listen."

"You better warn them about me! Soon my husband and my children become citizens. They'll have their rights!" She faltered as the enormity of this occurred to her.

"That's really wonderful, Inez. But what about you?"

"There was a problem with my file. I have to wait!"

"I'm sorry. Anything I can do?"

"Hmmph."

His gentle response irritated her even more. Inez glowered at him with annoyance. She stomped back through the gate. Inside he could hear her back door slam.

Kenny lit a cigarette, squatted down, and paused for a few minutes. Somewhere in the neighborhood a baby cried, a dog barked. Kenny stood up, dropped the cigarette to the ground, and squashed it out with a greasy boot. Then he went inside to lock up.

When Kenny opened the front door of their house, Nick was curled on the sofa watching a game show. In one hand he held the remote control and the other a Campari and soda. Candles were burning all over the house. The air conditioner blasted as a breeze floated in from the open sliding glass doors framing the patio area, where the pool shimmered. The terrace speakers bleated jazz into the night air. In the kitchen a rerun of a sitcom was blaring.

Nick hated to be alone, hated silence. Kenny stopped to examine a stack of bills on a table in the entry hall. He picked up a red envelope. He opened it up. A threatening notice from the Department of Water and Power.

"Shit," Kenny said softly. He looked over to where Nick lounged on the sofa. "Here's a hundred dollars. Pay the utilities tomorrow or they'll cut us off. Okay? You won't forget? I'd do it but I have to go to Indio. You won't forget?"

"No," Nick said without turning around, but his shoulders slumped slightly, as if in defeat. "I'm courting several investors as we speak."

Kenny felt bad so he changed the subject.

"Did you cancel Inez? We can't pay her this week."

"The house is a mess."

"We can't pay her. Did you cancel her?"

"I'll call her first thing in the morning." Nick shrugged.

Kenny struggled to swallow back his irritation. "I had to fire the new waiter."

"*What?* I just hired him."

"He was turning tricks in the alley. I caught him just outside of Soila Quintero's window. Inez was furious." Kenny told him the story in detail.

"Jesus, can't we give him another chance? The customers love him."

"Now we know why." Kenny studied him. "You eat anything?"

"No." Nick replied, barely a whisper. He looked like he was about to pass out. His arms and his legs were matchstick thin.

"You have to eat. I'll make you something."

And then Kenny walked through the house, turning off noise, finally ending up in the kitchen where he ran water, filling a pan. He turned on a burner, setting the water to boil. Then Kenny stepped out on the patio, smoking a cigarette. After a moment, he wandered to the other side of the turquoise pool and contemplated the distant lights of Palm Springs.

He slumped to the edge of a dirty white chaise and put his head in his hands.

"Why don't you come inside and keep me company?" Nick called out to him. "You didn't even say hello! You just walked in here ordering me around."

Kenny gazes back through the house where Nick sat drinking. He took a deep breath and went inside. He dumped the contents of a box of penne into the hot rolling water. Ten minutes later he placed a plate of pasta with oil and garlic on the coffee table near Nick. Nick barely glances up from his crossword puzzle.

"What'sa capital of South Dakota?"

"I don't know."

"*Sure you know.*"

"I said I don't know."

"It's, it's . . . oh, *you know!*" He snapped his fingers at Kenny to prompt his memory.

"I told you I don't know!" Kenny shouted back. "*I don't know!*"

A surprised Nick looked up over his bifocals. "Well, *really . . .*" A minute later it came to him. "It's *Pierre!*"

"You pronounce it *Peer,*" Kenny corrected him. "Not *Pee-air.*" After a long silence they both began to laugh.

And later after dinner with Nick sprawled out on the sofa, Kenny moved to the workbench he'd set up in an alcove off the living room. It was here Kenny constructed and painted beautiful handmade porcelain dolls.

And as soon as Kenny settled in, opened his jars of paint, and selected the doll he wanted to paint, it would begin. The incessant chatter. The litany of inanities. The braying.

"We should get a nice review from the *Desert Sun*. I could tell she was *very* impressed with me. She asked me if we served homosexuals. I told her mostly steaks and chops! Get it? Wasn't that a good answer? Mostly steaks and chops?

"I was thinking about new promotions. The red shoe promotion went great. That pulled 'em in. Two for One if you wear red shoes. Marcella thought it was fabulous. She and Pablo went to the Good Will and bought *fifty* pairs of shoes. Got shit-faced and dyed 'em all red. Wasn't it a hoot? Red Shoe Day at Nick's."

As the barrage continued, Kenny's back and shoulders began to tighten. Alcoholic banter, all told to the air though Nick, in fact, thought he was in conversation with Kenny. Except Kenny never had to answer. Never was called upon to reply because Nick never listened. He only waited to speak.

That night Kenny began painting the face of a Hispanic woman, which he would later apply to a corresponding body. As Nick watched him dab paint in her cheeks, and contemplate her lips, something stirred in him which caused him a bit of sadness.

"You never look at me that way," he finally said, "and you haven't said a word to me all night."

"Friday's the first of the month. What are we gonna do about the rent?" Kenny asked.

"It's August."

"I'll tell Sam that."

"Tonight we did great. Seventy dinners."

"One good night doesn't make up for two slow weeks," Kenny murmured.

"I'm getting another drink," Nick said. "You want anything?"

Kenny looked up. Do I want anything? Three more wishes, Kenny thought. For starters. Answers would be a start, but to what questions? he thought greedily. He held up the doll to study it under the light.

"You didn't *answer* me . . ."

"Sorry," Kenny said, turning. "I'm okay for now."

"I'll run up an investor or two. I have some very good prospects."

"How can you sell more shares than we have left?"

"Create new stock. Declare a split." Then Nick slumped hard like an old cat on a soft cushion. His breathing was labored. Kenny knew he would shortly fall asleep.

"Put your cigarette in the ashtray. You're about to burn a hole in the couch."

Nick complied. He leaned forward to take a sip of his fresh drink. He passed out in an upright position.

Later that night as Nick snored on the sofa, with Letterman blaring and a sultry chlorine breeze rising off the pool, Kenny got up to help him to bed. Watching Nick sleep never failed to move Kenny, always renewed his affection. Maybe it was the vulnerability. Or the relief on his face. Kenny knew Nick was nervous about the bar. Was feeling pressure to stimulate new business. But Nick never verbalized doubt, or showed ordinary fear.

He was very superstitious about all of that, thinking that it drew everything negative right to him like a magnet.

This felt like Nick's last chance, and both of them knew it. Kenny helped him to bed, half carrying, half dragging him the length of the hall, Nick seemed fast asleep when his head hit the pillow.

"You have to do something about your drinking." Kenny smoothed out the sheets.

"I will tomorrow, I promise," Nick offered sincerely.

"You say that every night . . ."

"I mean it every night."

"I know you do," Kenny said, and bent down to tuck him in.

"Stay with me till I fall asleep," Nick said. "And then you can move onto the couch."

"Tomorrow I thought I'd drive down to Mexicali," Kenny whispered in the dark.

Nick grunted in reply. He rolled away, looking into the wall. "So I got hassled at the liquor store."

"*What?*"

"Kids from Palm Springs. Soila Quintero ran 'em off."

Kenny knew Soila Quintero. He didn't ask how or why.

"What were you wearing?"

They both knew he was wearing his red loafers.

"What'd you expect?"

"I *expect* them to learn to accept me," Nick explained with a weary but patient tone in his voice. "To have a sense of humor."

Kenny didn't say anything. Every tendon in his body synapsed, firing energy into his muscles. Kenny had a bad temper which he was always trying to control.

"Let it go. They've been trying to kill me for years. I'm used to it. I'm tougher than they are . . ." He began to drift off. "I'm thinking of buying a limousine, to pick customers up from the hotels or the airport and bring 'em straight to Nick's. A guy came in the other day said he knew of a used one in good condition. We can paint it chocolate brown . . ."

Kenny undressed in the darkness. He reached for a pillow. Stood over Nick. Hesitated about what he should do.

"Nicky?" Kenny whispered, but Nick was snoring slightly, fast asleep. "Nick?"

Kenny knelt by the bed, near Nick's sleeping face. *Pray*, he ordered himself. You were in a fucking church today. *So pray*. The visit to the church had been positive, he thought. He was glad he'd had the courage to talk to the priest. Hadn't told him anything, but the old man seemed kind. Seemed understanding, yet how could he admit what the power of his imagination had lapsed to lately?

His hands struggled with the thick pillow as if it were filled with a heaving, imprisoned wild animal, struggling to be let free. "*No, God,*" Kenny prayed as the contents of the pillow fought upward from the side of the bed toward Nick's face. Kenny didn't want Nick to wake up, but he wanted to quiet the soft whistle of his snoring, to calm the nervous tic in his eyes while he slept. He wanted the night air to be free from fumes of alcohol.

"Help me," Kenny whined. "Please help me. Please make him stop. Give me the power to stop . . ."

And now the pillow was filled with wild falcons, wings beating furiously, talons ripping at the fabric of the pillowcase, and Kenny wrestled to keep the bag from rising, and away from Nick's face, struggled with all the power he could muster to keep Nick safe.

Hadn't he managed all these years? What was this? Just one more night. One more night to keep him safe. That's all that was required. All.

Exhausted, Kenny fell asleep on the floor and began dreaming.

*   *   *

A half hour later he rose wearily and stood naked in the bedroom doorway, looking out at the floodlit pool as if uncertain where he belonged. He'd been dreaming about the two men having sex in the alley. He was surprised to discover he had an erection.

"Come back to bed," Nick murmured into the darkness.

"Go back to sleep," Kenny said softly. "I love you."

He considered returning to bed but instead turned away and disappeared down the long dark hallway that had become their lives.

2

Desierto Peligroso

The name of the park was Los Niños Heroes. As Kenny studied it, he paused to get his bearings. On the other side of Francisco Madero, over a narrow patch of dusty lawn and trees flanked by westbound Avenue Cristobal Colon, a ten-foot chain-link fence, many times repaired by rusty patchwork steel panels, ran the east-west length of the international sister cities of Calexico and Mexicali. Kenny noticed many loiterers pondering the appeal of the north side of the fence, the American side.

El Norte.

The fence looked easy enough to scale, but Kenny knew well enough that the recently stepped-up Imperial Valley border patrol presence—the surveillance cameras combined with the omnipresent green-and-white four-wheel-drive border patrol vehicles buzzing the Calexico side of the fence—discouraged even the most ardent border jumper.

Kenny also understood the temptation, that need to cross over from one place to another, so he empathized with their frustration. He wanted a quick fix, to get away, even for the day. So early this morning Kenny drove the two hours south to the California border town of Calexico, parked his rusty old Scout on a side street, and after flashing his driver's license, strode through the United States Border Inspection Station and walked himself into Mexico. He decided to amuse himself by wandering through the streets of Mexicali.

He loved Mexican folk art and was delighted to discover a beautiful collection of *retablos* in his favorite open air marketplace on Calle Morelos, only blocks south from the U.S.-Mexico Port of

Entry. The *retablos* were small, colorful images, painted on tin expressing in picture form a perilous event for which the grateful petitioners, many of them migrants, had been miraculously delivered, or for which they were seeking divine intervention.

"How much is this one?" Kenny asked the vendor in Spanish.

"It's very beautiful, no?" The vendor beamed. Then he rattled off a quick barrage of adjectives in Spanish to confirm his opinion.

Kenny looked up questioningly, as if he didn't understand.

"You're Mexican, of course."

"No." Kenny shook his head. "American."

"You have Latin blood from somewhere," he pressed.

"I'm Black Irish by descent. Maybe that's it." A Spaniard in Kenny's distant Irish past.

"Ah, I thought so. You must have a very good ear. You speak Spanish with a Mexican accent. Where do you live?"

"In the desert near Palm Springs. Two hours north of here."

The vendor wanted to engage him. Sell him more. He was a short, regal little man and moved floridly as he waited for Kenny to make up his mind. Solidly built but not cosmetically muscular, Kenny was big boned with a broad back, strong forearms, and full, solid hips. His hair was shaggy and black as the vendor's, but unlike the vendor he gazed into the world with mournfully brooding blue eyes. His features were large—a strong prominent forehead, a long straight nose, and a thick, sensual lower lip. The vendor knew the more he made Kenny uncomfortable, the tighter and more exciting Kenny's body would become.

"Maybe I can show you some ceramics. I have some very beautiful patterns—"

"On a budget. Maybe next time."

"Some silver perhaps? I can offer you a very reasonable price. A third of what you'd pay across the border."

"Sorry." Kenny shook his head. "This is all I can do."

"Is business so bad, señor?"

Kenny nodded wearily. "Please."

"Where do you work?"

"I'm a . . . chef."

"A chef. Which restaurant? I know the desert very well. Maybe I've heard of it."

"It's called Nick's. Out in Cathedral City."

"Well of course I've been there," the vendor beamed.

Kenny was beginning to get exasperated. It was very hot, easily in the low hundreds. All he wanted to do was buy some inexpensive craft work, treat himself to a few hours exploring downtown Mexicali, and then start back. It was only a day trip. A chance to get away from the restaurant. Now here he was explaining himself to a complete stranger just to get a few cents knocked off for possibly fake folk art he could buy at Pier 1 Imports in Palm Desert for the same price.

"Ah yes, Nick." The vendor rolled his eyes. "Nick is the personality of the place. It wouldn't be Nick's without him. Is he still drinking?" He'd obviously been in. He was being snide now. Making fun of Nick.

Kenny wanted to walk away, not spend his money with the vicious little queen but instead pressed him for a price on a particularly beautiful little painting. It depicted a solitary man standing on the border, with one foot in Mexico and the other in the United States. The man was clearly perplexed and held his hands up to the heavens as if beseeching the Virgin of Guadalupe to help him decide which way to step, which country to claim.

"How much?" Kenny asked, this time in English.

"It must be difficult for you. Working with so flamboyant a personality. You live together, too?"

"I've lived with Nick for eighteen years," Kenny muttered absently. He was clearly distracted by the painting. *"How much?"*

"Does anyone tell you how much you look like Antonio Banderas? But his eyes are brown and yours are blue."

The vendor shrugged, knowing he wasn't going to get anywhere with this handsome, dark-haired, lapis-eyed man. He finally quoted him a good price and Kenny bought the little *retablo*. Then he walked happily with his purchase half a block back to the corner of Morelos and Avenida Francisco Madero, a busy one-way street running east along the Mexicali-Calexico border.

Once again Kenny studied the fence. The park seemed to be a place to procure illicit things. Although not particularly worldly, Kenny knew by his own eyes that sex, drugs, and travel could all be had for a price in this dusty park. It was obviously a place for buyer and seller to meet, all in the shadow of the United States Border Inspection Station in Calexico, the U.S. sister city to Mexicali.

Until he'd gotten to know his crew at the restaurant, Kenny knew little to nothing about border politics or the mechanics of illegal immigration. Occasionally there might be some mention on the news of the death of some immigrant trying to sneak across the border;

maybe a drowning in the Rio Grande—or heatstroke in the desert. Then the graphic imagery of the border patrol agents yanking a Hispanic woman, a suspected illegal, from the front seat of a van and beating her in full view of television cameras, not to mention her children back home. Marlon Brando had even come forward and offered her twenty-five thousand dollars to try to make right the injustice.

The stories Kenny heard from his kitchen help had enlightened him tremendously. He now knew, thanks to Carmen, the tall smiling salad chef Kenny was helping to get her U.S. citizenship, that each year over a quarter of a million people were arrested and turned back in the Southern California desert alone! Not counting San Diego, Arizona, or Texas.

Kenny believed the anti–illegal immigration climate was thinly disguised racism. California's sagging economy had to be blamed on someone, some specific group. Why not poor immigrants? Many claimed they were sapping the California economy for free services, education, medical care, and welfare.

Carmen informed Kenny that it was best to arrange for a *coyote*, a paid guide, to drive you west of Mexicali and then off north, traversing bumpy single-lane desert roads as close as possible to the U.S. border, finally to drop you off; leading you by foot under cover of night the twenty or so miles into the barren California desert; to be rejoined by an awaiting van to whisk you off to Los Angeles.

"Do you pay them before or after?" Kenny had asked her.

"After!" she laughed mirthfully. "If you pay them before, they can ditch you! No, after."

"What do they charge?"

"One thousand dollars! Maybe more! Your relatives pay."

"Relatives in Mexico?"

"No! Here."

"Who has that kind of money?"

"Is very hard. But if you want to help your brother, or your mother . . . you pay," she observed solemnly.

"Did anybody pay for you?"

"No! Who'd want me?" she laughed. "I save and pay for myself! But I paid for Miguel . . . and he's working to pay me back."

"Carmen." Kenny winked at her mischievously. He liked to flirt with her. "I'd pay big money for you."

"Big money," she laughed merrily and he noticed she'd lost another tooth. "Big money, sure!"

*   *   *

After purchasing the *retablo,* Kenny found himself wanting to stay awhile longer. He liked old mission churches and asked the vendor where he might find a cathedral. He was directed several blocks over to a small, beautiful church called *La Catedral.* Kenny took a deep breath and went inside.

It had been many years since Kenny had been willing to enter a Catholic church, and this would be his second visit in two days. He thought about the old priest in Cathedral City. Emotion flooded over him as he entered the sanctuary, his presence disturbing a flock of mourning doves, high in the rough wooden beams overhead. They scattered along the slatted rooftop of the cathedral, their feathered wings whooshing softly till they came to rest in the balcony overhead. Without kneeling, he slid into a pew. He folded his hands and pondered his surroundings.

What's this about? he wondered to himself. They made it quite clear he wasn't wanted. Why punish himself by coming back? He stretched, allowing himself to luxuriate in the peacefulness of the old wooden sanctuary. The missals and hymnbooks were in Spanish. Confusion and comfort began to conflict inside of him. He closed his eyes and began to daydream.

His was a typical Irish Catholic upbringing. His father was agnostic but his mother, though not an ardent believer, brought him up in the church. Catechism, parochial school in grades 1 to 6—his foundation in the teachings of Catholicism was solid, a respectable base, at least in his formative years. He had no childhood horror stories to tell. The nuns were kind. The priests kept their hands to themselves.

He fell away due to boredom and rebellion in junior high and high school. But the typical loneliness of being a first-year college student, combined with his unshakable shyness, fomented a return to the Catholic faith. Out walking early one fall weekday morning, he noticed a small group of parishioners, maybe ten or twelve, assembling for an early morning Mass outside a pretty little hillside church, and he impulsively decided to join them.

Nothing he encountered that morning after so many years away conflicted with his current core beliefs. He wasn't a Jesus freak. He *never* proselytized. He drank, smoked pot on weekends, enjoyed an occasional sexual dalliance when it presented itself, but never got serious about any one girl. And he continued to go to Mass.

But the weekly mass evolved to twice weekly, then daily, and finally, twice daily. They were only thirty gentle minutes out of his day. Coeds practicing Transcendental Meditation put as much time into their meditations as he did attending Mass.

He kept these visits to himself, but he found himself really needing them. He didn't socialize with other parishioners more than to say hello during the service. He did, however, enjoy speaking to the several parish priests. He went to confession regularly, and one evening was invited to dine with the fathers in the rectory dining room, enjoying himself immensely. This set about his thinking that perhaps he should consider being a candidate for the priesthood, and the priests sensed it.

In the privacy of his own prayers, he'd lately been marveling over the simple fact that whatever spiritual connection he was making, be it with God the Father, Jesus Christ, the Holy Spirit—he couldn't really differentiate, but incredibly, a lifetime of estrangement was ebbing. His heart had quietly filled with the presence of a loving, powerful, and supernatural force.

He moved through his days in a pronounced state of spiritual ecstasy. His grades didn't improve. Women weren't falling in love with him. Financial opportunities weren't dropping from the sky. Kenny found he didn't require one bit of tangible proof that God existed. For him, the quiet, humble, private, mystical experience of the day-to-day joy of God's unconditional love was enough.

Then a shocking incident disrupted the carefully cultivated peace he'd been enjoying. A deeply confused Kenny arrived at the office of the campus priest to discuss the incident. The kindly cleric had been old like Father Gene. Father Tom was quiet, given to long pauses, liked to tell jokes. Kenny believed him to be an intellectual. He was very popular among the student population from the university. As Kenny spoke, the old man tended to the plants in his window box, snipping and dead-heading with purpose. Kenny was candid, certain to leave nothing out.

"I love coming to the church, Father," Kenny told him. "I attend Mass, sometimes twice a day."

"Why so often?" the priest murmured.

"I suppose it gives me comfort."

"So you take comfort from the church."

"I do, yes."

"What gifts do you offer in return?" he asked Kenny. "In exchange for this *comfort* . . ."

"I tithe. I donate my time to parish functions." Kenny taught art to preschoolers. He was good with them and they liked him very much.

"Tithing means nothing," the priest answered, somewhat sharply, surprising Kenny. "Everybody tithes. As for the art classes, I've been opposed to them for years. We aren't day care. The children should be limited to catechism classes. You remind me to take up the issue again. Now, what's really troubling you?"

And Kenny told him about a recent, highly startling anonymous sexual encounter with a fellow male student in a campus locker room.

Father Tom continued pruning a small indoor plant with tiny sheers. Kenny waited, taken aback by his comments. After a long moment of silence, Kenny spoke up: "What advice do you have for me?"

"Leave the church."

"What?"

"You're an abomination before God. Leave his church."

"Father!"

And the old man put down his clippers and turned to face Kenny, his eyes burning with hot fury, "You don't deserve a relationship with God. You disgust God. There's nothing in scripture to defend your nature."

Kenny stood up. Emotion engulfed him. As a kid, he'd endured all kinds of negative gay epithets, straightening up taller and taller with each assault. Not since junior high had anyone suspected, let alone accused, him of being gay. The priest's reaction hurled toward him like a debris-clotted freak storm. Kenny was furious with himself for feeling so hurt. Surely this was some aberration on the part of the old priest. Perhaps he was actually senile.

"You have no right to judge me as an abomination to God!" Kenny retorted. He was stunned to tears. This isolated incident had only been an anomaly.

"Of course I have a right! I'm a priest," he roared. He shouted so loudly a passerby knocked on his door, asking if everything was all right. "You can try other parishes, other clergymen, but if *one* disagrees with me, then you'll have found yourself a liar. Homosexuality is an abomination before God," the old priest thundered, and Kenny was forced to leave, fearing the old man might have a stroke.

"I have a place here," Kenny affirmed, "I was *called* here," and he lurched from the office and, wracked with heartache, staggered home to contemplate the day's events. He sat stupefied in his bedroom and wondered if he'd imagined the whole thing. As for his concerns about being gay, he'd never had a homosexual encounter before, let alone an overt fantasy. In the recreation center locker room a fellow next to him was toweling off and Kenny had looked over, noticed he had an erection. Without any hesitation, Kenny followed him into the sauna, and in seconds, it was over. They parted without another word. Was that, too, a dream?

A week later, a stubborn, still-smarting Kenny attended an evening Mass. Another younger priest whom Kenny knew officiated. When it came time to accept the host, Kenny took his place in line and waited his turn, just as he had done twice a day for the last year.

Just as the priest turned to proffer the communion wafer, he was startled to find Kenny standing before him. "Move along," he whispered.

And Kenny refused as the line bottlenecked behind him.

"Look, Kenny, you have to move along," the young priest insisted breathlessly. "I *can't* give it to you. He's watching. Please move along."

And Kenny could see the old priest, watching him through a side door. To make it easier on the young priest, Kenny relinquished his spot. As he turned to leave, the other parishioners were bent in prayer. When he left the church, head down, aghast, silent, without protest and filled with shame, nobody noticed that he was gone. Because Kenny went quietly, he now realized, nobody stood to intercede for him.

Shortly thereafter, his sexual experimentation continued.

To one side of the sacristy, Kenny noticed a collection of *retablos*. Kenny moved forward to study them.

As he knelt before a flickering row of votive candles in the Virgin's Chamber, Kenny heard the huge door to the cathedral creak open, the splay of bright morning light from the street causing the flock of doves to scatter again. The birds fluttered to rest in the wooden cross beams of a magnificent stained glass window, high over the crucifix.

He could hear footsteps, and soon a young woman was kneeling beside him, producing her own *retablo,* covered in brown paper and tied with string, which quickly she unwrapped. Kenny feigned interest in lighting a candle, but out of the corner of his eye he could see that the *retablo* was extremely beautiful.

It depicted two women, one young, one old, crossing a desert and guided by torches held from above by a man and woman resting in the clouds. A smaller image of a Blessed Virgin seemed to suspend them. He couldn't make out the Spanish text in the lower corner, but he assumed it was some sort of prayer.

He found a lone scorched wooden taper jutting up from a box of sand and lit a candle. He could feel her eyes on him. He turned, realizing that she, too, wanted to light a candle but had no matches. He offered her the still burning taper. After nodding her thanks, she took the liberty of lighting the candle in the votive holder next to Kenny's. She bowed her head in prayer. Kenny, too, lowered his head but, instead of meditation, stole another glance at her and then contemplated the ornate, creaking sanctuary.

From her profile he could see she had long dark hair and looked to be in her midtwenties. Her expression was somewhat grave, though she was quietly beautiful in profile. Behind them the door to the cathedral opened again, but this time an old woman's voice echoed through the sanctuary.

"*Maria,*" she hiss-whispered. "We have to go!"

Maria Lourdes Castillo crossed herself, glanced over at him, and stood up, somewhat unsteadily. He offered his hand, which she accepted briefly. He squeezed it gently and released her. Soon she was rushing down the aisle toward the door. After a moment, Kenny stood up without crossing himself and ambled past the rows of polished pews toward the door of the church. Behind him their candles flickered together.

Kenny stepped from the church onto the dusty Mexicali street, and was blinded by the red bougainvillea clinging to the whitewashed clay walls of the church. He took a moment to adjust to the light.

As Kenny made his way down the steps of the cathedral, he noticed the young woman from the sanctuary assisting an ancient old lady as she sipped delicately from a small canteen. She was wearing a crisp white sleeveless blouse and a mid-length faded denim skirt. Next to them was a small bag, loaded with belongings. The old lady was insisting that she was all right. Maria reached for the bag and they began to walk down the hill toward town. Kenny watched them for a moment, and then, as if she felt his eyes upon them, Maria turned, smiling ruefully when she saw him, and the two of them hurried away.

Shortly thereafter, Kenny wandered westward down Avenida Cristobal Colon, toward the U.S. Port of Entry into Calexico. In Los

Niños Heroes, the hot patchy park was crowded with milling people, all trying to escape the scorching sun, trying to do business in the fragmenting shade of the trees. The visit to the cathedral had moved him unexpectedly.

He found himself thinking about the girl who had knelt next to him, *Maria,* the old lady had called her, and suddenly, over traffic, as if conjuring her up, Kenny saw her in the park, towering gracefully over the head of the old woman, the two of them maneuvering hesitantly among the throng of drug dealers, prostitutes, teenage hustlers, and lastly recruiters, *talones,* Carmen had called them.

Guides who would put them in taxis and take them to safe houses where they would become the chattel of highly sophisticated, extremely dangerous smuggling cartels. Maria and her grandmother weren't the only ones seeking *coyotes,* but because of her height, because they were obviously women alone and lastly because of her noticeably beautiful face, knit with intimidation and confusion, they swarmed her: a pack of aggressive, smallish teenage boys wearing extravagantly colored shirts, striving for height in cheap cowboy boots. Maria blinked back tears, overwhelmed. They tugged at her hands, while simultaneously pulling at the old lady, separating them for several moments, probably assuming the old lady carried the family cash.

"Mamita!" She screamed so loudly Kenny could hear her from the street. The boys yanked so hard the old lady stumbled, at which time Kenny rushed into the park, pushing and elbowing his way through the crowd till he was nearly behind her. She was crying, struggling to steady the confused but angry old woman while holding on to her bag.

"Hey!" Kenny shouted in English. "Leave them alone!"

He gripped her shoulders to pull her back, startling her so much she flung wildly around, slapping and clawing at him with her fingernails.

"No!" he protested, now in Spanish. "I saw you in the church! Just now? Remember? The candles? *Recuerda?"*

Now the *talones* fell back. Probably her boyfriend, or worse her husband. Obviously some kind of family dispute. He looked too tough, too rich to mess with. This bitch and the old lady were a waste of time. They drifted away and Maria collected herself, struggling to reconcile the kind, handsome face with the rivulets of blood pouring from his cheek where she had slashed him.

She studied him in bewilderment.

"Do you remember me?"

"What do you want?" she finally stammered.

Behind her the grandmother appraised him with critical admiration. She was cunning, Kenny saw. Cunning and very strong.

"I saw you from the sidewalk. You looked—" He was gasping for breath. "You looked like you were in trouble."

"He's *bleeding*," the old lady chastised her. "He only wanted to help." She introduced herself. Her name was Concha. Her hysterical granddaughter's name was Maria.

His hand went to his cheek. "I'm okay. My name is Kenny."

They all stared at each other. Maria's eyes were wild but she struggled to compose herself.

"What are you trying to do?" he finally asked her.

"Nothing!" she exclaimed. "Thank you for helping us." She turned to go. The old lady remained rooted defiantly to her spot, all eyes for Kenny. The girl pushed her gently. When she saw that she wasn't going to cooperate, she threw up her hands.

"*Abuelita. Please.*"

"He wants to help," she observed. "Let him help. We can pay you five hundred dollars each!"

"*Abue!*" Maria reacted. "She doesn't know what she's saying . . ."

"No. You don't understand. I'm not a *coyote.*"

"What then, *la policia?*" Concha shrank back.

"No." Kenny protested. "I'm nobody." He glanced through the fence to the bustling American side of the border. "Look, I have to get back to my truck. It's across in Calexico. I saw you at the church. That's all. You looked like you needed help. Nothing more to it. I've got to get going."

"Why don't you go get your truck and come back?" Concha asked slyly.

"*Abuelita!* We'll stick to our plan."

Kenny smiled at the old lady. She clearly wanted him to sneak them across.

A lone tear rolled down her granddaughter's cheek. "I can take of everything," Maria insisted. "She still sees me as a little girl."

"Let's get a lemonade." Kenny suggested kindly. "Let's talk this out. Okay?"

Maria was exhausted and could expect no cooperation from the old lady. "Okay," she relented. "Okay."

Sitting at a small table near the back of the air-cooled coffee shop, Kenny observed that with her long neck, slightly aquiline nose, and large eyes, Maria was quite beautiful. Her eyes and her smile could reflect conflicting emotions simultaneously. He sensed that she desperately wanted to relax but needed to get on to the business at hand.

"You ever done this before?" He looked at her with concern. "Crossed over?"

She shook her head.

"They told us at the bus station to come to the park," Concha observed. She was sipping lemonade. Maria's eyes fell to Kenny's wrapped *retablo*.

"I paint them as a hobby," Maria explained softly.

"*Una retablista!*" Concha interjected with emphasis. "She makes many pesos for her paintings."

"I noticed the one you left in the church. It was very beautiful. I collect them," he added hesitantly. He unwrapped his package and showed her his painting.

Maria studied it with interest. "Why did you pick this one?" she asked curiously. "Are you between countries? I thought you were American."

"Maybe he's between lives," the old lady studied him. "Which way will he go?" she asked, referring to the figure in the painting.

Kenny shifted uncomfortably.

"Why do you want to come to California so badly?" he asked, wanting to change the subject.

"After I'm gone, Maria will have no family left. Mexico is not safe for a young woman alone. She needs to be established in the United States."

"She said if I didn't come with her, she'd go on her own."

The old woman's smile confirmed Maria's assessment of the facts.

"Can't you qualify for a visitor's permit?"

"No. She's too old. She has few assets. They think she's too high of a risk."

"I sold my house," the old woman bragged.

"Without advising me—" Maria scolded.

" I now have over three thousand dollars in my brassiere," she cackled. "Enough for a new start."

"*Sshhh . . .*" Maria admonished her as she looked around. Several men were staring openly at their table. After exchanging an irritated glance with Kenny, she contemplated her grandmother. Her annoyance faded. She patted Concha's hand. She was wolfing down a plate of *carnitas*.

"She's having a wonderful time," Maria smiled at Kenny. "This is all very exciting for her. Thank you."

"So you have no other family?"

"My daughter and son-in-law were missionaries and teachers," Concha explained matter-of-factly. "My daughter married well. Her husband was a brilliant man. He spoke many languages. Maria's English is as perfect as her Spanish. They were murdered in the mountains. The entire population was massacred by soldiers . . ."

"The images in your painting. They were your parents. It was very beautiful."

Maria nodded wistfully. "I was very young. They'd left me with my grandmother."

Looking at Concha slurping her straw, Maria shook her head. "You must think I'm taking a terrible chance. That I'm doing something very ridiculous. She's so stubborn. She would come alone. Just to make me come after her."

"I would, *nietas.*" Concha blinked gravely. "Of that you can be certain."

Studying Concha's ancient face, Kenny uttered softly, "She seems to want to do this one last thing."

"Where do you live in California?" Maria asked him softly.

"Cathedral City. In the desert east of Los Angeles."

"Cathedral City," Maria repeated. "It sounds like a beautiful place."

"Are you married?" Concha demanded.

"No, *señora* . . ." Kenny shrugged apologetically. "And I don't think I ever will be."

"What are you, then, a priest?"

"*Abuela!* Leave him alone," but she studied him curiously.

Kenny laughed and shook his head.

Several moments later a laconic middle-aged man in a leisure suit and a cowboy hat wandered up. "I couldn't help overhearing you. I know of a reputable young man, my nephew, who might be able to help you. I could drive you. You could escort the ladies to see if everything is in order. I'd bring you back. He's leaving this evening. I'd be happy to call him. Of course, *señor*, I want *nothing* in return."

Kenny and Maria looked at each other and blinked.

He introduced himself as Señor Juel Ramirez. He drove a large red Chevrolet sedan. Kenny rode in front. When he thought Kenny wasn't looking, Ramirez would stare lasciviously at Maria's legs as she sat with her arm protectively around her grandmother's shoulder. Of the three of them, Concha was the least intimidated. To her, Kenny noticed, this was great theater, great adventure.

Several times Kenny and Maria exchanged shy, curious glances. They were bonded now by Señor Ramirez; wed in concern for their mutual safety. Kenny figured she was wondering why he had elected to ride with them. The thought flickered through his mind that she might even suspect that it was he who had set the whole thing up. Perhaps he was a *coyote*. Why else would he intervene in that dangerous park, offer to buy them cold drinks and then proceed with a seemingly total stranger into the barrios of Mexicali?

Who else would do such a thing?

He looked out the window. Ordinarily someone with something to gain or little to lose. He studied Maria in the rearview mirror. She looked like she was going to be ill. She was clearly ashamed of what they were about to attempt. Occasionally her doubtful eyes would shimmer with tears and she would kiss the top of her grandmother's head. The old woman would respond and pat her hand.

"This is the right thing to do, *nietas*," he overheard Concha whisper. "Don't worry so much . . ."

She caught Kenny's eye and winked at him. This was the proper thing to be done, her excited manner seemed to assure Kenny. The old lady was tough, that was plain. She infused Kenny with resolve. Kenny, who until two hours ago was a complete stranger to them both. Of the entire entourage, he was the most mysterious and suspicious of the lot.

They roamed the tight dirt avenues of the barrio, looking for the *coyote's* address as street kids eyed the big red car and wondered if the passengers were armed and how far would they go to protect themselves. Kenny had donned mirrored sunglasses, his muscled arms gleaming with sweat as they wended their way through a makeshift plywood and cardboard migrant squatter's camp to find this girl her *coyote*. All along the dusty streets, hordes of migrants huddled in patches of shade, some tending pots of beans, some hanging off trees, all studying the passing vehicle with hollow curiosity, grateful for a break in the monotony.

The ominous sunglasses, his shaggy black hair, and his puffed-up chest all combined to make Kenny look pretty fierce. Señor Ramirez glanced over at him. Kenny stared coldly at the older man. Senor Ramirez's eyes flickered with concern. As they neared their destination, Kenny knew Ramirez was hoping he hadn't misjudged him. For his own protection, as well as the two women riding in back, it was better that the Mexican remained wary of Kenny's motives.

Behind the protection of his mirrored persona, Kenny's thoughts were racing. What could he be thinking? He was expected at the restaurant by five. The soonest he could hope to be back was eight. And they were busy tonight. He glanced at his watch. Carmen and Miguel would have to open. What would they think when he didn't show up? What would Nick think?

Maybe he should tell Ramirez to turn around, take them back. Kenny could cross the border and come back with the Scout. They could drive east of town and he could four-wheel the two of them across the border, make a run for it. Kenny's heart was pounding, and when he came out of his daydream, he could see Maria staring at him with concerned, frightened eyes. She didn't exactly trust him, that was for sure. But next to her the tiny old woman smiled at him with satisfaction as if she could read his mind and approved of his thoughts.

The big Chevrolet lumbered to a halt. A makeshift hut, a little nicer than the rest, with a gang of shifty loiterers hanging around in a junk-strewn yard, teasing a yelping pit bull tied to a rope. Tipped off by the call from Señor Ramirez, they were waiting for Maria and her grandmother.

He pulled to a halt as the apparent *coyote* stepped from the group, whistling as he appraised Maria, huddled in the back seat of the big red car.

"Hey, we been waiteen for you."

"We got lost." Ramirez shrugged from the driver's window. He picked his teeth with a matchbook. There was no love lost between these two. "Okay," he turned to his passengers. "Get out." All solicitation had drained from his voice. He had them where he wanted them now.

Maria glanced nervously at Kenny. He looked at Ramirez and opened his own door. "You're waiting for me," Kenny affirmed to Ramirez. "You're taking me back." .

Ramirez checks at his watch. "If you hurry." Maria's expression registered her disappointment. The *coyote* barked an order to a subordinate and suddenly a group of wary, nervous immigrants, maybe ten or twelve, emerged from the hut, shielding their eyes as if they hadn't seen the light of day for a week. All were quickly herded into the back of a beat-up old van.

Maria moistened a handkerchief with a bit of water from her canteen and wiped her grandmother's face. The old woman had lost her verve, was nervous with the noise and dirt. Kenny observed this despairingly. He and Maria regarded each other. He got out of the car to help them alight. Concha crawled out first. As Maria stepped from the car into the dusty yard, catcalls swelled from onlookers.

"What do they pay you?" Maria whispered to Kenny. "To hide in the church."

"*What?*" He was shocked by the question.

"You heard me," she replied bitterly. Maria wouldn't look at him. She had new faces to study and memorize. She had her grandmother to consider. The old woman shuffled past him slowly.

"Thank you for the lemonade," Concha muttered wistfully, gently touching his hand.

"Hurry up!" the *coyote* shouted.

Kenny looked after them, still stung by her accusation. "Hey, how long will the trip take?"

The *coyote* turned to study Kenny. His look of concern about Maria might cause potential problems.

"You her husband?"

"No."

"What's she to you?" He scrutinized Kenny skeptically. Maybe some *Migra* spy.

"She's a friend. They're both friends," he stammered.

Maria looked at him skeptically. Now what was he up to?

The *coyote* grinned. He was too green to be a cop.

"Three hours, *tops.*"

"We gotta go!" Ramirez honked his horn.

"Do you provide provisions?" Kenny ignored Ramirez.

The *coyote* laughed heartily. His mouth was filled with silver caps. He shook his head. He appraised Maria and Concha.

"You gotta pay me up front."

Concha started to reach into her bra.

"*No,*" Kenny barked, thinking of Carmen. "They'll pay you when they get there."

"I'm warning you, *señor!*" Ramirez honked his horn again. "I have another appointment!" Then he began to swear angrily.

Kenny studied Maria. She was perspiring under her eyes. He could almost hear her heart pounding. Even Concha seemed intimidated, unnerving her further.

"*Maybe we should go back with you!*" Maria cried out, surprising them both, desperately surveying Kenny's crestfallen face. Kenny's shoulders sagged.

"I—"

But she composed herself before he was forced to refuse. And with that, Ramirez revved the engine of the big Chevrolet and peeled out of the dusty yard, leaving Kenny, Maria, and Concha behind.

Maria's doubts about Kenny completely dissipated. Now he was trapped in this horrible place and seemed completely inept, an inexperienced Anglo surrounded by Mexicans.

"Why did he leave?" she demanded of the *coyote*.

"Why do you think?" the *coyote* laughed. "So you couldn't change your mind."

"He has no way to get back!" Maria protested.

"He has feet," the *coyote* smirked. "He has a thumb."

Exasperated, Maria was clearly angry that, on top of everything else, she now had to concern herself with his safety.

"You comeen or not?" the *coyote* demanded.

"Let's go," Concha urged her. "We've come this far."

"Don't go," Kenny urged her, though not very convincingly. Maria was now outraged. Her *abuela* was correct. What did they have a right to expect? She drew herself up. She would take charge from here on out.

"Okay, *Abuelita*, this is what you wanted!" Maria said sharply. Concha looked up, surprised by her tone. She helped her up into the crowded van. When it was Maria's turn to climb up, the *coyote* groped her ass. She turned around and slapped him. He fell back in mock fear. He and his friends laughed.

In that moment Maria locked eyes with Kenny. She drew a deep breath. Then she disappeared behind the rusty metal doors of the van.

Kenny hesitated. Fragmented thoughts hurtled through his mind. He couldn't risk taking them across. Kenny had a face which betrayed deceit. A border guard would read his guilt a mile away. Getting them all detained and thrown into jail would solve nothing. Still, what were they to him? He should walk back to town. Cross the border, get in his Scout, and drive away. She disrespected him now. She saw him for what he was.

A dilettante. A weakling. An armchair liberal making himself feel good for the price of a lemonade.

He began to justify himself as he stood contemplating the rusty old van, rumbling in the dusty yard in the squalid migrant squatter's camp just west of Mexicali. The angry beautiful Mexican woman inside didn't understand that he needed a day off. He had responsibilities back home. He might lose his business. His house. She didn't know about Nick. That Nick was sick. Alcoholic, but sick nevertheless. She didn't know that the responsibility for Nick fell squarely on Kenny's shoulders, not to mention the kids who worked in his kitchen, *all immigrants,* he might add, who loved him dearly for raising them up, giving them jobs, overlooking phony green cards, standing up for them in two days when Carmen, Miguel, and Gabriel all would become U.S. citizens.

She was asking too much, Kenny shook his head. She had judged him too harshly. Kenny was entitled to forget his troubles. Where before he had fancied himself a missionary or a soldier of some honorable underground movement, he was just a tourist here. He was just being honest with himself.

If he believed Carmen, a thousand people tried this same thing every day. These *coyote*s were experienced. Motivated by greed. They had to deliver to collect the money. And if they got caught, turned back, they'd try again tomorrow. He should get to his Scout and drive away. He'd never see them again.

Kenny turned to walk away but stopped.

He didn't trust this *coyote.*

A short drive, a three-hour hike through the desert. Just to make certain they'd leave her alone. He could help with the old lady. Once they were across, made their connection to L.A., he could hitchhike back to Calexico, reclaim his Scout.

His heart was pounding. He should call Nick, say what he was doing. Or Sam Singer, their landlord. Sam had connections everywhere. Just so somebody would know his whereabouts but there wasn't any time. Carmen, Miguel, and Gabriel would have to take care of the kitchen tonight.

"Wait!" he called out to the *coyote.*

"Yeah?" He turned. "For what?"

"One more passenger."

"It'll cost you."

"How much?"

"Fifteen hundred bucks."

After paying for the *retablo,* Kenny didn't even have fifteen dollars left.

"Don't have it. But look, I'm your insurance policy. We get caught, you'll say I'm the *coyote.* "

The *coyote* laughed and popped opened the back of the van. Kenny sprinted toward it.

That night as an ancient nun knelt to say her evening prayers, the votive candles lit by Kenny and Maria began to extinguish. The nun liked to be in the sanctuary when the candles began to flicker, as if the devil himself was blowing them out. One by one they gave up. Soon she was kneeling in darkness.

"The petitioners are now without protection," she observed. She crossed herself and stood up to go for her supper. The skirt of her robe whisked softly across the tile floor as she departed.

It was nearly pitch black inside the van and Kenny found himself wedged between the van door, a broken-off handle poking him at the small of his back, and face to face with a very surprised and angry Maria. They were so close he could hear her heart pounding.

"What can you be *thinking?*" she demanded in the quietest possible way. "I never asked you to do such a crazy thing. You're frightening me. What do you want?"

"I couldn't let you go alone!" he stammered.

"He was concerned about us," Concha observed frankly, in full voice. "It's really quite commendable."

"I can take care of us!"

"*Shut up* back there!" The *coyote* peered through a curtain separating the front compartment with the cargo section. "You wanna get everybody thrown in *jail?* We can stop right now and kick you out! You understand, fuckeen gringo?"

"Sorry."

"We got two hours on bumpy roads before we start walking. I don't wanna hear another fuckeen sound out of you. Any of you!" He let the curtain drop. They could all hear him muttering profanities. Then he turned on the radio.

Kenny's leg was starting to fall asleep. He was desperate to change positions. Sensing it, Maria adjusted herself slightly and he fell into her, against her breasts. The tingling began to subside in his leg and he sighed with relief. They were nearly lip to lip.

"You shouldn't have done this," she whispered. But she reached out and found his hand, clasped it, and held it against her racing heart. Concha could make this out and blinked in approval. To her, the trip was thus far a bona fide success. No one spoke, not when the van veered north, bouncing along bumpy treacherous desert roads.

Kenny figured they had driven west on Mexico Highway 2 and were now cutting north the ten or so miles toward the international border. The sun would be setting now.

Last night, Kenny remembered, the moon was full. He'd worked till ten, closing alone after keeping the kitchen open till ten-fifteen after serving only twenty-four dinners all night, most of them early bird specials. At least eighteen before seven o'clock, mostly locals from the Sun Town Trailer Park.

Kenny grimaced as he remembered telling the vendor in the marketplace that he was a chef. He was a fry cook, and nothing more. Never came out of the kitchen. That much was true. The kitchen, no bigger than ten by twelve, was his domain. The lounge and the dining room were Nick's.

A swinging door with a murky porthole was the line of demarcation, but it is in every restaurant. Different worlds inhabited either side; and not always peacefully. Not always without resentment. It all had to do with money and status. One waiter usually made more than three kitchen workers combined in a night, and then always complained about lousy tips, but Kenny's kitchen crew never complained. Not Carmen, not Gabriel or Miguel.

The waiters were allowed to wear whatever they liked as long as it was fashionable. The kids in Kenny's kitchen, Kenny included, wore jeans, T-shirts, and greasy tennis shoes. Instead of hair nets, they sported baseball caps turned backward and walked home together stinking of onions, grease, and Clorox.

Last night Kenny let his crew leave at nine. They were good-natured about it, but they all hated losing the extra hours, especially Carmen, because she was sending extra money home to her mother, who was sick. Carmen was the matriarch of her family, at only twenty-six. It was Carmen who urged her brothers and cousins to go to school, get English, to work as hard as she worked.

It incensed her that they'd all fought so hard to come to the United States yet were satisfied to remain busboys or day laborers. In two more days Carmen, Miguel, and Gabriel would all become citizens of the United States. Kenny hoped to be there with them. Attend the swearing-in ceremony in Indio.

It occurred to him that he had made a terrible mistake, jumping in this van. He didn't know, couldn't explain what had possessed him.

The van hit a deep pothole. The *coyote* swore. Several people murmured. A young girl began to cry and her mother shushed her, *quiet, little one,* and luckily the child calmed down.

Kenny thought again about the moon. It was probably six-thirty now, and Nick would be dressing for a night at the club, worrying a little about where Kenny was, but the worry wouldn't manifest itself the way it would for a normal person. Nick would drink a little earlier to assuage his fear. A little earlier and much faster. *Kenny got held up at the border; the INS was probably cracking down. That was it. That's what the delay was most likely about.*

The van lurched to a halt and Kenny thought again about the moon. Tonight it would be waning slightly, but enough for them to see. They waited in silence for a good five minutes. Up in front the *coyote* and the driver now conferred in hushed, urgent whispers. The front doors popped open. They could hear footsteps round the side of the van to the back. The rear doors were unlatched so quickly Kenny was unprepared and fell backward, falling three feet and landing in the dirt with a thud, much to the amusement of the *coyote* and his driver.

As Kenny lay there, staring up at them in impotent bewilderment, the driver turned abruptly, walked back to the van, and climbed up behind the wheel. The engine sputtered to life, spewing exhaust over Kenny and Maria and then took off, without lights, back down the road that led them to where Kenny lay sprawled in the dirt.

The wind was knocked out of him. He looked up in utter amazement, unable to breathe, but shortly Maria was kneeling beside him, gently urging him to sit up, with Concha's face looming worriedly over Maria's shoulder.

"Does he need water? Give him some water." Concha instructed her.

"I *will,* Mamita," Maria responded. She opened her canteen, offering it to Kenny. He took a sip. He didn't even have his own water, he thought. Some protector. Now he was a liability.

"Take more," she urged.

"No. I'm okay."

"He should get up," Concha advised. "Scorpions."

Kenny allowed Maria to ease him up and finally stood to his feet. His back was killing him. They looked around. They were standing alone. The air was thick with the sweet, musty smell of creosote and desert lavender. Kenny could barely make out several figures drifting wordlessly into the darkness. They stood at the mouth of a bajada, a broad, flood-created, slanting plain of rising sand dunes clustered with rock and spidery desert bushes and smoke trees. If they didn't start walking, they'd be left behind. Slowly they began to make their way up through the rocks of the ascending bajada. Several yards into the rocks, a weathered sign loomed up in the darkness.

It was a picture of the desert with a coiled snake in the center. Stenciled letters admonished the following: DESIERTO PELIGROSO

"What's it mean?" Kenny asked Maria.

"The desert is treacherous," she whispered.

"So am I," Concha observed. "Let's *go.*"

By late evening, Cathedral City was drenched. The smell of the rain caused the dozing old priest to look up from his book. He decided to treat himself to the pleasure of the church sanctuary so he left his rooms in the rectory and wandered over.

The heavy rain cascading above him on the vaulted roof was particularly comforting. So were the lighted candles of the many petitioners of all the patron saints. In moments like these he was happy to be a priest. He opted to seat himself in Kenny's pew, reflecting that yesterday Kenny had sat in this very spot. He was disappointed not to see him this morning. Would he ever return?

How to minister to gay men and women? Father Gene grieved deeply about this issue; had, in fact the entire length of his career. He wasn't asking anything of them he hadn't asked of himself. He had successfully survived his private temptations through prayer, some days a second at a time. He had come to believe his urges were a blessing from God.

Still . . . this young man had moved him deeply. Whenever a parishioner so filled the old priest's thoughts, he felt obliged to remember them in his personal prayers.

Father Gene lowered the brocaded hassock and fell to his knees to pray.

Kenny never dreamed they would be driven so savagely. The band of Mexicans were now officially *mojados,* illegals, trespassers on the property of the citizens of the United States of America, and the *coyote* assigned to their group was vicious and agitated, rushing them down a footpath alongside a deep arroyo at top speed. The sky overhead had been blackening now for several hours.

His three-hour quote had expanded to twice that, and Kenny sensed they were nowhere near their destination. The clouds clustered wickedly, covering the moon. Then the wind picked up, hot dust devils enveloping them, and this was particularly difficult for Concha.

Occasionally she had to stop to clear her wind passages, the small particles of dirt collecting in her nose and throat. Maria tied a bandanna over the old woman's face. She looked like a wizened *bandido* and the others laughed, but the *coyote* ordered them to hurry with such ferocity that they had to run to get caught up.

This was his first solo trip, and the *coyote* was particularly worried about making good time; about pleasing his superiors who would be waiting to pick them up at their designated meeting spot off Highway 98 between the Mexico border and U.S. Interstate 8. The Interstate was heavily patrolled by the border patrol, so a late-night pickup on a small two-lane highway was the only option.

Maria knew the little *coyote* hated them, had it out for the slow-moving old woman. Spindly and frail, Concha was nonetheless relatively spry, but she was no match for the speed of the young boys comprising the bulk of this group of pilgrims.

"Can't you make her move faster?" he demanded of Maria. "You'll make us all late!"

"She's moving as fast as she can!" Maria insisted. Maria was a head taller than the *coyote* and was too tired to take any abuse. Behind her, Kenny scowled at him. They paused briefly.

"Anybody waiting for you at home?" Maria held out her canteen.

"I was expected at my restaurant. My crew can handle it." He took a delicate sip of her precious water and handed the canteen back to her.

"Your crew," she repeated. "Mostly Latinos, I expect?"

"Mostly," Kenny nodded.

"They'll worry about you," she said softly.

"I expect."

"And your family?"

"My family lives in another state. My mother and my brother and sister. They'd have no reason to worry. Not unless someone called."

Maria studied him with interest. He seemed to be keeping a secret from her. "Anybody else who might be concerned?"

"My partner," he sighed, giving her that much. "My partner and I are close friends. He's somewhat disabled."

"Disabled?"

"He's an alcoholic," Kenny admitted miserably.

"So you look out for him, eh?" She smiled and patted his hand. She liked him for it. "I'm sorry we're causing people worry," she said simply, not pursuing it anymore. "Maybe it explains why you came along. Put yourself at such unnecessary risk."

She'd also brought up a good point. Nick would call his mother if he was still gone by morning. He'll call her shit-faced drunk and crying and scare the hell out of her. His father died several years ago. His parents had met Nick, even came for summer vacations to stay with them in Laguna. Kenny's father was also an alcoholic, and his mother martyred her life to his unpredictable mood swings. She had taught Kenny how to stay. She was a master in the art of staying.

Concha's laughter brought Kenny to his senses. He still owed Maria an explanation as to why he'd opted to come along.

"Maybe I'm like your grandmother. Maybe I wanted a little adventure." In the background Concha was in deep discussion with two lovesick teenagers. She seemed to be lecturing them.

"My grandmother is a very strong woman," Maria commented, reading Kenny's thoughts. "She was wonderful to me after my parents were killed. I was very young but I remember them vividly. They spoke Spanish and English to me. I was fluent by the time I was eight."

"How do you cope with the way they died?"

"Violence isn't such a stranger in Mexico. I pray that my mother didn't suffer. She was quite pretty. The soldiers would have noticed that."

"Pretty as you?"

"I am nothing compared to her." Sadness filled her face. "Sometimes I have nightmares. I ask God for only one thing, every night. That she died quickly. My father was very strong. I'm sure he must have fought for her. Gave her his very last breath. I'm sure she must have been so worried about me. I'm proud of what they were trying to achieve. No matter what. And I know we'll see each other again."

"You think God answers prayers?"

"If we wear him down enough," she smiled simply.

The *coyote* felt a drop of rain. Looked up. He studied the angry sky. Rain would slow them considerably, and this he could not allow. He surveyed the arroyo. For many of his clients, this was a second or third return trip. They all knew that a footbridge, perhaps a mile or more down the path, was the object of this mad run along the arroyo. The footbridge was constructed to eliminate the established danger of falling while descending into the arroyo or drowning by flash flood. The arroyo was also rife with scorpions and snakes. Two more strikes against any premature passage, which was exactly what they all sensed that this nervous little *coyote* was contemplating.

"We cross here!" he announced. They sagged in disbelief. Concha was happy enough to rest while the suggestion was being digested. Maria critically studied the deep ravine, jagged with rock and cactus. Spindly soccoro branches jutted up from the sides. Descending into such angry terrain would be impossible for Concha. Before Maria could object, others stepped forward in protest.

"We'll be at the footbridge in less than a hour!"

More drops of rain. The *coyote* pulled out the pistol. This was a test of wills he did not intend to lose. End of discussion. They go.

He held Maria behind.

"Let her go," Kenny shouted.

The *coyote* waved the gun.

"You and the old lady go first. She'll slow us down. You gotta push her."

Maria nodded, concerned that Concha might slip. "Please go with her."

Kenny grimaced and followed after her. It was obvious that the *coyote* would like the old woman to stumble. A light rain began to fall. The others dropped into the arroyo, moving nimbly downward over rock and brush. Maria panicked as she watched Concha and Kenny slowly pick their way down the ravine.

"Maria? Where are you?" Conch called up.

Maria yanked herself free from the *coyote* and he struck her. To his amazement, she struck him back so hard he fell. She rushed down ahead of him and he followed, screaming obscenities, furious that she had hit him back. Kenny looked up.

"Leave her alone!" he yelled at the *coyote*. He started up toward them.

"No!" Maria ordered him. "Stay with her. Mamita! Slow down!"

But below them they could see the arroyo slowly filling with water. Concha had moved several yards closer to the water's edge and Kenny couldn't lose sight of her. Slick wet rocks undulated like giant black bloodsuckers on the bed of a shallow creek. Her fellow travelers gingerly moved around them. The thick angry clouds made it impossible to see. A deep rumbling increased as the rain picked up. All of them looked up in panic. The arroyo was beginning to flood.

"Come back! The arroyo is flooding!" cried the *coyote,* and his charges scrambled up the walls for safety. He grabbed Maria by the back of her shirt. Concha gazed at her in miserable bewilderment, rivulets of rain tracing the lines of worry in her wrinkled face. There was no way she could quickly scale the side of the arroyo to safety.

"Maria?"

"*Let go!*" Maria struggled to pull away from his grasp. "She has our money!" He released her instantly. He pointed his gun at her.

"Go get her!"

"I'll get her!" Kenny yelled.

Kenny quickly made his way to Concha. A low roar was swelling. They all heard it. Most had made it safely to the top. Maria stared anxiously down at Kenny and her grandmother. As Kenny urged Concha up the ravine, the roaring deafened them. They looked up. A wall of water ripping through the ravine was bearing directly down on them. Above them, Maria screamed.

Kenny flattened himself against the rock wall of the arroyo and reached for Concha's outstretched fingers. Concha steadied herself near an ancient tamarisk tree, stealing herself for the rush of water.

"Save us!" Concha cried out to heaven.

Suddenly they were submerged.

The panicked onlookers watched them disappear beneath the surface of the raging water, the *coyote* fingering his pistol in case his companions decided to avenge these unnecessary deaths. Suddenly Kenny's head popped into view, his eyes closed, coughing and spitting up liquid. Maria cried with relief, because it was apparent that he was holding on to her grandmother with one submerged hand, though Concha was still covered in foaming, raging water.

As the water subsided below Kenny's shoulders, his eyes opened and he yanked Concha's arm to bring her to the surface. She stumbled, nearly toppling into the river, but she caught her balance and he yanked again. This time it worked and Maria managed to reach forward, grab Concha's hand, and fall back, dragging her grandmother up over the embankment of the muddy arroyo and to safety.

But to her horror, and the horror of her fellow travelers, even the offending little *coyote,* over Concha's panting shoulder Maria saw Kenny fall back, arms and hands outstretched, his eyes widening, yet locking calmly again with Maria's.

For a moment Kenny felt suspended in midair as if some invisible supernatural force held him under each outstretched arm while the floodwater raged beneath him. He could see the amazement in the eyes and faces of his concerned Mexican companions. Only Concha didn't look up, lying lifeless in a heap on the ground near the edge. Maria was frantically trying to revive her. She forced her eyes to look away from Kenny and leaned in to attend to her grandmother.

It was then that suspension gave way.

Fatigue was filling Kenny, in waves of resolve so peaceful he felt ecstatic. His head lolled to one side and his eyes closed wearily. In the hollow distance he heard screams, though with all certainty they came from the horrified mouths of nearby onlookers. Arms still outstretched, Kenny allowed his body to let go, keeling back. The last thing he saw was the confused assurance in Maria's eyes.

"Nicky . . ." Kenny uttered.

Nothing he felt approximated fear. Only peace and coolness beneath the surface of the black tormented floodwaters and his relief to be, at long last, swept away.

3

The Drowning

With her grandmother choking and spitting up filthy water, Maria had to immediately attend to clearing her windpipe, had to relinquish Kenny to the floodwaters, as a drenched Concha convulsed and vomited on her knees while Maria attempted to resuscitate her. Out of the corner of her eye she saw several boys racing along the flood plane of the arroyo hoping to catch a glimpse of him, but without ropes, even if they did, there was certainly nothing they could do.

They returned several moments later. When she looked up, they shrugged. Kenny most certainly had drowned. As Concha began to revive, she began to inquire about his whereabouts.

"Where's the boy?" she whimpered.

"He saved your life, Abuelita," Maria smoothed back her hair. "You nearly drowned."

"Where is he?" Concha's face and skin were damp, though hot to the touch.

"He pushed you to safety and fell back, Mamita . . . He was lost."

And Concha screamed in remorse. Others began wailing with her, even the men.

"Why not me!" she wailed.

"No! Don't say such a thing!" Maria protested, erupting in hysterical tears. "I thought you were dead! I couldn't bear it!"

"But he only came along because of us!" She grabbed Maria's arms. "He was so young and I'm just an old woman. Him for me! *Him for me!*"

And all Maria could do was try to hold her.

"Many people die crossing the border, *señora,*" a solemn young boy observed after she quieted.

Others nodded. Some crossed themselves. Behind them the *coyote* shifted one foot to another, disgusted about all the carrying-on. "There's nothing to be done! Feeleen sorry gets us all arrested or killed. We rest one hour and move out. As it is, we're already late, thanks to these two bitches!"

When Nick came in the next morning, Marcella stood leaning against the back of the bar with her arms folded, her expression satisfied but grim. Carmen, Miguel, and Santiago all sat on stools at the end of the bar nearest the kitchen. Other than staff meetings, Nick couldn't recall a time he ever saw them come purposefully through the porthole doors.

"What's happened to Kenny?" Nick asked.

"He's in a hospital in El Centro," and the three Latinos crossed themselves. Carmen had been crying. Miguel and Santiago flanked her, ashen with concern.

Nick staggered toward them. "Is he in danger?"

"They found a card in his wallet."

"Tell me if he's all right!"

"Border patrol called." Marcella continued to mete out portions of information, to keep him at her mercy for as long as she could possibly delay.

"What happened? Please tell me what happened."

"He was found in an arroyo this morning."

"What's an arroyo?" Nick asked.

"A ditch," Carmen offered.

"A Mexican ditch," Marcella confirmed. Miguel and Santiago nodded in agreement.

"Was he robbed? Attacked? Is he dead? Will somebody *please* tell me if he's okay!"

Marcella paused to make him a drink. He sat on a stool and drank it all down, sure they were about to tell him Kenny was dead. She made him another. Down the hatch.

"They wouldn't tell me. They want someone responsible to come down and make arrangements."

"I'll leave now."

"I'll drive you, Mr. Nick." Miguel stood up.

"And I'll watch the front. Carmen and Santiago can handle the kitchen."

"Call Sam and let him know." Sam was Nick and Kenny's landlord. Nick ran toward the kitchen, Miguel trotting behind.

"We already lit him a candle," Carmen called after him. "You call when you find out."

"What was he doing down there?" Marcella queried. "Do you think he was smuggling?"

"Smuggling?" Nick asked incredulously. "Smuggling what?"

"Drugs? Money?" She eyed Carmen and Miguel. "Illegals? Lotta money in trafficking illegals . . . I hear."

"Lotta money," Carmen echoed softly.

"That's absurd."

"Do you think he was leaving you? Running away?"

"Fuck *you!*" Nick raged. "Let's go, Miguel."

"It could be anything," Marcella called after him. "All of the above." She shrugged her shoulders as the door separating the kitchen and the dining room swung madly back and forth till it came to an unsteady rest on its hinges.

As the sun began to rise, and they were huddled together among the rocks away from the other travelers, Maria contemplated her sleeping grandmother with great worry. A slight wheezing in her breath had arisen. She was fearful it might be the early stages of pneumonia. Thoughts of Kenny kept appearing and reappearing in her mind. What had possessed him to come along? Where was he now? Had he managed to clamber to safety or had he perished, submerged in the muddy water? She could still see his eyes as he fell back into the water; beatifying Kenny for all time in her thoughts.

His outstretched muscular arms, a calm swan dive backward into the water; graceful even in chaos and then gone.

She had known him less than twenty-four hours and she would never close her eyes again without seeing first his image flicker briefly before fading; Kenny would always be in her mind. Without him the *coyote* would have certainly abandoned them or worse. She might have been raped. As horrible as she felt about his accident, the rescue of her grandmother was so perversely thrilling she felt guilty to even utter a prayer of gratitude. She also knew because of the tragedy they would go easier on her and her grandmother tomorrow. The group had been saddened by the unnecessary death of the beautiful, cultivated man. They, too, regarded Concha's rescue as being divine intervention.

There was a reason to spare one, take another, and who were they to question God's will?

Something divine had intervened last night in the arroyo, and had filled Maria with humility. Perhaps as in her *retablo*, her parents were up in heaven, guiding their paths, interceding on their behalf. Concha's faith has always been so simple, so easy for her. She had raised Maria to pray to the Virgin Mary, to go to Mass, to say her rosary. Maria's faith had been mechanical until last night, and as she held her grandmother, she had felt like rejoicing.

"Thank you, Blessed Virgin," she whispered fiercely. "Thank you for saving her."

And then the long shadow of the *coyote* blanketed her view of the sky. He loomed over them menacingly, and didn't say anything for the longest time.

Then.

"What kind of granddaughter would bring such an old lady on a trip like this? Are you crazy or just stupid?"

"I'm all she has. She wanted to come! I couldn't leave her!"

"She held us up last night."

"We made it, didn't we? Our friend *died* because of your mistake!"

"He died because of you! Well, let me warn you, if your grandmother has to die, or I have to die, I can promise you it's gonna be *her* . . ." He tossed a burning cigarette in the sand near Concha.

He laughed and disappeared into the rocks.

As a nervous Miguel drove an emotional and highly intoxicated Nick south below the desert cities toward the international border, he fell to wondering about the nature of Nick and Kenny's relationship. He knew they were gay, but nothing like *los maricones* he remembered from his youth in Mexico. It was unthinkable that an openly homosexual man could also be a *patron*, a boss like Kenny was, or own an important business like Nick's the way he perceived Nick did. He didn't understand that Kenny was an equal partner, because the bar was named for Nick.

Sneaking a glance at Nick, huddled in the corner of the car, he pondered over the fact that, as kids, he and his friends routinely brutalized local transvestites. Now, living in Cathedral City, he reflected that such behavior would be reprehensible, but he didn't have the words to explain why. It seemed to Miguel that the gay and Latino communities had much in common. Both were beleaguered politically. They had all heard about Pat Buchanan's speech at the 1992 Republican National Convention. Gays and Latinos had been derided equally in that speech. It also seemed, having primarily observed Kenny, that homosexuals had a certain spiritual yearning, not dissimilar to his own culture. It made him sad that they were an abomination to God and the Catholic faith.

Where did they have to go when they wanted to pray?

Although he and Nick had never exchanged little more than a greeting or a request for more ice, Miguel was fond of him, and felt bad that he was hurting and concerned. What would they do if Kenny was dead? What would happen to the restaurant? To their jobs? Within forty-eight hours, Miguel was scheduled to take his oath as a citizen of the United States. Kenny had been instrumental to that end. He helped with their paperwork, their filings. He paid legal fees when he could. He drove them to countless interviews. He made calls for them when paperwork was lost, or filled out incorrectly.

Even now as they roared south on Highway 86, Miguel shuddered each time he passed a green and white Border Patrol vehicle. *La Migra* was everywhere. A green card didn't guarantee freedom from harassment. It was possible they'd pull them over today, just because he was Mexican and Nick was Anglo. He was glad they weren't driving below El Centro.

"So Nick, how'd you and Kenny meet?" Miguel was shocked at his balls. What a personal question! But Nick didn't seem to take it wrong. He seemed relieved to make conversation. His silence, so uncharacteristically Nick, made Miguel understand how fearful he was of what they'd find in El Centro.

"We met in Denver. In 1980. Kenny had just graduated from college. I was in town trying to decide if I should open a restaurant there or stay and make another stab at the failing one I owned in Laguna." Nick paused to reflect. Then he blurted out, "Do you think Marcella was right? Do you think Kenny was leaving me?"

Miguel shook his head. "No."

"He didn't warn you? Or Carmen? He'd never leave without taking care of you."

"Or you," Miguel reasoned kindly.

This quieted Nick. He felt momentarily reassured. An INS chase car pulled up behind them, roaring past. They were after an older-model gray cargo van. The two vehicles rounded a corner and were out of sight. Perspiring, Miguel clutched the wheel.

"Kenny was unique," Nick began to recall. "Different from anyone I'd ever met. He rented a room in the attic of an old Victorian house of some friends of mine. He was working as a waiter at the Palace Arms in the Brown Palace Hotel in Denver. He'd just graduated from college with an art history degree. He has religious hangups. He was sensitive. And very sensual," Nick winked at Miguel. "He had curly black hair and blue, blue eyes. When I first laid eyes on him, I knew he was the one. He wasn't so sure about me."

"No?" Miguel asked politely.

"I was *so* California. I arrived tanner and blonder than I'd ever been. I'd just had my teeth capped because I broke them in a bad fall. He thought I was shallow. But opposites attract. I asked him to move to California within twenty-four hours. He saved my life, you know."

"How?" Miguel asked.

"I was drunk, and standing on the landing outside his room above a flight of stairs. I fell back and he grabbed me by the lapels of my jacket. He pulled me so hard we crashed to his floor."

"I've heard," Miguel volunteered, "that when you save a man's life, you're responsible for that man for the rest of his life."

"I've heard that, too," Nick ruminated, and wondered if that was on Kenny's mind as he drove away the other day.

So I'm dying, Kenny thought. He'd heard drowning was peaceful. He'd see if they were correct. The girl gave him the courage. He could have saved himself but this seemed like a good place to get off, slip away unnoticed in the midst of what would be remembered as a heroic moment. They'd find his truck in Calexico. His body in some ditch, five miles from here. They always did, always found the bodies, and this whole area was so heavily patrolled. Kenny was certain they'd find his.

He was spinning around. He could feel his head hitting the rocks, his hands scraping the walls of the arroyo but it didn't hurt. His lungs filled with water but he wasn't uncomfortable, not panicked at all. Just rolling along.

He couldn't make sense of it at all. Just couldn't go back, not with an opportunity like this. The girl and the old lady would be okay. They'd made it into the United States. The grandmother got her wish. If they got caught and deported, at least she'd have done what she set out to do, which is more than Kenny could say for himself.

Nick. Can you hear me? Do you know what's happening? I'm leaving you but not because I don't love you. I do love you. But I've been so unhappy, see? The stress is too great. I'm so afraid for you, and so unable to help you I'd rather die than face another day.

When Nick had asked Kenny to join him in California, he promised Kenny that everything would be blue. Blue skies, blue ocean, blue like Kenny's eyes. Laguna was the *Riviera* of Southern California. Nick had a home high on a hill overlooking the sea. The restaurant had great potential, because it was located on Pacific Coast Highway and situated directly across the street from the prestigious Surf and Sand Hotel.

Kenny argued that he didn't have the experience Nick needed to help him run a restaurant. He was only an assistant waiter. "But I trust you," Nick assured him. "I have all the experience I need, but I can't be up front, meeting and greeting our customers, if I have to worry about what's walking out the back door of the kitchen. The kitchen will be yours. You can hire and fire—"

"I could never fire anyone," said Kenny. "I don't like to give orders, and I don't like to be told what to do."

"You'll learn how to manage people."

They were lying in Kenny's bed listening to Carmen McRae. Nick sat up to smoke a cigarette. He paused to admire Kenny's craftsmanship. The room was cluttered with half-finished projects. Carvings here, painted boxes there. An old sewing machine was set up in the corner. Bags of old fabric leaned against the wall. Nick was comfortable with clutter.

"I collect old things," he observed. "Vintage *objets* from garage sales and swap meets. Our belongings would live well together."

"I'd be moving in on top of your already established life. I'd be a guest in your house."

Nick turned back to face him. "You'd be my life. This isn't an offer I'm making lightly. I came to Denver to evaluate whether I should make a fresh start here or go back to California and finish what I started. You need a fresh start. Come to California with me, Kenny. You'll never regret it and neither will I." Nick had a habit of winking when sentiment overcame him, as if he were trying to check a tear.

"You really want me."

"I do. Since the night I stood on the landing outside that very door. I saw in an instant how special you were and what a bad fit this house and Denver are for you. I saw it all in an instant. You don't know me that well, but you'll learn, I make quick decisions based on my gut feelings. I never change my mind. I love you, Kenny. When you come to California, everything will be blue. The sky, the water—these eyes if you don't come."

"Those are cosmetic contacts."

"I wanted green eyes and I have them. I fight to get what I want. I'll fight for you." And then he smiled gently, not big and loud like he usually smiled, but apologetically. Hat in his hand. "But I have one condition."

"What's that?"

"We've both done our share of fucking around. I want a marriage. I want a family with you. Nobody else interferes. We stay faithful. Can you do that?"

"Yeah," said Kenny. "I could."

"Then you'll come?"

"I will."

And so he did.

As Kenny gave himself up to the raging water in the flooding arroyo, he calmly reminded himself to spend his remaining waking moments wisely, to be a good steward of his memory, to serve himself up only what was beautiful and beloved, so of course he dreamed about Laguna and Cathedral City, and of Nick, and the years they'd spent together.

The house in Laguna turned out to be a converted studio apartment on the lower deck of someone else's house, but Kenny didn't mind. It had a fireplace, a sleeping loft, and a deck which overlooked Laguna and the ocean beyond. It was filled with Nick's collection of stuff, some of it junk and some rare and worth hanging on to.

Kenny brought his sewing machine, his paint supplies, and a few family photos. He owned little more than a couple pairs of jeans, a few tie-dyed T-shirts, black waiter's pants, and one good white shirt.

In a month of mornings Kenny awoke to mourning doves cooing and Nick stroking his face. In the distance he could hear the crashing of the surf. After a few Bloody Marys they'd drive to West Street; Laguna's gay beach, get some sun, come home, and make love. Later Nicky's oldest friends would visit—Molly, a trim chic dyke who loved the beach, always dressed for water in a black tank suit with a scarf wrapped around her waist. Molly was a Laguna artist whom Kenny liked instantly. And then there were Nellie and Tony. Nellie, a Vanessa Redgrave look-alike, who'd just divorced her husband after twenty years of marriage. She always arrived with caviar and cracked crab and bottles of champagne. And Tony, kind, affable, bearded, the new love of her life. On weekends they'd all go together to the swap meet in Anaheim. Kenny had never been to a swap meet. Acres of recycled junk. Every Sunday night they'd return to their already overcrowded studio, loaded with treasures to admire.

Then they might drive down to the Little Shrimp, one of three Laguna gay restaurants, have cocktails, eat steaks. Kenny would laugh in wonder at Nick's popularity, as eccentric after eccentric would approach their table to say hello and meet Kenny, whom Nick was always touching and kissing with pride. Kenny never thought being out and gay would be this fun. They were in love; the whole of Laguna knew it, and Kenny thought he'd burst with happiness. Celebrity was an aphrodisiac. These were their lustiest days.

Nick was in no hurry to restore the restaurant, which Kenny agreed had potential but now was little more than a bar. Nick was having too much fun with Kenny, wanted to spend all his time with him. And while Kenny liked to drink, he wasn't used to drinking in the mornings, as Nick liked to do. Or all through the day or night for that matter.

They took weekend trips to San Francisco, and out to Palm Springs. They spent ten days exploring Maui and Kauai. When Nick and Kenny were alone, Nick was a different, much more vulnerable man, dropping his act, his need to be the center of attention. These trips solidified their relationship, because what Nick had initially sensed about Kenny was now confirmed as fact: Kenny's humility and integrity freed Nick up enough to let down his guard. They could be quiet together—like family.

Then one day Kenny came home from the local Albertson's Market to find Nick drunk and huddled on the floor of the bathroom with a pile of bills and legal-looking documents.

"Please forgive me," was all Nick could chatter. "Please forgive me but I've lost everything. It's gone. They've taken it away."

Nick, Kenny came to find out, owed everyone in town. He also had a silent partner in the restaurant, Hal Green, a straight real estate developer who lived in Newport Beach. As Nick needed advances to cover his living expenses, he'd sign percentages over to his partner on cocktail napkins. He had delayed making improvements, breaking promises to come in every night, to meet and greet, to make the customers feel welcome and want to come back. That was Nick's allure to Hal in the first place. He was the personality, the draw to locals and summer tourists. When Nick didn't come in, neither did his customers.

Earlier that day Hal came into the restaurant and presented Nick with all his signed cocktail napkins and receipts for the accumulated cash he had advanced. Nick had invaded his entire share of the restaurant. And now he owed Hal twenty-two thousand dollars. It would be forgiven if he walked without a fight. If not, he'd be sued.

What was clear to Kenny more than Nick's concern about the loss of the restaurant was his fear that Kenny would leave him. "This isn't what you came to California for. I promised you so much more."

"I've gotten more than I expected in other ways," Kenny smiled kindly.

"I'm humiliated. I'm ruined in Laguna. I don't think I have another start-up in me."

"So we'll move." Kenny sank down to the floor and cradled him. "We'll go somewhere else."

"But you love it here."

"Because you're here. Now where can we go where it's cheap?"

"The desert is cheap. Remember, I used to live out there."

Kenny loved the desert. "Let's go."

"Really? I have an old friend I can call. Her name is Ruthie. Her husband owns a lot of property. She might have some ideas."

"Call her," Kenny said simply.

Later that night Nick came out of the bathroom and found Kenny kneeling by the stairs to the sleeping loft. He looked up, somewhat embarrassed. Then he stood.

"What are you *doing?*"

"Praying," Kenny offered.

"What?" Nick asked in amazement. "Things aren't that desperate."

"I pray every night before I go to bed."

Nick guffawed. "I haven't seen you."

"It's a private thing with me."

Nick studied him. "I was raised in a Catholic orphanage. We can talk about *that.*" By his tone, Kenny knew Nick's experiences hadn't been positive.

"That's why I thought it might be a turnoff for you. It usually is."

"Not as long as you pray for me . . ." Nick smiled quietly. He moved past Kenny into the kitchen.

"I do," Kenny called after him.

Kenny could hear Nick fixing a drink.

"And you aren't offended if I don't believe as you do," Nick called out to him.

"No," Kenny nodded.

Nick came back to where Kenny was standing. "Nightcap? It's been a long day."

"I don't think so, Nicky. I may be cutting back myself."

"Suit yourself," Nick murmured. "Mind if I go ahead?"

As Kenny tumbled along, his only thoughts were of Nick's well-being, fearful that he'd been so angry and judgmental these last few years that Nick would think he'd just up and left. Just driven away, not to come back.

The distance certainly grew in the years after they left Laguna and moved to Cathedral City. The swinging door from the kitchen to the dining room represented more than the class and cultural differences between the Latinos working their asses off in the back and the well-heeled desert rat clientele drinking and laughing in the air-conditioned front lounge.

Kenny and Nick had staked out their territories, and for one to visit the other was tantamount to traversing an international border. Both worlds rarely mixed it up at Nick's. When they did, it usually resulted in a public showdown, embarrassing them both.

The fights were usually about drinking and driving. And money. Always the lack of money. Or the terrible financial decisions made and implemented when Nick drank. Or Kenny's antisocial behavior. He refused to be political, let alone polite. Nick would have loved it if Kenny were more gregarious, more social. He longed to be out more, to frequent other clubs, to network in the desert gay community, but Kenny refused.

He'd fought shyness since he was a child, and one day several years ago, he looked up and accepted himself just as he was. Later Nick verbalized it. Kenny wasn't really shy. He was judgmental.

Kenny liked things much simpler than most people. He appreciated humility. His own and in others. He liked music and art. He drove an old truck and wanted few belongings. Where Nick needed the house on the hill with a pool, Kenny did not aspire to the admiration or envy of his fellow men. He preferred his solitude and de-

cided to no longer fight it or make excuses for it. Not wanting attention, he most likely chose a partner who, by virtue of childhood
trauma and abandonment issues, absolutely craved it.

But all the unspoken compromise between a couple could not over-
ride other very important and necessary components to what make up
a relationship.

Sex, for instance. Kenny's ebbing sexual desire. Kenny hated to be
grabbed when he could smell alcohol on Nick's breath. *Hated it*.
Hence the nights spent on the couch in the living room, which
started every so often and evolved to every night. For Kenny to move
in to one of the spare bedrooms would have been too provocative,
too hurtful, and too truthful.

So they came to a truce. At work they stayed out of each other's
way. Nick could drink and glad-hand his regulars if he didn't drink
and drive and allowed Kenny to handle all the money. In exchange,
Kenny could stay out of sight, back in the kitchen with his crew,
Latin music blaring on the radio, the *retablos* and votive candles,
and the alley filled with the disparate comings and goings of gay men
and Latino families.

And now, with the river water rushing around him, Kenny was
mindful to be grateful for the constancy they'd had in each other's
lives. That he'd opted to hang on, to not lose his faith, for even if the
emotion of love had faded, the knowledge, the *fact* of loving Nick,
had never wavered. Nick loved having a home with Kenny, would
never discuss any details of childhood, but Kenny knew Nick had
been horribly scarred by those events.

And most of it had been good. They were used to each other.
Loyal. As a couple, they were as committed as any two human beings could be. Different as night and day but a team, and now Kenny
found himself praying for one more day to give. A day to make up
for the last few bad years. He wondered how Nick would feel if he
didn't come back.

And Kenny began to fight the river.

As he struggled, he dreamed of Carmen, Miguel, and Gabriel, and
other desperate hopeful immigrants who had preceded him on this
arid desert path. Lastly Maria's face loomed overhead, like a rising
iridescent lunar Virgin of Guadalupe, a *retablo* saint, and from her
vista she could see across the desert, she could see the scorpions and
rattlesnakes, she could see the parched, cracking sand, the spindly
skeletal salt cedar trees.

Maria could see ahead and she was crying, and suddenly Kenny woke coughing up water, the distant *chop, chop, chop* of a Border Patrol helicopter veering southeast toward him. A group of worried-looking Mexican day laborers were trying to revive him and Kenny sat up, not knowing where he was. Then he recognized the silhouette of Mount Signal rising behind them to the southwest where Mexico lay; and the twinkling dawn lights of Mexicali, Calexico, and El Centro to the southeast; and ahead of them, the vast flat Yuha Desert of Southern California, and the splintering desert dirt roads, patrolled hourly by the U.S. Border Patrol; and the spidery canal system fed by rains and the deceptively treacherous All American Canal, which teamed to irrigate the vast El Centro agricultural economy of the Imperial Valley.

Highway 98 lay out there. Interstate 8. With checkpoints and 120-degree temperatures.

El Norte.

"Sir? Can you hear me, sir?"

A young Latino border patrol agent was kneeling down, shaking him awake. A medical helicopter had set down on the nearby desert floor and Kenny was being loaded onto a stretcher.

"What's he doing out here?" another voice asked, this time a female border patrol agent.

"Smuggling? But what? Tonks or drugs." 'Tonk' was the sound of a flashlight hitting the head of an undocumented alien. An illegal was a tonk.

"Sir, can you hear me? What are you doing out here in the middle of the desert?"

"I don't remember," and Kenny passed out.

When he woke up, six hours later in an El Centro hospital room, Nick was sitting next to his bed. Unshaven. Disheveled blond hair. Roaring drunk. Classic looking, even in despair.

"Nick?"

Nick started in. "They think you're a *coyote.*"

"What'd you tell them?"

"I told them that you were my lover of eighteen years, and if you were a *coyote*, I most certainly would have known about it."

Kenny sank miserably back into his pillows. "Then what did they say?"

"Lucky for you they laughed and said I could take you *home.*" Nick perched himself on the edge of the mattress. "They figure you were dragged by the water for six miles. Some Mexicans found you in an alfalfa field. They say it's a miracle you didn't drown, let alone no broken bones. Your wallet was still in your pocket. Your Scout was recovered in Mexicali. Stripped, I might add. Miguel drove down with me. He went across the border and drove it back for you."

"What day is it?"

"You left on Tuesday. This is Wednesday afternoon."

"Who's running the restaurant?"

"Gabriel and Carmen are handling the kitchen and Marcella is behind the bar." Nick's hands were trembling. "Think I can smoke in here?"

"It's a hospital."

"Oh, right." He patted Kenny's hand. His brow was furrowed with concern. He looked old, Kenny thought. And crippled with alcohol.

"Nick, were you worried about me? When I didn't come home?"

"They say its a *miracle* you weren't killed. They never saw anything like it. I was worried sick about you. What were you doing out there?"

"I don't remember anything. Nothing at all. Except I wanted you to know where I was."

"You probably got knocked on the head. You were delirious. You were calling out for the Virgin Mary. That's what the border patrol said." He gazed at Kenny with relieved anger. "I feel like I don't know you anymore. But I'm so glad you're okay. I was so worried. I don't know who I'd be without you."

And then Nick put his head down on the bed.

In the mirror over the hospital room sink Kenny saw them reflected back. He recognized Nick, but his own self-image was hazy. How had he survived? he marveled. And why? Six miles down a flooding arroyo. With no broken bones.

He didn't have any answers. All he knew to do was to stroke Nick's hair, speak soothingly, reassure him.

"I love you, Nicky . . ."

Be grateful to God for that extra day.

4

The Mayor of Cathedral City

"Ruthie?"

No answer.

"I'm going out to Cathedral City. It's the first of the month."

"Say hello to the boys."

Ruthie tried to ignore him as Sam stood at the door of her bedroom, his cigar smoke wafting toward her as she lay huddled under her blanket at two-thirty in the afternoon.

"Ruthie, I want you to get dressed today."

No answer. He moved to the side of the bed and sat next to her, his big hand reaching over her side and resting just under her breasts.

"I really mean it. You can't stay in bed all day. It isn't healthy. You hear me?"

"I have to go to the grocery store later," she finally acknowledged. "Tell Kenny and Nicky I said hello." She pulled the comforter over her face and rolled away from him.

"Inez is here. She needs to make up our bedroom."

Again, no answer. He studied her intently. After a moment he patted her gently, stood up, and left her alone. He lingered for a moment at the door. She was relieved when she felt him withdraw.

"Work around her," she heard him tell Inez, the cleaning lady. "Your *esposo* have your rent this month?" Moments later Ruthie saw a flash of light behind her drapes as Sam's white Lincoln Continental pulled out of the driveway.

When Sam and Ruthie moved to Las Palmas, Sam bought her interior-designed furniture for thousands and thousands of dollars.

Everything white, chrome, and Lucite, and though they'd never admit it to each other, they hated it. It only created worry—scratches on the Lucite, stains on the sofas—so Ruthie kept one room like the happy old times, a small converted maid's room with a beat-up old couch and easy chair where they both hung out to watch TV.

The bedrooms were more of a white nightmare, a blizzard of white dressers, chaise longues, and in the master, twin orthopedic beds, and they made Ruthie think of illness and death. The first time she lay down on them, her fingers dangled over the side, and when she felt the cold metal controls, she was speechless with horror.

The day the beds arrived, Sam pushed them together for appearances' sakes, because appearances were his department, but anybody knows twin beds pushed together create the best excuse to avoid intimacy. The crack down the middle represents a coupling separate but still unified. A unity separate, but still contained under a false committed plane of a pure white top sheet and comforter.

"I wish I had a rich husband who let me lie in bed all day," Inez muttered into the darkness as she stomped into the bedroom. Ruthie could hear her move into the dressing area and begin organizing her vanity. Tiny, homely, and formidable, Inez was so terrifying that most of her clients disappeared on the days she came to clean.

"When I lived in Mexico, I had my own maids," she grumbled. "Now *I'm* a maid! A maid for a loca lazy woman."

The only person who refused to be intimidated by her was Ruthie. Today, even in the cloudy grip of terrible depression, Ruthie planned to make Inez change the bed without getting out of it. A silent contest of wills between them.

"I need to change the sheets," Inez admonished her. "Mr. Sam ordered me."

No answer.

Inez contemplated the bed. Undoing one side of the fitted sheet on Sam's side, she rolled it toward the center of the mattress where Ruthie lay. Then she reached for the clean sheet and began making Sam's side of the bed. Marching to Ruthie's side, she undid her side of the used sheet, and after vigorously raising it up, rolled Ruthie's slender body onto the side of the mattress with the new sheet already in place. Quickly snatching up the soiled sheets and blankets, she fitted the remaining edge of the clean sheet onto Ruthie's side of the mattress.

"Hah!" she cried triumphantly but Ruthie didn't acknowledge

her. Instead she lay catatonically where Inez had deposited her. Inez shook her head. "Get up, today, missus . . ." she urged her. Still Ruthie failed to show any sign of life. Inez shook her head forlornly and gathered the pile of dirty sheets into the plastic laundry basket.

She liked Ruthie but she didn't know why. Perhaps it was her palpable sorrow. Inez rarely had the luxury of pitying anyone. Not from her station in life.

"Lazy cow," muttered Inez as she uprighted several silver-framed photographs on Ruthie's dressing table. They were glamour shots of Ruthie in the sixties. Inez's favorite was Ruthie at a microphone, singing in the club Sam owned in Cathedral City, wearing a slinky low-cut gown. Inez always polished the intricate silver frame extra carefully on this one. It fascinated her that the woman in the picture was the same lump of potatoes lying nearby in the blacked-out bedroom.

"You like that one, don't you, Inez?" Ruthie loomed up behind her from the darkness. Even with her hair flattened and her face puffy from sleep, Ruthie at fifty-five was still a remarkable woman. Inez could see that she'd stuffed pillows under the blankets to make her think Ruthie was still sleeping.

"Lazy *cow*, huh? That part about having maids when you were in Mexico . . ."

Inez bit her lip.

"You aren't *in* Mexico anymore, are you, Inez?" She pushed past her to go to the enclosed lavatory. Winking good-naturedly at a scowling Inez, Ruthie closed the door with a snap.

Inez finished polishing the frame and set it down among the other photographs of Ruthie and Sam; Ruthie and Nick at the old bar when it was Sam's; Nick and Kenny in the front of the bar with the new sign *Nick's*.

This one Inez studied carefully, because pictured behind it, across the alley, was a little row of beat-up houses, and the neatest one, peeking out just to the right of the bar, was the one that her family rented from Ruthie's husband, Sam Singer.

This was a picture of her house twenty years ago, and Inez, who was saving to buy it, liked the fact that it was framed in silver.

"Fucking goddam *Mexies.*"
Never without a cigar jammed in his face, Sam Singer was a solid, short, block of a man—very rakish, very handsome, even at seventy-two. Be they Salvadoran, Guatemalan, Equadoran, or Mexican, Sam

called all of the Hispanics who lived in the desert *Mexies,* but in Sam's mind, he didn't really mean anything by it.

Ruthie and Sam lived in Las Palmas, a lush, shady enclave of modern, white, midcentury homes designed by architectural greats such as Richard Nuetra and Albert Frey or single-story Spanish rancheros, with paint-peeling pink tile roofs, huddled against the tawny razor-backed San Gorgonio Mountain Range overlooking old Palm Springs. Shimmering palm trees wafted overhead, sprouting up from iridescent, Day-Glo green lawns surrounded by low, whitewashed adobe walls.

Over the past twenty-five years, homes on neighboring streets laconically named Via Las Palmas, Vereda Sur, and Tuxedo Drive had provided refuge for the likes of Elizabeth Taylor, Lucille Ball, Trini Lopez, Loretta Young, Robert Wagner, and Natalie Wood. Sam Singer liked having illustrious neighbors. Although they never socialized, at least being ignored by them beat the stinging ostracism of many of the desert's anti-Semitic country club cliques—gated communities which came in vogue to keep out the likes of Sam Singer.

Sam was tailing a beat-up Toyota pickup loaded down with gardening equipment. Lawn mowers, rakes, shovels, and leaf blowers— the whole shebang. The driver of the pickup was a Mexie gardener, and he and his buddy were crawling up Palm Canyon Drive in front of him. One of their rear tires was low on air. Sam tried to pass, but when he wheeled the big Lincoln into the inside lane, another flatbed truck loaded with Mexie laborers was blocking his escape. The occupants of both vehicles were talking and laughing with each other. Mexie music blared out of both vehicles.

"C'mon now!"

Sam honked his horn but they didn't acknowledge him. They were looking for an address, all of them craning their necks, scratching their heads, looking to each other for reinforcement. Finally Sam swore and roared across the double yellow line and passed them.

When he raised his finger and gave them the bird, they waved and smiled sweetly in return.

Sam always allowed twenty-five minutes for the drive from Palm Springs to Cathedral City, where he owned a valuable parcel of property. As Sam drove down palm tree–laden Palm Canyon Drive, he had to pass several Palm Springs landmarks: La Casa de Liberace, the original Las Casuelas Mexican Restaurant, Louise's Pantry, The Biltmore Hotel, and The Occotillo Lodge.

On a park bench where Palm Canyon curved east at Lyons English Grille, Sam noted several cronies from years ago, sitting like idiots with nothing to do. He slowed up next to them and lowered his power window.

"Hey, Sandy. Hiya, Mortie! Aincha got anything better to do with your time?"

"We just had lunch, Sam. We're waiting for Ethel to pick us up." Ethel was Sandy's ball-busting fat blond wife.

"She still not letting you behind the wheel?"

Sandy grinned. "What can I do?" Ethel wouldn't let him drive after cataract surgery even though his doctor swore he had twenty-twenty vision.

"Then where ya' going after?" Sam took a drag off his cigar.

They looked at each other.

"Probably to the park till dinner, Sam," Mort shrugged.

"Yeah, well, take it easy." Sam waved, shaking his head in disgust. He punched the power window button, and with cigar clamped between his teeth, Sam veered the Lincoln back into traffic away from them.

This wasn't for him, he'd seen to that. The desert was filled with old people, which was why he vowed never to retire. You wouldn't catch him hanging around in parks balancing checkerboards on his knees or griping for more cream cheese in the delicatessens which lined Indian Canyon Avenue. He didn't eat early bird, was insulted if offered a senior citizen movie ticket, and kept himself interested by looking ahead. Sam Singer prided himself by not getting stuck in the past.

He had his properties to manage, his tenants to look out for; hence the trip to Cathedral City.

He suffered mixed emotions at how the desert was changing as he passed Bob Hope's flying saucer house. Gone were many of the date palm groves, replaced with poorly constructed condo complexes. Gone was the dry desert air. So were the old hangouts: Now mall after mall was being constructed from Palm Springs to Indio, as if erected to hold the encroaching desert at bay.

Only Cathedral City remained somewhat pristine.

Cathedral City was a service town, the poor cousin situated between toney Palm Springs and Rancho Mirage. It was the kind of town you drove out to for shoe repair; to get your vacuum cleaner fixed; to poke around in thrift stores—or maybe to have a drink with a whore.

It housed primarily the desert working class, the service population forced to stay through the scorching desert summers unlike the rich snow birds who could leave in the middle of June. The population was a third Hispanic. It boasted more gay bars than churches and the most prime, underdeveloped real estate in the desert. Five blocks of low-slung wood-and-stucco-framed shops, all built in the thirties, forties, and fifties, and Sam owned the best parcel, the one in the center of town fronting the highway.

"The blighted area mentioned in the report is represented by the red-lined quadrant as seen on the city map at the front of the room." Cathedral City renewal attorney Ralph Zola was lecturing to a small group of landowners, businessmen, and residents, Sam Singer among them. Several reporters were taking notes. Zola pointed to a map of Cathedral City.

"This area is the section that we consider our top priority. For those of you who can't see, I'm referring to the segment of land south of Highway 111 through the alphabet streets, A through J, and west and east between Cathedral Canyon and Van Fleet. The lower end of the Cathedral Canyon Cove."

"What makes it a higher priority than the other side of 111?" a reporter asked.

"The northern quadrant was already mostly industrial except for the Sun Town Trailer Park, occupied primarily by retirees, all who agreed to be relocated." He smiled beatifically at the reporters. Zola was a former wrestler in a navy blue suit. Big handed with large feet, he was midforties attractive—wavy black hair, sensual looking, a man in a constant state of semierection. A man whose balls were always churning.

"Why is Cathedral Canyon Road still the only major artery from Palm Springs to Indio without a bridge over the wash? Wasn't it a case of move or be flooded?" The same reporter waited for him to reply.

Ralph Zola smiled calmly. "No intimidation tactics were ever employed on any senior citizen in that park. I am particularly proud to note that all have been successfully relocated."

"In rest homes and public shelters—" said Sam.

"All were stipended according to county guidelines."

"What about the south side?" asked a reporter.

"The southern quadrant is much more problematic. The residents and business owners are highly unique, among the most unique of any area we've studied in recent memory."

"Unique?"

"He means Mexicans and *gays*," said Sam. Everyone turned, most in laughter. Sam Singer lit a cigar. "I own most of the parcel and these people are my tenants. The Mexies want no trouble, so they keep their noses clean, right? They mind their own business. The gays come in and right away they want to fix things up, redecorate, plant shrubbery . . . all at their own expense so's they don't have to compromise on quality."

"So what constitutes blighting?" A reporter was taking notes.

"There's no blighting on my property," Sam asserted.

"Blighting is more than a broken window here and there," said Zola. "It's illegal activity attracting undesirables. It's more than esthetics, though we all agree the area is an eyesore—"

"*I* don't agree," said Sam Singer, eyeballing the reporter. "It's just desert architecture. Been okay for fifty years."

"Mr. Zola," the reporter asked, "is it true you served as one of the chief fund-raisers for the governor's reelection campaign?"

"That's right. And he promises to attend our unveiling ceremonies, once the renewal effort has been completed. He's watching our efforts carefully. He's hoping Cathedral City will serve as a model for future renewal efforts in the State of California. It deserves to be brought up to the quality and character of Rancho Mirage and Palm Desert. These cities have been beautifully redeveloped."

"It'll all look alike, from Palm Springs to Thermal," Sam interrupted. "That what you want? Huh? This is the Coachella Valley. Not downtown Sante Fe." Sam was pleased to see the reporter noting his objections.

Ralph Zola contemplated the renewal committee businessmen, who were all watching Sam Singer. He knew what they were thinking. Sam Singer didn't seem like a typical liberal activist, worried about preserving authenticity and community character. He seemed more like a street-smart old Jew, mounting public resistance to set the developer up to pay him off big-time.

Zola smiled. If he wanted to play that game, there were ways to obtain property other than by buying it. The pressure from the wealthy homeowners, high up in the cove, added with that of the industrial park flourishing only one block north of Highway 111 by the wash, was enormous. A few gay businesses and eight blocks of Hispanic slum housing would be no match for that kind of pressure.

After the meeting, Sam Singer wandered over to Ralph to blow smoke up his ass. "You gotta understand, some of us like Cathedral

City just like it is. And I intend to take care of my kids." Sam's eyes twinkled merrily.

"Your 'kids'?" Ralph Zola snorted.

"Yeah," said Sam, "Me and my wife, Ruthie, we have no kids of our own, so we treat our tenants like family."

"I wouldn't put my dog in one of your houses, Sam."

Sam's eyes twinkled. "A dog of yours would be very comfortable in one of my houses, Ralphie. Stop by the restaurant down on Highway 111. Tell 'em I sent you. I'm the landlord there, and my tenants treat me real good."

"At the gay restaurant?"

"Oh, you know it then. You a regular there? Well, that's okay, live and let live, that's my motto, but fact is, everybody's welcome at Nick's."

"I've never been there in my life."

"They make a great martini. How 'bout it, Ralphie?"

Sam Singer would never admit to anyone that his dreams were now coming true. He'd been the laughingstock of Palm Springs when he started buying up the main drag of Cathedral City, and then the little cinder block houses on the streets behind it. He got the property for next to nothing, consisting of seven houses, a restaurant with a liquor license, a diner, a convenience store, an empty gas station, and a bead shop or two. Now Sam Singer was poised for profit, but it would mean selling the entire parcel, including Nick's and the dream house of Inez and Thomas Quintero.

After the meeting, Sam Singer pulled his big white Mark IV into the alley behind Nick's, blasting the horn three times. This was his monthly signal for the Hispanic families who occupied the seven beat-up houses he owned between Grove Street and A in Cathedral City. When his tenants heard the horn of the Lincoln, they all knew to come to the alley: Sam Singer was here to collect his rents.

While he cooled his heels in his air-conditioned car, the alley gates unlocked like rifles cocking; a family member from each house assigned the task of paying the rent ambled toward the car. They stood in line, emissaries from the seven shacks, a grandmother here, a teenage girl there, but never the head of the household.

Sam stayed in the car, opening the window only slightly so no cool air could escape. Cigar smoke smarted the eyes of the renter stuffing cash into his thick hairy hands, which he didn't need to count because he knew they'd never risk cheating him.

All the while he took the cash, he muttered greetings through his cigar.

"How are ya? How's school? Are ya snaking the septic tanks like I taught ya? Anybody nosing around I should know about?" Then he stuffed the cash in the inside coat pocket, revealing a concealed pistol in a shoulder harness, in plain view for all to see.

Today his tenant Quintero didn't send his little girl out with the rent. Sam blasted the horn again and, annoyed, decided to drop in on Kenny at the bar to pick up his rent from the boys. He'd take care of Quintero later.

"Hi, Kenny boy." Sam's frame filled the doorway as he surveyed the kitchen. Shoddy but immaculate. Sam sucked on his cigar.

Kenny glanced up. He was organizing paperwork at a tiny steel desk cluttered with bills and arguing on the telephone with his meat purveyor.

"I have the cash. Yeah, I'll give it to the driver. It's ready now, but I need my meat. No, you promised me! No! Gotta be today. Please." He hung up the phone and swung around in his chair, facing Sam.

"Heard you had a little trouble, kid."

"A little."

"You don't look too worse for wear. A cut on your face. A few bruises."

"You should see the one on my rear end, Sam," Kenny managed to tease him. He was so stiff he could barely move.

"No thanks," Sam deadpanned. He relit his cigar. "The way Nick tells it, you went over Niagara Falls in a barrel. What were you up to down there?"

"If I knew, I'd tell you. But I don't. Rent day, huh?"

"You heard the horn."

"It's rude to make them come to the car, Sam."

"I don't make you come to the car."

"That's because you know I wouldn't." Kenny stood up. He moved to the grill to light a cigarette.

"You would if you had something to hide. They don't want me knocking on their doors, nosing around."

"You want anything to eat?" Kenny grew bored by the banter. He leaned against a cutting board and smiled wearily at Sam.

"I had lunch at home."

"How's Ruthie?"

"Low," Sam said quietly. "Maybe you'll call her."

"Sure, Sam."

"I like to think of you and Nick as the sons I never had."

"Well, I hate to break this to you, Sam, but both of your sons are gay."

"I don't care," Sam said, chewing his cigar. Then, his ordinary deadpan response to their banter, "I love you just the same."

Then a long pause. Down to business.

"Quite a pile of bills you got there."

"It's been slow. I don't have the rent, Sam. I'm sorry."

"It's thirty days past due!" Sam was genuinely angry. "You're taking advantage."

"I'm COD with my purveyors," Kenny replied evenly. "I can either pay the rent or not serve food. If I don't serve food, we lose our liquor license."

"This is no way to do business!"

"I have enough cash here for the meat guy. I haven't taken a draw for a month, and I haven't paid my crew for two weeks. It's August, Sam. Nobody's in town."

"So you plan for August in May." Sam was breathing heavily. He mopped his forehead with his handkerchief. "It's hot back here! Swamp cooler broken? If it is, you gotta pay for it. Any other trouble I should know about?"

"What kind of trouble?"

"I mean trouble with the Mexies."

"Not that I'd tell you about."

"I'd take care of it. You call me." He patted the pocket with the gun in it.

"You like to think of yourself as the Godfather of Grove Street." Kenny shook his head.

"More like the mayor. I'm the mayor of Cathedral City." Sam dragged on his cigar.

Sam's eyes focused on a wooden wine box hanging on the wall with a tin painting of the Virgin Mary, a candle, and a small spray of dried flowers in a vase.

"Whazat?" He motioned with his cigar.

"It's an altar. For special intentions."

"You Catholic? I didn't think they took your kind."

"No. I built it for my kitchen crew when Carmen lost her cat." Kenny motioned him over. "See, I put a ceramic cat up here and then Carmen got to light the candle. Kinda like a prayer."

"Cat come back?"

"Dragging both hind legs. It was hit by a car. Cost me three hundred dollars and we still had to put it to sleep."

"You paid for it?"

"It was her *pet,* Sam."

Sam took a long drag on his cigar.

"It's bad business, smuggling illegals. You probably think because you're a liberal that it's okay. But it's not. I used to be a liberal, but now that I'm old and rich, I see things more conservatively."

"I figured as much, Sam."

Sam studied him intently.

"I had to pull a few strings from this end to cut you loose. Nicky-boy tell you that? I had to call Sacramento."

"I wasn't smuggling illegals."

"Border patrol says they think you were."

"I *wasn't.*"

"It's no secret you're a friend to these Mexies."

"If I have that reputation, I'm *glad,* Sam." Kenny folded his arms.

"I like to think I have the same reputation," Sam drawled. "They have it tough. I'm a minority too. Remember that." Sam gestured with his cigar. A few ashes dropped to Kenny's clean floor. "I lived here in the forties. They had signs in certain establishments in Palm Springs, you know what they said?"

"What, Sam?"

"No Dogs No Jews," Sam said matter-of-factly.

"I'm sorry," Kenny said softly. "It must have been hurtful."

"You bet it was hurtful. It hurt plenty bad. Still does when I think about it. That's why Frank Sinatra and his buddies built outside the city limits. He wouldn't stand for no discrimination."

Sam's grammar, Kenny knew, was perfectly fine. He just talked that way to sound tough.

Sam could see that Kenny felt pretty bad about the rent. "Look, we can ride this out, but I don't want you thinking I'm soft. I expect to be paid when you get caught up."

"Thanks, Sam." Kenny folded his arms and smiled wearily.

Sam focused on the altar. Then he looked carefully around the kitchen as if calculating the value of the equipment. After a long moment he said before leaving:

"When it comes to prayer, you gotta be pretty specific."

He disappeared into the hot desert light of the alley.

*   *   *

Kenny breathed a huge sigh of relief. He knew he had only a few more moments alone. He reached for his wallet and removed a photograph of him and Nick, the oldest picture he had of the two of them sitting on the old deck in Laguna. Both of them were that much younger, sheltering their eyes from the sun. They squinted into the camera.

He placed the picture on the altar, flicking a BIC lighter, lighting the candle with one hand. Then he lit a cigarette, took a drag, and contemplated their likeness. When his crew arrived, they'd see the candle and look at the picture and know Kenny was depressed about Nick.

Kenny picked up the phone to call Ruthie. She answered in the same seductive little girl voice which hadn't changed since she was a teenager. "Hello?"

"Heat got you down?"

"Oh, honey," said Ruthie, recognizing Kenny's soothing voice. "These desert summers are murder on me."

"Why don't you come in later? Have dinner on me." Ruthie hadn't been out to Cathedral City in years.

"I'll think about it. I'm on a new jag. Got me low."

"What's that?"

"Posterity. No one to remember me when I'm gone."

"I'll remember you."

"But who'll remember you?"

Kenny felt stung by the finality of her observation.

"We're in the same boat," Ruthie ventured. "Are you going to tell me what happened down in Mexicali? I don't believe you don't remember."

"I don't remember everything . . ." He hesitated. He knew he could trust Ruthie.

"But you remember *something*," she pressed. "I know about Mexicali. I've *been* to Mexicali, I'll have you know."

"I think I died in the water," he whispered. He glanced up at the flickering votive. "I haven't told anyone. I think I was dead and something brought me back to life."

"Did I ever tell you Frank Sinatra once asked me out?"

"Did you go for it?" Her segue didn't throw him. For some reason it made perfect sense.

Gently Ruthie hung up the phone.

5

Inez Quintero

After morning Mass, Inez Quintero crossed the parking lot and began her walk up Glenn Avenue past the alphabet streets of Cathedral City till she reached H Street and cut over to Chuperosa. She was hurrying to avoid the impending downpour. She was still angry about the other day when Father Gene had snubbed her for Kenny.

She snarled at the very injustice of it. What had Kenny been doing there anyway? What was the world coming to? That old priest had never once asked her to stay for coffee. Never inquired about her family though in confession she reported every intimate detail of their lives. Her hopes and dreams. Her disappointments.

To Inez, every barking dog was growling at her.

As she stalked the gently inclining streets toward Cathedral City's "cove" section of privately owned nicer homes, the neighborhood was howling with attack dogs on short leases, contained behind tall chain-link fences. What were they protecting? she huffed and puffed. Would she steal an old car on cement blocks? A rusty refrigerator with no door? A clothesline of colorful but ratty Mexican blankets?

Inez Quintero had her standards.

A pit bull without a chain raged at her from behind a short wooden fence. Inez stopped to rage back. *"Idioto!"* she laughed as it ran full force against the fence, never learning its lesson, yelping and falling backward in pain and shock, more incensed with each assault. She laughed heartily, looked at the sky, and hurried on.

This would remain the highlight of Inez's day. Another living creature far more frustrated than she. She regarded the enormity of his pain as answered prayer. The prospect of cleaning Kenny and Nick's house loomed less daunting now, and if Inez Quintero hated anything, it was cleaning the house of *los maricones,* the homosexuals who owned the gay bar across the alley from where she lived.

As it was, to her great dismay, she owed her livelihood to the homosexuals of Cathedral City. In addition to one or two private jobs which were exceptionally well paying, she worked as a maid for one of Cathedral City's several gay hotels.

Every penny she earned was promptly handed over to her husband, Thomas, a highly prized furniture maker employed by Arte de Sonora, which was owned and operated by a muscular gay man whom Thomas admired very much. *Pincha Puto,* she thought. He had instigated Thomas's drive to become an American citizen by promising him higher wages and a share of the business once he was sworn in.

Thomas wouldn't allow one word of complaint to be spoken against him.

So what? she shrugged. Thomas didn't control her thoughts. She could think whatever she thought, and even he couldn't tell her not to. In America the godless controlled all the purse strings. The homosexuals and the Jews. Only the blacks were worse off than the Hispanics.

As she marched up Chuperosa and turned onto Las Tunas, the sight of Kenny and Nick's three-bedroom ranch house filled her with envy and refueled her resentment. Two men living in such a big house when six Quinteros including Inez, Thomas, three children, and one old aunt were all crammed into a tiny two-bedroom shack facing an alley, and what was worse, an alley where the unspeakable was committed every night within full view of her bedroom windows.

Inez inserted her key and kicked the front door open.

The house shuddered on its foundation but she failed to wake Nick, who customarily would be sleeping it off till well past noon. Grimly Inez's eyes darted around the living room. Another pigsty, she thought disgustedly. She immediately reached for the money they always left in the bowl by the door. It was empty.

She studied the cluttered living room and resisted the impulse to cry.

Back in his bedroom Nick woke up. His hair was matted, his eyes swollen. His hands shook as he reached for the remainder of a warm vodka water. He threw off the cover and attempted to get up, but his head felt filled with sand—sand and hard bits of jagged rock, pressing from within to points under his left eye, his right temple, and the base of his neck. He glanced up. Inez Quintero stood at the bedroom door.

"Inez," he said. "Is it Thursday?"

"I need my pay."

Nick's mouth fell open. "Isn't it in the bowl?"

"No."

"Here," he said, scrambling for his pants. He found the five twenties Kenny had given him two days ago for the overdue utility bill. "The house is a mess. Take an extra twenty for your trouble."

"Hmphh," she said. Her ordinary pay was eighty dollars a day. A hundred dollars for four hours work. Twenty extra dollars for the mess. She was insulted by the extravagance but the extra twenty would help. She'd give it to the priest tomorrow before the citizenship swearing-in ceremony in Indio. Ask him to pray for her. Maybe money would make him notice her.

She disappeared down the hall. Nick could hear her pull out the vacuum cleaner. He ran for the bathroom to throw up.

No power. Inez shook her head. She tried another plug. Nothing.

"You have no electricity!" she bellowed. As Inez waited, her eyes wandered over the thousands of individual objects placed in friendly chaos throughout the living room. Kenny collected dolls, and these dolls always especially gave Inez the creeps. Many were dismembered, a basket of arms here, heads there . . . she had no idea what such a mind could be thinking.

In the den, jutting off the living room, Kenny had a worktable set up, with paints and brushes, and a sewing machine to make doll clothes. There must have been over two hundred dolls, some confined to glass cases, some out in the open, but all with shining doll eyes, staring at Inez, judging the quality of her work.

In addition to dolls, Kenny and Nick collected pottery and art deco glass they'd purchased at swap meets since the early seventies. The walls were also adorned with Nick's collection of posters with celebrities all wearing white clothes and assorted varieties of shoes. Who were these people in the red shoes? Inez wondered as she half-heartedly feather-dusted the Plexiglas frames.

Finally she tipped a few slightly to give the impression that they had all been cleaned.

Outside, the pool shimmered in the midday sun.

"If the pool was filled with Tequila, it would be empty by now," she observed.

As she studied the pool, several objects rained down from the neighbor's side of the fence and landed in the water. Nick ran to the sliding glass door, opened it, and emerged caterwauling onto the patio. He reached for the pool skimmer, retrieved the foreign objects, and hurled them back over the fence.

"Hey, *faggot!*" Buddy his neighbor, popped his head over the fence.

"You throw dog turds in my pool again, Kenny will *burn you out!* He's itching to go to prison, just to get away from *me.*"

"Fuck you."

"Okay." Nick turned around and lifted up his robe. Buddy's cheeks reddened and he dropped out of sight. Nick turned to see Inez watching him, her face distorted in amazement and disdain. Nick went into the bathroom to finish his toilette.

An hour later the last thing Nick applied were eye drops, and eyes blinking, he emerged fully dressed from the bedroom, shaved and showered and reeking of YSL Cologne. Inez was just finishing up. She stared at him in disbelief. How did he manage, she wondered, day after day after day to raise himself up from the dead? Now he looked as handsome as the day he turned twenty-one.

"Amazing, isn't it?" Nick grinned as if reading her thoughts. He swaggered to the kitchen for a drink.

"Mister. You have no power," she admonished him.

"They must have just cut us off." Nick shrugged. "Better use the ice while we have it." She watched him disappeared into the kitchen to make a Bloody Mary.

Later did he offer her a ride home? *No.* Instead he let her risk the rain. At least it was all downhill. Downhill in 111-degree heat and 98 percent humidity. Block by block dogs picked up her scent and howled like banshees. She felt like a Mexican Cruella De Vil.

Inez stomped into the little house on A Street they had rented ever since they crossed the border. It was the nicest house on the block. Thomas Quintero kept his house the neatest because he was a proud man and wanted to set an example for his neighbors.

Inside the house was cool. At least the purring swamp cooler worked. She was surprised to see her entire family gathered around the dining room table. Thomas held out his hand. Inez reached inside her bra strap and handed him over the money. He counted out eighty dollars, folded it neatly, and placed it in his own wallet.

Inez folded her arms. She could scarcely hide her resentment. She flicked the side of her old aunt's head with her fingers.

"*Aiii . . .*" cried the old aunt. She ran into the kitchen and returned with a glass of cold, lightly sweetened lemon water. Inez accepted the glass and sat down.

Thomas had always given Sam Singer his rent on time like everybody else, but yesterday did not send his little girl out to the white car to pay it. Normally when the horn honked, they would all look to Thomas, who, as was his custom, would reach in his pocket and peel off the rent from the roll of bills he kept there.

Thomas would solemnly count out eight hundred dollars in crisp twenties, and hand it over to Soila, his oldest girl of fourteen. But he surprised them by deliberately opening the lid of a small wooden box, hand-carved by his great grandfather and passed down father to son since then.

The box had photographs from Mexico, the family Bible, catechism papers, marriage certificates, death certificates, immigration paperwork, and now the Quintero family checkbook. It was the checkbook he reached for with callused hands, and then began to write out his first rent check to Sam Singer. The family gathered behind him as he inscribed the amount, $800.00 numerically, and then spelled out, Eight hundred and 00/100.

Pay to the order of *Sam Singer.*

When he had signed the check, he fanned it, teasing his daughters. He'd used a ball point pen and there was no need to fear that the ink would run. Then he sat down to wait.

A knock came at the door, which Soila opened to reveal a very annoyed, very sweaty Sam Singer. Thomas and his family observed him, squinting through the screen door, puffing away on the cigar with the Lincoln parked in the street behind him.

"Hey, Quintero, what gives? Dincha hear me yesterday? I blasted the horn three times. Everybody else paid like they was supposed to. You guys sick in here?" He stepped back as the possibility occurred to him.

"*Soila, abra la puerto para el señor!*"

Sam was frightened. He backed away even farther. Thomas smiled and approached the door with his check. He stepped outside.

Thomas had learned hundreds of phrases of English words in

complete sets, and never tended to admit when a new set of words came at him. When he didn't understand a question or a statement, he tended to smile a little wider, or freeze ever so slightly as he struggled to come up with a meaning.

When Thomas strode out on the porch, Sam relaxed, because his best tenant was smiling.

"Here is your rent," he said to Sam. Inside the house his family held its breath as Thomas offered up his check. The number on the check was 001.

Sam saw no cash and looked completely bewildered. "What's this? You paying me by check this month? I don't take checks! This is a cash deal!"

The hand holding the check out to Sam didn't waver.

"This month I am paying by check as I will continue to do from now on. It's all here," he said with finality. "Take it, please."

Sam's hands splayed out from his body involuntarily. Without intending to, he knocked the check from Thomas's hand. It fluttered to the lawn behind him. Inside, Inez's hands flew to her face. Why was he refusing a check being issued by the Quintero family? What was wrong with Thomas Quintero's check?

Sam was taken by surprise and had to think quickly. He knew how to think on his feet and how bad this must have looked. He could also see Mexics gathering on either side of the yard next to the Quintero shack, and improvements aside—neat lawn, a ceramic donkey or two—it was still a shack that pulled him a hefty profit every year. He'd paid only sixteen thousand dollars for these seven houses, and that was eleven years ago. Eight hundred times seven times twelve times eleven was seven hundred thirty-nine thousand two hundred dollars. In cash. Even Ruthie had no idea how much he'd socked away.

He could see the umbrage in Thomas Quintero's eyes, so he moved as quickly as Sam Singer could, and stooped to pick up the check. A slow stoop would give him time to plan, to think of a solution, because he couldn't have these Mexics paying him by check. Therefore, Sam stooped long and low.

"I'm sorry, Quintero," he came up slowly, talking through his cigar, "but you had me a little worried. I thought something was wrong with you. I know I came on a little strong, but see, I can't cash this check. Our deal was cash. Eight hundred dollars was a cash price, and if you pay by check, I need to charge you more."

Thomas became nervous, because he wasn't understanding what the old man was saying.

"Soila!"

Anticipating that he would need his daughter, who was the only one who spoke fluent English, Soila was sent flying though the screen door. The weight of her body sent it smacking against the house. To Sam, who was looking at the check and the rest of the neighbors, who were all watching him, it sounded like a shot from a rifle.

It made them all jump, and then they laughed, even Sam, who was really sweating in the hot August sun. Soila stepped forward rather importantly, Sam noted with irritation. Because of her birthmark, it made him uncomfortable to look at her.

Her father gestured for her to translate.

"Tomorrow we get sworn in. He says now that we'll be citizens, we can pay like everybody else." Soila was clever and always added a little in her translations. "You even promised to sell us the house when we became citizens."

"Look, honey, tell your daddy that I give him and the other Mexies a deal because they pay cash. If he pays me by check, he has to pay more, thirty percent more because then I have to pay taxes. That's another two hundred forty dollars." His verbal skills suffered but mathematically he was bar none. Privately he'd only offered to sell them the house to encourage them to save. To inspire a goal. He never thought they'd take him seriously. "You'd need to put at least five thousand down to buy a fine property like this."

Soila rattled off some explanation to her father, some Mex gibberish that apparently made Sam's point. Thomas was stumped and didn't know what to do. He now had over thirty people staring at him if he counted Sam, Soila, his family inside, and the smattering of neighbors.

Ever since he opened the checking account, he had been savoring this moment. Now it was ruined unless he insisted that Sam take the check. Thomas was very proud and he didn't want to lose face with his community. If he acted with authority, this would establish him and his children in a way he never could have orchestrated on his own.

Quietly he told Soila that he would agree to the additional rent if he could continue to pay by check. His employers raised his wages when they paid him by check. It was fair of Sam Singer to ask him to do the same, he reasoned.

Sam's eyes bugged when Soila asked him to return the check and that Thomas would go inside and make one up for the right amount.

"Tell him to leave the name blank," Sam called after her when he'd recovered. "Nobody can spell what I'm usually called."

Kenny had come to collect his trio of kitchen workers. Together they were all driving down to Indio. Today they were being sworn in as citizens of the United States of America—Gabriel and his cousins Carmen and Miguel. All had worked for him since he opened.

When they met in the alley behind the restaurant, Kenny had them line up so he could take their picture. They all wore white gauzy shirts. Kenny had a red flower for Carmen's hair. This was a huge day for them. Citizens at last.

They drove in Kenny's Scout to Indio. Carmen rode in front with him, and Gabriel and Miguel grinned happily behind them in the back. The drive down the main business artery of the desert took about forty minutes from Cathedral City to Indio. After they had passed Rancho Mirage's restaurant row, The Kobe Steak House, Las Casuelas Nuevas, and The Chart House, they came upon Thunderbird Estates, a magnificent cache of homes nestled in the erupting desert foothills south of the highway.

"President Ford lives there . . ." Kenny explained to Carmen as they passed the guarded kiosk with an impressive iron gate.

"The president now?"

"No . . ." Kenny corrected her. "President Clinton is the president now. Aren't you supposed to know that?"

She looked at him and laughed. "Does he live there too?"

"No. He lives in Washington."

"Where does the governor live?"

"Sacramento."

"No. Somebody should kill him," she observed casually. "He's a very bad man."

"*Carmen!* That wouldn't solve anything."

Carmen shook her head vehemently. "People *die* because of him. Somebody should kill him," she affirmed philosophically. Then she waved gaily to Miguel and Gabriel in the back.

Kenny drove the rest of the way in silence, distressed about her nonchalant remark. Soon they passed Palm Desert, Bermuda Dunes, and La Quinta. In many areas the desert was obstructed by new construction. Shopping malls, movie theaters, and parking lots. Finally they arrived in Indio.

*   *   *

"—that I will support and defend the Constitution and laws of the United States of America against all enemies, foreign and domestic—"

In Indio the swearing-in room was actually a high school gymnasium. Kenny stood among two thousand new citizens, all reciting the "Oath of Allegiance to the United States of America." Several rows ahead of him he noticed Inez, who was so short she stood on a metal folding chair. She was standing with her husband, Thomas. Next to them stood Soila; her older brother, a handsome *chollo* named Alex; and her little sister, Anita.

When the pledge was completed, the entire audience sang "America the Beautiful," many in Spanish. Kenny's eyes glistened as he studied the blissful faces of his three friends. Inez turned momentarily, saw him, and before she could conceal her emotions, Kenny could see that she was crying. When she recognized him, her face hardened. She turned instantly away. Later they ran into each other on the sidewalk. Thomas nodded gravely, as was his way, Inez, Alex, and Anita ignored him, and only Soila called out a sweet "Hello . . ."

Kenny focused his attention on his own friends.

"Was it hard to give up Mexico?" he asked.

They looked at each other and laughed.

When Inez Quintero heard the "Oath of Allegiance," she was surprised to find herself utter, *"Perdona estos, Mexico,"* Forgive them, Mexico, she was thinking, referring to her husband and the others, all forsaking their Mexican heritage in favor of Los Estados Unidos. Instead of such romantic nonsense she should be worrying about her own questionable status, the piece of paper which came from the Immigration Department requesting a second blood test before they could process her application for legal residency.

She was angry to find her thoughts being read by Kenny, her nemesis, who now held the vicar at St. Louis completely under his spell.

This morning she had attended Mass, with the hopes of gaining the favor of the old priest. She clutched the twenty-dollar bill so tightly it was damp from her anxiety about the day. All through the Mass she noticed Father Gene frantically searching every face in the congregation, and then glancing furtively at all the exits.

He's not here, she wanted to scream. But *I* am, Father. I came. What about me? Why aren't I worthy? When will you invite me for conversation? A cup of tea?

When the Mass was ended, the priest glumly wished everyone the peace of Christ and said his goodbyes. An old, old lady was whining to him about an eviction notice. Inez wanted to grab her by the hair and throw her down.

"I'm sorry," Father Gene explained to her. "It means you have to move. They're tearing down your house."

"They're tearing down my house?" she repeated. "Why?" Her skin was so thin she was almost blue with veins. Inez let out an impatient sigh of irritation.

"They're tearing down all the houses. Have you called your son? Does he know about this?"

"Why are they tearing down my house?"

"Your landlord apparently sold it," he continued patiently. "They're rebuilding all of downtown Cathedral City."

"Even the big houses?" the old lady asked. "My son lives up there."

"No," the priest said. "Just the smaller ones at the bottom of the hill. Listen, I think it would be best if you called your son."

"It's true then." She began to cry. "I'll call him." Finally she wandered away.

The priest's eyes lit up when he saw Inez.

"Father," she was about to implore him, and pressed her twenty into his hand.

"The young man from the other day! You spoke to him, remember?"

"Yes." Her smile shriveled to a thin line of deep disappointment.

"Do you know much about him?" He didn't even acknowledge the money in his hand. To her horror, the priest absentmindedly stuffed it in his pocket as if she had repaid him a loan.

"Well," Inez offered, "I do know that he owns the bar down on the highway."

She was just about to tell him what kind of bar it was when the priest smiled happily and said, "Yes, Nick's. I've been there!"

Her faith disintegrated.

"What is it? What's wrong?"

"I live across the alley from the bar," she said evenly. She assumed he knew what she was getting at.

"Then you must see him now and then. Tell him to come back to church. Tell him that I asked after him." Then he rushed happily out the side door and left her standing alone in the sanctuary.

* * *

Although she was only thirty-three, Inez looked much older and knew how handsome other women found her husband. Inez's face was already lined with worry, worry about holding on to what she had. She knew Thomas wanted to buy their little house, and thought if she worked extra hard and contributed more than her share, then her industry would secure her position.

Inez had married Thomas when she was fifteen and had her first child seven months later. Her father was a local police captain with six sons and one daughter, his youngest.

Inez's father loved his baby daughter very much. Although she was short on looks, he treated her like the sun rose and set on her beauty. He spoiled her, and encouraged aggressive, demanding behavior so she could defend herself in later life. Her homeliness was a family secret, although, with so many brothers as body guards, Inez enjoyed a certain stature in her neighborhood.

With her brothers off working, Inez was left to take care of the home with her frail, ailing mother. Her father employed a maid and a cook to assist her, and little Inez quickly learned how to give orders. She knew what a well-run household could be. As the daughter of a police captain, by all rights Inez should have been considered a good catch, but for reasons she didn't understand, men weren't interested in her. In her mind, it must be God's will. She was his best kept secret; at least that's what her father told her until Thomas Quintero came into her life.

At nineteen, Thomas was a bright, handsome young man, great with his hands; able to build anything with a piece of old wood and some nails. Everything he touched felt sensual to him, hence his growing interest in woodworking.

Thomas's family was very poor, and he worked very hard to help support them. One day Captain Sanchez hired Thomas to refinish furniture left to him by his uncle. Among the pieces were a beautiful mahogany armoire, a dining table and ten chairs, and a hope chest which belonged to his grandmother. The house was opulent by Thomas's standards. The rooms were dark and cool, and most of the furnishings were antiques. Thomas would have given anything to be part of such a fine family.

After Thomas had been working for a while, Inez shyly asked him if he'd like a Coca-Cola or a lemonade. He accepted the Coke. He knew she was Captain Sanchez's only daughter. From what he and his friends had observed, Inez did little else other than go to Mass or stay home to care for her mother. She was very lonely, with few prospects in sight. She could also be easily persuaded to fall in love with him, judging by the grave way in which she smiled at him while she watched him drink his Coke.

He took his time to finish the table, which Captain Sanchez didn't mind because he declared the work masterful. During this time Thomas urged Inez to sit and watch him work, keep him company. To impress her, he even began to attend daily Mass, always maintaining a respectful distance but making certain she noticed him. And Inez began to battle smoldering feelings for him.

The seduction of her by Thomas Quintero was accomplished rather quickly. He began to sit next to her, holding her tiny hand in his. She was a young, careful girl and she trusted him, trusted that he was a good man and had sincere intentions. Because she kept him a secret, her brothers and her father were unaware of Thomas's interest, for if they'd known, he certainly would have been driven away.

One hot afternoon, Inez lost her virginity, her most precious gift, in a quiet, furtive struggle with Thomas Quintero in the choir loft of the small cathedral. Her passions quickly evolved to shame. No husband would ever want her. She'd betrayed the trust of her father. She defiled the house of God. Her behavior was inconceivable to her. To this day, she'd been unable to confess her sin.

And just as he was pulling up his trousers, her father and three of her seven brothers burst into the choir loft, tipped off by a priest who had been suspicious of Thomas's intentions. Her father gave her two options. He would force Thomas to marry her, or he would have him killed.

Within seventy-two hours Inez Sanchez became the wife of Thomas Quintero, both knowing that a shot gun was pointing at his head. Hence Inez started life in a loveless marriage, and left her comfortable childhood home to move into the poor rooms of her husband's family, since he couldn't support himself on his own. Whereas before Thomas might have expected to move in with Captain Sanchez, his bad behavior had precluded it.

Her mother-in-law immediately put her to work, and instead of running the household, she became her husband's personal maid. There was nothing her father could do to intercede for her, for Thomas had done right by her and saved her reputation. He was working hard, his celebrity as a furniture maker more and more renowned among local craftsman and dealers, even though they paid him so little for his skills.

Soon Inez gave birth to her handsome son, Alex, and then a

daughter, Soila, deformed by a horrible birthmark, provoking bitterness among her in-laws. Thomas himself had reached his limit with both families. When the offer from the American Anglo from Palm Springs was proposed, he consulted Inez and proposed a truce. They could relocate to the United States as a true family. They'd be able to afford a home of their own if she agreed to work and the in-laws would all be left behind.

Fearing the cruelty which faced her daughter, Inez agreed at once, infuriating her father. Although they were being sponsored, she'd be nothing but another *mojada,* a wetback, and so would her children.

Inez's Mexico of myth was no longer obtainable. But on the off chance that Thomas meant what he said, a new beginning for them as husband and wife, she agreed. They made the move north, but soon enough he was the same old Thomas. He enjoyed increased status and the appreciation of his new boss who paid him more, but not enough to buy a house.

Life lost all its grace with the exception of her son and especially her daughter Soila, whom every day Inez told was the most beautiful girl in Cathedral City. The only work Inez could find, after the gentile upbringing of her childhood, was that of a maid in a hotel frequented only by men.

Tonight at El Gallito, a small Mexican cantina on a side street across the highway from Nick's, a group of new Americans were celebrating their elevated status. Inez found it ironic to be singing and dancing Spanish songs after being sworn in as U.S. citizens. Mostly talk grew wistful of Mexico, of families and friends in villages far, far away. They drank cervezas from cans, and passed around a bottle of tequila in a brown paper bag.

Thomas began bragging about his plans for the future. He held up his new checkbook and announced plans to buy his little house. A new car would follow, and perhaps education for his son. Soila's face briefly reflected her sadness. Of the three children, she was the best student. Her brother Alex had little or no interest in an academic future. The reach of Indio's gangs was now extending into Cathedral City and soon would ensnare him, if they hadn't already.

"Now that we're citizens, almost all of us," he corrected himself, eyeing his wife, "We'll all have to work very hard. Much harder than before." This last remark he directed at Inez, and then swatted the bottom of the pretty young waitress as she brought them a fresh pitcher of beer.

"Maybe we'll turn Mom in," smirked Alex. "Get her deported if she doesn't pull her own weight."

Soila swore at him under her breath. He was always teasing her or her mother.

The waitress sashayed away. Her name tag read RUBY, Inez noted angrily, and Thomas's action stung her so badly she averted her gaze through the side window of the restaurant, before he could see that it hurt her. To her astonishment, Inez noted that the Sun Town Trailer Park was being ripped out, with nearly half of the coaches already missing. She knew it well because she had cleaned for an old lady who lived there for a year before she died.

Later that night in their bedroom facing the alley, a drunken Thomas fucked Inez as the neon lights from Nick's flashed on.

"Ruby!" he cried, and shot his stuff into her, rolling over exhausted from the excitement of the day.

"My name isn't Ruby," Inez admonished him quietly, and was suddenly seized by sadness as happy memories of life in Mexico overwhelmed her and caused her to cry, just as the bar emptied out in the alley across from their bedroom window. Inez and her family were used to the sounds of happy, drunken homosexual men coming and going from the gay bar.

Now their laughter particularly angered her, because laughter of any kind evoked jealous rage in Inez, Inez who worked so hard and was devoid of humor. Soon the laughter died down, but Inez was awake, awake with resentment and fear.

Resentful because she never laughed.

Fearful that no one would ever really like her.

Positive she would die unloved.

She woke up an hour later, her body drenched in sweat, as if in fever. Then she heard shouting in the alley.

6

Tenderly

When Ralph Zola arrived, he watched Nick move from table to table, a red grin stuck to his face like the sharp plastic lips from a childhood Mr. Potato Head set.

"How's that salmon? Fresh, huh?"

"It's not so great."

"I'm glad you're enjoying it, I'll tell the chef."

At another table. "Your hair is beautiful tonight. You know, I used to have the Hairhunters in LA. We did all the stars."

"I have cancer," a woman began to cry. "This is a wig."

"Well, it's a good one. Nice to see you."

"Hello," he cooed to another table. Then Nick snaked to the bar. "Fix me another drink, will you, honey?" Marcella served him a Campari and soda. Nick noticed Ralph Zola and nodded hello.

Ralph nodded back.

"Are you dining with us tonight?"

"No. Just having a drink."

"Fix him what he wants, honey. On the house."

"Thank you, thank you very much."

"This is Marcella. She's the backbone of my operation."

Marcella couldn't believe her luck. A good-looking straight man under fifty. She quivered with excitement.

"What'd you say the name was?" Marcella asked.

"I didn't." He offered his hand. "Ralph."

"What kind of work you in?"

"He's with the Cathedral City Renewal Agency." Nick smiled at Marcella.

Marcella reacted. "Is it true they want to tear Cathedral City down? This is my livelihood we're talking about."

"Sam Singer will never sell, and Mr. Zola here knows it," Nick grinned.

"So what's he doing here?" Marcella glared at Zola.

"Sam asked me to come in and see the operation," Ralph offered.

"Sam's already applied to have this building designated as a historical landmark," Nick informed him.

"That so?" Ralph Zola nodded. Marcella could smell false nonchalance a mile away. She shook her head at Nick.

"No offense, but do you sincerely think this is so great?" Ralph glanced around the room. His eyes focused on two men dancing passionately near the restroom. He gamely continued. "Wouldn't you prefer a new structure in a refurbished neighborhood? More lights, reduced crime? Less upkeep?"

Nick gaped in astonishment. "This building had been here since the *thirties*. This whole strip is completely pristine. You can't improve on that."

To Ralph Zola, the place was a matchbox, waiting to be struck. "Well, like you say, Sam will never sell." He and Marcella locked eyes. Several customers entered. They saw Nick and he ran to greet them, all smiles.

"So, you have many partners?" He smiled seductively at Marcella, pushing his card at her.

"You talking about me or the bar?" She tucked his card in the pocket of her little black skirt and smiled back. Over his shoulder, Marcella noted the arrival of Sam Singer and his wife, a very glamorous, reticent-looking Ruthie. Ralph Zola turned, following her gaze.

"That his girl friend?"

"His wife. She never comes out. Never."

"No kiddin' . . ." Zola studied her with interest. She looked uneasy. Almost sad. She brightened when Nick ran over to them. They kissed each other like old, old friends. Sam shook Nick's hand. He looked pleased to be out with his wife. "She makes Sam look pretty good. Like a rich man," Zola commented.

"She used to sing here." Marcella studied him.

"She friendly with Nicky boy?"

"They knew each other way back when. When Sam ran the place. Nick was just the manager. Ruthie sang. Then she and Sam got married. Nick said she was good, but she wanted to have kids. Raise a family."

"Sam said they don't have children."

A mournful Ruthie took in the happy patrons of the bar. Sam's eyes followed her protectively. He focused on Ralph Zola, sitting at the bar talking to Marcella, the bartender.

"Ralphie boy, I see you made it." Sam lit his cigar, winking at Marcella. "His money's no good here. Send his tab to me." Sam pulled Ruthie forward. "Ralphie, Ruthie . . ."

"Hello." Ruthie extended her hand. She didn't look too happy to meet anybody. Her diamond bracelet glimmered in the light from the bar.

"How do you do," Ralph murmured, taking her tiny hand in both of his big ones. Marcella's eyes narrowed with jealousy.

"Mrs. Singer, can I fix you something?" Marcella interrupted. Ruthie withdrew her hand. Ruthie had never trusted Marcella.

"Nothing at all," Ruthie smiled.

"I'll have a scotch rocks," Sam said. "Then I have to go in back to talk to Kenny. He owes me my rent."

Marcella moved to make Sam's drink.

"Kenny?" Zola asked.

"Nicky's boyfriend." Sam dragged on his cigar. "That okay with you?"

"Each to his own." Zola shrugged as Sam left. Behind Ruthie two women began kissing in a quiet corner booth. "Seems like an eclectic place."

"Eclectic?" Ruthie asked. "Is that what we're calling it now? Takes all kinds."

"I agree."

"My husband says you're a real estate developer."

"Well, actually I'm one of many attorneys who represent the developers who want to rehabilitate Cathedral City. "

"He says you plan to level every block south of here to Mexico." Ruthie sat opposite him on the stool.

"Maybe not that far. Only six blocks."

"We own two of them."

"That's right. The remaining two. The most important two. This building fronts the main drag. It's no secret this parcel is vital to the whole project. It isn't accurate to say all we want to do is level it. We want to rebuild something much more useful, more beneficial to the community."

"The desert doesn't need another indoor ice skating rink. Or movie theaters. The desert needs to maintain its own unique history."

Zola laughed. "Your husband coached you."

"No," Ruthie smiled. "I coached him. My husband very much wants to sell the parcel. He was a laughingstock when he bought it. Sam hates to be laughed at."

"Don't you ever laugh at Sam?" The question was insolent but she refused to be baited. Zola took another sip of his drink. "I hear you were a singer. I guess your children kept you too busy to go out on the road."

Marcella was serving a drink to a customer and stiffened at the cruelty of his comment. Ruthie followed this and directed her gaze at Zola.

"I don't have children," Ruthie smiled. "And for the record, I'm still a singer."

Zola's neck was beginning to tighten and he wanted to deescalate, cool things off. "I thought they had entertainment."

"She quit," Marcella volunteered.

They studied the silent piano. The smattering of customers looked restless. Many were looking at their watches.

"Any requests, Mr. Zola?" Ruthie stood up and took her place at the piano. "I think you just provoked me out of retirement."

Sam entered the lounge with Kenny in tow. He wanted Kenny to say hello to Ruthie. In the background Nick was laughing and joking with a few regulars. He looked up when Marcella canned the CD player. All eyes were on Ruthie at the piano.

"Now what's she up to?" Sam said warily.

Ruthie began to sing.

"I loved a man, truly I did. When he would touch me I'd act like a love hungry kid. Isn't this better?" Her voice was halting at first, until her audience recognized it as her style. Halting and breathy with perfect phrasing as if she were leaning forward to tell a very personal secret.

The room quieted. Sam and Kenny stayed rooted to their spot as she continued with the song. In the distance Kenny could see Nick, smiling with a faraway look in his eyes. Nick had often told Kenny about the early days of the bar. Hot desert nights, a Felini Circus of customers. Gangsters, movie stars, all types of desert rats, laughing, smoking, and drinking. *A place not to be seen,* Nick loved to say. Sam playing cards in the back booth with his cronies. Nick meeting and greeting. Ruth Harris at the piano.

Now the bar was filled with a smattering of losers. All listening to a very tremulous Ruthie.

"*Now I am calm, safe and serene. Heartache and hurt are no longer a part of the scene,*— Nicky, come and finish with me," Ruthie called from the piano. Nick floated to her side to sing the last refrain together after thirty years of silence, Ruthie to Sam; Nick to an emotional Kenny.

"*Isn't this better, the way it should be? Better for him and Oh, so much better for me . . .*"

Tenderly, Ruthie kissed Nick on the cheek, whispering. "*I'll always love you, Nicky.*"

Much to Ralph Zola's dismay, not to mention Sam Singer's, the room exploded with applause.

Nick and Kenny walked Ruthie and Sam to the Mark IV. Nick was very drunk, slurring his words.

"I'll manage her!" Nick was chattering, "First we'll cut a demo. Delores Hope did it. Why not Ruthie? Maybe we'll start slow. Three nights a week. Invite all the local concierges. Get the hotels worked up. I *told you* we needed a limo," he rebuked Kenny, who along with Sam was very uneasy about the night's events. "Remember those nights? Ruthie singing? The packed bar? Sam? Ruthie?" He was swaying on his feet. Eyes gleaming. "Remember?"

Behind him one of the marquee neon lights in his name burned out. —*ICK'S,* it read. Nick sagged at the sight of it. He suddenly felt very shabby, very old. He could see where the bar needed paint. Even the cactus in the window box was dying.

"You need to calm down," Kenny said quietly. "Let's go inside."

"Calm down! *Calm down?*" Nick slurred. "This *saves* us, don't you get it? They loved her—"

"This was a one-night performance," Sam interrupted him. To Ruthie. "Let's go. My wife ain't headlining a dump like this."

"Sam! *I'll* be the judge of that."

Kenny looked guiltily over at Nick. They were fighting because of him.

"Now look here, all of you!" Sam brayed. "Ruthie was a class act! The club isn't up to her standards." They all shrank back, because he was obviously very angry.

"But—"

Ruthie spoke gently, trying to placate Nick but she was very angry at Sam. "I think what Sam's trying to say, sweetheart, is that maybe we shouldn't play around in the past. Those were golden nights." She smiled kindly at Nick, who wavered slightly on his feet. She exchanged a sympathetic glance with Kenny, whose eyes were filled with pain for him. "I wish you could have seen us all then," she said for his benefit. "We were the best."

"We're *still* the best!" Nick insisted.

Sam opened Ruthie's door. "We gotta get going."

"I love you with all of my heart." Ruthie leaned forward and kissed Nick on the cheek. "Take care of him," she whispered to Kenny. "He needs you."

"Ruthie!"

She slipped into her seat and Sam reached over her lap, pulling her door shut in their faces. As the Lincoln maneuvered its way down the alley, several small Hispanic boys sporting cowboy hats loitered in the shadows. Ruthie studied the neatest of the beat-up old houses.

"That's Inez's house," she said.

"So?"

They drove in silence toward Palm Springs. Finally at the city limit, Ruthie erupted in fury. "Did you have to be so cruel to him? What'd he ever do to you?"

"He's a drunk and the place is a dump," Sam ranted. "He ran it into the ground. They're late with suppliers. Always late with the rent. I just gotta keep him going for one more season."

"We could fix it up. At least give it a coat of paint."

"That's what you know about business!" He fumbled with his cigar. "It's in his lease to keep up appearances. It's a leasehold expense. Look, I know what you're up to and it won't work. You aren't singing in the bar. It's not dignified. That's why I turned it over to him in the first place. To get us both out of there. To get us respect."

"Respect!" she shot back. "Who do you think you're talking to? We aren't the Annenbergs, Sam. We aren't Bob and Delores Hope. Our neighbors don't even acknowledge us! Nick was right. We had fun in those days. Good times."

"Well, the good times are over. I have our future to consider. Our security."

"Sam," she laughed. "We're millionaires. And we're getting old."

"I'm getting old," he shouted. "Not you."

Ruthie shook her head and smiled ruefully. "Look at me, Sam." She switched on the makeup light in the visor mirror over the passenger side of the Lincoln. The effect illuminated every tiny line in her face. "Face facts, kiddo. I'm getting old too. And I'd trade respect for a laugh any day of the week." She took a deep breath. "I read the papers, Sam. I know what you're up to, too. I know enough about business to know that you'll need my signature. I'll never sell Cathedral City out from under the boys. Or Inez either, for that matter."

"You may have no choice," Sam observed. "There are bigger forces at work than you or me."

The Lincoln roared up the palm-lighted highway toward Palm Springs.

Somewhere near the intersection of Ramon Road and Cathedral Canyon, a Chevy Blazer cruised into unincorporated Cathedral City. The young occupants were drunk, young, and mean. They were all teens; two males and one female, and hungry for a little excitement. Misty, Logan, and Drew. It was after one in the morning, which was the best time to stir up trouble.

They wheeled up Cathedral Canyon. When they reached Perez Road, they hung a right, because a gay dance club called CC Construction was just around the corner, hidden away in an industrial complex. They roared to a halt and surveyed the parking lot.

Mostly empty.

Then they scanned the few cars parked ahead of them down Perez, looking for single people who had already left the bar.

"This is too wide open. Even if somebody comes," said Drew. Misty sat in the middle. Riding next to her and holding a paint pellet gun sat Logan.

"Let's try the alley in Cathedral City . . . Let's try Nick's." said Logan. Drew whipped the Blazer around and roared past the parking lot to CC, just as two biker guys emerged from the bar. One wore chaps with no jeans. His bare butt jiggled in the moonlight.

"*Faggots!*" shrieked the kids from the Blazer. One of the biker guys grabbed his cod piece and wagged his groin at them. The Blazer swerved back around. Drew gunned the engine. The men realized something serious was up and began running toward their own Scout Cherokee. Logan took aim with the pellet gun.

He fired.

Bull's-eye. Red paint exploded on the jiggling white ass. The stricken man looked down, horrified.

"He thinks he really got shot. Shoot him again!" Misty howled.

Logan fired again, but his partner, having bent down to examine the friend's wound, took a shot in the side of the neck. It stung so bad he stumbled. For a horrible instant they believed they were dying.

The Blazer honked its horn and, tires screeching, kids laughing, peeled away, back to the intersection of Perez and Cathedral Canyon Drive. Then it whipped right and headed toward Highway 111.

When Ralph Zola left the bar, he had to think for a moment where he parked his car. The night was hot and quiet, and Zola recoiled momentarily, like anyone unused to the ferocity of the desert heat. His eyes focused on a stenciled warning on the brick wall opposite the side door of Nick's.

NO LOITERING.
DO NOT WALK ALONE TO CARS PARKED IN ALLEY.

He paused. Then he stepped jauntily into the alley where he parked his rented Park Avenue. The visit to Nick's had been a huge success. Nick told him most everything he might have wanted to know, and now Ralph had Marcella to fill in the blanks. He gave her three days to call him at his hotel. He liked black women and she must have been pretty frustrated, given that her options in Cathedral City seemed slim.

Ralph Zola never expected such a mixed clientele. A smattering of older straight couples sitting among gay men and women kissing and dancing together. He had never seen anything of the sort.

Ralph was so deep in thought he failed to notice the Chevy Blazer, parked opposite the Buick in the shadows of a concrete wall. He was stunned when three teenagers loomed out from behind it—two boys and one very beautiful girl. They looked stoned and highly menacing.

"Hey," Ralph said calmly. "You've got the wrong guy."

"What?" said one of the boys. Drew.

"I'm not who you think I am," Ralph said conspiratorially. He held up his hands. He needed to meet those punks on their own level. Negotiation was his specialty.

"Who says you're a queer?" the girl smiled. "That's what you meant, isn't it?" She reached out and glanced his nose with the heel of her hand. "Did we call you a queer?"

The pushing of him by the girl took him so by surprise he tumbled back like an old woman. He was immediately righted by a fist in his kidney which had been jammed there by the tallest boy.

"We didn't call you a queer," the boy said from behind. "We haven't started any name calling yet." He slugged him again and he fell toward the ground. He was righted by another male, and shoved back toward the third one.

"You have a big nose, maybe you're a Jew. You a Jew, Mister Big Nose?"

"You a Kike, mister?"

"A Yid?"

"What would you rather be, a Kike or a fag?"

"Yeah," they pushed him again, "fag or Kike?"

"I'm half-Italian . . ." he muttered, so confused now that he was numbed by the confrontation. A big man, even muscular, it seemed as though the evil intent of their actions was immobilizing him, and not the collective power of their force.

"A Wop?" said the girl. "You're lying," she added, shoving him hard, and with that he tumbled to the ground.

Just as they began to kick him, Gabriel rounded the corner with a load of trash.

"Hey!" he cried. He rushed into the kitchen. With that, Kenny emerged and the rest of the workers spilled out behind him. Marcella and Nick followed.

When Kenny saw Zola on the ground, surrounded by the teen-agers, he charged toward them, bellowing like a crazed animal. The sound was so horrific the kids leapt back, spilling into the Blazer like some film reel in reverse. Marcella quickly appraised the situation. She studied the waiting Blazer in the distance. In a second they peeled down the alley, lights out, leaving Ralph Zola weeping in a heap behind them.

When Kenny reached him, he knew Zola had shit his pants. Gabriel recoiled as Kenny stooped to help him up.

"Go get me a tablecloth," he ordered Gabriel.

"They were gonna kill me." Zola's teeth chattered.

"Were you hurt?"

Gabriel returned with a tablecloth. Zola wrapped it around his waist. In the distance sirens could be heard. He came to life when he heard them. "I don't need an ambulance."

"It may be the police."

"I'm not pressing charges. It was a mistake. They thought—they thought I was one of you."

Kenny's mouth dropped open. "That excuses what they did to you?"

By now Nick and Marcella were standing over them. Clutching

the blanket around his waist, Zola reached for his keys. He opened the door to the Buick and slid in.

He surveyed the alley. "Give Sam Singer a message for me."

"What?" said Nick.

"Tell him I'm going to destroy this area whether he cooperates or not."

Marcella caught his eye before he turned back to the wheel. He started the engine as the police car rounded the corner, two blocks down. He sped away in the darkness, the deeply disturbed expressions of Kenny and Nick reflected in the windows.

In Marcella's face, something far more calculating.

Later that night Ralph Zola lay huddled in the bottom of his shower, shaking with the realization that he was not in control of his circumstances and could apparently, at any given moment, fall prey to darker forces which heretofore he never really believed existed. In short, he had never been so frightened in his life. Then the telephone began ringing; he could hear it even with the water running and reached around the plastic shower curtain to answer the lavatory telephone.

"Hello . . ." he said, shivering.

"What's it like for a straight man to be taken for a fag?"

"*Who is this?*" he demanded.

"You know who it is. I think I can make you feel like a man again. I have a friend at the DMV if you want to make it worth my while."

"You got those bastard kids' license number?"

Marcella laughed and hung up on him.

That night Kenny stayed in bed with Nick for the first time in a year. Kenny didn't have the first idea as to how to make sense of everything that had happened. The threat of being sold out. The fight with Sam. The beating in the alley.

So tonight he shivered under the cotton blanket, his back to Nick, allowing his nearness to soothe some of their horror away. Nick was still smarting from Sam's remarks. Kenny had also been alarmed by his conversation with Sam Singer. He knew that changes were imminent, but had not, until this afternoon, really suspected that Sam was capable of selling out. The fact that he let the issue of the late rent go unchallenged, and the way his eyes appraised Kenny's kitchen fixtures, made Kenny aware that he was, in fact, considering a sale.

Kenny said into the darkness, "If you have any ideas about an investor, maybe you'd better make a call."

"This is all my fault," Nick whispered. "I'm sorry."

"No, it isn't."

"Yes," Nick affirmed, but without artifice. "I'm going to make it up to you."

"Nicky," Kenny called softly into the dark. "No matter what, we still have each other. We've survived . . . a lot."

Kenny reflected for a moment. In addition to the constant money worries, the eccentric and often bad choices Nick had made in and around his drinking, they'd fought off the advances of other gay men, jealous of their longevity, the closeness they had. They'd warded off the initial objection of Kenny's family, who thought Nick too old and too extreme to be involved with their son.

"What do you *see* in him?" his mother once asked, seven years into their relationship, her hands knotted against her face as she'd crept into the kitchen over his drunken body to find a cup of coffee.

"He's hopeful," Kenny said without hesitation. "I'm not. I don't have an ounce of optimism in me. And he dreams. Something goes wrong, no matter how bad he wanted it, he always has a new idea. I haven't had a new idea in ten years."

"You weren't always that way. Is there any coffee?" she asked shrilly, the anxiety so prominent that Kenny had laughed. He microwaved last night's dinner coffee and handed her a steaming cup.

"You call that hopeful?" She motioned to Nick, facedown into the carpet with an old dog blanket thrown over him. He was dreaming, protesting something to someone in his sleep.

"Not while he sleeps. He has nightmares when he sleeps."

She studied him, compassion hurrying across her brow. "Nightmares? About what?"

"I told you he grew up in an orphanage. He didn't get placed till he was thirteen."

"Why not?"

Kenny hesitated. He knew, but he didn't want to embarrass Nick by telling her. He decided to trust her. "He was effeminate. The fathers-to-be couldn't stand him. He'd eventually get returned. I think he dreams about that. About getting sent back."

"Does he remember his mother?"

"Won't talk about her."

"Not even with you?"

"No." Kenny started to clean up the kitchen but stopped. "Mom?"

"Yes?"

"You mean a lot to him. He's very curious about you. Can you?" Kenny's voice broke. "Can you give him a break? Make more of an effort?"

"Yes," she told him wryly and sighed. "Yes, I can. I'm just sorry that you got saddled with a drinker."

"I'm sorry you were saddled with one, too."

"Will you take a little advice?"

"Sure."

"Get your own life, have interests. Make friends. Don't pretend it doesn't exist. Don't wait for change. Change yourself. He won't ever quit."

Kenny knew Nick was emotionally drained. The violence had actually sobered him up. But to what? His own failure? Tonight Nick seemed particularly afraid. Kenny huddled up against the hollow of Nick's back. Then he reached over Nick's shoulder and tenderly patted his hand.

The next morning when Kenny parked his truck in the shady spot next to the abandoned garage near the restaurant, a swath of low-hanging snowy clouds hugged the ragged peaks of the barren San Gorgonio Mountains. Above the cloud layer a milky blue sky. At eight-thirty the air was already sultry with humidity. It was ninety-three degrees.

For several days Kenny had neglected to drop his box of new dolls at Arte de Sonora. Kenny thought he'd better bring them over today. When he lifted the box over the passenger door of his truck, he was startled to find Anita Quintero standing in the alley watching him.

Anita was only eight. She studied the box of dolls with great interest. Kenny balanced it on his knee so she could get a better look. Her calm brown eyes widened with intrigue.

"Pick one," Kenny smiled.

She looked at him doubtfully.

"Go ahead. Whichever one you like."

Her hand went immediately to the newest one, the beautiful doll with the red satin skirt. Kenny tried to hide his disappointment. He had struggled with the idea of even bringing it along. It was the best doll he'd ever made.

She sensed his reticence and withdrew her hand.

"No," he said quickly, feeling bad because she looked terribly disappointed. "Take her. She's yours." He reached into the box and pulled out the doll. He handed it to her after gently adjusting her hair.

Anita quivered with happiness. She took the doll and scooted away. In a moment he could hear the gate to her house open and then slam shut. As Kenny crossed the alley to unlock the kitchen door, he heard the gate open behind him. When he turned, Soila Quintero stood holding it open and looking at him.

"Hello," Kenny nodded, balancing the box of dolls.

"Did you give my sister a doll?"

"Yes. Would you like one, too?"

"No," she smiled shyly. "I just wanted to say thank you." Then she quickly withdrew behind her fence.

Kenny unlocked the door and kicked it open. As light flooded the linoleum floor, several roaches scattered under the stove. Kenny shook his head and set the box of dolls down on the cluttered desk. Maybe they'd sell a few this month. They paid him fifty dollars apiece and sold them for three times that amount.

Behind him Carmen entered the kitchen. She was here to help with the prep. This meant chopping vegetables and starting soup stocks. Carmen made the best soups of the three crew members.

Carmen lived with Miguel and his family in a tiny house across the highway from Nick's. She often invited Kenny for special occasions. A baptism, a wedding, or even just a weekend get-together.

The garage would be set up with card tables and paper tablecloths. The little girls would be dressed in pink or white frilly dresses, their long black hair braided down their backs. They would generally pursue the little boys, equally cute in little shirts and shorts, and by the end of the party they'd all be coated in sandy ice cream paste.

Kenny wondered if Carmen's friends thought it was odd that she invited her Anglo boss to these events. He knew he must seem strange. He always came alone, since the one time he brought Nick it didn't work out so great. Nick drank too much, was nervous around small children, and didn't follow baseball.

Carmen's boyfriend Hector didn't know anything about old movies or musical theater. He also had never heard of Ethel Merman or Angela Lansbury but nodded agreeably when Nick offered to go out for more beer.

When Nick left, Kenny noticed Hector and the other men whispering and snickering in the corner of the garage. Nick had elected to wear white slacks, a white tennis sweater, and red espadrilles to this function. When the men looked up and noticed Kenny watching them, they were embarrassed, but Kenny thought they were mostly embarrassed for him.

"How are you today, Carmen?"

"I'm okay, okay . . ." Carmen smiled brightly at him. "How's Nick?"

"He's okay," Kenny smiled conspiratorially. Whenever Carmen asked about Nick, Kenny always responded the same way. A shrug, as if what could he possibly say? Then they'd both laugh.

She moved to place her purse in a small locker near the sinks. She turned and smiled at him again. She hesitated, smiling brightly. "So Kenny, I was wondering, any way I can get part of my check this week?"

It pained her to ask him. She wanted to keep the request light. Give him an out if he needed it. Kenny had given her many advances in the past. Even an outright gift of several hundred dollars when she needed money to bail out Hector from the local jail.

She was very frugal and he knew she sent nearly half of her check back to relatives in Mexico. Her mother was old. She needed a cataract operation and without money would be severely impaired.

"Yeah," Kenny said. "We look booked for tonight. Can you wait till the end of the day?"

"Oh sure, sure," she nodded vehemently.

"I feel really bad about asking you guys to wait. I appreciate it, Carmen."

"Oh Kenny," she smiled. "You've helped us all so much. It's okay. We're like family. We know business is bad. You want me to start with the vegetables?"

"Yeah," he answered, chagrined. Then he went to the envelope with the cash for the food purveyor. He took out a hundred-dollar bill and handed it to Carmen.

"No, Kenny." She shook her head. "I can wait."

"No. Take it. Don't say anything, okay?"

"Noooo," she laughed, flapping her rag at him. "I won't say nothing! They'd ask me for a loan." She laughed heartily again. Then she went to her locker and slipped the money into her purse. "Thank you very much."

Kenny flipped on the swamp cooler. Overhead they could hear it purr. The dining room had frigid central air conditioning but there wasn't enough money to duct the kitchen as well. This meant that on hot summer days, when the temperatures soared into the triple digits, Kenny and his crew would swelter at just below ninety-five degrees while the dining room and lounge would bask at seventy-eight, but none of the kitchen crew complained.

Instead they listened to the desert Spanish stations, made fun of the waiters, talked about fucking the temporary hostess, told Kenny stories about life in the barrios of Cathedral City. He, in turn, brought presents for their babies, teased them about their girlfriends or boyfriends, and urged them to tell him their problems.

Now Kenny and Carmen were interrupted by Sam Singer, storming through the open kitchen door, waving the *Desert Sun* newspaper in Kenny's face. "This fucks it all up, I hope you know that! I had them right where I wanted them. You know what kinda pressure this puts on Zola to force me to sell?"

"What are you talking about?"

"This! Don't you read the newspapers?" Sam brandished the article. "They'll blame it on the neighborhood, the *Mexies,* that's who. Sorry, dear," he nodded politely to Carmen. "They'll have feds crawling all over this place."

"I'm an American citizen," Carmen corrected him. "Let them come."

Irritated, Sam looked back at Kenny.

"They were white teenagers, Sam." He looked over at Carmen and winked at her.

"You tell the cops that?"

"The cops never came. I don't know who made this report."

"Well, it sure as hell wasn't Zola. You think this looks good for him?"

"He threatened us before he left."

Sam's eyes narrowed. He grew very quiet, very patient. He made a major production of acting nonchalant.

"What'd he say?"

"He said to tell you he'd destroy this neighborhood whether you liked it or not."

Sam took out his cigar and lit it. "That so."

"You meant what you said, right, Sam?" Kenny was kneading dough for biscuits. "You won't sell Cathedral City, will you?"

"I gave you my word, didn't I? Fucking kids, fucking bastard kids. You need protection out in the alley. Those kids will be back. They hate gays. That's what this is all about."

"Actually, they also thought he was Jewish. Zola's ethnic looking. They used Jewish epithets too."

"What kinda epaulets?"

"Epithets." Kenny turned with his tray of biscuits and placed them in the oven. "The usual ones," he said, and dusted the flour off his hands.

"Well, you need protection back here, that's all there is to it."

"How can we afford a security guard? I can't pay Carmen as it is."

Carmen perked up at the mention of her name.

"I'll do it," Sam patted his pocket. "I'll be your security. Bastard kids will have another thing coming."

Kenny scowled scornfully. "That makes me feel a whole lot better."

Sam surveyed the kitchen. He studied a small tin painting resting against the back of Kenny's altar.

"So whatsit today?"

"It's a *retablo,*" Kenny explained.

"A prayer for the dead," Carmen observed without being addressed. For some reason she and Kenny looked at each other and laughed.

Sam contemplated the little painting. It depicted a Mexican funeral with a casket being lowered into the ground. Many mourners crowded around the open grave.

The subject made him uncomfortable so he left.

7

Ruthie

Ruthie opened her front door and screamed from the blast of heat. It was just past noon and over a hundred degrees outside. She bolted from the house to her car, which was parked in the shade under the carport.

This morning as she lay huddled under her blankets, the day loomed so long ahead of her she forced herself to get out of bed and take a shower. Sam was out. The house was quiet. She decided to go to the market.

Ruthie had a rule about going out. She always dressed up. Nothing about her public appearance ever betrayed her desperation. Even a trip to the nearby Ralph's at Smoke Tree required makeup, coifed hair—a dress. Her legs were as good as ever. Men turned when she passed. When Ruthie Singer entered a room, she knew she was still a beautiful woman.

Every day or so, Ruthie took a few minutes to hang around the grocery store, where she pushed a nearly empty cart and followed busy mothers with babies. If she'd had a therapist, she would think this worth mentioning, but she didn't have a therapist. Now she didn't even have any close friends. The urge to snatch a baby had been with her off and on since her early forties. It started as a game but had since expanded to a full-blown compulsion.

Sam didn't know it, but in the suitcase on the upper shelf of her closet, she'd embezzled enough cash from their rents to live for several years. She could take a baby, drive to Arizona, and disappear to parts unknown.

She never went through with it, though, and the time for doing it had long since past. As good as she looked, she could never fake being an older mother. She lost her chance for that ten years ago and she knew it.

Soon she had a young mother struggling with a toddler and a tiny baby in her sights. While feigning coincidence that everywhere the mother went, Ruthie needed to be there, too, the young woman finally turned, challenging her with nervous exasperation. At twenty-six she was already washed up.

"I'm sorry." Ruthie shrugged apologetically. "Your baby's beautiful. Do you know what it's like to be a Jewish woman in Palm Springs with no grandchildren?"

She threw up her hands good-naturedly. The woman smiled and moved away.

She returned to her car and removed the sun shade Sam had given her to protect the dash of her Cadillac. One side was an ad for Desert Realty. The other side, which she had unintentionally displayed read:

DRIVER IN NEED OF ASSISTANCE. PLEASE CALL POLICE.

Ruthie climbed into the car and remained hidden behind the cardboard shade while she collected herself from the day's events. Catching a glimpse of herself in the mirror, she was surprised to find the deranged eyes of a stalker staring back at her. She didn't even need to turn around. No one was lying in wait behind her in the backseat. These were her own green eyes.

"You'd better get your shit together, girly-girl . . ." she admonished herself sternly. Then she looked forward to tomorrow, when she could come back again for that odd jar of artichoke hearts, follow a few young mothers, indulge in a little wishful thinking.

It was Ruthie's last game of Poker.

The old bats had always been jealous of her looks, that was true. So when they rubbed it in with those goddamned baby pictures, she retaliated by pretending she was in the early stages of Alzheimer's.

They were playing cards in the clubhouse near the pool when photographs of the grandchildren came out. There were several new women at the table, and Ruthie's friend Carolyn noticed Ruthie wasn't quite herself. She kept having to remind her whose turn it was. It started when Ruthie would bet out of turn, not a terrible faux paux but enough to ruffle the feathers of a few diehards. Carolyn was a retired Vegas dealer, and she knew Ruthie knew better but was also mindful that this was Ruthie's first card game in a year.

Then she kept having to remind her to ante up, and Ruthie reacted as if she had been accused of cheating. After a tense minute Ruthie relented, tossing in a quarter instead of a dime.

"Are you raising the bet?"

"What?"

"The bet was ten cents. You threw in a quarter. Are you raising the bet?"

"I threw in a dime."

Carolyn held up the offending chip. "It's blue. It's a quarter. Did you need to make change?"

Ruthie shrugged. "I'm folding."

Exasperated, then concerned, the other women finished the hand in silence. Carolyn won. She pulled the chips toward her.

"Sure," said Ruthie.

"What do you mean by that?" Carolyn and the other women looked at each other.

"Ruthie, have you seen my grandchildren?" Norma, a smiling heavyset woman with a bright blond wig, pushed several baby photographs over at Ruthie. "These are Maureen's, my daughter married to the English professor."

Ruthie picked up a picture. She studied it critically. She snapped it facedown on the table. She picked up another one. She snorted. Norma reacted. Carolyn touched her hand to calm her down.

"Aren't they darling?" she offered for Norma's benefit.

Ruthie smiled brilliantly. Norma waited for her to reply. Instead, Ruthie gathered the photographs like a pile of junk mail and ripped them in half.

"What'd she do that for?" Norma demanded.

The women were shocked. Carolyn was so stupefied she didn't know what to say. With that, Ruthie stood up, pitched the torn photos into her purse, and walked away, heading first for a wall with no exit, spinning elegantly, and marching instead for the open sliding glass door. Later in the car when she rummaged through her purse for her keys, she found the torn photographs. She picked them out and held them in her lap while she drove.

She headed for the open desert, and when she reached the Interstate, Ruthie opened her window and let the torn photos flutter off in the hot wind. Ruthie was given to long drives in the desert, ever widening the distance she traveled from home.

"What good is it sitting, alone in your room? Come hear the music play . . ."

To cheer herself up, she played CDs from her favorite Broadway shows, or sometimes big band singers from the forties and fifties. Doris Day. Rosemary Clooney. Ella Fitzgerald. Julie London. Ruthie especially liked to sing along with Judi Dench. *"Life is a Cabaret, old chum. Come to the Cabaret!"*

Soon she was passing the exit to Indio. Thirteen minutes later she took the exit for Highway 86. At Thermal, California, Ruthie veered south toward the Anza Borrego Desert, the Salton Sea, El Centro. When she saw the sign for the international border and Mexicali, sadness trip-wired her system of self-defense. Fragmented memories from thirty years ago rushed in. Careening through the barren desert, Ruthie Singer began to cry. They hadn't known he would take all her future children from her.

"We're here to see Dr. Pena," Ruthie had whispered nervously. The waiting room was plain and clean. A few women held babies while older children played with toys from a toy chest.

She hadn't slept all night. The motel in Calexico had been horrible. Roaches clattering in the rust-stained bathtub. A condom dispenser over the toilet. The definite odor of mildew in the gummy orange shag carpet. Her worst nightmare. Punishment on top of shame.

"You want the other Dr. Pena, Señora. Three streets over." The stout Mexican nurse spoke fluent English. Her eyes registered utmost disapproval.

"How do you know which Dr. Pena she's come to see?" asked Nick. "She didn't tell you her name."

The nurse smirked at them. "My Dr. Pena is a pediatrician."

Behind Ruthie a child wailed.

"You're an American woman visiting a Mexican doctor. I don't think you need a pediatrician. That's how I know which Dr. Pena you want."

When Ruthie arrived at the Salton Sea, elevation -273 feet below sea level, she intended to turn around and head north to Palm Springs, but something compelled her to head south along the barren, canal-scarred slopes of Superstition Hills.

For kicks she veered east off the highway onto a sandy, one-lane desert road. Sam would kill her for taking such a chance, but she enjoyed gunning the engine of her big Cadillac, causing it to fishtail out, sending plumes of dust and sand spewing out behind her.

She would drive till she formulated her plan. When she got home, she planned to get out her music, sit at the piano, and reprise her repertoire for her extended engagement at Nick's. Deep in thought, she passed an eerie highway warning sign unique to Southern California highways.

"God, those road signs give me the creeps," Ruthie muttered.

Instead of a deer crossing, the image depicted a mother, a father, and a child, all of Hispanic origin, fleeing across the highway. The sign warned drivers to be careful of *human beings,* Ruthie shuddered, fleeing authorities and running for their lives.

With that, a young woman ran screaming in front of her car.

She was being hotly pursued by several smallish Hispanic men. Ruthie screamed, too, swerved the car, barely missing them, and nearly lost control of her car.

8

Maria

After spending three nights in a safe house in El Centro, Maria and Concha were now in a cargo van packed with seventeen other passengers, on a two-lane road heading for the Salton Sea. They'd just left Brawley, where they hid in a field until the van appeared and the drivers rounded them up.

"It's too small," Maria complained. "It's smaller than the van in Mexico!"

"Then don't come, *baybee* . . ." the *coyote* snapped. "I have your money. Maybe I won't take you anyway."

The driver of the van, the *raitero*, a pocked-marked teenager, whispered something in his ear and both of them laughed. On her look of irritation, the *coyote* explained, "He thought of a good reason to bring you along. Get in."

Everyone was loaded up but her and Concha.

"Come on, *Hija* . . ." Concha cajoled her. Concha had been very quiet this morning, her hands damp to Maria's touch. Maria could also hear her wheezing silently, but Concha denied it when asked and swore she felt fine. Maria helped her up. Then climbed up herself.

The *coyote* slammed the back door of the van behind her.

The stench in the van was ungodly, and all she could see were arms and legs. The *coyote* rode in front with the *raitero*. He turned around.

"From here on out, no one says notheen! I don't wanna even hear you breatheen. This is the most dangerous part of the trip. You thought the scorpions were bad? La Migra is much worse. If we get stopped, you don't whine, you don't cry, you don't do nothing but keep your mouths shut."

With that, Concha sneezed. He glared back into the darkness. "Okay, Americanos, we're takeen off." He yanked a curtain closed between them and the morning light. The van rumbled to a start, and after several minutes on a dirt road, Maria felt them pull onto the highway.

They drove for an hour in silence. Concha's head drifted into the curve of Maria's neck and shoulder. She listened to the sound of her grandmother's short breaths to keep herself calm.

"We made it, *Abuelita . . .*" Maria whispered.

"Whatever happens, keep going," Concha gently squeezed her hand.

The air was hot and dead.

Not a sound had been uttered for sixty miles. In the back of the van, the temperature was nearing 118 degrees. The *coyote* was happy that the trip was proceeding without incident. The young *raitero* had been hired to drive them to a safe house in Los Angeles. He picked at his tooth with a matchbook cover from his favorite whorehouse in Mexicali. Suddenly the silence was shattered with screams.

"I need water!" Maria cried. "She's dying! I need water!"

The passengers erupted into panicked lamentations.

"Shut up!" the *coyote* ordered. "Shut up!"

The curtain behind him was yanked from its hooks. Maria had clawed her way to the front compartment. "Water!" she screamed. "She isn't breathing! Stop the van! Stop the van!"

"We ain't stopping for nutheen!" the *coyote* turned, eyeball to eyeball with Maria. Behind her the other passengers began to wail. He pushed her back, but the sheer volume of bodies held her steady.

"You have to stop! She can't breathe! Stop the van," Maria screamed again. She clawed at the head of the *raitero*. The van swerved as he tried to shake her off. Now everybody was screaming.

Over all the cacophony, Maria thought she heard the voice of God.

The van fell silent.

"Lady," a little kid pulled at her skirt. "She's already gone. Lady."

"*What?*" Maria turned in horror.

"She's already dead, *señorita,*" his grandfather confirmed. In the bowels of the van, Maria could see Concha slumped in repose and knew in that instant it was true.

In the seconds following the death of her grandmother, Maria flailed through the sea of her fellow travelers to hold Concha's body against her breast. "Abuelita!" she cried, hoping Concha would respond.

"Mamacita!" she pleaded with her own mother in heaven. "Take me with you! Take me with you. Don't leave me here all alone!"

In the front of the van, other forces were at work.

"What are we gonna do?" the *coyote* demanded of the driver. The girl and her grandmother had been nothing but trouble, so when the driver offered a reasonable solution, the *coyote* was only too happy to comply.

"We gotta dump her," the *raitero* shrugged. And the other passengers—lives at stake, families needing money, wanting to avoid arrest—all made the sign of the cross in unison at the necessary horror of it.

The van screeched to a halt on a bridge over the Whitewater River, raging from yesterday's floods. The *coyote* hopped out. The heat blasted him in the face. Running around to the back, he popped open the rear doors. First they brutishly ejected a screaming Maria. Two men held her while Concha's still warm body was clumsily passed from the rear of the van to the ground.

Maria fought them wildly—hysterical, outraged—spitting, clawing, and screaming as she watched Concha's body being lugged to the side of the bridge.

"Hurry!" the *coyote* barked. "A car is comeen!" and in the distance they could see a white luxury car roaring down the hill toward them.

Thus Concha's tiny body was flung over the metal side rail of the bridge.

The body bounced once and sank from view. Maria was stunned into silent submission. Her captors relaxed their hold. The *coyote* pulled out his pistol. Behind him the *raitero* prayed for forgiveness.

And then as the car approached, Maria flailed out, knocking the gun of the *coyote* out of his hand. It clattered to the ground at her feet. She began to run, and several men cautiously pursued her. If they thought she intended to stop the car for help, they were wrong.

She wanted to be struck dead by it, to die on the front hood, to be trampled by its tires or thrown so far her head would explode on the blacktop like a melon. And she ran toward the oncoming car with all her strength. The *coyote* had been right. She was a negligent, horrible granddaughter. How could she have allowed the most precious person in all of her life to die in such disgraceful circumstances?

Maria hadn't been honest with herself. She'd blamed the entire idea on Concha, hiding behind the old woman's eccentricity to justify taking the risk. She wanted to come, too, and if she'd admitted it sooner, they could have devised a legal, orderly way to achieve it. Maybe she could have obtained a work permit, or applied to a school. There would have been a way, after she got established, to send for her grandmother. And now she was dead. She was sick with guilt. Would die of loneliness.

Abuelita! Abuelita!

The big white car jogged her memory.

"I'll come for you, *Nietas*," her mother had said. "Don't *cry* so. Your father and I have important things to do, please be brave, because it hurts my heart to see you so sad. Your grandmother loves you so much. Where we're going isn't a place for a little girl."

"But aren't there children there, too?"

"Yes," her mother was forced to admit.

"Then why can't I come?"

And her mother Pia hadn't wanted to frighten her by telling her it was dangerous, and evaded Maria's question by changing the subject to some nonsensical childish topic while Maria watched her pack. At eight years old she was certain her mother didn't love her, that her mother was traveling to meet her father in some exotic, beautiful mountain village where they'd find other little girls they preferred to her.

When Pia drove away in the family white Ford sedan, Maria refused to be placated, wouldn't wave goodbye even at the clucking of her grandmother. Instead she struggled out of her grasp and stomped angrily inside their house, slamming the door on her and her worried *Abuelita.*

Only now, on this hot California highway did it suddenly register that Concha had been afraid for the safety of Maria's parents, her daughter Pia and her son-in-law Ramòn. She hadn't immediately returned to the house, and little Maria had been angry about that as well. Concha'd stood watching the vehicle disappear in the distance and had wiped her eyes before turning to come back to the house.

A week later they both were killed.
Selfish.
Abuelita! Mamita!

Maria got close enough to see the driver, a pretty older woman with red hair, screaming with horror at the impending collision. For an instant Maria imagined that the woman driving the big white car was her own mother, sent from heaven to answer her prayer, to kill her and bring her home.

But the startled woman saw her in time, averted her doom by swerving around her, and after passing Maria and her pursuers, whipped the car screeching around and roared back up the highway to rescue her.

Concerned about Ruthie's whereabouts, Sam drove out to Nick's to ask if they'd seen her. He barged into the front of the bar, which even in his outraged haste, he noted happily, was packed tonight. After grilling Nick to no avail, Sam trudged into the kitchen to talk to Kenny.

"I haven't seen her, Sam. You want me to go home? Make a couple of calls?"

"I'd sure appreciate it if your gang can spare you." Sam mopped his brow. He really looked worried.

"We can take care of everything." Carmen looked up. "We know our jobs."

"Sure, sure . . ." Gabriel nodded.

Kenny smiled and pulled off his apron. "I'll call you if I hear anything."

Carmen, Miguel, and Gabriel all stared at Sam till he trudged back to the dining room. When Sam entered the lounge, he was surprised to find Ralph Zola sitting at the bar.

Ralph Zola put a hand on Sam's shoulder. "So, Sam, you have a minute to talk?"

He gestured to an empty booth in the lounge. Sam obliged him and they both sat down. Sam pulled out a cigar, offering him one. Zola accepted. Sam studied his face as he offered him a light.

"So what brings you back to the bar?"

"It's my job to get to know a few locals, Sam. What makes a neighborhood tick. You know that."

"Heard you made threats. That's a problem."

"C'mon, Sam. Let's drop the act. You want to sell the parcel. How much? I wanna get home to my family. What's your price?"

Sam blew his smoke in Zola's face.

"Ya know how long I've owned this property?"

"I know you've owned the houses for sixteen years."

"I've had the bar since 1957. You hear how I got it?"

"How?"

"I won it in a card game. Down in the basement. I bluffed with *two pair.* The guy was sure I had a boat. He folded."

"I won't fold, Sam."

"This is where I met my wife. She was a nightclub singer. She stood right over there." Sam gestured to the empty stage. "Night after night she sang right to me." For a moment Sam could imagine Ruthie standing in a tight blue silk dress, a spotlight illuminating her thick red hair.

"You happy with what the place has come to?"

"What's it come to?"

"Look around, Sam." Zola gestured to the raucous gay crowd. Two men were kissing in the booth opposite them.

"Look, Ralphie, if I was thinking about selling, your threat cooled me down. I can wait. I can wait a few more years. You must know I don't need the money. And I'm fond of the boys." He folded his hands in front of him. They were big. Hands that could strangle.

"You think of them like sons, I'll bet."

"That's right."

Zola stood up. "I'll be in touch, Sam. One way or another." He nodded and moved toward the front door.

"Ya never shoulda threatened me, Ralphie . . ."

Sam blew smoke rings into the air.

"We have to go back!" Maria was screaming. "We have to go back!"

Ruthie checked her rearview mirror. There was no sign of the men or their vehicle. "We can't go back! They were trying to hurt you."

"My grandmother is back there! They threw her in the river. We have to go back and find her!"

And Ruthie didn't know what to do. The girl was hysterical. On the CD player, a recording of Judy Garland singing live at Carnegie Hall. Ruthie ejected it. Over her shoulder, back down the empty barren road, lined on one side with dusty desert shrubbery and a raging arroyo on the other. She'd driven off so quickly she realized the car was speeding over a hundred miles an hour.

In a split second lives can change. Ruthie considered her options, all of them in those moments, and she decided that she simply could not go on living as the hollowed-out, self-obsessed, empty woman she had become. No matter what the price, she wasn't going back to bed.

"Okay," she announced, adrenaline coursing through her veins. "We're going back!" And she slowed down enough to turn the big Cadillac around. When she did, the van carrying Maria's *coyote* and the remainder of the human cargo was barreling toward them, with every intention of driving them off the road.

Maria screamed but Ruthie stepped on the gas. "Open the glove compartment. There's a pistol in it!"

And Maria complied, gingerly producing the 9mm Glock which Sam insisted Ruthie carry for her own safety.

"Hand it to me!"

Maria handed it over.

Ruthie lowered her power window, holding the steering wheel firmly with her bejeweled right hand. Holding the Glock in her left, she reached out over the side of the car and aimed the pistol right at the head of the *coyote* in the passenger seat of the old van, now only five hundred feet away from them.

"There are innocent people in the van!" Maria protested.

"Do you want me to pull over? Allow them to drive us off the road?"

"No!"

"Then fasten your seat belt," Ruthie ordered her. "We're going to finish this one way or another."

And the Cadillac sprang forward like a cruise missile.

"Try me!" Ruthie cried. "Try me, you fuckers!"

And when the *raitero* and the *coyote* saw that the redheaded woman holding the *pistola* and barreling toward them wasn't about to forfeit any game of chicken, they veered around her at the very last minute, perilously close to overturning; close enough for Ruthie to see the shocked respect in their eyes.

And moments later Ruthie allowed Maria to stand helplessly by the rushing water of the arroyo. She watched her walk up and down the water's edge, crying hysterically, searching for her grandmother, whom she finally admitted was already dead when they threw her body away.

"I know you want to jump!" she told Maria. "And I can't stop you. But she's gone and there's nothing we can do to help her. You have one gift to give her. Don't give up. Keep going."

"You didn't know her and you don't know me," Maria bitterly replied.

"That's where you're wrong," Ruthie admonished her, and after a moment Maria permitted Ruthie to lead her back to the car.

When Kenny opened the front door of the house, the lights were off. Only the blue light from the pool shimmered through the open patio door. He switched on a small lamp on a table in the entry hall. Then he began turning on other lights. He turned around. Ruthie was sitting at the piano.

"You scared the hell out of me. Sam has the cops looking for you. I came home to make a few calls. To try to find you."

"I need your help. Big time. You up for it?"

"What's wrong? Are you hurt?"

Ruthie nodded past him to the living room. He followed her gaze. His face blanched.

"What is it?" Ruthie asked. "You look like you've seen a ghost!"

Kenny was staring in amazement at a stunned Maria, sitting on the sofa holding a cold compress to her jaw. She stood up. She uttered something indecipherable in Spanish but it sounded very bitter.

"You know each other?" Ruthie was incredulous. "How's that possible?"

Then Maria charged him, slapping at his face, screaming obscenities, and collapsed to her knees in hysterical exhaustion. Kenny didn't defend himself, allowing her to place her blows, his face pinching with grateful shame. To Ruthie he was taking punishment, but why? She moved to pull her away.

"No," Kenny said. "Leave her alone. Let her finish."

And Maria looked up at him in astonishment. "You'll be happy to know God answered her prayer!"

"Whose prayer?"

"My grandmother's, *señora!*"

"What happened to her?" Kenny asked. His voice was hardly more than a whisper. Maria dropped her eyes and began to cry softly.

"I was driving. Down near the Salton Sea," Ruthie told him. "Men were chasing her. I pulled over." She glanced over at Maria. "Her grandmother died of dehydration. They apparently threw her body into a river."

"Now God has answered her prayer," Maria whispered wearily.

"What was her prayer?" Ruthie asked.

"When I told her he was lost. That he fell back into the water. '*Me for him,* she said.'" Maria replied. "Her for you."

Slowly she stood up. "If you hadn't interfered, she'd be alive now. You called too much attention to us. That *coyote* was *jealous* of you," she said, her rage cresting again. "*I wish it had been you!*" and she slapped him again. "You wanted to die. She didn't! *You wanted to die!*"

"What does she mean, 'you wanted to die'?" Ruthie demanded. Kenny and Maria exchanged a knowing glance.

"He fell back. I saw him. He didn't have to but he gave up, fell back into the water." The young woman challenged Kenny to dispute her. "He wanted to die."

Kenny stood very still. Maria stepped back. Maria and Ruthie looked at each other.

"There's nothing he can say, dear," Ruthie managed to stammer. And then to Kenny, "I'll make other arrangements, put her in a hotel."

"No," Kenny said. "She can stay here till we figure out what to do."

And regret finally flickered in Maria's eyes. She felt terribly ashamed. A lone tear rolled down her cheek. When it hit the floor, Kenny felt like he'd been slugged. A low moan erupted from his chest.

Kenny took two steps toward her and dropped to his knees, his body convulsing in great heaving sobs. To Ruthie's amazement, despite her own grief, Maria managed to lean forward to stroke his hair in a vain attempt to comfort him.

Later when Kenny suggested that Maria should lay down, Maria numbly reached down for her bag and realized that she had nothing.

"I had a bag. I had belongings."

Lost on the road where her grandmother had been disposed of. She was entering her new life with only the clothing on her back. But when she saw Kenny and Ruthie looking at her with such frank pity, she straightened up again. She remembered Concha's last words to her. *No matter what happens, keep going.* In that instant, as much as her heart ached, as poor as she was, Maria knew that the spirit of her family was with her and that she wasn't really alone.

She could elect to move on as a victim or a survivor. This was a defining moment in her character. As she gazed into the doleful eyes of the pretty woman who had rescued her, and the darkly grieving eyes of the somber man who was offering to shelter her, Maria made up her mind.

"Come, come, *Hija* . . ." Kenny held out his hand.

"What should I tell Nick?" Ruthie whispered.

"Tell him he has a daughter," Kenny said. He ushered Maria down the hall to her room.

Ruthie volunteered to go to the bar to fill Nick in. She also knew Sam would need extra special handling. This time she had gone too far. She'd never disappeared for longer than an hour without telling him where she was headed. Not in thirty years.

When she entered the lounge, she expected to find Nick drunk and Sam having a fit. Instead she found the two of them, calmly eating dinner together and discussing improvements for the bar. All at Sam's expense.

"We're redecorating," Nick smiled. "And I'm cutting back on my drinking. Tonight I only had one glass of wine. Isn't that right, Sam?"

"Whatever you say, sport."

"After what happened to Kenny, I see it as a wake-up call."

"That so," Ruthie said warily. She braced herself for a barrage of invective, but instead Sam stood up and kissed her tenderly. "Huh," she observed. "Maybe I ought to drive away more often."

"You had me real worried, kid."

"He was a nervous wreck!" Nick acknowledged. They were both acting so oddly she didn't know what to do. She sat next to Sam, who mopped the corner of his eye with his handkerchief.

"If you wanna sing here, a couple nights a week, it's okay by me."

"Well, I'm real happy to hear that," she smiled. "Frankly, I'd kind of come to the same conclusion on my drive. Whether it was okay with you or not."

He started to flare up but she smiled so beautifully he quieted. She leaned forward and kissed him gently. He started over.

"Nicky and I decided, that is, if you agree, that maybe we should fix the old joint up. Maybe paint the exterior, repair the booths. Put in a new carpet."

"I want air conditioning in Kenny's kitchen," Ruthie said flatly. Sam winced. "Okay."

"And a new sound system. And billing on the marquee. Ruth Harris."

"Now that's going too far!"

"*Ruth Harris Singer,*" Nick suggested.

Ruthie and Sam looked at each other.

"Deal."

"Now I have something to tell you both . . ." Ruthie began. "About my drive in the desert."

She slept fitfully, unused to her surroundings. Outside she heard a car pull up, and suddenly the front door of the house opened with a bang. An angry exchange of men's voices coming down the hall toward her room. She sat up fearfully.

"Don't go in there, she's asleep! You'll wake her up!"

"I won't wake her!"

Maria's bedroom door flew open with a bang.

"Goddammit!" Kenny exclaimed.

"Where is she?" Nick demanded. "I don't see her!" He switched on the bedroom light. He scanned the room with an impatient smirk on his lips. He reeked of alcohol. He softened when he saw Maria, cowering on her bed against the wall.

"Hullo," Nick said. "I'm *Nick.*"

"He lives here too," said Kenny sullenly.

"I'm very sorry about your tragedy." Nick said importantly. "I was an orphan till I met Kenny, and I want you to know that you can stay with us for as long as you like."

Maria didn't know what to say. Finally she whispered, "Thank you."

"Get some rest, dear." Nick smiled, adding, "And feel free to use the pool." He switched off the light and swaggered into the hallway. Kenny lingered for a moment. He seemed uneasy.

"I'm outside if you need anything."

"How can I stay here! I need to find work," Maria said. "I'll do *anything.*"

"First you need to rest. Sleep, now."

Later that night Maria dreamed that Concha was floating in the bottom of the swimming pool, looking for Kenny. She woke up screaming and ran down the hallway to find a way to get out to save her. Kenny was asleep on the couch in the living room. He bolted upright. He could see her struggling to open the sliding glass door. She flapped against the glass and draperies like a frantic bird, caught in the house and unable to fly away.

Kenny jumped up and opened the sliding glass door.

"I have to save her!" Maria screamed, rushing out onto the patio. "Abuelita, *Abuelita!*" She knelt by the edge of the pool, frantically looking for the body of her grandmother.

"No, *Hija,* she's not there," Kenny came up behind her. "Nobody's in the pool. No, no, no . . ."

"She's drowning!" Maria screamed. "Save her!"

"She's not down there," Kenny said softly. "You were dreaming."

She stared furtively into the water. The light from the pool reflected up onto her face. The look of sadness in her eyes caused the hair on the back of Kenny's neck to stand up. He'd never seen such loneliness before. He knelt down next to her and gently put his arm around her shoulders. Maria began to sob.

After a moment Kenny got an idea and stood up. He moved to a storage closet adjacent to the pool. Then he returned with a box of floating pool candles. She watched him as he lit one. He handed it to her, motioning for her to put it on the water.

She shook her head, thinking it would sink.

He took it from her and gently placed it on the surface of the water. It pitched slightly, the water threatening to douse the flame. Instead it burst back with a blaze of light. Once balanced, the candle floated courageously out to the center of the pool and sparkled.

Kenny continued to light candles, handing each one to her and allowing her to place it on the water. Soon the pool was ablaze with floating candles, illuminating Maria's comfort.

Maria lit the final candle.

"This is for you," she told him.

PART TWO

The Immigrants

9

Pablo

Pablo moved from Mexico to the California desert for several reasons, one being the new Gold's Gym, magnificently appointed overlooking the runways of the Palm Springs International Airport. In addition to all the latest equipment, Pablo could grind away on the second-floor Stairmasters and watch all manner of aircraft land and take off; from private Leer jets to huge commercial 737s. Set against the backdrop of the vast desert floor of the Coachella Valley and the distant, softly sloping foothills of the little San Bernardino Mountains, visually the experience was both romantic and spectacular.

The clientele of the gym was also intriguing, comprising equal parts of well-to-do, transitory tourists, always ensuring new faces, and a solid base of somewhat interesting locals; many having retired to Palm Springs prior to 1993 and the advent of the protease cocktail. Spurred by California's recession, the low cost of living, and diminishing T-cells, these well-ensured Persons With AIDS viaticated life insurance policies, declared disability, and retired to the desert seemingly to live out their final days. A three-bedroom ranch home with a pool could be purchased for under a hundred thousand dollars, and because Palm Springs was already an established retirement destination geared to a huge senior citizen population, excellent medical facilities lay ready to serve a growing HIV community.

Then the prognosis for HIV changed.

Conservative Palm Springs, so long opposed to gay businesses within its city limits, suddenly found itself courting the gay dollar. With a burgeoning gay population, by some estimates as much as thirty-eight percent, the city council found itself encouraging conferences and events which would have been unthinkable twenty years ago.

Pablo himself became acquainted with the desert when he traveled from his home in Mexico City to attend his first circuit event, the world famous "White Party" which was held at the Palm Springs Convention Center. Ten thousand well-heeled, sexy, muscle-bound gay men attended the three-day party—dancing, drugging, and fucking the desert nights away, engorging the local hotels, and overtaking every mom-and-pop restaurant situated along Palm Springs' famous Palm Canyon Drive. The cost of the weekend, between drugs, meals, and lodging, was estimated at a thousand dollars per head—ten million dollars lavished on the quaint desert hamlet in *one weekend*.

If the conservative old guard didn't approve of the gay lifestyle, they were happy enough to accept their money, and wasn't that *always* the way, Pablo observed. Pablo, too, benefited from the economics of the gay boom to the desert for he himself was in the service industry.

Call him what you want—trainer, masseur, physical therapist—amiable, articulately bilingual, amber-eyed, honey-bronzed, silken-haired, broad-shouldered, and magnificently well endowed, Pablo Seladon was a hustler. In addition he was educated, witty, self-effacing, and naive—it was difficult for Pablo to ever say no, and hence this set his story in motion.

Pablo was a pilgrim of sorts, an immigrant seeking asylum for reasons of sexual preference. He would not, of course, cite any such claim on his application for permanent residency. He would instead note the healthy bank account his father opened in his name in the City National Bank in New York. If the INS ever read the fine print, they would also find that Pablo's assets had been frozen—yes, he had funds in his name but they were frozen by order of his father, who also signed on the account.

Every personal choice Pablito made had something to do with needling his elderly father. He was the only child of very wealthy parents in Mexico. His father was a diplomat to the U.N.; his mother an elegant professor of literature at a very prestigious university. When after his first White Party he announced his desire to take a sabbatical from his own studies and return to Palm Springs, his angry father cut him off financially. If he remained in Mexico, finished his undergraduate degree, and then applied to graduate school at Harvard, Stanford, or Brown as had been previously discussed, money would never be an issue.

His mother wisely understood the forces driving his desire for autonomy, but she agreed with his father that if he wanted true independence, he should understand that it came with its own set of responsibilities. She believed her sensitive, handsome son was extraordinarily gifted. He belonged in the arts. His prose was particularly impressive, but without life experience to enhance it, the gift would be wasted.

It was she who convinced Pablo's father to allow him to emigrate, knowing also in her heart that the United States would probably be more accepting of Pablo's "gifts" than their conservative friends and family in Mexico. Central and South America, while progressing in this area, were not ever going to change in her lifetime or the lifetime of her beautiful young son.

Even the United States gave her grave misgivings, and she did her best to talk Pablo into considering Montreal or Toronto if he needed time for soul-searching. But he had been stubborn, as stubborn as his father. He would relocate to Southern California and earn his own way!

But the combination of Pablo's sexual appetite, his spirit of adventure, and the easy availability of designer party drugs—GHB, Special K, and Ecstasy—all conspired to cloud his judgment. His first paying job came quite by accident.

He had tricked with a wealthy investment banker he met one night at a dance club in Cathedral City. The guy took him back to his vacation rental, a small condo at the old Racquet Club in Palm Springs. The sex was great, and the trick seemed particularly grateful.

Pablo had not fallen victim to the sexual narcissism so common among many gay men his own age. He wasn't seeking a mirror image of himself in a sexual partner. In fact, he was actually attracted to loftier qualities: a sense of humor, a good intellect, kind eyes. Even in a noisy bar it was never too difficult to pick them out. They usually stood off by themselves, happy to watch the crowd, waiting to be chosen rather than choose. They were usually a few years older than Pablo. He preferred if they were well made, but in fact forgave much for what someone with his physical attributes could easily command. One body was no different from another. Bodies in general thrilled Pablo, but primarily every-man bodies appealed to him most.

So when they were finished and Pablo was dressing to leave, the guy asked him casually how much he owed him.

Was he joking? Pablo turned around in astonishment. "What do you take me for?"

And the guy started laughing. "Really," he said. "How much? Normally they always make you pay up front."

And Pablo didn't know how to respond. Pablo liked to experiment sexually as long as it was safe. He wasn't beyond a little role-playing. A little dirty talk. Some well-placed, lighthearted spanking. But he'd never considered sex for money. It eroticized him so quickly he grew excited.

The trick lay on the bed, the sheet pulled just up to his waist. "How much?" he asked again. "Is a hundred dollars okay?"

"Well, I guess a hundred dollars would be okay," Pablo smiled lazily. "If it makes you feel better."

And that night Pablo had driven home, the money burning in his pocket. Pablo looked at himself in his own rearview mirror and saw the eyes of a sonofabitch. *You're a bad boy,* he admonished himself, pointing his finger at his image, *you should go back, return his money,* but instead the black Jeep roared across the desert floor toward his encampment in the sandy foothills of the Little San Bernardino Mountains, fifteen miles east of Desert Hot Springs.

I should call him at least, insist on returning the money, Pablo's conscience told him, but when the Jeep rolled to a halt and he stepped onto the desert, the creosote smelled sweet and he was happy to be alone in his little trailer under a star-filled sky.

Pablo lived in Sky Valley, on land homesteaded by a gay porn star of such Joe Gage classics as *Kansas City Trucking Company, El Paso Wrecking Company, L.A. Tool and Die.* Pablo rented the old Airstream trailer, adding a screened-in porch and a greenhouse to grow orchids and pot. He'd get so high he'd start building footpaths, lined with small stones, and the end result was a crazy melange of trails leading all over the property and up to the mountain range behind the camp.

When he first moved in, Pablo broke into a padlocked metal chest he found hidden under the trailer, and to his delight discovered an old projector, a small screen, and the porn star's collection of his early films. That night Pablo treated himself to a Joe Gage Film Festival.

The projector started rolling and Pablo was amused to see such old actors in a porno film. Even women were present to eroticize a story line, and Pablo had never had sex with a woman. Used to fast-forwarding VCRs, he couldn't rush the projector to get to the sex scenes, so he decided to relax and see what this was all about.

The bodies were natural and hairy, no shaved groins or assholes, no steroid-pumped musculature. These were everyday men who couldn't always keep an erection, kissing each other passionately and fucking and sucking without condoms. Astonishing, Pablo thought, because Pablo always practiced safe sex.

Pablo shook his head sadly. He was smoking a joint. Normally grass turned him on, but tonight he was sleepy and drifted off to the sound of Richard Locke's laughter.

He awoke to the sound of film flapping. He looked at the clock. He must have been asleep for over an hour with the thing flapping away. He got up with a raging piss hard-on, and moved to turn off the projector. Outside he could hear coyotes chattering, yipping the way they do when one of them has made a kill.

When Pablo had to pee with an erection, his cock would get so thick and hard he couldn't bend it to aim for a toilet. It stuck straight up, running along the contour of his belly, and sometimes got so hard only he could pry it away from the cut of his abs. Since he lived so far out in the desert, whenever he had a hard-on and had to pee, he liked to step outside and piss in the wind, far enough from the trailer for sanitary reasons.

Wearing boxers and sweat socks, he pulled on his sweatshirt and a pair of work boots which he didn't bother to tie. His cock pressing against the shorts, he flung the trailer door open and was shocked by the burst of cold air. The sky was moonless, no clouds, and the stars were so brilliant they seemed to be reflecting up at him from the sand. The effect was so beautiful it intoxicated him, causing him to stagger. He wandered up a path where he liked to take a piss. An old smoke tree provided a little stability, and he hung on to it while he dropped his drawers. The piss worked its way up his cock and started flying, and he groaned as his bladder emptied. While he peed, he leaned against the arms of the tree like a drunk at a urinal in a bar. When he was done, his cock felt a little spongy, but when he shook it, it hardened again.

Suddenly he had the eerie sensation that he wasn't alone. Out of nowhere a warm hand touched his ass, rubbing the crack of it and wandering around the front of his belly to touch his cock. The other hand pulled his shorts down around his knees and slid them down to his boots. Almost in slow motion, Pablo stepped out of them. A bearded face slid up Pablo's body, a thick tongue tasting his skin. Soon the face was under his sweatshirt, emerging to kiss his neck and finally his mouth. As the stranger's hand jerked Pablo off, he penetrated him from behind while kissing him. The kissing was so deep he could feel it in the balls of his feet.

When Pablo woke up, the sun was coming up through the wooden slats of the trailer's venetian blinds. It was cold because the trailer door was open. His boots were sitting neatly by his bed. He was still wearing his sweatshirt but his boxers were off, and Pablo never slept without his underwear. He got out of bed feeling very refreshed. Wandering through the galley kitchen, he was awed to find the projector and films missing.

Gone. He flung open the storage unit. Empty. He stepped outside.

In the short distance up his pissing hill, he could see his boxers, hooked on a branch of the petrified tree, flapping in the breeze.

Several days later, Pablo began working at the Seven Palms Hotel, where he'd stayed when he first visited Cathedral City. The place had changed. Instead of a lazy small motel with a pool and a little coffee shop, new owners had expanded the number of rooms by adding a second floor and a wing of units on the other side of the pool area. They also built a huge lobby with a long bar and dance area, and a much larger restaurant where the coffee shop used to be.

Lee, the manager, a leather queen with a missing side tooth, remembered Pablo from several years ago. When Pablo jokingly asked if he needed a hand, Lee took him into his office and pulled out his dick.

"I meant that I need a job," Pablo resisted.

"Start with this and I'll train you to be a bartender."

Pablo thought for a minute, figured why not, reached out, and jerked Lee off. Later that night he was lugging beer from the shed to the bar.

"What brings you to the desert?" a bartender had asked him.

"I was hoping to find work in the service industry," Pablo smirked facetiously. He was really only taking time off between semesters. He had come to the desert to get laid.

"You'll do well in tips."

Two customers wandered up to the bar, well-heeled drinking buddies in the desert for a little sun. They observed the handsome Mexican boy bending down to stack the cases of beer.

"Look at his ass." one said to the other. Then he made a grunting noise, like he wanted to fuck him right on the bar.

"Jesus! He can hear you . . ." replied the friend.

"Hey, Paco. Pa-co—" the first guy sang. Pablo purposely doesn't turn around. The friend winked. "They never speak English. Hey Paco, *dos cervezas, por favor!*"

Pablo turned and smiled. "Foreign or domestic?"

"Uh, foreign, I guess."

"That's what I figured, but I wasn't certain. You seem like a fellow who appreciates the finer things in life. For instance, you seem to know a lot about asses." And then a crazy idea came into his head. "How much would you pay to see it for yourself?"

Most of the employees hustled the guests but never, ever openly discussed it. The hotel took ten percent. The Seven Palms attracted primarily single guests at inexpensive rates and rarely got a complaint about lack of service. A shuttle ran back and forth from the hotel to the airport and later to bars and the dance clubs in Cathedral City.

A visitor could arrive drunk, stay drunk, and leave drunk without ever getting behind the wheel of a car. The scene could get very intense for hotel employees, all young, good-looking men who had relocated to the desert till something better came along.

Pablo's parents would have been appalled if they'd known he was selling himself but he tried to maintain his sense of humor. He argued to himself that he'd still be having just as much sex, but this way everybody got a little something for his trouble.

Sex at the motel was frequent, sometimes with several different guys during the day. Often he found himself in the Jacuzzi, or the grove, and as many as six or seven guys would play. Those sessions were little more than jacking off. Harmless as peeing. Pablo thought nothing of it afterward.

There was also a steam room at the motel, and keys were issued only to the hottest guests by Lee himself, thereby assuring quality control. Pablo had a key, as did several other hot employees. He liked to take a steam after a workout at Gold's.

The keys were well-known among the regulars, and if you had to ask, the existence of them was denied. If Lee found out someone had loaned the keys to an unapproved guest, there was hell to pay.

Top on the unapproved list were 'A-Rabs' and 'Chinamen,' and the first week he arrived, Pablo had been in the sauna when a very handsome Asian man appeared. It was obvious to everybody that someone other than Lee had given him the key.

The man entered, allowed his eyes to adjust to the darkness. The room was packed, and at first he inadvertently sat on someone's naked lap. He popped up and quickly found a space. Pablo was seated across from him. Soon the group noticed he was Asian, and slowly but very deliberately gathered their towels and began to leave. Only Pablo was left with him.

Pablo felt ashamed. Even sex had racial guidelines.

"Was I late?" the Asian man asked nervously. "Did everybody come?"

"Not me." Pablo smiled givingly.

The man leaned forward to get a better look at Pablo. "I don't like Latins." He stood, his penis dragging halfway down his leg. "Will others be coming?"

At that point the sauna door flew open. It was Lee. "We're closing for maintenance. Changing the locks. I need your keys and I have to ask you to leave." The Asian man reached down for his towel and rather elegantly wrapped it around his waist. He nodded to Pablo and departed, apparently unaware of what was happening. He dropped his key in Lee's outstretched hand.

"A *Chinaman*," Lee growled. "In the sauna at the Seven Palms."

"One man's flavor is another man's poison," said Pablo gaily, stepping out into the sunshine.

Of the few remaining bars in Cathedral City, Nick's was Pablo's favorite, because like all of Cathedral City, it was a taste of time gone by. If Pablo ever became a writer, he'd write a book about the characters at Nick's, especially Nick himself, because Nick was truly unique, a gay archetype, the last surviving player from the boys in the band.

Nick liked to reminisce, and Pablo particularly encouraged him to talk about the gay history of the desert.

"Twenty years ago it was *unheard* of to operate an openly gay establishment in Palm Springs. Maybe one or two gay hotels but they had to be very discreet. A mixed bar. The city council would close you down. That's why the Desert Palms and Dave's are built just outside of the Palm Springs city limit."

He referred to the twin gay hotels, set back off the highway. "If you wanted quick sex, you just wandered naked into the date palm groves." Nick winked good-naturedly at Pablo. "Clothing was optional. The weather was much better then, too. It was hot, but *dry*. All the new golf courses and swimming pools changed the climate of the desert for the worse. It was never humid before."

"The clubs and restaurants were fun, too. The Aunt Hattie's down at 111 and Date Palm. His and Hers. Zak's. The Gaf. The original CC Construction was a beer bar then."

"It's still fun," Pablo chided him. "Look at all the hotels on Warm Sands up in Palm Springs. The InnTrigue. The El Mirasol Villas. And what about the White Party?"

"What *about* the White Party?" Nick snarled. "You young guys think you invented circuit parties? It's just another name for the *same* thing."

Nick tapped the counter with his empty glass. Marcella was talking to another customer. She looked over in irritation.

"Don't you go be tapping your empty glass at me!" she admonished him. "This isn't merry old England and you aren't Henry the fucking *Eighth*. I expect to be treated with dignity."

"*Fuck you*. Give Pablo what he wants," he told her. He was getting drunk, Pablo noticed. And sad.

"What do you want, baby?" Marcella asked Pablo.

"I'll have a shot of *Cuervo*," Pablo nodded. "And I'll buy Nick a round."

Marcella smirked at Nick. Pablo could tell she was happy he was getting drunk. She returned with a shot of tequila for Pablo and a strong Campari and soda for Nick. When Pablo paid her, he noticed she didn't ring up the sale. Instead she put the money in her tip jar. Nick didn't see a thing.

"Tell me more, sweetheart," Pablo asked, trying to keep him alert.

"Nowadays, everybody's a *clone*," Nick slurred. "You all have to look alike. Same pumped-up bodies, same short haircuts, same Jeep Cherokees. You know what you are?"

"What?" Pablo asked him.

"You're eleetishts." He stumbled over the word. "Eleeshits." Then he guffawed.

"I think you mean elitists," Pablo volunteered.

"I like my word better. Elee-shits. You leave people out who are *different* than you. The weak ones. The *vulnerable* ones. You ever been left out?" He leered into Pablo's face. Pablo didn't respond. "I *thought* so. You're just like all the rest of 'em. You're too good-looking for your own good. I know you're just slumming here."

He looked over at Pablo. "You think I'm camp. You young guys are dancing on the blood of a lot of drag queens. They took the heat. The blows. Just so you guys can march on Palm Canyon Drive in Palm Springs in your local gay pride parades. But don't be fooled. That's why I dress the way I do. Because I remember what it was like to be left out when I didn't know any better. And at this stage in my life, I'll be *goddamned* if I'll change for anybody, even if it means I can *suck your cock.*"

Marcella looked up and laughed. Nick blushed. "I'm sorry," he muttered.

"S'okay." Pablo patted Nick's hand.

"I'm so sorry," Nick said again. He felt so bad Pablo thought he was going to cry.

"He doesn't get much at home," Marcella interjected harshly.

"Fuck you," Nick said softly, staring into his glass.

Instead of bitter victory, Marcella's eyes were filled with uncustomary empathy.

"That's not him talking." She patted his hand. "It's just the way it is. You don't know what it's like to be black in the desert," she added. She hardened again, wiping down her counter with sharp, angry motion.

Pablo was thinking of the Asian man in the sauna. His own behavior in the alley.

Nick lay his head down on the counter.

"Listen," Marcella harshly interjected, "can you give him a ride home? If Kenny catches him passed out on my counter, he'll blame *me* again, and I've had just about all I can stand of his belly-aching today." On the drive home, Pablo commented on the demolition of all the businesses and little houses in Cathedral City.

"They're driving us out," Nick murmured tearfully. "The gay clubs. The Latino barrio. They don't see how special we are. They never did."

The next time Pablo came in, Nick had no recollection of their conversation. Instead he asked him if he wanted a job as a waiter. Pablo agreed, because it legitimized him to local acquaintances and gave him access to a solid base of potential customers.

By now Marcella was on to him, and if he tipped her well enough, she pimped for him behind the bar. The night he got fired, she'd connected him with a trick, a New Jersey tourist looking for a little company. Then she invoked Nick's rendition of "Strangers in the Night."

She did it primarily to goad Kenny. Pablo was surprised that, for lovers, two men could possibly be so different. Kenny, for Pablo, embodied everything he hoped to find in a lover if he was ever lucky enough to find one.

"His nickname is 'The Priest'," Marcella had told Pablo.

"Why?" Pablo had asked.

"Because he's always lighting candles, and he's given up his life for Nick."

And Pablo had yet to see him smile.

So after Kenny fired him, Pablo was deeply ashamed of himself. The admonishment from Kenny and the utter umbrage of the little woman in the alley had shaken him up.

One night when he was only fourteen, Pablo had seduced the son of one of his mother's most docile maids, who found them together in bed. The woman became hysterical, screaming at her son to go to the priest that very instant or surely she would go insane. Pablo and the boy quickly got dressed, but the entire household heard her cries, and soon his father and mother were standing in the doorway of his room demanding to know why she was screaming.

Although her son tried to silence her, unwittingly the maid blurt out what she had seen. She was too simple and naïve to anticipate the consequences. His father was furious with the maid, and although she remained impassive, Pablo could tell his mother believed her. But his proud father fired her on the spot.

The chaos in Pablo's bedroom that night, the hysterical maid, the shouting fury of his father that she should attempt to slander his own son, and her subsequent panic upon being fired were moments never far from his thoughts. He learned the importance of class differences and the power he could wield over the lives of others if and when he chose. This realization didn't intoxicate him as it might his contemporaries. Instead it filled him with shame. It was a seminal moment for Pablo, and now he found himself thinking about Inez Quintero in the very same way as the maid from his childhood.

His shame often interrupted his sleep and he would lie alone in the dark wondering why she so filled his thoughts.

10

The Deal

Sam woke up to hear Ruthie in the living room, playing the piano and singing, *singing* for criminy sakes. He looked at the clock on his nightstand. Seven-thirty. Ruthie never got up before eleven. Their bedroom window faced the western slope of the mountain, which slowly illuminated with the morning sunlight. The "drama of the desert dawn," the realtor had enthused when describing the views of this four-bedroom, five-bath executive home in luxurious and historical old Las Palmas.

"So how are the pipes?" Sam had responded, but now he had to begrudgingly allow that the effete fellow had been right on the money. The dawn light hitting the mountain was something to see; so majestic in scale it made Sam consider believing in God. They slept with their drapes open, and every morning since they moved in, Sam always thought of the funny little real estate agent, who later he heard had died of AIDS.

He climbed out of bed. Every joint in his body ached. It was hell being old. His toes cracked as he reached for a cigar. He lit it. Then he trudged into the bathroom to shave.

In all their early years of marriage, Sam and Ruthie never presented themselves to one another without grooming first. It was an unspoken ritual which kept their relationship very formal. To this day, Sam never allowed anyone to see him unshaven. He often showered twice a day.

When Ruthie began to sleep in, rising sometimes as late as two in the afternoon, and then appearing unkempt and swollen, Sam knew she was throwing in the towel. The sight of his immaculate wife wearing a dirty robe, with hair uncombed, barefoot, and badly in need of a pedicure filled him with great despair. Weeks might go by when she'd eat only a little cereal, or maybe a fried egg, and turn right around and go back to bed.

Despite his cajoling, she refused to see a doctor. She felt fine, she'd reassure him. She just had the blues. All her life Ruthie had suffered from depression. She had no faith in psychology, she told him. The sadness was part of her. She had no intention of artificially altering it. As a younger woman, she'd relied on it to give her singing ballast. A blues singer needed to feel blue, she reasoned to Sam. Dark days came with the territory. Nobody ever got into trouble while they were taking a nap.

Now Sam ran hot water in his sink. Ruthie appeared behind him holding a coffee cup. Her green eyes were sparkling. She smiled brilliantly. She was dressed to go out.

"So what's got into you?"

"I'm opening in a month! I have to rehearse, don't I?"

"Gimme a sip of your coffee."

"It isn't coffee. It's hot water with honey and lemon," she explained happily. "For my throat."

He sneaked a glance at her in the mirror. Ups and downs. When Ruthie got high, excited, a bad fall could be predicted.

"Pace yourself," was all he said. He began to apply his shaving cream. She was making him nervous, standing there and watching him. He wasn't one of those men who liked women to watch him shave. He'd annoyed her with his remark and felt bad. "So what's your day like today, old girl?"

She smiled again. "I found the box with all my old arrangements. The songs, they were so *good*, Sam. And I have to get the piano tuned."

"Sounded okay to me."

"Did it, Sam? Not the piano, but me? Do I sound okay?"

"Why sure," he offered. "You sounded swell."

"I thought I did too," she effused. "But I'm so rusty. And I've got to get a good accompanist. And maybe a voice coach. And a trainer. I think I should hire a trainer."

"A trainer!"

"I need to lose a few pounds. Or haven't you noticed. And I'll need new clothes. My clothes are all so subdued now." She hesitated. "It's gonna cost you, Sam."

"I never minded spending on you before," he reproached her.

"That's what it's for. That's what it's always been for. You know that."

"You've been very generous, Sam. I've appreciated it. I've been a lucky girl."

He watched her steal a glimpse of herself in the mirror.

"Girl," she added cynically under her breath.

"Didn't seem to do you much good," he commented. "I only wanted your happiness, Ruthie. It was the only thing I couldn't buy." He began to shave. She hung in the door frame to his bathroom and watched him. They didn't speak until he was finished and splashing his face with water.

The sparkle in her eyes dimmed. "It hasn't been easy for you, Sam. You could have had a much better time of it."

"I don't have any regrets."

"I know you missed having children."

"Don't, Ruthie. That's all in the past."

"I never told you this, but I know now—"

"No, Ruthie . . ."

But she kept talking, "I know that I should have agreed to adopt."

Sam froze.

"It was better that you were honest about your feelings, Ruthie. But you were wrong about something."

"What, Sam?"

"You would have been a terrific mother . . ."

She stood up straight. Suddenly sadness was creeping up through her body and she wanted to shake it off. "How did we get off on this?" She smiled her best false smile.

Sam turned around to face her. He studied her solemnly.

"This business about performing again. It might be disappointing, Ruthie."

"I *know*." She continued smiling.

"Nick's isn't the Chi-Chi. Or the Desert Inn. Remember your opening night?"

The Chi-Chi was a Palm Springs nightclub, a celebrity hangout which headlined the greatest big band and jazz singers in Southern California. Ruthie sang there a couple nights a week the last year before it closed. She was twenty years old and blew the roof off. Everyone said she had a great future. That was the first night Sam ever saw her. The most beautiful redhead in the world. He didn't see her again till ten years later when she walked into his club in Cathedral City and asked if she could sing for him.

He hired her on the spot.

"And it won't be Sam's either," Ruthie shrugged. "I'm just doing it for laughs, Sam. I promise you I won't be disappointed. I won't fall apart."

"If you are," Sam said as he passed her, "I'll be here to catch you."

Later in the kitchen, Ruthie picked up her keys and kissed him goodbye. They both were trying hard to shake off the strange sentimentality which had overcome them both. It made them feel awkward and vulnerable. He was smoking a cigar, drinking a cup of coffee, and watching the local news. The desert newspaper was spread out on the table in front of him.

"Nicky boy got reviewed today."

"Oh?"

She scanned the article. The headline read NO PLACE TO BE SEEN, *let alone be caught after dark*, the first line continued. Under Nick's picture the caption read, *Frank Sinatra is my biological father*. The article went on to say that if Nick's in Cathedral City was the apologia to desert renewal, bring on the bulldozer's, *please*. The final blow referred to Kenny's trailer park cafeteria quality food.

"I'm going out to Cathedral City."

"I thought you were going shopping."

"Well, I am, but not for me. The girl I found. It's tragic. I want to go visit her."

He put down his newspaper. "Now I know how you are, Ruthie. Don't go overboard. Don't go making her into some kinda special project." He puffed on his cigar. "In a way she's lucky, see?"

"How do you figure? She has nothing."

"So she starts over. I didn't have anything when I came to the desert. Maybe someday *she'll* own Cathedral City."

"Maybe she will," Ruthie affirmed. "But I don't think she'd want it for the price she's had to pay. You didn't see her face when she ran out in front of my car on the highway."

"It'll either make her strong or break her. Every Mexie bussing tables in Palm Springs has a story to tell."

"*Sam!* Do you have to talk that way? I really dislike it."

"Aw, it's just my way of talking. I have the greatest respect for anybody who wants to work hard, make his own way. I've helped plenty of people in my lifetime by providing them with opportunity. Plenty of people."

"I know, Sam. I know you have."

"So don't start giving her handouts. Handouts don't build character."

"Sure, sure," she said, disappearing into the hallway.

Then a local news item appeared on television about the redevelopment of Cathedral City. Ralph Zola, the unctuous lawyer from Nick's, was vowing to step up the pressure on local landowners to sell their parcels. He referred to a map of Cathedral City behind him. Ruthie reappeared in the doorway.

"It's a cesspool of undocumented aliens and deviant lifestyles. It's blighted beyond repair," he was saying. "I think the tax-paying homeowners and businesses which flank the targeted area have a right to expect it to be made habitable by all. Progress has arrived in Cathedral City whether undesirable elements and slumlords like it or not."

The interview was followed by an unrelated little-shown public service announcement featuring Bob Hope decrying the practice of gay bashing.

Sam feigned disinterest. Ruthie studied him knowingly. "So much for old times. This is all a big game to you, isn't it? This is why you agreed to fix up the property."

"What are you talking about?"

"You wiped a tear from your eye, Sam."

"I've been playing cards all my life, Ruthie." He couldn't look her in the eye. "I'm a born bluffer. You know that. But I've never bluffed about you and me."

"What were you going to do? Paint the bar, let me sing a couple of months, paper the house? Looks like you want to hang on and then sell out for even more of a profit? You can't just dangle hope on a string. Didn't you see the look on Nicky's face?"

"I told him we'd fix the joint up. It's up to him to make something of it or not."

"He loses either way. Either way he gets sold out."

"Not necessarily. He makes a go of it, keeps his rent paid, we hang on to it. Okay?"

Ruthie studied him mistrustfully.

"It's strictly a business proposition. I'll get 'em there opening night, but you gotta keep 'em coming. You, Nick, and the food. Kenny's gotta bring his food up to standard."

"You don't seem like you have very much confidence in us . . ."

"I win either way. We hang on to Cathedral City if it's a hit. We sell if it's a bust. It's our security. Yours and mine."

"Security. We can never spend all the money we already have, Sam! Nick and Kenny have no security. You should be thinking about them!"

"What're they to you?"

"They're *good*. They took that girl in without a moment's hesitation! They're like sons," she said incredulously. "You yourself are always saying, 'The boys are like sons to me.' "

"But they aren't sons," Sam shrugged, and turned back to his shaving. "They aren't really sons and that's the difference."

When Kenny woke up, the surface of the pool was clear of floating candles. The raft where Maria had slept lay neatly on its side against the storage shed behind the house. It promised to be a sultry, white-hot day.

He wandered into the house to look for her. He found her sitting on a straight-back chair near the front door, knees pressed together wearing the white blouse and the faded denim skirt which Kenny had laundered for her last night. She had taken a shower and her hair cascaded down to her shoulders in generous umber waves. The bruise on her cheek was beginning to mute. Kenny paused to ponder whether her lips were bruised from her travails or naturally ample. On her lap she clutched the doll Kenny had given her, now her only possession.

Kenny lingered in the frame of the terrace sliding door. Shyness overcame him. He ran his hand through his hair. He needed to use the bathroom, brush his teeth. For a moment her eyes rose and locked into his own, the same faded blue as her skirt.

"You hungry?" Kenny broke the silence.

She was ashamed to admit how hungry she was.

"Let me wash my face and I'll make us breakfast." He moved across the room in front of her. "Why are you sitting in that uncomfortable chair? Why don't you sit on the sofa?"

"I'm okay," she said softly.

"I'll be right back," he smiled at her. He disappeared down the hallway to the bathroom.

Every synapsing impulse she had informed her desire to throw open the door and run all the way back to Mexico. She was actively considering turning herself into U.S. Immigration. Deportation would be swift and she would be back in Vicente Guerrero in twenty-four hours. It was not as if any opportunity awaited her there.

Only questions about Concha and Maria's wanton neglect of her. It was also not the end result for which her grandmother would have wanted to lose her life. Guilt resonated through her thoughts like the ancient bell of a Mexican cathedral. She desperately needed to go to confession.

She was grateful for the throbbing pain on the side of her face. A missing limb would be better. As Kenny returned from the bathroom, refreshed from a quick shower, though still unshaven, he found her crying. She quickly tried to compose herself.

"Come and talk to me while I fix breakfast," he said gently. After a moment she stood up and followed him into the kitchen. The kitchen was a small compact square, badly in need of organization. Since they rarely ate at home, it was ill equipped with staples, but after opening and closing cupboards and the refrigerator, Kenny came up with alternatives.

She watched him as he routed around. He was physically well made, she thought, only slightly taller than she. Good-looking but troubled; difficult. His eyes were sleepy blue and his forehead knit automatically to deep worry. When he smiled, the transformation was magnetic. All the lines disappeared. She wondered why they weren't more self-conscious with each other. It was less than a week since they'd met.

She waited while he filled the coffeepot with cold water.

"You must feel lost."

She answered him silently in Spanish. *I feel worse than lost. I feel dead.*

Kenny reached around her to rummage through the refrigerator. "How about I just make us some scrambled eggs and toast?" He handed her a glass of orange juice.

She took a sip. Pain surged through her jaw like a wild splinter. She winced, and fresh tears formed in her eyes.

"Let me see. Did you lose a tooth?" Kenny asked her. "On the trip? Or before?"

Obediently she opened her mouth. Her back tooth was missing. It looked infected.

"It looks very angry. It must hurt. You'll have to see a dentist."

"I have no money," she said, horrified at the suggestion. What could he be thinking?

"We'll work it out."

"But—"

"We'll work it out," he said again easily and reached out to pat her shoulder. Her body stiffened. Her eyes narrowed with suspicion.

There it was. *Too good,* she thought, *too good to be true.* The ride from the accident, the cool bed. The kind man with the blue eyes. The short, short life span of kindness. *Too good to be true.*

Kenny noticed her visibly recoil from him and stepped quickly back to reassure her. His eyes widened with apology.

"Please." He held up his open hands. "Nothing at all is expected of you. You couldn't be safer. I just want to help you."

She glanced nervously down the hall toward the bedrooms. She didn't know what to make of the man who had burst into her room last night.

"What about the other?"

Kenny began to laugh.

Maria winced with embarrassed annoyance. What could she be thinking? A handsome man like Kenny with a restaurant and a big home desiring a poor girl with a broken smile? A *mojada* who owned nothing but a blouse and a dress and a small rag doll?

"I'm sorry," she replied miserably. "But anyone else might have turned me in."

"No," he said gently. "You're right to be curious." He cracked an egg with one hand into a mixing bowl. Then he cracked three more. He was out of practice explaining his thought process to anyone. It had been so long since anybody studied him patiently enough to question his choices.

"If you don't want anything, why are you helping me?"

He began whisking the eggs. Then he switched on the front burner to the gas range top. It clicked comfortingly and burst into flame.

"Can you hand me the butter?" He reached up for a hanging Calaphon pan.

When the eggs were done, Kenny turned around and noticed two places set at the bar looking into the kitchen, with utensils and napkins folded as elegantly as any restaurant. The toast was neatly sliced on a diagonal.

Instead of answering her question, he smiled at her. She smiled back wistfully. Then she whispered, "I miss her."

Kenny stood up and moved his chair next to hers. They ate breakfast silently. He put his arm around her. He didn't take it away until they finished eating.

"Don't you *ever* use a conditioner?"

When Ruthie arrived with bags from the Gap, she found Nick in a skimpy bathing suit, cutting Maria's hair out by the pool. Music was blaring, the cocktails were flowing, and he was laughing and telling her stories. The scissors were flying. Even with her broad command of English, he was talking so quickly Maria could only catch every third word. Kenny sat stonily in a chaise. When he glanced up and noticed Ruthie, he shrugged wearily.

"He's giving her a new look for her life in America."

Ruthie stood in the entry hall and shook her head in amazement. Nick was blow-drying Maria's hair.

"Now, stand up and let me show you."

Maria stood up uncertainly.

He led Maria into the house to the mirror over the fireplace. "What do you think?"

Maria gasped. Her hair looked wonderful. Parted in the middle, it curved down the sides of her face and curled inward at her shoulder. It made her look very sophisticated. She shook her head. It swirled out and back into place. She was very pleased. She smiled sweetly. Shyly she turned to show Ruthie.

"It's very becoming," Ruthie nodded.

Maria looked again. Then her eyes fell to her old blouse and skirt. They flickered with disappointment.

"I took the liberty of picking a few things up . . ." ventured Ruthie. "Maybe you'd like to try them on." She held up her bags.

"Go with her," Nick grinned.

Maria looked over to Kenny.

"Go," he affirmed, but he was somewhat subdued. "I've gotta get back to the restaurant. I'll be back toward the end of the afternoon. Then you can meet my crew."

Maria hesitated.

"You'll be safe with us," Nick assured her.

"C'mon, honey," Ruthie urged her.

Maria shook her head in bewilderment and turned to follow Ruthie into her bedroom.

*   *   *

Ruthie suddenly felt very shy with Maria. The young woman held herself with such restraint her very breathing seemed to pain her. All of Ruthie's maternal instincts came rushing out. She wanted to take her in her arms and comfort her, hug her hurting away. Then she remembered Sam's admonishment. In his way, without having met her, Sam was reminding her to respect Maria's dignity and now Ruthie felt ashamed. Was a bag of cotton clothing from the Gap supposed to compensate for the loss of her last surviving family member?

"Look at these tops, honey, aren't they darling? It's so hot in August, and I thought they'd be nice and cool. I thought the colors would complement you. Is this too red? I don't think so. And look at the light blue one. And this green tank top. I guessed your size. Try them on. And I bought a couple pairs of jeans, you know, you young girls have the figures for jeans. And look at these sandals. I got several sizes. Can't ever guess about anybody's foot size!"

Maria looked at Ruthie in amazement.

"What is it, sweetheart? Don't you like them?"

"Señora, I can't afford to pay you for these. "

"No, they're a gift."

"But why would you buy me so many things?"

"Oh please, please say you aren't offended. I know it's overkill but please humor me. I have no children or grandchildren. Try them on as a favor to me."

Maria studied the piles of clothing on the bed. She shook her head in bewilderment. She caught a glimpse of herself in a mirror over the dresser. She marveled at her new haircut. If Concha had been here, she would be throwing clothes on her back faster than Ruthie could count to ten. Reluctantly Maria picked up the red shirt. It was a shell top, with two thin straps.

"I'll pay you back," Maria said softly. "It's the only way."

"I have a little makeup, too," Ruthie said quickly. "Just a little eyeliner and lipstick. Will you let me help you? Let's get you ready and go out and surprise Nick. Wait till Kenny sees you."

"Kenny," Maria repeated. "Do you think he'd approve?"

Ruthie smiled at her, thinking it harmless that she may be attracted to Kenny. "Well, of course he'd approve. He'll love it."

Maria held the blouse up in front of her in the mirror and studied herself critically.

"Are you sure?" she asked again. "Are you sure, *señora?*"

*   *   *

That same afternoon Sam Singer pulled into the alley and honked his horn three times. Kenny poked his head outside. "You did this three days ago."

"But you still haven't paid your rent," Sam observed. "So I'm doing it again."

He popped the trunk of the Mark IV and began unloading gallons of paint. Several of his tenants appeared, lingering inside their gates, wondering what he was up to. Kenny moved closer to inspect.

"What are you doing with so much brown paint?"

"Sprucing up Cathedral City."

Kenny pried open a lid with a key. "Why'd you pick brown?"

"It was on sale."

"It's gonna look like a Japanese internment camp."

Sam took a drag on his cigar. "You got any better ideas?"

Kenny began loading the cans into the back of the trunk.

Sam and Kenny drove to Indio and returned the paint at the Army Surplus store where Sam bought all his supplies in bulk. Sam stood back and let Kenny pick what he wanted. It took two hours but finally Kenny emerged from the store lugging freshly mixed gallons of exterior paint. Sam could tell by some spillage that the colors were not uniform.

"Aw, whadya do here? This is green. I can't have green houses."

"It's *sage*," Kenny corrected him. "And this is taupe."

"Tope?"

"Light brown."

"Whyncha say so!"

"Trust me, Sam. It's gonna look beautiful. All the colors of the desert."

"Pink? You bought more pink paint?"

"Dusty rose. For the bar. All the colors together will make your property look like a sunset."

"It's income property. Not some goddamn view."

"It can be both, Sam. I'll supervise the whole thing. We'll take the whole weekend. Make a community event out of it. Everybody who paints their own house gets a rent break."

"That's going too far."

"Painters cost twenty bucks an hour."

Kenny could see the wheels turning in Sam's head.

When he came home after his trip to Indio with Sam, Ruthie and

Nick were sitting on the terrace, writing her opening act. To Kenny's surprise, Nick was somewhat sober. Kenny glanced around for Maria.

"She's been waiting to surprise you," Ruthie smiled.

"Look behind you, " grinned Nick.

Kenny turned. Maria stood hesitantly in the door. Nick and Ruthie redid her makeup. All natural tones. Whereas earlier today her pallor was papery and pale, now her skin was luminous. She wore jeans and the red shell Ruthie had chosen for her. On her feet were a pair of sandals which displayed painted toenails. Nick had even given her a pedicure.

Kenny was subdued. The only thing he recognized was the worry which lingered in her eyes. Emotion welled up inside him. He didn't want to upset them.

"I gotta get back down to the restaurant." he muttered.

"Doesn't she look great?" Nick queried after him.

"Beautiful," he said, catching her eye as he rushed past her. "Beautiful girl," she heard him say. Moments later she heard the bathroom door close. Nick and Ruthie stood up uncertainly and came into the house behind Maria.

"What's wrong?" Ruthie asked Nick. "I thought he'd get a kick out of it."

Maria was horrified at the thought that he might disapprove. Here her grandmother was dead only days and she had indulged herself in frivolous things.

Then the door opened down the hallway and a somber Kenny appeared. He'd splashed water on his face to disguise the fact that he'd been crying.

"You coming with me or what?" he asked Maria.

Maria looked at him uncertainly. He didn't seem angry at her. He just seemed sad. He held out his hand. Without hesitation, she stepped toward him. Moments later they were gone.

Maria's introduction to the kitchen crew was met with jealousy and suspicion. Dinner prep was in full swing when Kenny appeared in the doorway from the alley. Carmen, Miguel, and Gabriel were all smiles. The reservation book was packed. It would be a busy night after which Kenny, they knew, would pay them.

But when the pretty girl appeared in the screen door behind Kenny, their eyes narrowed in circumspection. Gabriel and Miguel immediately imagined fucking her, and Carmen, who could sense their ardor, was not happy at all to see her.

Kenny opened the creaking screen door and ushered her inside ahead of him.

"This is Maria." Kenny said reverently. "She's gonna help out."

How can you pay four when you can't pay three? Carmen wondered silently. Maria looked uncomfortably away.

"Maybe Maria can start by slicing the French bread. Making up the bread baskets."

Carmen, who was already half finished, dropped her knife on the cutting board. It bounced up once and then lay to rest. Kenny motioned for Maria to go over to where Carmen was standing.

"Show her," Kenny directed. He gave no sign that he was aware of any discord. "You just cut the slices about an inch-and-a-half thick and fill these baskets so the busboys can grab 'em. We need to keep doing it all night. Whenever an empty basket comes back, fill it right away. Okay?"

"Okay," Maria said meekly. She reached for Carmen's knife. Kenny turned around to check the ovens where the chickens were baking. Involuntarily, Maria glanced after him. His back was turned. Her eyes met the cheerful lasciviousness of Gabriel and Miguel. Miguel, who was married, winked at her.

She averted her eyes to Carmen, who hadn't given an inch from the time Maria joined her at the cutting board. Maria began slicing bread.

"Carmen, come here. I think it's time you knew how to bake the chicken."

The chicken was the house specialty. This was an honor for Carmen, who usually had to do the grunt work. Hmmph, she cleared her throat in satisfaction. Now she felt the jealous eyes of Miguel. The chickens were his territory.

But before she left Maria's side, she had one question to ask of her.

"So, Kenny likes you, huh? He gonna get you a green card?" she asked in Spanish. "We're all citizens." More of a threat than national pride.

Kenny heard her. "She already has a green card," he lied. Maria didn't reply.

That night the restaurant served seventy dinners. Maria worked effortlessly. Being so busy was a welcome relief. Every once in a while Kenny would glance up from the grill to watch her nervously, hoping she wasn't overwhelmed. Instead he saw her struggling doggedly to do her share, to not embarrass him in front of his crew.

She was helping Carmen on the side board, making salads, cutting bread, and washing dishes whenever she saw them stacking up. If anything, she was working faster than Carmen. Carmen noted this with irritation.

Later that evening Nick lay on the couch watching television and drinking Campari. Maria sat in the chair, politely listening to him tell her stories about the past.

"I danced on camera with Cyd Charise. Did you ever do any dancing?"

Maria smiled. "When I was a little girl."

"You certainly have the figure for it. Long beautiful legs. Doesn't she have beautiful legs?"

"They're okay," Kenny shrugged. "I've seen better." He grinned when Maria reacted. She smiled when she saw he was kidding.

"Kenny, maybe we should arrange for ballet lessons!"

On Kenny's look of irritation, Nick shut up.

Kenny stood up and moved to his worktable in the study. He began opening tubes of paint and wetting his brushes. He picked up a doll and started painting her face. When Nick got up to use the bathroom, Maria took the opportunity to move into the study to see what Kenny was doing. She stood behind him, fascinated by how gently he dabbed color into the faces of the dolls.

He reached to the right of him and dragged over another stool. He motioned for her to sit next to him. She glanced curiously over his cluttered worktable. She noticed a pile of unfinished doll clothes. She picked up a tiny skirt, reached for a spool of colorful thread, and quickly threaded a needle. Expertly she began to hem the skirt. Soon it was finished. She glanced over at him.

Okay to do another one?

He nodded, smiling slightly.

Pleased, she reached for a small shirt. She began to apply tiny snaps. Soon she was trying it on the body of the doll he was painting. It fit perfectly.

In the living room Nick was falling asleep. In one hand was a full glass of Campari and soda, and in the other, a lighted cigarette.

"*Go to bed*," Kenny said sharply.

Nick shook himself awake. He looked around in confusion. He saw the cigarette and reached toward the ashtray. He smashed his cigarette out on the glass coffee table. Then he hoisted himself up and staggering slightly, rounded the couch, and trudged back down the hall toward the bedroom.

"G'night, everybody," he said over his shoulder.

"I'll help him," Maria murmured.

When she came up behind him, he smiled up in happiness, thinking she was Kenny. "Oh," he said softly, "it's you."

She put her arm around his waist and led him down the hall to his bedroom.

The bedclothes were strewn and tangled on the floor by the bed. As Nick wandered into the bathroom, Maria quickly made up the bed. When she turned around, he was leaning heavily against the wall, wearing only his underwear. He was terribly thin, and she could see the outline of his ribs.

"Come to bed . . ." she offered gently.

He obeyed her, sitting with a thud onto the mattress. He swung his legs up and she covered him. He drifted in and out of consciousness. "I hope you're as lucky as I've been," he commented.

"How so?" she asked.

"I hope you find your own Kenny someday."

She didn't say anything. She went into the bathroom and returned with a glass of water. Nick was already asleep and snoring softly.

"Thank you." Maria switched off the light. "For everything."

When she came back into the living room, Kenny avoided her eyes, involving himself with cleaning his paintbrushes. She moved to the stool next to him. They resumed working. They sat silently, side by side, stitching and painting, occasionally stopping to admire the other one's handiwork. Late into the evening Kenny was surprised to look up at the clock and see that is was half past three in the morning.

"Go to bed, *Hija*. I'm gonna sleep on the couch."

She obeyed him, but later, after she knew he was sleeping, she crept back into the living room with her pillow and blanket. Near dawn Kenny awoke to find her, holding his dangling hand, sleeping peacefully curled on the soft carpeted floor to be near him.

11

Fate

On Mondays, Wednesdays, and Fridays it was Inez Quintero's custom to take the bus from the intersection of Cathedral Canyon Road and East Palm Canyon Drive, two blocks from where she lived, and travel a mile west to the entrance of the Seven Palms Hotel. She did this after walking the eight or nine blocks from her church, having already attended morning Mass.

The old priest was miserable, because, as Inez fully well knew, Kenny had not returned to worship at St. Louis Parish. Father Gene had initially been all smiles, full of conversation when he saw her, but now that he saw she was little or no use as a conduit of communication with his beloved *Kenny,* he treated her with indifference, even hostility, she thought. He was like another fenced dog, eager to rip at her throat, but he was too high-profile to show his true spots.

And he mistakenly got her name mixed up. He always referred to her as *Annette.*

"Hello, Annette," he said again this morning. "God bless, see you tomorrow . . ."

And she was tempted to rifle through the pockets of his robe for her misspent twenty-dollar bill.

So today she took a new tack, went on the offensive, and when he offered his limp hand for a kiss, she said, "Father Gene, I saw Mister Kenny yesterday!"

"You did, Annette? Really?" He seemed to shake with pleasure. "How is he? Did you tell him we miss him here? Did you tell him I've been asking about him? Did he say anything?"

"No," she replied belligerently. "It didn't come up."

"Oh? That so?"

"I'll remember next time . . ."

"But he seems well?"

"Confused," Inez clucked. "Well, I have to catch my bus. Today I work at the Seven Palms . . . I'll come to confession on Saturday as usual." Inez mistakenly believed Father Gene looked forward to her confessions. *How,* he wondered, could the little Quintero woman possibly be on to him?

Bless me, Father, for I have sinned.

What is the nature of your transgression?

At my job I see many deviant things. Sometimes I don't turn away my eyes.

Silence. Then—

What deviant things?

Men with men.

Yes?

I can't go on.

How can I expiate your sins if I don't know the true nature of them? You may not have sinned at all.

Well—sometimes when I clean rooms I see them—like a husband and wife.

Oh.

One on top of the other.

Ahhh . . . And you didn't avert your eyes?

No, Father.

Hmm. Three Hail Marys and sin no more.

I'll tell you more next time.

That won't be necessary. Next!

The bus let her off at a kiosk just off the highway at the Rite-Aid parking lot. The Seven Palms was a gay hotel, nestled in a grove of palm trees behind the major pharmacy. The hotel had been there for years, long before Rite-Aid was even a chain. It used to sit isolated in the middle of the desert, just outside the Palm Springs city limits and jurisdiction of the Palms Springs city police.

Once in her supply closet, Inez donned her green palm printed smock and pushed her housekeeping cart down the patio to the last room on the ground floor. This was Room 18. When cleaning rooms her instructions were as follows. Knock loudly, several times. Wait. If no answer, knock loudly again. Wait a few moments more. Then it was okay to let herself in with her master key.

She had learned to follow her instructions to the letter. Several other maids reported seeing deviant things, too shocking to mention. She herself had suffered a bad experience. She hesitated.

She knocked once, waited, and knocked again. Like they taught her. Just as she was trying her key, the door pulled open away from her. She was confronted by two huge men, one Anglo, one Latino, both in skimpy swimsuits, each rippling with muscle. They were giggling as they left. The blond Anglo pushed past her without any acknowledgment. The Latino's eyes flickered with recognition. He nodded and kept going. Inez looked back after him as they walked across the green lawn to the pool area. She thought she knew him too.

Inez entered their room. The curtains were closed, and the room smelled of soiled socks. She often encountered this odor, and found it emanating from small brown bottles she'd find spilled under the bed, or caught up in the sheets.

She moved around the bed, first stripping off the blankets. When she shook out the sheets, something fell to the carpet and hit the top of her foot. She bent down to pick it up. It was rubber, and felt gooey to her fingers.

She held it up to the light. A used condom.

"Ugghhh . . ." She dropped it, stepping quickly back. Then she cried out in pain. Something had pierced the back of her heel. It hurt so badly she staggered momentarily. Then she hobbled to the door.

Out on the hotel patio, adjacent to the turquoise pool, Inez limped past a sea of tanned, Speedo-clad gay men, laughing, drinking, and telling jokes. By the time she reached the main building, she was crying.

"Honey, what do you want?" the desk clerk challenged her. "You aren't allowed up here."

"My foot," she shuddered.

He looked down at her foot. A needle protruded from her heel. He nearly passed out.

"Jesus Christ! You gotta go to a free clinic or something but you can't stand in my lobby!"

"But sir," Inez fought back tears, "it hurts."

Behind her the Latino man from the room she was cleaning entered the office. Pablo.

"What are you waiting for?" the clerk pleaded with her.

"I'll lose a day's pay," she stammered. The thought of her husband's wrath gave Inez great courage.

"You want money? Here. Here's fifty bucks. On me. Go to a doctor, but take it outta here, now. Please . . . " His teeth chattered with revulsion.

Pablo noticed her heel.

"Yeow," he gulped, startled but sympathetic. "I'll help her," and Pablo assisted Inez through the patio door to her housekeeping closet. By the time he sat her down on a stool, she was pale from pain.

"We need to pull this out," he said gently. "I know how to do it. I've seen this many times. I want you to hold on to my shoulders. As tight as you can while I remove the needle. Okay?"

Even in her agony Inez was overwhelmed by Pablo's physical beauty. His eyes were the most beautiful gentle eyes she had ever seen. She felt embarrassed to have him touch her.

"What's your name?" he asked her.

"Inez," she whimpered.

"I love the name Inez," he said eloquently. "I always wanted to name my daughter Inez, if I ever had one," he added, smiling at her. "Okay, hold tight. This may hurt and I don't want you to move your foot." She grasped his shoulders. They were taut as coiled ropes. Pablo pulled.

For an instant, Inez passed out from the pain, but when she fell forward, he caught her, and to Inez it was like being held by an angel.

"You need to go to the doctor," Pablo told her. "You gotta get a shot or something. Where did this happen? Which room number?"

"Number 18."

"Yeah?" He glanced over his shoulder. He studied the row of motel rooms. "Near the end?"

"The last one on the lower level. Where I saw you."

Pablo's eyes flickered. "Well, it's really important you go to a doctor. And tell them exactly what happened."

"Yes, I'll go," Inez pleaded contritely. "Don't say nothing to anybody, okay?"

"Well, sure," he hesitated, wondering whom he might tell. "Look. I have a Jeep. I'll take you."

"No. I'll take the bus."

"It's no problem." He searched her face with concern. Then he checked his watch like he had a meeting to go to. "You promise me you'll go?"

"Yes. I'll go. *No diga nada, señor. Por favor.*"

"Wait," he called after her. "How can I reach you? I want to know what the doctor says."

The incident in the alley replayed itself in her mind. The younger Mexican man. The handsome one with his pants around his ankles. *Pablo.* The boy she got fired from Nick's.

"You know where I live." Her mouth inverted to an upside-down crescent moon. "In the alley behind the bar in Cathedral City. I got you fired from your job."

"Oh," he said softly. "The woman in the alley. But you didn't get me fired . . . I got myself fired."

Inez stood up and hobbled away till she crossed the patio and disappeared through the lobby and out the front door.

Pablo wandered across the grass to Vance, a steroid-bulked Chicago tourist who'd picked Pablo up in the sauna. Vance was sitting in the middle of a group of friends. He looked up and sniffed the air. Chlorine and suntan oil.

"Hey."

"I gotta talk to you," Pablo said.

"So talk." Vance stretched languidly on his chaise longue. He was clearly over Pablo. His friends smirked in Pablo's direction. They obviously knew they'd just fucked.

"Privately would be better."

Vance looked at his friends and begrudgingly got up. They wandered out of the pool area to the shade.

"I like you but I'm not looking for a lover. That's why I pay."

"No," said Pablo. "That's not what this is about."

"You have the clap."

"No. Let me finish. Are you on the juice? Did you use a needle earlier today?"

"What if I am? What if I did?" His body rippled with muscle.

"I didn't see you shoot up."

"What are you *getting* at?" Vance whined. "I'm losing *sun.*"

"You must have dropped the needle. The maid who came in. She stepped on it."

He blanched visibly. "She okay?"

"I dunno." Pablo shook his head. "You tell me."

"She call the cops?"

"They sent her home with fifty bucks."

"They *know?*"

Pablo threw up his hands.

"We were safe—"

Pablo began to rush away. He wanted to find Inez. Get her to a hospital.

"Look, airborne it dies within *seconds!*" Vance called after him. "She's got nothing to worry about. Hazard of the trade."

Pablo raised his hand as if in acknowledgment but flipped him off as he sprinted around the corner. Pablo hurried across the lobby and out the front door to where his Jeep was parked. He tried to keep his eye on Inez, who was sitting forlornly across the street at the kiosk. The bus was pulling up. The sun reflected brilliantly on the white bench. One minute Pablo could see her and in the next, like a vaporizing mirage, Inez Quintero began to disappear.

By the time he had traversed the highway in his Jeep, the bench was empty. He scanned the highway for the municipal bus to Cathedral City. Nothing but the usual passenger cars.

As Pablo drove back to Cathedral City, he ruminated over all that had just transpired. The likelihood of infection was next to nil. The idiot back at the hotel was right. The needle had been exposed for at least sixty seconds.

Hazard of the trade. Pablo held his breath and begged God to spare Inez Quintero.

Inez sat on the bus and clutched her fifty-dollar bill. Good, she thought. No taxes taken out. Her weekly pay stubs from the motel would qualify her for her papers. Mr. Sam told her to work at least one day a week on the books if she ever wanted to establish residency. Today no taxes would be paid.

Her foot throbbed but she wouldn't waste her good luck on any doctor. Inez was afraid of doctors. Especially in this country. She'd go home and make her old aunt heat some water. She'd soak her foot in a bucket.

She placed the fifty in her bra and stood up to get off at her stop.

"Thomas? Can you help us up here?" Thomas's boss Andy was talking to a customer in the showroom of Arte de Sonora. The customer had driven up from Palm Desert, a tall blond woman with big hips, big hair, and a big attitude. She wanted to buy a large mirror to hang over a credenza. She just couldn't decide on which mirror or which credenza.

Thomas had been working on a copy of an antique Mexican bookcase. Thomas was a master furniture maker. It was likely that his very own ancestors had built the original shelf which Thomas was doing his best to duplicate in the hot workroom of Arte de Sonora.

"Yes, Mr. Andy." In the presence of his employers, Thomas was all shuffle and nod.

"Tell him to hold this mirror over that credenza," the woman said.

"I'll help you," Andy offered.

"No, don't help him, I need you to help me decide." Her fingers danced on Andy's thick forearm. Andy shrugged apologetically to Thomas.

"S'okay." Thomas smiled. He picked up the heavy mirror. "Which?"

"This one," she barked.

Thomas obliged. When he moved to rest it on the table, she said, "No. I need to see it floating. Hold it up, please!" Thomas complied, raising the mirror several inches higher than the credenza.

The mirror reflected the image of the woman back to her and she immediately tilted her head up and sucked in her cheeks. Her hand went to her chin. "Hmm," she said. Thomas, perspiring under the weight of the mirror, shuffled to keep his balance.

"Don't put it down yet. I haven't made up my mind. Try it with this one, please."

Because Thomas was hidden behind the mirror, he couldn't see what she was talking about.

"He can't see what you mean," Andy said a bit testily.

She marched over to Thomas and pulled at his arm, which was vibrating now from the weight of the mirror. "Over here." She led him to a more ornate credenza. "Up. Up."

"Thomas, do you need to rest?"

Exasperated, the customer looked askance at Andy. "He's strong as a burro. *Copeesh, señor?*" She laughed.

Behind the mirror Thomas was sweating. His arms were going numb.

"What do you think?" she asked Andy. "Honestly."

"I like this one."

"Well, I love the mirror. I just can't decide on the table." She spun around, looking for options. Behind her, Thomas's strength gave out. He began to stagger. Since he was grasping the mirror toward the bottom of the frame, he couldn't easily set it down. The mirror fell forward, smashing the table and shattering to the floor.

The woman, a good distance away, began swearing her head off. Andy was rushing toward Thomas, who fell after it, hand down into the debris.

"Why didn't he put it down, for Christ's sakes! Is he a complete moron?"

"He was trying to help you," Andy said, scrambling to help Thomas up.

"What are you helping him for?" she shrieked. "You didn't even ask if I was all right." Quickly she did an inventory of her entire body. Then she shook out her hair for chards of glass.

Andy now had a shaken Thomas standing up. The back of the mirror had protected him from flying glass, but his hand was cut from a jagged piece of splintered wood.

"My mirror! You broke my mirror! And the table. What a stupid idiot! I may have wanted the table, too!"

"I need to get him cleaned up," Andy told his hysterical customer. "He may need stitches. Come back another time."

"Don't you have anyone else to help me?" She stamped her foot in frustration.

"It's August. Everybody takes their vacation. Please. He's bleeding."

"Well, I hope he doesn't have AIDS."

"Sorry, miss," Thomas muttered as Andy led him away.

"You cost your boss a very big sale, that's all I can say."

"Sorry," Thomas said.

Behind him the woman stopped to admire a row of Kenny's dolls. "Oh, these are lovely," she exclaimed. "How much are they?" She paused to read a tag.

Handmade in the State of Sonora, Mexico
by Genuine Mexican Peasant Women

When Thomas came home, his family made a big deal about his bandaged hand. Inez was limping but no one noticed. Soila ran to fetch him a lemonade, and the old aunt fluffed a pillow to put behind his head. Little Anita came in and ran to his lap, and cried when she saw that his hand was hurt.

"You gonna sue him?" Alex wanted to know.

"It wasn't his fault."

"He's the owner, he's responsible. What if you can't use your hand for a while? What if they fucked it up for good!"

Thomas spewed his disapproval in rapid Spanish. No one swore in his house.

"I'm just saying," Alex observed. "You deserve something."

Inez trudged from the room. She went into the bathroom and closed the door. She sat on the edge of the toilet. Her face was wet with perspiration. The bone in her foot seemed to be throbbing. It was all she could do not to cry.

She opened the door and returned to the living room. Thomas looked up at her expectantly. "What's eating you?" he challenged her.

"Nothing," she said tersely.

"Only you." He shook his head, the mask of his face spreading with sneering displeasure.

"Only Mom *what*, Pop?" Alex asked. Alex liked to stir things up whenever he could. Liked to start fights.

"Only your mother pays no attention. Doesn't seem concerned that her husband is injured. That I'm in pain."

"I'm concerned," Inez offered weakly.

"You think only of yourself." He was finished discussing it. Alex grinned at his sisters. Inez hobbled into the kitchen to start dinner.

Instead of eating with her family, Inez and the old aunt sat in the kitchen so she could soak her foot. Her husband and son and daughters were framed in the open doorway. Only Soila occasionally glanced up, smiling sympathetically as Inez swathed her foot in the warm water. As the others chatted, each about his own day's events, Soila and Inez contemplated each other with the seriousness of comrades with sad business between them.

I don't want this for you, Inez seemed to shrug.

I don't want it for you, either, Soila answered silently. She was allowing her hair to grow, and subconsciously would drape it over her deformed cheek. In the candlelight, one romantic concession Thomas continued to allow, Soila looked lovely, Inez noted. She had memorized her beautiful side and managed to present it artfully whenever she could. Like an aging movie queen, Soila at fifteen knew how to augment her best features and deemphasize her flaws.

Soila had been so fascinated to learn about Doctors Without Borders, but these humanitarians seemed only concerned about deformed children from third world countries. It was her bad luck to be transported to the richest country in the world when so much could be done for her back in Mexico.

Now Inez fell to studying her son, so jocular and handsome. So mean. Even now he taunted Soila to tears. She flounced off, hurt and bitter. A wave of shame washed over Inez as she realized that he must have learned his unkindness from her, when he was little and she was so bitter. She never held him. More accurately she held him away. He embodied all that she had forfeited that afternoon in the choir loft. The loss of her innocence. Her stature in her father's eyes. In God's.

She rubbed her foot. To her amazement, it still throbbed. She sighed so heavily Thomas gazed up in concern, but when he saw that it was she, he grimaced and looked away. Inez suspected him of decency when he was away from her. Not flirting or cruelty—but decency. This hurt her the most. That to strangers, Thomas might open doors, or pet a little cat, or chuck the chin of a sad child. To them he would present decency, an open heart—a countenance which wished the best for others.

Why for her the other? Soila, avoiding the taunting fingers of her dreaded older brother, came into the kitchen to kiss her mother. When she did, she tasted tears on her cheek.

She knelt in front of Inez.

"Mamita! Why are you crying?"

"It's just my foot," she whispered, shuddering in agony as the hulking frame of her husband reflected in her eyes. In the other room he shifted in his chair—turned his cold shoulder to her.

12

La Mojada

Kenny arrived early on Friday morning to do his paperwork and prep for lunch. It was just after dawn, and he decided to walk instead of drive. The sun was only just beginning to creep across the desert floor, and he looked with wonder at the shimmering palm trees, wafting in the morning breeze. The desert, for Kenny, had truly been an acquired taste. He was raised in the outskirts of Denver, in the foothills of the Rockies. He was used to pine trees—not date palm groves and miles of open desert.

From his family's small brick house on Green Mountain, Kenny and his brother could bike to the Morrison Foundation, a short hogback mountain range with dinosaur footprints still intact. His mom and dad were quiet, altruistic people, enjoying their backyard garden, family barbecues, and the company of their children over that of coworkers and contemporaries. His father was a sportswriter with a daily column in the *Rocky Mountain News*. A man's man, in his spare time he carved wild birds, liked to hunt, liked his beer too much, eventually giving it up, along with the early morning martinis he'd grown accustomed to having in a small bar on Broadway in downtown Denver.

Kenny felt bad when his dad had to quit drinking. He was a happy drunk, maybe a tad too sentimental when he overindulged, but not a stereotypical alcoholic. He didn't succumb to rages, or blackouts. He just got sweet and a little talkative. One afternoon two coworkers brought him home from the newspaper office. Kenny's mother was so horrified to learn he was a secret morning drinker, his dad, who loved her, had no choice but to quit at age fifty-eight, just when drinking was looking like a good friend to buddy around with when he retired.

After all, he couldn't talk much about his son. The same questions invariably would come up. When will Kenny get married? Is he dating yet? And the invariable office jokes about gays and lesbians.

While knowing that alcoholism was a disease, Kenny still blamed his candor about his confused sexuality as the culprit which pushed his father from being an alcohol abuser to a full-blown drunk. His parents always told him Kenny could tell them anything, but this was too much. Way too much, though they never said anything.

One by one they cut friend after friend out of their lives, stopping the questions. Increasing their dependence on each other. Their distress certainly fueled Kenny's desire to move away, to give them more space. It was only years later, after his father had died, that Kenny could admit that he moved partly because of them; that and because his Catholic mother had urged that Kenny speak to her own priest, a surly old Irishman who told him in no uncertain terms that he would be driven from heaven with whips and chains and to never show his face in a Catholic church again.

So of course, in defiance, his parents left the church, too. Not only had he damned himself, he had condemned them to hell as well. Hence Kenny's self-imposed solitude. Following their lead, he owed them that.

The desert was a place of scented visions for Kenny. Rainstorms excited him most. The smell of the desert after a rain intoxicated him. Desert light was equally magnificent, the way colors muted as light refracted through the vapors rising from the warming desert floor. From his vista he could look north to the upper Coachella Valley where the spinning windmills whirred. This was the threshold to Los Angeles, on Interstate 10.

Looking southward he thought of Mexico—two hundred miles away—and wondered if people like Maria were running right now along dry arroyos, hoping to connect with their rides, hoping to avoid detection by *La Migra*.

Maria had been with them for over a month. He hadn't regretted the decision to take her in for one instant. The week after she'd arrived, he went to Indio and arranged for a phony green card. The remark from Carmen made him edgy and he asked Gabriel to tell him where to go to get her good-quality paperwork. Kenny hooked up with a counterfeiter in an Indio park, paid him fifty bucks, went for a beer and a taco, and came back an hour later to pick it up.

It was all going very smoothly. If anything, his patience for Nick had increased since she'd arrived. Perhaps because she diffused some of his responsibility. Maria was exceptionally polite and sensitive. She would listen sweetly to endless stories. Later she even acknowledged learning a great deal about American culture as a result of his diatribes.

But the best part was when he began to drift off, either falling asleep on the couch or padding softly back to the bedroom, one too many drinks making him drowsy. Then either Kenny or Maria would tuck him in. Make sure his cigarette was out. Take off his reading glasses. Cover him gently with a light blanket.

Then Kenny and Maria would begin to work on the dolls. The television would be turned off. Classical music would be turned on. He would carve and paint. She would sew. For hours they would sit side by side without a word passing between them. Occasionally their shoulders might touch. Her knee might fall lightly against his.

Often they would share a rung on a stool until finally Kenny might announce that it was time for bed. Lights would be turned off. He would go back to the bedroom to brush his teeth. She would disappear into hers. Soon he'd return, in gym shorts and a T-shirt, pillows in tow. He'd plop them on the sofa and stretch out.

Then, five minutes later, her door would open. She, too, would appear with her pillow under her arm. A blanket. Her doll. Then she'd make her way down the dark hallway, study his sleeping form on the sofa, and curl up on the soft carpet below him.

His hand would fall to her side and she would clasp it while they slept.

Night after night like that.

It didn't take Inez Quintero long to realize that an interloper had infiltrated her territory, and probably an illegal interloper at that. Her file was delayed at immigration and now some *mojada* was trying to steal her American job. This very morning she trudged up the hill from her house on Sam Singer's alley, sighing and scowling at the prospect of having to clean Kenny and Nick's pigsty of a house. As a habit Inez sighed like an iron letting off built-up steam, and Maria heard her doing exactly this when she opened the front door with her key.

When Inez entered, Maria was folding Kenny's underwear, her lustrous hair freshly washed and pulled to the side with a silver comb Inez had coveted the first day she ever set foot in this house. Inez had thin frizzy hair. At first she thought Maria was Italian or Spanish, but when Maria greeted her cheerfully in an unmistakable Mexican accent, Inez's eyes narrowed in mistrust.

"What are you doing?" she demanded. "This is my job! When did they hire you and why wasn't I told?"

Maria laughed, a big mistake with Inez.

"I'm not getting paid," Maria explained. "You aren't being replaced." She motioned to Inez's money lying in the bowl where Nick always left it. Inez marched straight over and snapped the cash under the strap of her bra.

"If you aren't working, then what are you doing here?"

"I live here," Maria smiled. She wanted to win Inez over. She hadn't met another Mexican outside of Kenny's kitchen since she arrived. "I was only trying to help."

"Why do you live here?" Inez demanded. "Why don't you live with your family?" Maria stiffened at the question. Her lack of family was a source of great sensitivity to her. She glared at Inez, deciding that she didn't warrant further discussion. Inez waited for her answer. Maria continued to fold socks.

"Kenny and Nick are my family now."

"Queers," Inez said with satisfaction.

"*Mande?*" Maria was incredulous.

"They fuck each other." Inez folded her arms.

Maria snapped. She flew at Inez and began slapping at her ears, slapping so wildly that Inez could only cover her head with her hands and run screaming for the door.

"I'll kill you!" Maria cried. "I'll kill you if you ever say that about them again." To the neighbors' amusement, she chased Inez to the end of the block. When Maria came back to the house, she closed the door behind her, looked around the living room. Cluttered with photographs of Nick and Kenny on holidays. At their house in Laguna. With Kenny's parents. And Maria knew what Inez had said was true. That Kenny and Nick were lovers. And she was some ridiculous interloper.

She sat on the edge of the sofa and cried. She hurt primarily for them, for the wickedness in Inez's voice. She'd had gay friends in Mexico, and she'd observed what hardships the weaker, more effeminate boys faced. A girlfriend's brother had been savagely raped and beaten by a gang of neighborhood boys for wearing his sister's blouse as a joke on the street in front of their house.

While she'd noted Nick's sometimes outrageous behavior, she dismissed it to his drinking. He wasn't effeminate. Just exaggerated in dress and his way of moving. The artist in her liked to study him when no one was looking. He was unlike anyone she'd ever known. Physically he was beautifully made, and even the layer of alcohol abuse really couldn't attach itself to him. It floated high enough above him, a panting opaque viscous sheath to allow her to see what was underneath.

And in rare moments, when Nick was out of motion, or not talking, she'd noticed him contemplating Kenny while he sat captivated at his workbench; the gentle way he'd apply paint to a doll's hands. Or smooth out fabric to a dress. For being so big—Kenny's hands were quite large and not suited to the delicacy of these tasks—his careful regard for his work was poignant. Like Geppetto and his puppets.

Sometimes Maria observed Nick watching Kenny, and one recent evening he turned and caught her, but her eyes, like Nick's, were on Kenny, who continued working, unaware that his friends were loving him.

So now Maria stood up, wiped her eyes, and went to her bathroom to wash her face. The evil little woman was ignorant. Uneducated. Kenny was not like her friend's poor brother. He was strong and studied. He was kind, as was Nick. She would forgive herself any fleeting dreams about a future she might have with Kenny. She already had a home with him—with *them*, she corrected herself as she brushed her hair. She should grow up, she admonished herself. If there were forces outside that would try to harm them, then she, Maria, would always come to their defense.

Inez continued running long after she rounded the corner onto Chuperosa. The heat pounded down on her forehead and she grew increasingly lightheaded. She could hear dogs barking, and kids laughing, and she imagined that the girl at the house was still chasing her, still beating at her head and swearing to kill her.

When Inez finally came to her own block, she relaxed a little, but her head felt whoozy and she had to stop to vomit. By now she was within reach of her own gate. When she entered, her daughters were sitting in chairs on the porch. They looked at her, surprised to see her back so soon.

And then the ground came hurtling toward her.

Inez passed out only steps from the safety of her own front door. Faintly she heard the screams from her daughters, but in her mind they sounded more like the caws of attacking crows.

Later that afternoon Kenny was teaching Maria how to make soup stock. Although he noticed she was particularly quiet, they were behind on prep and tonight the restaurant was booked solid. He couldn't take the time to pull her aside and ask her what was wrong. Carmen, Miguel, and Gabriel were all working furiously to keep up. Overhead, music blared gently from the radio.

More than once he caught her studying him, but each time he did, her cheeks would flush and she'd quickly avert her eyes to her cutting board where she was chopping onions.

"Do onions make you cry?" Kenny asked her.

"Yes."

"Here. I'm used to them," he said. He pulled the bowl of raw onion away from her. "You do potatoes."

"No. I can manage." She reached for the bowl and continued chopping.

Several moments of silence passed between them. It was in silence that they typically communicated the most. Today Kenny couldn't read anything from her. He placed his knife on the cutting board. He looked over at her. When she felt his eyes searching her face for some clue as to what he was thinking, she couldn't look at him. She was relieved when his attention was drawn to a figure standing in the screen door to the alley.

Alex Quintero. An object dangled from his right hand.

"Go see what he wants," Kenny said to Miguel. Kenny continued with his peeling.

Miguel obliged. He knew Alex from the alley.

"*Que quieres?*"

Alex uttered a litany of profanities in Spanish at Miguel.

Maria heard them and looked up. Kenny continued to peel. Carmen and Gabriel also stopped cold in their places. They looked at Alex in astonishment.

"*Mande?*" Miguel said in horror.

Alex thrust whatever he was holding against the screen. Kenny turned. He recognized it immediately. The doll Kenny had given to his younger sister Anita. It was dirty and torn. The red dress was torn away from the figure of the doll, as if it had been sexually assaulted. Alex spewed more insults.

"What's he saying?"

Miguel blanched white. Kenny looked over at Carmen.

"What'd he say!"

Carmen struggled for the words. "He say that if you give presents to his little sister again, his parents will call the police . . ."

"*What?*"

"He says his father is a citizen now and doesn't have to be afraid."

Kenny advanced toward the door.

"Faggot!" Alex shouted at Kenny. Like boiling water thrown in his face, he reeled back.

"Get that guy," Maria said in a low, urgent voice. Her face darkened with such fury that Carmen turned to see where such a strange voice had come from. Miguel and Gabriel were equally amazed. They weren't even certain if she'd spoke in Spanish or English.

Alex opened the screen door and tossed the doll at Kenny's feet. Kenny bent down to pick it up.

Even though the doll was badly mutilated, Maria could plainly tell that Kenny had crafted the image in her likeness. She watched him study it as grieved as though he held a dead child in his hands.

"*Get him,*" Maria ordered again.

Miguel and Gabriel lunged at the door for Alex, who then had turned his back and was striding quickly down the alley to his own gate.

"No!" Kenny cried. He followed them, as did Maria, and when they emerged in the alley, Alex was down on the ground being pummeled by Kenny's employees. Even Carmen marched over and began kicking him.

"No," Kenny cried out. "*Let him up!*"

"He insulted you!" Gabriel explained. We have to defend you!"

"No," Kenny said softly. "No you don't."

They allowed Alex to stand and face Kenny.

Kenny stared at him for a long tense moment. He was twice Alex's size and could have easily torn him to pieces. Instead he pulled his cap low over his eyes.

"Back to the kitchen," he ordered his crew. When he gazed up, Maria was standing at the screen door. He looked at her for a long instant. Long enough to tell him what had been bothering her earlier.

Then Nick stumbled into the alley, roaring drunk at five o'clock.

"*What's going on out here?*" Nick came up to Kenny. "I just put out a fire in the kitchen!"

"Faggot," yelled Alex when he saw him. "Everybody who works

for you is a faggot!" he added in Spanish. This was an insult which could not be overlooked. Gabriel and Miguel gave chase. They all disappeared around the corner in hot pursuit.

"They'll be back," assured Carmen. "Once the matter is settled."

Kenny turned back and headed for the kitchen, with Nick hobbling after him in red espadrilles. Thomas Quintero rushed into the alley uncertain as to what to do. He wasn't used to fighting battles, especially with Anglo-Americans. Alex stood behind him, goading him to do something.

Dejected, Kenny passed Maria and stepped into the kitchen. Nick followed nonplussed, and didn't see what all the fuss was about.

Maria paused in the alley by the kitchen door, waiting for Thomas and Alex to make a move. Behind her, from the other end of the alley, Kenny's crew returned, laughing and joking about the fight. They came to a halt when they saw Thomas and Alex.

Alex made a charge at them.

Alarmed, Thomas pulled his son back. "We have more to lose," he advised him. "We can't have trouble with the police."

"It was better when we were illegal. We could settle this like before," said Alex. *"Pincha puta!"* He spat onto the ground.

Maria folded her arms and stood her ground.

Thomas pushed Alex behind his gate and locked it.

13

Whitewater

"You here to prove your manhood?"

Ralph Zola climbed on top of her, propping himself up on one hand and peeling back his underwear, which Marcella hooked with her big toe and dragged down his thighs to the scramble of sheets at her feet. Now that he was naked, he began to prod her and she relaxed, rocking slightly. She smiled with pleasure as he pushed himself into her. He was a big man, but when he began thrusting her like a jackhammer, she began to resist him.

"Take it easy," she wheedled between clenched teeth. "I'm not a guy. You gotta be gentle or I'll break." At her suggestion that he was hurting her, Ralph Zola climaxed in a matter of seconds. He pulled out and flopped next to her.

"Hey!" she exclaimed. "What about *me?*"

"So what do you know about Sam Singer?"

She stood up angrily and stomped to the bathroom to douche. "That's a hell of a question to ask me now!" Through her window she could see her elderly landlady strolling down the path, pruning back the wild bougainvillea near the dry creek bed.

Marcella lived in a small cabin in an enclave called Whitewater, at the throat of the Whitewater River. Whitewater was owned by Mrs. Ridley, and consisted of sixteen cabins and small trailers which she rented to a select chosen few. Mrs. Ridley considered herself a keen judge of character, and refused to rent to anyone deemed spiritually deficit. Marcella was her only black tenant, and had rented from her the day she arrived in the desert and began working for Nick and Kenny over ten long years ago.

Fear of poverty had made Marcella very frugal. She banked every cent she earned or stole. She paid two hundred thirty dollars per month for her cabin, and to date had four hundred thirty-nine thousand five hundred eighty dollars in securities. She hoped to have three times that amount by the time she was sixty.

Keeping Nick drunk and off guard was her main purpose in life.

She had been taught better but her mother observed often that God was not finished with Marcella yet. Her mother had been a reformed alcoholic since the day Marcella was born six weeks premature and weighing only four pounds. Any real damage done to her daughter had probably been inside her womb, and the only alcohol Marcella had ever imbibed had most likely come from her mother's umbilical cord.

Since her birth, Marcella and her mother had never taken another drink, but Marcella was always very comfortable around alcohol. Although her mother never drank, she didn't ban alcohol in her house. She loved the company of men, especially high-spirited fun-loving men. Handling booze tempted her, so she taught little Marcella early on how to mix drinks for assorted appreciative "uncles" and older cousins. Marcella associated affection with drinking. She was always getting called honey and having her ass fondled, and since she never knew her father, she was starved for affection from men, and men with rheumy eyes and whiskeyed laughter always provided it for her whenever she served them a drink.

She had one particular uncle who liked to slide his right hand under her dress. He never lingered long enough to be caught—only as long as it took to accept his cocktail from the sweet-looking young girl who had learned to serve him half hidden behind the arm of an old stuffed easy chair.

She never wore underwear on the days he visited.

A good bartender likes to think that if things had been different, they'd probably have made a great therapist. The preparation of a drink is secondary to listening, making a customer feel at ease, getting him to want to come back for another session.

The separation of the customer by the bar empowers the bartender. A good bartender can control the mood of his regulars, and a self-pitying customer makes for the best tipping to be had. A good bartender maintains control by watching and remembering the habits of others. Especially the boss. An alcoholic owner is the best friend a wicked bartender can have.

*   *   *

Marcella returned to where Ralph Zola lay outstretched on her bed, naked and still erect. He had a wrestler's stocky muscular body. An ultrathin layer of fat coated his muscles, giving him a rounded, generous appearance. He folded his hands behind his bed. She was wearing a green silk robe which clung to the curves of her body.

"You should always wear that color. It's beautiful with your skin."

She looked at his erect penis in disgust. She tossed a sheet up over him to cover him. "So what's in it for me?" she demanded. "You aren't here for a girlfriend. You aren't planning to move me to Los Angeles after you leave your wife and kids. You see a horny little black girl working her ass off in some shithole, and you think if you fuck her, she'll be so grateful she'll give you all the dirt for free."

"What are you looking for?" he asked calmly. He stroked himself gently while he waited for her answer.

"You want dirt on Sam Singer so he'll sell you the property that the bar sits on, right?"

"I want dirt on Sam Singer so he'll give me the property to go away."

"He's smart. He's way smarter than you."

Zola shrugged. "That may be so. He's waited for years for the day progress would come to Cathedral City. Cathedral City hasn't always been so Hispanic. He didn't buy the whole parcel all at once. He says he won the bar in a poker game. Later on he probably intimidated one of the white senior citizens in the alley behind him to sell him a house. Or maybe he was just ready when they died and the heirs wanted to cash out."

"So," Marcella said. She straddled a chair. Now she was getting intrigued.

"So when the first one caves, he rents to illegals. Maybe on purpose, or maybe by design. Naturally he wants to get his money back. So ten or fifteen people move into a small two-bedroom house. Scares the crap out of the next-door neighbors. Probably another old lady. He buys that house. Rents to more Hispanics. The next neighbor caves. Sells for even less. More Spanish-speaking tenants. All hardworking. Scared of trouble. Eager to maintain a low profile. Don't want to be deported. Do you see his plan?"

"Spell it out."

"He played on racism. He purposely devalued the neighborhood by infecting it. Sam's shrewd, all right. White fear. He buys more houses. He finally gets enough property to build a big hotel. Or maybe a shopping complex. He knew where the desert was headed twenty-five years ago."

"And his best attribute is patience."

"So what matters to Sam Singer?" Zola asks her.

"His wife," she answered without hesitation.

"She's a great-looking woman."

"She's okay," Marcella shrugged. "But she's got mental problems."

"Yeah?"

"She's been friends with Nick for years. Nick used to work for Sam when Sam ran the club. Nick told me Sam was kind of a small-time gangster."

"He carries himself like a gangster."

"There were big ties to the mob in the desert. He show you his pistol?"

"No kidding, he wears a piece?"

"In a shoulder harness. He loves to show it off."

"Is Sam known for being a ladies man?"

"He talks a good game with me, but he never goes through with it."

"You think he ever killed someone?"

"Not that I've heard."

"Think he could be goaded into using the gun?"

"If he felt threatened enough. Who wouldn't?"

"So other than his wife, what else does he care about?"

"The bar. It was his baby."

"So why'd he let it get so run-down?"

"He's fixing it up, or haven't you noticed?"

"It's all set dressing. When I see plumbers or electricians pull into the parking lot, then I'll know he's fixing it up." Ralph looked at her. "So why'd he let it go gay?"

"That's where you're wrong. You see a few gay men and women, and you think it's a gay bar. You see me in there and you probably think you're in Harlem. It's a neighborhood bar. All types come and go. Live and let live. That's the mentality of the true desert rat."

"Desert rat?"

"Live and let live. No questions asked. Honor among thieves. People come to Cathedral City to be left alone. For privacy. You'd be amazed at the people I've served at Nick's."

"Like who?"

"Like politicians with their girl friends or boy friends. Movie stars on honeymoons. Priests in plain clothes. Anything goes. It has that reputation. It always did. And that's your main problem. That's why he may never sell."

"Yeah?"

"You want to know what to remember about Sam Singer?"

"Yeah."

"He isn't predictable. You think he's been laying plans to ultimately sell Cathedral City?"

"From what I can piece together, sure."

"He's already a rich man. And he's old. He doesn't need money. I've been a bartender for a long time. I watch people. You know what they start worrying about if they get sick or old?"

"What?"

"They worry about getting to heaven and how they'll be remembered."

"He's hardly a devout Jew."

"But he doesn't have children."

"So. He'll sell the property and leave the cash to a synagogue."

"Or he'll save a town. Leave it for the future. Spoil your plans. And remember, Ruthie is younger by twenty years. She's only fifty-five. And aside from bad depression, she looks in pretty good shape to me. And one other thing."

"What's that?"

"She loves Nick and Kenny. She'll never agree to sell Cathedral City. Not unless she was forced."

"What might change her mind?"

"What's in it for me?"

"Huh?"

"What's in it for me? This is my livelihood we're talking about. If Sam Singer sells his property, where does that leave me? You think it's easy to find a job in the desert?"

Zola waited for her to name her terms.

"What's the parcel worth without the bar? It's street front. You can't build an ice-skating rink behind a gay bar, motherfucker. This is three million bucks' worth of property. I want one percent of that."

"Thirty thousand dollars?"

"Pay me or I tip Sam off. You never should have lost your cool in the alley. You never should have threatened him in front of anybody. You lost a year because of that. You'll lose ten after I get through with you."

Ralph lost his erection.

"This deal is worth ten percent to you. I want one. *One*, mutherfucker! That leaves you with nine. Cathedral City is a house of cards. You have to know which one to pull away." She stood up and moved to a small desk she kept in the hallway. She returned with a contract.

"I took the liberty of having my lawyer draw up this contract. It's a finder's fee. If you obtain Sam's parcel, I get thirty thousand."

"What are you going to do with thirty thousand dollars?"

"I'm moving to Las Vegas." She smiled triumphantly. "I could go now but I want a two-bedroom condo. Sign it."

"You really think you can deliver?"

"If you have the guts."

"Hand me the paper."

She handed it over. He scanned it quickly, a smile breaking across his lips. Then he signed it.

"So what's your secret weapon?"

"Those kids who beat you up." She smiled. "I've been in touch with them."

Several days later Drew was pouring water at Las Casuelas Nuevas, the outdoor Mexican restaurant where he worked as a waiter. When he paused at the table of a beautiful black girl sitting with a middle-aged white man, wearing a baseball cap, he jumped back when the girl stroked his scrotum through his jeans.

"Yow!" he cried.

Marcella looked up. "You wanna make a little money?"

"Or would you rather go to jail?" Ralph asked, pulling off his baseball cap, looking frankly into the blue eyes of the young man who had beaten him so badly behind the gay bar in Cathedral City.

14

The Priest

At Father Gene's morning Mass he noted several new and interesting faces in the congregation, intermingled among his small, but shrinking loyal group of regular parishioners. The displacement of the senior citizens residing at the Sun Town Trailer Park and the now dwindling housing for the Latino migrant population were having a serious effect on church attendance. Intermittent sections of small houses between the church and the highway were disappearing as if leveled by a tornado. Why three houses would be torn down and one left standing was a mystery to Father Gene. One day he paid a charity visit to an ailing parishioner, and when he returned two days later, her entire house was missing.

Anxiety remained acutely high for both groups. Many senior citizens had lived in Cathedral City for over thirty years. Some longer. Not a lifetime spent, but a retirement budget planned with inexpensive rent as the cornerstone of a limited income. Sometimes he felt helpless to alleviate their fears.

Today attending Mass was the Cathedral City renewal attorney. Father Gene recognized him from TV, but he couldn't recall his name. He was seated near the back, alone, and seemed to be a practicing Catholic. When Father Gene administered the Eucharist, he accepted it. He was an intense, calculating man. He seemed inordinately interested in his fellow parishioners and spent more time observing them than concentrating on the sacraments.

In the back on the other side, after Mass had begun, an exceedingly winsome Latin man entered, casually dressed in shorts and sneakers, looked around sheepishly, and finally took a pew near the door. He remained on his knees for the entire Mass and didn't receive Holy Communion.

He was joined in the same pew by a tall somber young woman, so close to his own age and appearance that Father Gene at first thought they had to be siblings; but she remained on her end of the pew without acknowledging him.

Father Gene was pleased. A few new faces. And several younger ones. Perhaps there was hope after all. In the weeks since Kenny had visited the church, Father Gene could not exorcise him from his thoughts. He took it to mean that God intended for his obsession to be converted into prayer, so Father Gene spent most of his waking moments in silent meditation for Kenny. But still he didn't return.

In addition to his newcomers were his regular regulars, little Annette Quintero and her subdued but bright daughter with the birthmark who Father Gene admired and was hoping to convert to a life of service to the church. She already donated her time to the Sunday morning nursery. Her disgruntled mother was a handful but she was raising a well-mannered, very devout daughter.

After Mass, Father Gene made it a point to corral the newcomers and welcome them to St. Louis Parish. He particularly wanted the redevelopment attorney to know that he recognized him; and also to recommend that his company better prepare local residents before any drastic impending demolition.

"But Father," Ralph Zola explained at the door to the sanctuary, "we had a town meeting only a month ago."

"I believe only property owners were invited to attend," Father Gene chided him gently.

"Who else would attend? It's the landlords who have the obligation to give notice to their tenants. Most of them are month to month anyway."

"I'm not talking legalities, Mr. Zola. A more aggressive outreach for the community would be greatly advantageous. Most of my parishioners are very poor, and some quite elderly. Many speak little to no English at all. A *Notice to Quit* is hardly compassionate under the circumstances."

"I certainly agree," Zola nodded condescendingly, but Father Gene could see that he didn't care at all. "Listen, Father, I need to confess, and I'm wondering—"

"Confession is on Saturdays between nine and twelve." And out of the corner of his eye Father Gene saw Kenny's Scout pull up. He thought he must be imagining it. Out from behind Mr. Zola, the pretty young woman Father Gene had noticed on the back row darted from the shade and hurried down the walk toward it.

Then Kenny climbed down from the driver's side and rounded the vehicle to open her door. They kissed briefly, cheek to cheek, and he helped her up to the passenger seat. They seemed to enjoy a high level of intimacy, and he moved as though he cared deeply for her. She, however, seemed distracted and solemn. Distinctly unhappy or worried about something.

Why would he expect anything different of one of his parishioners?

"Look, Father, see I'm kind of in a bind. My wife is coming out for a visit, and before I see her, I kinda wanted to come clean about something."

Father Gene looked at Zola with mild surprise. Had the man been talking the whole time? Now the Scout was pulling away.

"Somebody you know, Padre?"

"Yes," he answered coldly.

"Maybe I can make it worth your while if you'll hear me out now."

"I'll hear you out now if you'll agree to a community meeting to discuss relocation options with concerned tenants. You can have it here. I'll announce it on Sunday."

"Gee, Padre, by Sunday ten more houses will already be gone."

"Those are my terms, Mr. Zola."

"Is blackmail part of sanctioned church doctrine?" Zola grinned at him. "Okay, so be it. We'll have your town meeting. Now, can you allow me to unload here?"

"Let's go back into a confessional."

"I can tell you right here. Bless me, Father, for I have sinned. I committed the sin of adultery to obtain information about a property I'm having trouble acquiring."

"Which property?"

"Aren't you supposed to forgive me and give me my penance?"

"No. I want to know which property you're after."

"If you must know, the gay bar on the highway."

"Nick's?"

"This is highly irregular, Father. Can you please give me my sentence so I can sleep with my wife?"

Father Gene looked at him disapprovingly. "Your *life* is your *sentence,*" he commented.

*   *   *

The young woman attended morning Mass every day, and each day the same ritual was performed. She always sat at the back and never accepted Holy Communion. She usually dressed casually—jeans, T-shirt—and looked very anglicized, but in the few brief words he managed to coerce from her, she was definitely Mexican, though her English was impeccable.

Each time after the service, she would wait in the shadows near the open door of the church sanctuary. Then the Scout would pull up in the same spot, she'd bound down the walk toward it, and Kenny would ceremoniously open her door for her. He never gazed in Father Gene's direction, though clearly he could see him standing there.

To Father Gene's credit, he didn't leave his spot, and tried to give his attending parishioners the semblance of his full attention. He didn't question the young woman about Kenny's well-being, or indicate in any way that he knew him.

And just when he allowed himself a glance in Kenny's direction, the little Quintero woman would loom up into his face, reading his discomfort as easily as if his face was a street signal. Today he noticed that her pallor was gray.

"Hello, Annette," he greeted her breezily. "How are you doing today?"

"Her name is *Inez,* Father."

Father Gene and Inez both turned in the direction of the voice who had corrected him. It was the smiling, good-looking young man he'd noticed days ago, sitting in the same pew as the woman who knew Kenny.

Father Gene nodded. "You know each other then."

"Oh, yes." Pablo grinned. "I'm certain that Inez knows more about me than she'd care to admit."

"Is that right, Inez? If I was calling you by the wrong name, why didn't you correct me?"

Inez was stumped. This was the first full attention he was paying her in all the years she attended his church and now she couldn't find her words. This morning she had woken up feeling so ill. She was light-headed and nauseated. Even in the intense desert heat, she knew she had a temperature. Worse, she suffered from a growing, prevailing fatigue, a malaise which caused her to conserve any movement whatsoever. The only client she continued to work for was Mrs. Singer.

After the incident with Kenny's doll, she couldn't go back to work for him and Señor Nick. As strange as she found his hobby, and as much as dolls made her feel uneasy, she could never in her heart imagine that Kenny intended anything but kindness. He was generous, and Anita was so bold she had probably asked him for the doll.

Inez had spent too many years watching him come and go past her bedroom window not to have developed a sense of his character. He always walked hunkered against the elements—hot sunlight, wind, even despair. With Kenny she had one important thing in common, she now reflected. He never laughed either.

And she'd seen his dolls for sale in the showroom where Thomas worked. It had impressed her that she knew instantly that they were Kenny's, and that he could command such a price for them—as long as Thomas's boss pretended they were crafted by poor Mexican women. This galled her and further fueled her general resentment.

But the doll Kenny had given Anita was special, and Inez was pleased she could have something so beautiful and expensive. Even Thomas was impressed, but handed it to Alex to make something sinister out of the gesture.

And the incident with the needle at the hotel was too horrible to contemplate. She didn't like to admit to fear, but Pablo's reaction had filled her with unspeakable dread. She wondered if it had anything to do with the way she was feeling.

So she hadn't gone back and they never called to ask after her. Four lost days of employment did not make her husband very happy. They needed her money to save for the house. Sam Singer had offered them a fair deal, Thomas explained. And he'd already put so much work into renovating it to their liking. He'd completely rebuilt the cabinetry in the kitchen and bathroom and laid down all new Mexican tile.

Where walls were rotting and had previously been repaired with painted plywood, Thomas had painstakingly replaced them with drywall and plaster. The old painted beams on the ceiling he'd stripped and stained, restoring them to their original splendor. All in anticipation of owning the house. His American dream.

And because she was ill, Inez was slowing them down.

Now she contemplated the boy and the priest. She unsuccessfully stifled a cough and the boy's eyes filled with concern.

"Did you see a doctor?"

"Yes," she lied, and coughed again.

"Maybe you should go *back*," he said pointedly. "I could take you right this instant."

"My husband will take me if I need to go," she asserted.

Father Gene watched this exchange with interest. "How do you know one another? Are you related?"

Inez glared at him like he was a complete idiot.

"We met in the alley behind the restaurant where I was working." Then to Inez Pablo said, "If I can't take you to the doctor, can I at least give you a ride home? It's very hot today."

He scanned the scorching desert floor. The distant rolling foothills were varying shades of soft pink and purple. Some afternoons they were so soothing and beautiful, he had to catch his breath.

"I'll *walk*," Inez's eyes narrowed. They watched her trudge down the sidewalk to the street.

Pablo and Father Gene were the last two standing at the door to the sanctuary. Pablo's friendly sexuality made Father Gene ill at ease.

"She didn't go to the doctor. She'll probably confess on Saturday."

"It was kind of you to offer to take her. Where are you from?"

"Mexico. Cuernavaca, to be exact."

"I've heard it's a beautiful city. In the mountains near Mexico City."

"I'm thinking about relocating here permanently, however. My parents won't approve but they travel frequently to the States. They'll probably see me more than ever."

"What line of work are you in? You say you work in a restaurant?"

"It would be more precise to say that I operated out of a restaurant. But they didn't appreciate it."

Father Gene studied him intently. Things were getting more interesting by the day. "What brings you to Mass, young man?"

"I'm conflicted about my profession, Father. And trying to reconcile it with my faith. Or," he added, smiling ruefully, "I might just be wasting our time."

"You're always welcome to worship at St. Louis. By the way, which restaurant were you . . . subcontracting out of?"

"Nick's."

"I could have guessed. Good day, young man."

"Peace of Christ, Father."

"And also with you."

"Father, I need to ask for advice."

The priest paused to study the worried expression on Maria's face. She had arrived for morning Mass, and waited till he bid the other parishioners the peace of Christ. He knew she wanted to speak with him by the fervent way in which she looked at him during Mass.

"How can I help you?"

"It's very difficult." Maria hesitated. "Father, is there really a hell?"

Father Gene hated this question.

"I would find it easier to reassure you about the existence of heaven. Then you can draw your own conclusions."

"But what if someone you know is kind and generous but differed from the church in only one way. Would this person go to heaven?"

"It would depend on how significant the difference."

Her silence indicated that she thought the difference highly significant.

"Sin is the thing that can separate us from God. Confession is the only way to expiate sin. And not only in word, but deed. Is your friend willing to confess? And to sin no longer?"

Maria's shoulders sagged. "I don't know."

"Are we perhaps talking about the young man who brought you first to this parish?"

"Kenny? Yes. But I know he loves the church, Father."

"I can't speak about him specifically, but I think you're correct. He's trying to find some answers. And I can tell you this. He's in my prayers."

The priest wiped his brow. He felt ridiculous. Who was he to reassure this young woman who sat earnestly before him, worried about preserving Kenny's place in heaven. She should be the priest. Not him!

"He's in my prayers also, Father. But what else can I do?"

"Have faith in the mercy of God and the power of the Holy Trinity. Beyond that, love him with all of your heart."

"I do, Father!"

"You mean as a brother."

"Yes!"

He searched her face. "By his nature alone, he isn't in conflict with the Catholic Church. The Church recognizes his . . . predicament as a given—not a matter of choice. But we are judged, rewarded, and condemned by our actions."

She looked at him as if she didn't understand.

"I don't think you have much to worry about."

Her face reflected her relief.

The priest had to mask his own.

*   *   *

That evening after the kitchen closed, Maria and Kenny drove up the hill in Kenny's truck. It was a sultry desert evening. The amber lights of the desert cities shimmered in the distance. The sky was ink-black with tiny pinpoints of starlight.

"No moon tonight," Kenny said.

Maria didn't reply, but he could feel her sneak a glance at him and look away.

"Would you mind if we took a drive up into the hills? I don't want to go home just yet."

"Okay."

He continued past the turn to their street. The truck climbed the winding hill past the larger homes in the Cathedral Canyon cove. Soon they were bouncing along on a dirt road with a magnificent view of the desert floor. Kenny shifted gears into four-wheel drive. He looked over at her. Her profile was somberly beautiful against the backdrop of the desert sky. Her hair swayed with each bump in the road. It sparkled with starlight.

Kenny hesitated.

"I know the incident with the Quintero kid upset you—but something was bothering you before he showed up. You wanna talk about it?"

She looked at him. She didn't know what to say.

"You didn't understand about me and Nick, right?"

Silence. They rode along. Then, "No, Kenny. But I do now."

"I thought it was obvious. I guess I don't show Nick much affection."

Maria was very uncomfortable. "I'm to blame. I wasn't seeing."

The truck came to the top of the mountain, near a posted overlook. Several other cars were already parked. As Kenny pulled in, he could see lovers entwined in passionate embraces. He was suddenly very embarrassed.

"I haven't been up here for ten years. I didn't expect this. We'll go back."

"Could we sit for a few minutes? It's beautiful."

Kenny turned off the engine. He was very nervous. His hands trembled.

They were silent for several minutes.

"Have you ever been in love?" he asked her.

"Yes. But my grandmother didn't approve of him."

"Handsome?"

Maria smiled. "Very."

"But you wouldn't disobey her?"

"No. Part of the reason we left Mexico was to get away from him. When I refused to marry him, he changed. He became very bitter. I was frightened of him. He threatened to kill himself. My grandmother thought he'd kidnap me."

"Do you think he would have?"

"Yes."

"He sounds pretty passionate." After a long moment Kenny added, "It doesn't surprise me."

"Were you ever in love—with a woman?"

Kenny spoke without hesitation. "Yes."

"Pretty?" Maria teased him.

"Very."

"Oh." She feigned jealousy. She folded her arms and waited. Then she tossed her hair for good measure.

"She was very . . . special. And kind."

"Ahh. So what happened to such a wonderful woman?"

"She got married and has a child. A little girl. Then she got divorced. She wrote me about it. I never answered." His voice grew wistful. Maria softened, shifting in her seat.

"Why didn't you stay in touch with her?"

"I didn't think it would be fair to Nick. Or her."

Nick.

They sat up, jolted into reality.

In the rocking car next to them, two lovers were making violent love. Their ardor culminated in gasps and groans. Finally the driver's side door popped open. A heavyset man got out. He walked to the edge of the overlook and lit a cigarette. After some rustling around inside, the passenger door opened. His partner joined him, a slender man, adjusting his trousers.

He glanced over at a mutually surprised Kenny and Maria.

"We're everywhere," he observed haughtily. "Get used to it."

An embarrassed silence.

"Each to his own," Kenny shrugged. In agreement, Maria threw up her hands. Maria and Kenny burst into laughter. The man sniffed and strode over to the cliff to join his companion. Together they held hands against the night sky.

Kenny and Maria watched them in silence.

"I guess we should be getting back."

"Yes."

Looking directly ahead, he reached over to the gear shift and found her hand resting gently on it as though waiting for him. Instead of withdrawing his own, he allowed it to rest over hers for an instant. Without turning and without words he asked her to pretend that they were alone in the world and could he kiss her just once, in this spot, high above the desert floor under the ink-black sky with the pinpoints of starlight, without any bad will, with no adverse ramifications, no one getting hurt, no expectations, just a kiss to express their love—just a kiss—just one.

Since he wasn't looking at her, he couldn't see her nodding yes.

So Kenny lifted his hand to allow Maria to withdraw her own. He started the engine. The truck roared to life, and Kenny and Maria backed away.

15

Indio

Pablo had come to a decision. Although he was in the country on a temporary work visa, he had come to the conclusion that he wanted to apply for permanent residency. He decided to file the necessary paperwork, and today had an appointment with a preapproved doctor for the medical portion of his application.

The doctor's clinic was in Indio in a mostly Latino ghetto on the south side of town. Pablo parked and went inside. He was surprised to see Inez Quintero sitting in a chair by the door. She pretended not to recognize him.

"Hey," Pablo called to her. "Remember me?"

"Hmmph," she said.

The woman next to her was called by an attendant, and Pablo quickly assumed her vacated chair.

"So how's your foot?"

Inez grimaced.

"What did the doctor say? Everything okay?"

"S'okay."

"He give you a shot?"

Inez was a good Catholic and incapable of lying. She also clearly didn't feel well. She looked at him with daggers in her eyes.

"You never went . . ." Pablo shifted in his chair. The room was filled with other applicants, all here to get blood tests and examinations for green cards. "I tried to find you. I should have taken you. Made you go."

"What do you care about me?"

Pablo composed himself. His thoughts were spinning. If she had a blood test and a problem came up, she might forever be on record and never get legal residence in this country.

"Well, see, I do care. That's all there is to it. And I need to give you some advice," he added, looking around the room. "They take a blood test. Did you know that?"

Inez shifted uncomfortably. What was he driving at?

"If there's any problem, they put it on a computer. You can't ever get it off. Now, I'm sure it's nothing, but maybe it would be better for you to get your own blood test—*before*. So you know what's on it."

"What could be on it?" she demanded. "You're very stupid," she added. "Leave me alone!"

And then she looked up and saw it. On the wall across the room. A poster about SIDA. A long needle in the background. She looked at him in horror.

"It's probably nothing. But you should know for sure. I could take you. We could go right now."

"*Never!*" And she stood up and fled the room.

Several days later Pablo stopped into Nick's to pick up his last pay-check. It had been months since Kenny fired him. Kenny and Nick weren't in, but a tall striking *Latina* was working in the kitchen, and when he explained what he needed, she shuffled through some papers on Kenny's small overloaded desk and pulled out an envelope with his name on it.

"When did you start working?" he asked her in Spanish.

"In August."

"Yeah? Right when I got fired." He smiled ruefully, like it was not as funny as it sounded.

"Kenny *fired* you?" She looked at him in amazement and laughed good-naturedly. He was so cute and charming.

"What's so funny?" he demanded, feigning umbrage.

"I can't imagine Kenny firing anybody!" she laughed again. "What could you have done?"

He shook his head sheepishly. "You don't want to know. He's a good guy, though, Kenny. Huh?"

"Yes," she answered softly and a flush of color rushed to her cheeks. "A very good guy."

"Where you from?"

"Mexico. Vicente Guillermo . . ."

"You married? Do you have a boyfriend?" he teased her.

"No, no, no." She shook her head.

"Have your eye on anyone?"

"What's with all these questions? I don't know if I can trust anybody Kenny fired. You must be a very bad boy." She looked at him and grinned. They were flirting with each other, and she was having fun. He never stopped smiling at her.

"I have a new calling. A mission in life. I'm gonna find a man good enough for you to marry."

"Why don't *you* marry me?" This was daring of her but it felt good.

"Oh, I'm so sorry, but you see, I'm not the marrying kind," he clucked his tongue, "but if I did marry you, you'd have very beautiful children!"

"So you have a big head on top of everything." Maria pretended to pout. She knew he was telling her he was gay. Then she added, "Well, I hope you have someone nice in your life."

"No," he shook his head. "I'm all alone."

She realized she'd struck a nerve. "That's a waste. You should come by and say hello again. Kenny won't mind. Kenny forgives anything."

"I know," Pablo nodded. "That's why I was so surprised he fired me. He really hurt my feelings." He pretended to wipe a tear away.

"Poor baby."

"Well, I've got to get going. I'll see you around, eh? What's your name?"

"Maria."

"I'll see you around, Maria." He winked at her and retreated into the alley. When Kenny and the rest of the crew arrived several hours later, Maria was still smiling. She told him that Pablo had come in to pick up his check.

"How'd he seem?"

"Like he regretted whatever he did that made you angry." She fell silent.

"Oh." On her look he asked her what was wrong.

"It's not my place, but he seemed like such a nice, funny boy. What could he have done that made you fire him?"

Kenny blanched with embarrassment.

"You don't want to tell me."

"It's too delicate."

Annoyance flickered in her eyes. He hesitated. He didn't want to hold anything back from her, and now the others were watching them. He leaned over and whispered in her ear.

She looked at him in amazement. "In front of *Inez?*"

"Yes."

"You should forgive him," she admonished Kenny. "That was punishment enough." And she laughed again, pleased that she'd made a new friend today, but happier still because Kenny wouldn't keep a secret from her.

Pablo rounded the back of the restaurant to the alley where his Jeep was parked in the shade. He felt good, too. The fresh paint job on the little shacks sparkled in the hot desert sun. The alley dwellings looked like a movie set—not a mean little barrio in the doomed section of a sleepy desert town.

The most well-kept house he knew belonged to Inez. He remembered her crying softly and squirming from his touch when he offered to pull out the needle in her foot. Then he winced as he recalled her charging into the darkness, swinging her broom, and shouting for him and his trick to get away from her daughter's window.

Shame flooded him. It felt as hot on his back as the burning rays of the afternoon sun. He began to walk toward his Jeep. A few Mexican boys loitering in the alley jeered softly but he ignored them and kept walking.

He often wondered what the Catholic maids thought of the conditions they encountered when they made up the rooms. He was curious if they talked among themselves, the more experienced ones cautioning the new maids about the dangers of handling unclean linens, used condoms—misplaced drug paraphernalia. These concerns would be true of any hotel, gay or straight, but the juxtaposing cultures of an openly gay sex motel and the pious Catholic upbringing of the mostly naïve women who were hired to clean them intrigued Pablo greatly.

Inez Quintero was certainly not highly regarded by the managers of the hotel, or she would have been issued gloves and required to wear protective footwear. It was true, Pablo knew, that infections were few among medical and dental health care workers except in the case of accidental stabs, which were more frequent than anyone cared to admit. At least these professionals were armed with education and preventative remedies.

Not so Inez at her job at this particular gay motel.

He paused for a moment, studying her gate. He wondered if he should pull his Jeep around the block to her front door and ask how she was doing. Ask if she went to the free clinic.

More jeers from the boys. They wriggled against the fence, pulling at their crotches.

They were small, ignorant, and jealous of his Jeep. He climbed into the driver's seat and adjusted the mirror. Glancing over in the direction of the boys, he started the engine. He roared down the alley past them, making certain to blanket them, in a cloud of dust from his wheels.

When he came to the street, he made his decision, whipped to the left, and soon found himself standing on the porch of her newly painted cottage.

Pablo took courage and knocked.

Inside, Inez saw his approach and prayed as follows:

I have been expecting him but intend to make him go away. I beg you, mother of Jesus, that my husband won't turn me out. The house is empty, quiet, and sufficiently calm for prayer. I petition you, Saint Theresa, that my children will not cry for a mother, that my passing will cause them no sorrow. I make it my business to be as evil as possible, that their love for me will fade in my lifetime, that my death will please and not grieve them. I pray that Soila will continue her studies, and be compelled to marry God. I pray that my body will be returned to Mexico, if I can ask him anything I may ask him this, that my body be buried in the land where I was born, that I be returned to my mother and father.

"Go away!"

"I only want to help. Please, let me talk to you. I know you're alone."

"My husband is here!"

"Your husband is at work. I know how alone you must feel."

"He'll be back soon, and chase you off!"

Pablo leaned heavily against her door. She could see his shadow, casting its weight across the polished wooden slats of her floor.

"Please—I want to help you."

Slowly she opened the door. She glanced nervously behind him to see if he was alone. She waved him in and closed the door.

"Have you seen a doctor?"

Her wild eyes said no.

"You have to see somebody. Get a test."

"Never!" she spat. The door opened. Her old aunt was returning. Nearly blind with cataracts, the old woman glanced around the room and narrowed on the presence of a different body. A man with a big frame. She couldn't see Inez.

"Aaaaiiiiiiiiiiiiiiiiiiiiiiiiii!" she screamed, so loud and shrill Pablo couldn't believe any old woman could be capable of making such a noise.

Inez flapped her handkerchief. "Be quiet, he's a cousin from Guaymas. He's in medicine, he's going to help me with a few things."

"*Sí?*" The old crow woman quieted.

"Where are my provisions?"

"It was too hot. I'm tired and I need to rest." She waved her hand, dismissing them. She moved to the kitchen where Pablo could see her kick off her shoes and curl up on a pad under the table like an old black dog.

A look of great distress crossed Inez's brow.

"Give me the list."

"*Estas un puto,*" Inez said grimly.

Pablo had never heard it put exactly that way. He shrugged. "*Sí.*"

"I don't approve," she said, folding her arms.

Pablo bristled. "I'm not asking for your approval."

Inez thought for a moment. She was very ill, her complexion waxy and gray. She perspired under her eyes.

"Give me your list. *Que quieres?*"

Inez's lips were cracking and dry. "I really wanted lemonade."

"I'll go at once."

"The old lady has the money." She moved into the kitchen. The old woman snored on her pad. "*Da me el dinero!*"

She didn't move so Inez kicked her, but not hard.

"I have enough money for this list," Pablo intervened.

"*Sí?*" Inez left the old woman to her rest.

Pablo returned ten minutes later. Inez opened the door, snatching the brown paper bag. She closed the door without a word.

"I'll take you," he whispered through the door. "Tomorrow at the same time. Send your aunt to the drugstore."

"No! Go away!"

"I'll see you tomorrow." He stroked the glass windowpane of her door. His words resonated through wood and glass to her heart.

* * *

Later that night Pablo reclined on a chaise longue he dragged away from the trailer to better observe the stars. A falling star streaked across the sky, and inside Pablo could hear his telephone ringing. He never gave his number out to tricks from the hotel, so a call at this hour might be his mother, wanting to say good night. He hurried over sand and cactus to answer the telephone.

His mother Elena spent many nights alone while Pablo's father traveled between Mexico and New York City. A professor of literature, she was a chic woman in her early fifties, and had married Pablo's father late in life. Pablo was born when she was thirty-four, and other children were not possible after his difficult childbirth.

Pablo was a miracle baby for her, inasmuch as she had truly forsworn marriage and children in favor of a distinguished but lonely career. She met her husband at a dinner for the president of Mexico, a widowed man twenty years her senior. If a child surprised her, it staggered him completely, but Pablo proved to be a source of pride and happiness to them both.

They knew fully well why he wanted to relocate in the United States, and privately never disagreed that the choice made good sense. But they didn't want Pablo to fall victim to opportunists who might be impressed with his wealth, and decided to withhold money for that very reason. He could go if he worked, and come back if he wanted to continue his studies. They would have been horrified by his circumstances. A rented trailer in the high desert; tending bar and hustling in a gay motel, one step up from a bathhouse.

"Pablo, I've had a dream," said his mother, "and you mustn't be angry because you know I'm not superstitious. It's better if I ask you outright, because as my son, it's your job to reassure me as I grow older and more ridiculous."

Pablo laughed. "Anything." He knew she was dead earnest and wanted to infuse it with humor.

"I dreamed last night that you were selling yourself, and I want you to tell me this very minute that it isn't so."

Pablo was speechless. He couldn't find words, not in the face of her honesty.

"Pablo?"

A very long silence. He still could not speak.

"I see now there must be something to clairvoyance," she whispered. "I want you to come home immediately."

He could picture her in her bedroom, surrounded by books and exquisite paintings, her hair hanging softly around her shoulders after all day in a high tight bun.

"How can a son talk about such things with his mother?"

"How can a mother refuse to have dialogue with her son when it's so important—"

"This is impossible—"

"You must not refuse to talk to me! I need to know why you've chosen such a path, why you don't understand the danger when every opportunity has been made available to you!"

"On your terms!"

"Are you saying you do this for money?"

"I don't do it to survive. I make real money as a waiter. I guess I do it for adventure." He mistakenly thought she might be impressed with his reasoning.

"Pablo! We were fearful of others preying on you, but it would seem that you are the predator in this circumstance. Is that what you've become?"

"I'm no predator!"

"You offer your body to lonely strangers for *money?*" Her voice grew shrill. He could hear her take a deep breath, struggled for control. "You could be killed."

"I'm very safe . . ." His voice trailed away as he thought of Inez Quintero.

"Safe! Have you been tested for HIV?"

"No. But I'm very safe."

Pablo began to cry and told his mother how unprepared he was for the way they treat Hispanics in this country. For the way peasants are treated in Mexico by the upper class. He cried when he suggested that he wasn't even certain how they would treat her, his beautiful mother, if all they heard was her name and saw her skin color, or the brisk accent with which she spoke fluent English.

She grew silent. She allowed him to calm down.

"My heart is broken," she said.

"I'm sorry I broke your heart," he whispered.

"No, you misunderstand me, my heart is broken for you, for your lost innocence." Gently she hung up the telephone.

When Pablo knocked on Inez's door, exactly twenty-four hours later, he was surprised when she answered so quickly. Her head was covered with a scarf, and she wheezed slightly as he helped her toward his Jeep. When she hesitated about climbing up to her seat, he leaned down and helped her up, placing her securely next to where he would sit. She gazed fearfully around her, wondering who was watching, and then contemplated the distance to the ground. He reached up and fastened her seat belt, closing her door and locking it.

"Are you still working at the motel?" she asked moments later, nervously watching the other cars zoom past them. He was driving slowly so she wouldn't be frightened.

"No. *Yes.*"

A car honked as it roared past. "You're a very bad driver! Speed up."

He shook his head at her rancor. He stepped on the gas.

"They never called me when I didn't come back."

"The manager is afraid you'll sue him."

"*Sí?*" Inez looked at him. "Could I do that?"

"Maybe," said Pablo.

"My husband wouldn't approve." Resentment flickered in her eyes. They drove the rest of the way to Indio in silence.

The Indio Free Clinic parking lot was packed with pickups, low riders, and old cars, and Pablo had to let Inez off to find a place to park on the street. Hundreds of clients spilled from the doorways, old people, young people, children, and screaming babies. Pablo had never seen anything like it, and lunged for a chair just as it emptied so Inez wouldn't have to stand in the sun.

"You aren't used to waiting," she said.

"No," he admitted. "I have private insurance."

"Spoiled rich kid," she observed, and settled into the chair he'd provided.

He stood in line to sign them both in, and when he returned, he found her trembling.

"What is it?" he asked, kneeling next to her.

"*Nada,*" she said, but opposite them was a poster with photos of needles, urging the use of clean ones and warning about the dangers of SIDA. She allowed him to place his arm around her, and his temper about the crowd and chaotic conditions evaporated as he began to experience her fear. They both wished her turn would never come.

In the examining room, Inez was stalwart as an attendant took her vital signs.

"Is this your son?" she asked, trying to make small talk.

"No," Pablo replied for her when Inez didn't answer. She was glaring at the girl sullenly.

"She's a babbling idiot, like most of the maids at the motel," Inez interjected.

The attendant disappeared and forty minutes later a pretty Latina doctor breezed in, apologizing automatically for their wait.

"You don't know how long we've been waiting," Pablo chided her.

"As a matter of fact I do. See? They write your arrival time on the chart, Mr. Smarty Pants." She grinned at Pablo. She touched Inez on her shoulder while she studied the chart. To Pablo's dismay, her humor faded.

"She had an accident where she worked about a month ago," he explained. "She stepped on a hypodermic needle."

"Where does she work?" the doctor asked, "In a medical facility?"

"She's a maid at a hotel."

"Why are loose needles floating around in hotel rooms?" She glanced up at Pablo, slightly suspicious. She studied Inez. "You're very pale, and you have a high temperature. How long have you been feeling this way?"

Inez shrugged, "A long time."

"Before you stepped on the needle?"

Inez looked at Pablo. "A long time before."

"I want to listen to your lungs." After the examination, the doctor studied her chart. "I think you might have pneumonia. Why didn't you come in sooner? We could have made you more comfortable." She studied Inez with interest. "Your chart says you're married." As if sizing her up. She clearly wanted information but wanted to be delicate.

"I have to ask some personal questions, Mrs. Quintero. Do you want your friend to leave the room?"

When Pablo automatically stood up to leave, Inez abruptly took his hand.

"He can stay . . ." Her voice trailed away. She began to quiver from fear.

"Okay," the doctor began. "Have you ever had a blood transfusion as a result of surgery or medical emergency?"

Inez considered her questions.

"After my last daughter was born, there were complications. But no transfusion. I was unable to have more children." She looked up nervously. "Is that bad? Should I have had this transfusion?"

"No. Not at all. Do you use IV drugs?" the doctor continued, making a note on her chart.

Inez shook her head.

"To your knowledge, Mrs. Quintero, have there been any incidents of sexual relations outside of your marriage? Either you or your husband?"

Inez became angry. She jumped up.

"I *need* to know," the doctor said calmly. Pablo looked at his hands in embarrassment. Inez swore angrily in unintelligible Spanish. She hopped off the table and disappeared across the hall into a small lavatory.

"In so many words, *yes,*" Pablo translated as she slammed the door.

"She's very ill. She might have contracted hepatitis from the needle, but I can't be certain. She's clearly been ill for much longer than a month. Maybe she was lucky to be bitten by the needle."

"How so?" Pablo queried, and for some reason, relief swept over him. He felt responsible for the part he played at the hotel.

"Without it, she may not have agreed to come in." The doctor shook her head. Commiserating with Pablo she added, "The paranoia about hospitals and doctors is still epidemic in these migrant communities. I go out, I speak at churches, but they're so stubborn. They either think they'll get deported or we're infecting them with mysterious viruses . . ."

The doctor spoke plainly to Pablo. "This needle, was it yours?"

"No," Pablo shrugged.

"What kind of a hotel does she work at?"

He looked at her miserably. "A gay hotel in Cathedral City."

"Ah, the Seven Palms?" She smiled. "My brother and his boyfriend stay there when they come to town. So anyway, Pablito, regardless of what might have been on that needle, the chances of it living after being exposed to air are pretty nil. Whatever she has, she got from somewhere else. You know her husband?"

"I've seen him," he shrugged.

"Will he agree to come in and be tested?"

Pablo blanched. "He's very proud."

"Ah, *muy machismo,* no? Mrs. Quintero is the third Latina housewife I've had this month *alone* with the symptoms of severe pneumonia."

"You never get Latino men?"

"Openly gay ones. It's rare that a heterosexual Latino man volunteers for an HIV test. As it is, they'd rather contract AIDS and die before they'll use a condom. They only come in for advanced cases of gonorrhea because they can no longer urinate."

The toilet flushed in the lavatory.

"I think she knows something she's not telling us. You think she'll let me test her for HIV?"

"I think she'll agree if I do it first."

"Have you ever been tested for HIV?"

"I'm a literature major . . ." He was clearly ashamed.

"Unfortunately, that won't be enough to protect you." She folded her arms.

The door opened. Inez gazed solemnly across the hall to where Pablo and the doctor stood waiting for her. Her face was glistening with perspiration. She was holding her rosary beads in her right hand.

"I'll take the test," she volunteered. "If he will."

After drawing blood from Pablo, the doctor flicked his needle into a red plastic container marked *Hazardous Materials*. Then she prepared a new IV for Inez. "It only pinches a little. You can look away if you need to."

Pablo studied Inez kindly. "I could barely feel it. Move over on your chair. Let me sit next to you."

"You're very forward," Inez clucked nervously.

"Move over." He edged himself next to her, placing his arm around her frail shoulders. She felt damp to his touch. While the doctor prepared the injection, he began to tickle her.

"Stop it!" she squirmed, annoyed but grinning. "Must I bear *so much* in my miserable life?" She caught the doctor's eye. "You know, he resembles my husband when he was younger."

The doctor looked up and smiled. She moved to insert the IV needle in a large blue vein on Inez's rough, freckled hand. Pablo squeezed her shoulders.

"This will only take a second, señora," the doctor murmured. "We'll test for everything."

"So I look like your husband? How lucky you are!" Pablo grinned, primping in the mirror to make her laugh. They both watched her blood coil through a tiny plastic tube and collect in a clear plastic bag.

"Yes," said Inez. Her eyes grew distant, as if she were deep in thought. "That night in the alley, I thought it was him again."

The doctor looked up questioningly. Pablo blanched, but continued to smile.

Why, he wondered, would Inez think her husband could possibly be caught with his pants down behind her house in the alley with another man? How could she even make such a mistake?

On the way out, the doctor patted Inez sweetly on the shoulder. "Results will be ready in two weeks."

"Thank you." Inez drifted ahead of them.

To Pablo the doctor whispered, "You'll bring her back? We have counseling services available, but she adores you. You make her feel secure."

"Why are you telling me all of this?" Pablo whispered.

"Her husband. I saw your reaction. If she's infected, it's *him*. Can you get him in here for a test?"

16

Thomas Quintero

His extramarital activity notwithstanding, Thomas Quintero had always been a faithful husband, and never in his dreams would have considered cheating on his wife, though he was lately disappointed in her for several important reasons. First and foremost, Inez was not a beautiful or affectionate woman. She had grown bitter and cynical, and complained often that she missed her family in Mexico.

This had been a sore subject for thirteen years. They had immigrated to the United States shortly after Soila was born. Thomas had been discovered by his current boss, Andy, on holiday in *Baja*. The son of a master craftsman, Thomas loved working with fine wood, which he likened to the skin of a beautiful woman. When Andy had admired a small chest Thomas had built, and asked if it was nineteenth century, the owner of the shop unwisely brought its creator forward to receive his just accolades. Later Andy snuck around back and offered Thomas a job in Los Estados Unidos. Because his skills were so unique, Andy felt certain he could assist Thomas to obtain a work permit and enter legally. Three months later the Quintero family—Thomas, Inez, eight-year-old Alex, and four-year-old Soila—found themselves residing in Cathedral City, two blocks from where Thomas would be working. Inez's aunt followed the next year.

They rented a tiny Spanish-style cottage in a Latino barrio, with a beautiful white clay tile roof and an enclosed yard, all for a price well within their budget at the time. Thomas would fix up the house in lieu of a higher rent, though Andy advised him time after time not to trust his landlord, and sure enough, after the improvements, Sam raised his rent commensurately, but Thomas loved his little house.

Of course, Inez spoiled everything with her disagreeable attitude and complaints. For one, she was incensed by the fact that they shared an alley with a row of businesses, particularly a bar.

But because Inez was so devout, she thought the influence highly negative, and since she was an early riser, the late-night comings and goings, music, laughter, fistfights, and lovemaking in the alley all kept her up. Each morning she woke up surly and withdrawn and only softened the slightest bit as she headed out the door to attend morning Mass at St. Louis Parish.

Thomas couldn't see that she had any reason to complain. He had a plan, a vision for his future, and she, his wife, was lucky to be able to share it with him. It didn't take her long to find work, though in Mexico she hadn't had to. In Mexico she had her own maids, who always quit because her standards were too high and she was far too demanding. Thus, she knew how to satisfy her employers in the United States. She knew what aggravated *La Dona* of a fine house, for she, Inez, had once held such a station.

While his stature improved with the move to *El Norte,* hers had diminished. But Thomas saw a future here, where his son and younger daughter would grow up, return with their own families, and he would live to a ripe old age in his Cathedral City hacienda. Soila, of course, would become a nun, because her birthmark was so disfiguring no one would ever want her.

Because he was *macho,* the fact that Inez could bear him only three children was keenly embarrassing. He thought it reflected badly on him as a potent man. Complications had resulted from the birth of Anita and ultimately the doctors had to perform an emergency hysterectomy. Three would be the limit of their offspring.

Thomas had hoped for a family as large as the one he grew up in. Seven children his mother bore, and without the assistance of a doctor. Inez's body had betrayed his dreams, and now because she seemed listless and ill, it was betraying him again. It had always been their agreement that they would live on his wages and save hers.

Loving Ruby had never been part of his scheme, but there it was anyway. The move north, the well-paying job, the chance to buy a house, and his United States citizenship all cascaded into a sense of entitlement for Thomas Quintero. They were all gifts from God, though he was hardly devout. He attended Mass only on special holidays. And other than Inez, no one was more surprised by Ruby's interest than he.

Ruby was short like Inez, but beautiful and feminine; ten years younger than his wife. They first noticed each other at El Gallito where Ruby started working after her young husband had died in an auto accident. A small insurance policy of five thousand dollars had provided for her immediate needs, but she wanted to work and be out among people. She banked it and got her job at El Gallito.

When she started to flirt with him, he naturally thought she was interested in Alex, because Alex at seventeen looked much older. But to his astonishment and Alex's annoyance, it was Thomas she later admitted she liked. Her old man, she called him.

She had been hurt by the death of her husband, but found solace in the fact that in the way things lined up, she was lucky to be free of him. He was young and immature; driving a delivery truck and had no future as far as Ruby could see. In addition to being extremely attractive—a full head of black wavy hair, a thick lower lip, and huge forearms—Thomas also seemed solid and safe. He had dreams, as did Ruby.

His wife had no dreams in her eyes, no inner stardust, and because of that, Ruby felt entitled to take her husband.

For Thomas, the most attractive and seductive thing about Ruby was her sense of fun. She laughed more than any woman he had ever known. When he made love to her, she talked and stroked his face; giggling and undulating under the weight of his muscular body, stroking his back and tracing out the hollow of his buttocks with her fingernails, all as he pounded away; even making fun of the way he bit his lip and tensed his forehead until finally reaching a simultaneous orgasm, and laughing raucously, Thomas Quintero collapsed on top of her.

When Thomas fucked Inez, she mostly lay like a stump and cried.

Pablo took his seat in the cubicle and realized that he could hear his heart pounding. He first noted a box of tissues within reach of his chair. A pretty picture of a calm sea hung on the padded wall behind the chair where the nurse would sit. Other than the tissue and the picture, the tiny space offered no other personal amenities. He suspected that the desk drawers were probably crammed with pamphlets. He wondered if he'd be offered English or Spanish. He wondered if they even had them in Spanish and then he began to despair about Inez. How would she read her pamphlet in English? His head began to spin.

What if he were positive? What would he tell his mother? His father? He was their only son. How would they cope? How would he cope? He had many acquaintances who had HIV or AIDS. He saw them around Palm Springs and Cathedral City. Sometimes the sick ones would have a lover, or friend, who seemed perfectly healthy and he was always touched by the tenderness he perceived between them.

But he also saw sick, middle-aged men alone, in the market or waiting in line at the Thrifty Pharmacy. Sometimes they leaned on canes. Sometimes their skin was translucent, or ruddy from steroids. Sometimes their bellies were swollen yet they were always hiking up Bermuda shorts because their asses were wasting away. They were lucky if they had a friend to help them. Or a mother.

And Pablo began to quiver just as the door opened. A male nurse entered with his chart. During the past weeks Pablo had gone over and over this moment in his mind. He tried to read the nurse's face to see if he could guess what his results would be, like a sexual defendant waiting to hear what the jury had to say.

Pablo had been free with his beautiful body. It gave him and others enormous pleasure. He had always insisted on safe sexual practices. He learned early on from other hustlers to maintain control of each and every sexual encounter, even if you pretended you weren't. No kissing, no fucking without condoms, no blow jobs without condoms, never come inside— He idly flashed to the encounter in the desert behind his trailer. That was only a fantasy, he wanted to blurt out to the nurse. From watching the film.

He could tell he made the nurse nervous. He was thin and a little effeminate. He wore a wedding ring. His face remained impassive but his hands trembled when he opened the folder. Trembled because he was in Pablo's presence or trembling because he had bad news?

On the drive home they rode in silence, Pablo trying to focus on the road. As they passed the city limit of La Quinta, Inez looked over at him calmly.

"What were your results?"

Pablo didn't answer for a very long time. He looked at her sadly. Inez's chin began to waver.

"I feel so guilty," he broke down, pulling the Jeep to the side of the road. She leaned over and allowed him to hug her, patting his heaving back as he sobbed into her bony shoulder.

"I was worried no one would cry," Inez observed.

17

The Kiss

"Is Kenny having a thing with Maria?"

Nick glanced up from his crossword puzzle. His bifocals were dangling on the edge of his nose. It was just after three and the bar was empty except for Marcella and Nick. The regulars usually started rolling in around four o'clock. This was a favorite time of day for Nick. He liked to pick a sunny booth in the corner of the lounge, eat lunch, drink Campari, and read or do the daily crossword puzzle.

"Now that's ridiculous," Nick snarled at Marcella. "Whatever gave you that idea? You're just trying to start trouble because you're jealous."

"Jealous! Now you're the crazy one! What do I have to be jealous of?" She was drying glasses and putting them back on the mirrored shelf over the bar.

"You're jealous of my relationship with Kenny. You can't stand to see anybody else be happy. You never could."

"I only know what I see with my own eyes. She's a beautiful girl. *More* beautiful after *you* got hold of her. Every pachuco gang member from here to Indio wants to fuck her and she won't give any of 'em the time of day. Who's she holding out for?"

"She's just been through a terrible ordeal."

"She must be mighty grateful for everything Kenny has done for her."

"She's grateful to both of us. She tells me every night."

"But she doesn't look at you the way she looks at Kenny. She never leaves his side. Carmen said Maria ordered the attack on Alex Quintero after he returned Kenny's homemade doll."

"If she did, I'm glad. Alex Quintero had no right to insult Kenny that way. She knows better. It was disgusting what they did to that doll."

Marcella finished stacking the glasses and reached for an empty bucket. "It's created a lot of tension in the alley in case you haven't noticed. Nobody trusts her. They wonder why she's hanging on to Kenny instead of mingling in with her own kind. They even go to church together."

"He drives her. He doesn't go in."

"But they really resent that Maria is aligned with this bar and not with them. Carmen told me so."

"Since when did you and Carmen get to be so buddy-buddy?"

"Since *always*. People always seek out my friendship."

"Oh really?" Nick shook his head.

"I just think it's something you should watch. I bet she doesn't even know you're gay."

The point on Nick's pencil broke.

"Kenny sleeping with you now? Or is he still falling asleep on the couch?"

"He sleeps on the couch because he says I *snore*." Nick was getting really rattled. He picked up his glass and downed his drink. He slammed it down on the bar and Marcella quickly refilled it.

"Maybe you guys should be more affectionate in public." She studied him critically. She knew she had him going. "For a gay couple, you guys are kinda old-fashioned. Except for the arguing."

"We haven't been fighting as much since she moved in," Nick admitted after a long, long silence.

"Hmmm," said Marcella, wiping down the counter. "How much sex do you guys have?"

Nick said nothing.

"I thought so!" cried Marcella. "If you can't see that Kenny is going through a second puberty, I don't know what to tell you. He shaves every day. He wears *cologne*. She's never out of his sight."

Behind them the door to the kitchen swung open. They both turned. Kenny stood in the doorway, his normally unruly hair combed neatly back out of his eyes.

"What?" he asked, after nobody said anything.

They continued to stare.

"I want a kiss," said Nick, slightly slurring his words.

Kenny looked at Nick in amazement.

"What?"

"He said he wants a kiss, baby," Marcella repeated lightly.

Nick studied Kenny hopefully. "Kiss me."

Nick stood up. He was very drunk. He began to make his way along the bar toward the spot where Kenny stood. Marcella watched with hateful pleasure.

Then Maria appeared in the doorway behind Kenny.

Nick stopped in his tracks.

"Hi." She smiled, placing her hand gently on Kenny's shoulder. Then she leaned around him and pecked Nick innocently on his cheek. Nick stared at her hand on Kenny's shoulder. They looked magnificent together.

"Kiss me," Nick said again.

"Maria already did," said Kenny, and he and Maria disappeared into the kitchen.

Sam sat on his usual stool having breakfast at the horseshoe-shaped counter in Michael's Coffee Shop, which was a half a block down from Nick's. Sam watched the sunlight play off the passing cars zipping by on Highway 111. A tinny jukebox churned out a shaky rendition of Gloria Gaynor singing "I Will Survive."

At 7 A.M. the café was already packed with a mixture of local Cathedral City regulars—a few white senior citizens from the small houses up near the Catholic church; some Mexie laborers eating breakfast before heading off to do roadwork or garden at one of the local golf courses; and a few uniformed Cathedral City cops slurping coffee and donuts before starting their daily rounds.

Several athletic-looking gay men entered the café and took a booth behind two cops having breakfast. Sam could see them whisper and giggle as they contemplated the sturdy uniformed backs of Cathedral City's finest. The cops heard them, too, and one of them looked over his shoulder and shot off a look of warning. More gales of laughter. The cops shook their heads and ignored them.

Sam smiled as he watched his favorite waitress walk over to the table of gay men with a fresh pot of coffee. She smirked over their heads at the cops. Sara knew everybody in Cathedral City. These new guys were obviously tourists from the local gay motel, and soon enough she had them laughing and joking and feeling as comfortable as anyone else in the room.

Then Sam's gaze drifted to the row of empty shops across the street from Michael's.

A torn awning flapped in the October breeze. Remnants of a shabby appliance repair store, a Christian Science Reading Room, a tax service, and a small café called Judy's shimmered in the morning sun. Waves of heat wavered up from the blacktop and momentarily caused Sam sufficient dizziness that he had to shield his watering eyes.

When he looked back, the tableau through the window gave him the impression that these old buildings were growing increasingly transparent. Sam rubbed his eyes.

For an instant it was as if Sam could look into the future and see these old buildings gone and him with them. Either that or he was gazing into the past, when the California desert was void of buildings and people and home to sage and insects.

Sam knew the truth. This was the cycle of life. The old days were passing into the new. So it would all be gone. The shifting desert winds would gradually reclaim it all.

Sam Singer had watched the renovation of his Cathedral City properties with mounting anxiety. The paint job and the minor repairs renewed optimism in his tenants that at least his parcel would be there to stay, which was important because Sam's storefront properties and the row of old desert houses were the last vestige of old Cathedral City left standing.

All the old shops across the street had been purchased by Ralph Zola and were scheduled to be torn down. In particular Sam would be sorry to see Judy's go. To Sam, Judy's, like Nick's, was a desert historical landmark. A long narrow room, it offered six padded booths with Formica tops, twelve stools at the counter, and a lone Formica table with shiny chrome chairs sitting in the front window.

Judy was short and blond and very beautiful in a Lana Turner sort of way. She was also cold, with no sense of humor—didn't like to talk and wouldn't tolerate any profanity. The café had always been an after-hours place. Judy only served from midnight till four, even in her heyday.

Years ago Sam and his cronies would close his club and walk across the street to Judy's for breakfast. It was said that Judy, a confirmed spinster and a New York ex-patriot, thought the desert needed a place where revelers could get a hamburger or bacon and eggs and sober up before they went home to waiting wives.

She worked alone, waiting tables, cooking the food, clearing the dishes and washing them by hand, and didn't take another order till she repeated every step. To keep everybody quiet she prepared hot biscuits and coffee in individual thermoses, all ready and waiting at each table before she opened. She operated for twenty-five years, opening only for three nights a week, Thursday, Friday, and Saturday. Finally a Thursday came along and no Judy. No closed sign, no note, just the restaurant waiting pristinely in the darkness.

Sam sipped his coffee and recalled watching big stars wait their turn, just like everybody else. At Judy's in Cathedral City, nobody got preferential treatment, and the gardener was as good as Frank Sinatra.

And now Michael's followed Judy's tradition for service. Sara stood over Sam's shoulder with a hot pot of coffee, saw that he was emotional, and patted his shoulder before moving on.

Although she hadn't been open for years, for as long as Sam and other desert rats could remember, Judy had hired Inez Quintero to maintain the café on a daily basis. Floors were mopped, booths wiped down, windows washed, and the grill oiled. Judy never came to supervise Inez's work. Every morning for years, Sam watched Inez enter the café, raise the blinds, and do her work. Often tourists would stop, thinking Judy was about to open, and tap on the window with their keys till Inez would look up in irritation and mouth the words,

No open!

When? they would respond. *What time?*

And Inez would reply, *Nunca, nunca, never,* then stomp to the window and rudely drop the blinds till finally the hungry visitors would give up and cross the street to Michael's.

Now even Inez didn't show up.

"You seen Inez Quintero lately?" Sam asked as Sara was scrawling out his check.

"I hear she's kinda sick . . ."

"That so?" Sam wondered. "She keeps canceling. It isn't like her. Ruthie's getting concerned."

"Thomas doesn't come in anymore, but I think because he's been working a lot of overtime at the furniture store. He says he's saving to buy his house from you." Sara studied Sam for a long moment. "You made your decision? You gonna sell out, Sam?"

"You mean to Quintero?"

"You know what I mean."

"I'm fixing everything up. Haven't you noticed?"

Sara scrunched up her forehead. She knew he was dodging her question.

"That developer has been in asking questions. He made us a good offer. Don't tell anybody but I think we're gonna accept."

Sam tried to hide his reaction. Now Michael's would be gone.

"At my age it won't be easy to find another breakfast place, Sara." He pulled out his cigars and lit one.

"It's only a matter of time before you get your price, Sam."

"What are you gonna do?" Sam dragged on his cigar. One of the gay men sitting nearby frantically waved away the smoke. Sara shrugged as if there was nothing she could do. "After you sell?"

"Jimmy wants us to retire. We might buy a houseboat up at Lake Havasu. While we're young enough to enjoy it."

"I'm twice your age," Sam blinked. "And I think I'm too young to retire."

"It's somethin' to think about, that's for sure. I'm afraid of getting bored. I figure if it gets to be too much, we'll open a place out there."

"Won't you miss Cathedral City?"

"It won't be the same Cathedral City, even if we hold out. They're building a shopping mall across the street with an ice-skating rink! In the desert, for Chrissakes. Look at the traffic now. Next thing you know they'll take our street parking. How do you fight all that?"

Sam didn't say anything. He didn't know how to fight it or even if he wanted to. He reached for the check. "You gonna come to Nick's grand reopening? Ruthie's coming out of retirement."

"I never heard her sing. Was she good, Sam?"

"She was the best."

"You can count on us," Sara assured him. "Me and Jimmy would love to be there."

"We're fixing it up like the old days. It'll be like walking into the fifties."

"That's what it's like now."

"No. A few movie star pictures don't make it like the fifties. Trust me. I had a much higher standard. There was no place like it."

"Maybe it isn't such a good idea to try to recreate the past."

"Ruthie would never forgive me if at least I didn't try," he said slowly, as if he himself was luckily just coming to that realization now. "Nothing is too good for my wife."

Sam paused as he watched Nick enter the café. He seemed to be looking for someone. When he saw Sam, he nervously came over.

"Sam, I have to talk to you. Can I sit down?"

"Sure," Sam said. Nick slumped onto the stool next to him. Sara offered him a cup of coffee which he took.

"I need some advice."

"Fire away," said Sam. It pleased him to be sought out for his opinions.

"You once offered to help me with my drinking . . . I think it's time I think about quitting."

Sam dragged on his cigar.

"I've told you all along you drank too much."

"Maybe I wasn't ready to pay attention. Maybe something is waking me up." Nick shifted uncomfortably in his chair.

"Things okay at home?"

"Why?" Nick said quickly. "Have you heard anything?"

"I have eyes," Sam observed, but actually he was bluffing. He didn't like to ever admit being the last to know.

"Do you really think he loves her? Don't you think it might just be the attention?"

"You have to ask him."

"I can't. I can't. I couldn't take it if he said it was true. I have to change. To keep him."

"You gotta change to keep yourself."

18

The Opening

The day of Nick's grand reopening, Ralph Zola called Sam Singer to make him an offer on his land. He was looking at his map of Cathedral City which detailed the status of his acquisitions effort. Red tacks pocked the parcels of properties surrounding Sam Singer's quadrant.

The four blocks east of Cathedral Canyon Drive and south of A Street to Grove had all been purchased, with the present owners or occupants in the process of moving or making plans to shortly do so.

This left Sam's parcel, extending north by two blocks to Highway 111, which was now picturesquely renamed East Palm Canyon Drive to unify it with all the desert cities. Cathedral City, so long held in such low esteem by its richer and more prestigious neighbors, was now a full-fledged member of the desert community.

This morning Ralph and the city architects had presented the highly detailed and impressive proposed model for the huge City Hall designated for construction on the north side of Palm Canyon Drive. A ten-story clock tower would be visible from the Interstate, five miles away. A mighty pyramid of stores, restaurants, and theaters, the largest shopping mall in Coachella Valley would inspire desert travelers to leave the freeway and drive to Cathedral City for lunch and ice skating, prior to the hot trip west to the discount surplus stores of Cabazon.

An air-conditioned pedestrian walkway connecting the north and south sides of the Cathedral City mall would permit shoppers to easily traverse Palm Canyon Drive. But the map Ralph examined posed a difficulty that was becoming increasingly imperative to resolve.

Instead of finding more shops, fast-food halls, and an Imax theater, the mall patron would be subjected to a small barrio of Hispanic housing and a sixty-year-old pink bar operated by a flamboyant gay restaurateur. In short, before construction could really begin, Ralph Zola had to come to terms with Sam Singer and decided to give him a call.

"Look, Sam, I know you have affection for the place. The new paint job. Showcasing your wife. You don't have to go to such lengths to impress me. What's your price?"

"I'm thinking of a number between three and five."

"Million?" Zola laughed and hung up the phone.

"Am I making a terrible mistake?" Ruthie demanded of a distracted Kenny when he answered the door. She breezed into the house with a hanging bag, a makeup case, and a shoe box. "You'd tell me if you thought I was. You would, wouldn't you?"

It was decided that Ruthie would dress for her opening night at Nick and Kenny's. Nick had promised to do her hair and makeup and then he, Kenny, and Maria would go on ahead of her.

"You're making a terrible mistake," he smirked at her.

"So what do you know!" She looked around. "Where is everybody?"

"Nick's getting ready. Maria's lying down."

"Wake her up! This is a party. It's our opening night. We owe everything to her! We all changed the day she arrived!"

Kenny winced in reaction to her observation.

"I brought three outfits. I want you all to help me decide. We'll take a vote."

"Where's Sam?"

"He's home taking a nap." She looked at her watch. "Remind me to call him around six. He'll meet me here and we'll drive down together."

Nick emerged from the bedroom. He was dressed in dark brown bell-bottoms and a paisley shirt. Kenny and Ruthie looked at him, aghast.

"What the hell do you have on? Go put on your linen suit. Plain loafers. Nothing crazy, okay?"

"It happens to be the *exact* outfit I was wearing the day Ruthie and Sam eloped."

"They probably eloped just to get away from you."

Ruthie laughed.

"It still fits perfectly." Nick paused in the mirror.

"You know, Nicky," Ruthie began, wanting to be gentle, "Sam's arranged for reporters. There may even be a TV crew. You look great, but maybe Kenny's right. Maybe something a little more subdued."

Nick sighed and stalked down the hall.

"Nicky—I'll change, too, and then you can comb my hair."

Moments later Nick reemerged from the bedroom more sedately dressed in a linen suit. Smirking at Kenny, he marched up to the mirror and flipped up the lapels. Kenny came up behind him and flipped them down.

"Better," he murmured, patting Nick's shoulders. "You look great, Nicky. Big night ahead. I hope they all show for Ruthie's sake."

"What about for *our* sake?" The animation drained from his expression. His eyes were pained. "I miss you Kenny."

"I'm right here."

Maria's face drifted up in the reflection of the mirror between them. She smiled and slipped down the hallway to the bathroom.

"You haven't been the same since Maria arrived, and frankly, I don't think you'll ever be the same again. It isn't her fault or your fault. It's my fault and I know it. I've been drunk for the last ten years. You stuck it out and I appreciate it but I don't know how you justify it to yourself at the end of the day."

Kenny's eyes flickered with irritation. "I don't want to have this conversation now. Not with two hundred dinners to cook."

"I just think you should be prepared," said Nick. "I've had to be. Relationships change. Most of them end. I've been a big-mouth *bore*. You've always gone along with whatever I wanted to do. What are you going to do when you have to make choices for yourself?"

Kenny laughed. "I *want* to be here with you."

"Well, maybe I don't want to be here with you."

"You're drunk."

"You're in love with somebody else, Kenny. Hasn't anybody told you?"

"In love," he said in astonishment.

"With who?" Ruthie echoed. She was barefoot and wearing a slip.

"*Maria,*" Nick retorted.

"Nicky! You're being idiotic," Ruthie observed. "They have a little crush on each other. What's the big deal? We've had a crush on each other for thirty years and you don't see Kenny or Sam griping."

"Yeah, but you and I know who we are."

"We don't have a crush on each other," Kenny protested quietly. What could they possibly be talking about?

"No," Nick observed. "It's gone *way* beyond puppy love. Everybody's talking about it."

"It's like the love a brother and sister have for each other," Ruthie observed. "They bonded out of tragedy. Who *wouldn't?* Now *look,* can we get back to me for a minute? This is supposed to be my night! What do you think of this?" She held up a green pantsuit.

The room resonated with discomfort.

"That bad, huh?"

She disappeared down the hallway into the room where she was changing. Maria emerged from the bathroom and began walking timidly up the hallway toward them. She was wearing jeans and a white T-shirt. Dressed exactly like Kenny.

"Are you ready for our *grand opening?*" Nick asked her brightly. She nodded her head. She stole a glance at Kenny.

"We'd better go," said Kenny. "I guess we'll meet you down there," he said to Nick. The three of them ambled out the front door.

"How do I look?" Ruthie emerged into the hallway in a new outfit. "Hey, where'd everybody go?"

Tonight after dark Inez planned to have Soila help her across the alley to watch Ruthie singing in the lounge like the old photographs on her dressing table. She could see the new marquee from her bedroom window, where she spent most of her time these days.

No one dared ask her the nature of her affliction though she was obviously very ill. The clinic had requested her papers. She had no insurance. Her residency was tenuous. Today had been unforgettable. She could never go to the INS doctor for another blood test now.

As for visits to the free clinic, Inez decided not to return. They gave her bottles and bottles of strange pills. The pills weren't going to save her, although the boy assured they would help. Mostly she decided it would be better to die quickly so Ruby from El Gallito could marry Thomas and the two of them could raise little Anita as their own.

With Inez ill, her aunt old and senile, the care of Anita would fall squarely on Soila. Soila was a good girl. Every day Soila attended church school up at St. Louis where she learned about the saints and the generosity of Frank Sinatra.

Inez knew Soila prayed fervently for her to get better. She worried that her continuing decline would cause Soila to lose faith and stumble, so she always maintained a beatific countenance whenever Soila was around. Tonight Inez was particularly uncomfortable.

Thomas was over at El Gallito visiting with Ruby and Alex was probably down in Indio running with his gang, so Inez felt free to confide in Soila.

She cried when Inez explained everything to her, a response which filled Inez with wonderment.

"Of my children, I love you the most."

"Why, Mommy?" Soila asked her.

"Because we look the most alike."

Soila self-consciously touched her birthmark. "That isn't true."

"As a baby you were affectionate and I knew how clever you would be. I love Alex and Anita but I know they'll be okay in the world without me."

"Are you worried that I won't be okay without you?"

Inez was perspiring so heavily her bedclothes were drenched in sweat.

"Mommy," Soila lamented quietly, "I need to change your gown and your sheets." Soila went to Inez's bureau and pulled out a fresh cotton nightgown. Then she moved to the small linen closet in the hallway near the bathroom and returned with a set of clean sheets.

After helping Inez pull her nightgown over her head, Soila grasped her mother tightly with both arms and eased her onto a nearby chair. Inez sagged tiredly, her head so heavy she could scarcely hold it up. Soila quickly sponged away her perspiration and dried her with a warm towel.

"Lift your arms, Mommy."

"I'm so tired," Inez began to whimper, but she complied, allowing Soila to pull the clean nightshirt over her head.

"Let me make your bed, Mommy. Then you can go back to sleep." And she tore the damp sheets from her mother's bed, briskly remade it, and soon was easing Inez back under her covers.

"You'll wake me later, right? I want to see her sing." Outside in the alley they could hear cars pulling into Nick's parking lot. Car doors slammed, voices conversed, and the muffled sounds of music and laughter came from inside the bar.

"Yes, Mommy, I promise."

"Thank you, Soila. When I'm in heaven, I'll take better care of you." And she rolled over on her side while Soila sat next to her, holding her hand till her mother could fall asleep.

*   *   *

True to his word, Sam saw to it the bar was packed, having bribed a Rancho Mirage Senior Citizen director to bring a busload of Jewish seniors up to Cathedral City for the early bird supper.

Sam's retirees and Nick's regular desert rats made for an eclectic but invigorating mix. Even Father Gene attended, taking a stool at the back of the bar where he could see Kenny working furiously through the portholes. The kitchen would close in thirty-five minutes and then Ruthie would start her first set.

Father Gene watched Nick seating customers, telling old jokes, and working the room like the good old days. He noticed that Marcella, the bartender, kept looking nervously at the clock.

"You worried about the time?" he asked good-naturedly.

"No," she responded so guiltily he wondered what she could be possibly cooking up. She decided to try to make conversation. "So what brings you to the desert?"

"I'm not a tourist. I live here."

"Yeah?" she glanced up at the clock. "What do you do?"

"I'm a priest from your local parish."

"Huh?" Marcella wanted to throw up.

It had been pandemonium in the kitchen. Kenny and his crew worked furiously. Maria worked silently next to him and Kenny allowed himself the mirage that everything would turn out for the best. Nick's would be saved, Ruthie's career would take off, Cathedral City would be preserved in time, and Maria would live with them forever.

And then Kenny shuddered, his entire body firing electrical impulses to his brain. His thinking was insane, crazier than Nick's had ever been. What possible evidence did Kenny have, what *right,* to believe that everything was changing for the better. He'd lived most of his adult life reeling in the tornado force back draft of a practicing alcoholic. When in Kenny's life had he acquiesced to nothing more than purgatory?

Maria reached around him for a saucepan. Her hand grazed the small of his lower back. Startled, he glanced down at her. She smiled up at him, somewhat playfully.

Was he *in love* with Maria as Nick had charged?

He certainly cared deeply for her. She was loving. Exquisitely beautiful. Artistic. Intelligent. Humble. Gentle. Silent . . . Hadn't they bonded by fate, as if each were marionettes in some heavenly play?

"Kenny," he heard her whisper. "Kenny!"

He started out of his silent ranting. She touched his hand.

"What?" he asked her.

"You were talking to yourself," she smirked, somewhat embarrassed for him.

Carmen and Miguel had stopped what they were doing. They, too, watched him, eyes knitting with curiosity.

Kenny smiled briefly into Maria's face, but his eyes were bright, no longer veiled by self-deceit. "It's *true*," he whispered in astonishment.

Quickly she turned away.

Nick entered the kitchen. The whole crew cheered and he waved them off good-naturedly. "Ruthie starts her set in fifteen minutes, and I want all of you out in the bar to welcome her. A news crew is outside!" He grinned breathlessly at Kenny. "They interviewed me in the parking lot!" He ran back into the dining room.

"Okay." Kenny clapped his hands. "Let's wrap it up!" and happily they began to close the kitchen.

Moments later a knock came at the kitchen door. It was Sam and Ruthie arriving for her first set. Ruthie wanted to say hello to Kenny and Maria before she sneaked through the alley to the entrance leading from the parking lot into the lounge. Sam stood proudly behind her. Several times he pulled out a handkerchief to wipe his eyes.

"It's like old times. I can't tell you how nervous I am!"

When Kenny hugged her, her hands were like ice through his T-shirt. Over his shoulder his crew grinned at her approvingly. She'd driven back home and changed into a light blue cocktail dress and matching patent leather pumps. Nick had cut her hair into a glamorous bouffant. Maria never saw anyone look more beautiful.

"This dress is thirty-five years old. I wore it the last night I sang. It still *fits*."

"All you need is a scotch and a cigarette," Kenny mused.

"Honey! This is it. Hug me for luck." She opened her arms for Maria. "We've come a long way since that night on the highway." Maria clutched her tightly. "You brought me so much luck!"

Nick flew back into the kitchen. "Are you ready? I'm just about to make the announcement. You gotta go around to the alley and come from the hallway!" Then he was gone again.

"Let's go, Ruthie." Sam held the door.

"I'm *coming!*" Ruthie assured him, and after another kiss for a laughing Kenny, she disappeared into the alley. He and Maria hurried to the porthole to watch Nick announce Ruthie's entrance. Their hands grazed lightly. To help her see, Kenny put his arm around her waist and pulled her up in front of him, where she teetered on his work boots to give her a better vantage point to see into the dining room.

In the darkened hallway leading into the lounge, Sam held Ruthie while they waited for Nick to announce her set.

"Thank you, Sammy. I love you." She stared nervously up the hallway to the packed lounge.

"I love *you,* Ruthie."

Sam released her and watched Ruthie float up the hall to greet the past.

19

Homily

They were three blocks away, hidden behind a shopping mall at the intersection of Cathedral Canyon Road and Palm Canyon Drive. Misty had just confirmed with a very nervous Marcella that all systems were go. She could tell by the background laughter that the bar was packed, with some woman singing in the background, and the sound of customers ordering drinks.

"It's getting late and people are starting to leave. You gotta come now!" Marcella hissed, covering the receiver. *"I'll be right with you, baby!"* Misty heard her assuage an impatient customer. She came back on the line.

"Remember, no one gets hurt! Just enough fuss to get us in the papers."

"Oh, you can count on us, miss!" Misty screamed hysterically into the telephone. Then she staggered back to the rumbling Mustang and toppled over the side into the front seat.

"Just remember, no one gets hurt!" she mocked Marcella, surveying her companions and squealing with laughter. Logan handed her the bottle of Cuervo.

"Your *mask,* Misty," Drew admonished her and then he maneuvered the muscle car stealthily through the back streets of Cathedral City. When he got to A Street, he cut the lights and the rumbling, trembling car lingered at the mouth of the alley separating the gay bar from the Hispanic barrio of Cathedral City.

"Ladies and gentlemen, back by popular demand, the songs of *Ruth Harris Singer!*"

Ruthie made her entrance from the blacked-out hallway, and when the lights came up behind her, Sam dissolved into tears.

"That's her," he began to clap, cigar hanging from his mouth. "That's my girl."

She made her way through the packed audience of the lounge, smiling and greeting well-wishers. Her accompanist smiled widely from the baby grand Sam had rented for her opening night.

In the background, up against the wall near the kitchen, Nick applauded wildly. Kenny and Maria emerged to stand next to him. Behind them Carmen, Gabriel, and Miguel. Marcella moodily kept watching the clock.

Ruthie's piano player began to play a medley of jazz.

"I want to thank you all for your support tonight. It's been a long time since we got together," she smiled. "Before I get started, I want to say how much I love Nick and Kenny, and the swell job they did in patching the old girl up." Then in mock umbrage she added, *"I'm talking about the refurbished bar!"*

The audience laughed and clapped. Kenny nudged Nick, but Nick refused to acknowledge him. He couldn't take his eyes off Ruthie.

"I have a lot of good memories of this old place," she said to the crowd. "I wish you all could have seen it then. Cathedral City was a small desert town way out in the middle of nowhere. To drive out here from old Palm Springs felt like quite an adventure. It made you feel a little mischievous." Ruthie studied her audience, her jacket sparkling in the spotlight. "Kinda loose and bad. But let me assure you, I was a *good girl* then!

"In those days you never knew who you'd run into out here. That's what made it fun. It could be a movie star or a politician, and if it was, nobody *ever* told. Here in Cathedral City we respected each other's privacy. We didn't ask questions. In those days this place was called Sam's and I ought to know because Sam's the man I married"—she gestured to him—"and years later, well, the rest is history, ladies and gentlemen."

Then the music stopped. The lights went down. Ruthie stepped forward to her microphone and began to sing softly, the lyrics of Sam's favorite song, "Tenderly" . . .

When Soila woke Inez, she was in a deep, deep sleep and was dreaming she had gone to heaven. But instead of looking like Inez, her heavenly form resembled Maria. In her dream she was also pregnant and a beautiful angel told her she was carrying the second Christ child, and Inez felt very relieved.

But then Soila was waking her up saying, *"Mommy, Mommy, you said to wake you, you wanted to hear the lady sing."* Inez nodded wearily.

Inez glanced over to where Thomas usually slept, but Soila shook her head that he hadn't come home again and was no doubt curled up next to Ruby, satisfied that he wouldn't have to die a lonely old man after the SIDA took his wife.

Of course, Thomas didn't know she had the SIDA and didn't want to know because it certainly wouldn't sit well with Ruby. This even Inez could reason, even in her diminished state.

So Soila helped her out of bed, and placed around her shoulders a cotton overcoat with which to hide her nightgown. Then she knelt on the ground and took Inez's slippers and placed them one by one on her tiny feet.

"Are you sure you want to go, Mommy?"

"Sí," Inez wheezed. "I've dreamed of this."

And for some reason Soila found this touching and funny.

So she assisted her mother into the kitchen past the table under which the old aunt lay snoring on her mat.

"Watch Anita." Inez kicked her gently, but the old woman was fast asleep.

Now in the backyard Soila led Inez with her arm around her shoulders, and the two of them stepped gingerly into the alley. It was quiet tonight with the exception of Nick's busy parking lot, and the air was exceptionally still.

"We'll stay for one song," Soila admonished her mother and secretly feared she might faint in the bar. They made their way across the alley without incident and entered the forbidden sanctum of the homosexual restaurant.

Soila was tingling with excitement.

When she opened the door to the lounge, they were greeted with an assault of laughter, music, and smoke. The room wasn't filled with horned devils as Soila had been led to expect. Instead it looked like a church revival meeting, with a hundred people clapping in response to Mrs. Singer.

Soila had only met her twice—once as a little girl when Inez couldn't leave her alone and took her with her to Palm Springs on the bus. It was on a day when Ruthie was in a bad depression, and

Soila had only seen the top of her head, her dirty red hair, stringy and gray at the roots and poking out from the blanket, and Soila ran from the bedroom in terror.

The second time had been only last week, when a beautiful lady in a form-fitting blue dress had stopped her big car in front of their house and came to the door with flowers for Inez.

Soila and Anita were playing on the porch and watched agape as Ruthie walked up the sidewalk toward them. Soila had never seen such a pretty woman before, who smelled like flowers and stroked Soila's hair and, after coming out from speaking to Inez, told Soila to call her if her mother needed anything.

It was that evening Inez announced her plans to hear Ruthie sing, because Mrs. Singer was the only client she had who ever treated Inez like she mattered.

So when the crowd shifted a little and Inez saw Ruthie looking as beautiful as the picture she polished every week in the silver frame, for some reason Inez felt like her life was complete. And to please her even more, Ruthie announced that the next song was for her.

Anita Quintero woke up to discover Soila gone. Looking around her tiny bedroom, she surmised that her sister was probably in the kitchen having something to eat. Anita was hungry too, and thought she'd go inspect. Through the window of her bedroom, she heard music and laughter and was surprised to see her own mother, assisted by Soila, just as they were leaving the bar across the alley.

Pulling a dress over her slip, and sliding into a pair of sandals, Anita decided to join them. Slipping down the narrow hallway past her parents' bedroom, she sneaked through the dining room to the kitchen, being careful not to wake her great-aunt, who lay sleeping on a foam pad under the kitchen table. She was happy to see that the back door was already open.

She slipped though the small backyard to the gate, which was also unlatched. No need to find a box to stand on to unhook it. She opened the gate and peered outside. Her mother was leaning against the wall of the bar, trying to catch her breath. Soila, ever vigilant, was urging her to relax.

Behind them the mixed patronage of Nick's began to filter into the parking lot. Kenny and Maria were just leaving the kitchen, Kenny fiddling with the lock and Maria surveying the busy alley. She suddenly found herself face to face with Inez Quintero and her daughter, the sweet girl with the birthmark.

An uncomfortable silent exchange passed between them.

"Okay," Inez wheezed. "We can go."

Just as they were about to step into the alley, a speeding black convertible rounded the corner, headlights off, and came roaring down the alley. The faces of the occupants were all concealed under grisly Halloween masks, and screaming obscenities at the crowd.

Soila looked up and to her horror saw Anita smiling gleefully at her as she peered out from the gate.

"Anita! *Cuidado!*" she shrieked.

The car sprang toward them. Even at fifty miles per hour in the narrow alley, it all seemed to unfold in slow motion.

When Kenny saw the speeding car at the throat of the alley as they were locking the kitchen door, he pulled Maria into him, twisted around, and pushed her against the wall, shielding her with the entire expanse of his body. He heard the whining of projectiles as red liquid exploded over his head against the wall of the freshly painted bar, raining down upon them. Then a stinging sensation ripped through his back so painfully his body shuddered, and he slid to the ground to his knees.

Still the car approached.

Several yards away, Inez and Soila were screaming at Anita to stay where she was, to go back inside their gate.

"Anita," Inez protested. "*El coche!*"

And the car thundered toward them, just as a grinning Anita took a step into the alley. Then a look of surprise crossed her face, and blood splattered across the front of her white dress.

"Anita!" Soila cried as the car roared past, the occupants, faces covered with hideous masks, screaming ugly words and firing into the crowd with guns. The alley erupted into a cacophony of cries and screams. Over twenty people must have witnessed the assault, older married couples from Sam's Jewish retirement home, a few gay men on their way to the dance clubs, neighboring Latinos hanging in the alley because it was too hot inside their houses—and now many had been shot and were crying hysterically as the marauding car roared around the corner and drove off into the darkness.

In the din, Inez and Soila could see Anita lying facedown on the pavement in a pool of red liquid, just as Thomas Quintero rounded the corner, coming home from his evening at El Gallito. He was hurrying across the highway because he'd seen the black Mustang leave the alley, and heard all the commotion behind Nick's.

"*Anita!*" Soila screamed again, and Thomas saw the body of his little girl as she lay crumpled in a heap outside his gate.

Maria, too, thought Kenny had been shot.

"*Help us!*" she screamed in terror. "*Help us!*"

The alley began filling with occupants from the houses and the remainder of the patrons from the bar, all responding to the screams for help.

Inside the lounge, Nick and Ruthie sat at the bar drinking Perrier served by a very nervous Marcella.

"Your hands are shaking," Nick observed. "Why do you keep looking at the clock?"

"I have a date," she shrugged. "He was already supposed to be here by now." She was very nervous.

Ruthie and Nick were too happy to notice. The night had been utter perfection for both of them. The reporter from the *Desert Sun* was sitting in a quiet booth at the front of the restaurant interviewing Sam, who was glowing from the obvious success of the evening.

Father Gene, sitting unnoticed at the end of the bar, was eavesdropping.

"Word on the street has it that you aren't being totally sincere— that you only want to give the impression that Cathedral City isn't for sale. How do you respond?"

"This place has been my life for fifty years," Sam observed calmly. "My own wife will be performing here Thursday, Friday, and Saturday nights. I just spent nearly eighty thousand dollars fixing it up."

And then came the sounds from the alley.

First screaming and crying. The unmistakable running of feet. The bar began to flood with people. An older man and his wife came first.

"Kids in a car! Shooting. My wife has been shot!" and he led her to a booth, a pretty old lady had a red splotch across her dress, doubled over in pain. Behind them came many others, and soon the lounge was filled with agitated patrons and neighbors, all calling for help.

"Call 911! *Call 911!*"

Marcella stood frozen behind the bar, unable to believe her eyes. When she didn't react, Nick ran around the bar and punched out the numbers himself.

"They were shooting people?" she kept asking over and over to herself. Then she hugged herself and sank to the floor behind the bar. Then Kenny came through the kitchen, assisted by Maria, and Nick thought he was going to pass out.

"It's paint!" Kenny shouted when he saw the look in Nick's eyes. "They were shooting paint pellets! Fucking goddam kids. Fucking goddam monsters." And Maria winced from his anger as she surveyed the room and wondered what kind of place Cathedral City really was.

And as sirens became audible in the distance, Thomas Quintero's voice could be heard outside, and then he and a band of Latino men charged into the bar, his son Alex among them.

"*This is all your fault!*" He shook his finger at them. "They shot my little girl!"

"What?" Nick asked.

"They shot her! She was coming out of the house, looking for her mother, and they shot her! *Jotos!*" He wailed in anguish.

"But it's only paint," Marcella protested. "They weren't real bullets!"

"*Negros!*" he cried, his imperious gaze falling upon her.

"Hold your horses! " Sam tried to calm him.

"*Judios!*" Thomas ranted. "Better it should have been one of you!" And his small army of men nodded in sinister agreement.

"Better it should be no one," Father Gene corrected him.

"*You'll all pay!*" Thomas hissed at them and the angry horde ambled from the bar with the exception of Alex, who lingered menacingly and after a moment disappeared up the ramp to the parking lot.

Later that night Kenny paused in the darkened alley and stopped to smoke a cigarette. After the assault the police arrived, along with camera crews tipped off by the reporter and photographed a sullen Kenny and a hysterical Nick, trying to explain what had happened.

Tonight when Kenny drove Maria home, he flipped on the local news to see all of them on TV, including interviews with a few of the Latino neighbors stating that the overt nature of the bar attracted the trouble, that they were quiet and observed their customs quietly.

"Are you saying the customers who frequent the bar haven't been the best of neighbors?"

"Yes," the interviewee nodded. Kenny recognized him from a house several streets above near the church. "That's what I'm saying, see, sometimes late at night I seen 'em having sex in the alley, you know, out in the open and everything, like they don't care whose looking or nothing."

"And you think that's what's creating the tension here in Cathedral City?"

"Like maybe it's part of it. I dunno, some of 'em are okay, but sometimes I think they're asking for it."

"Asking for this kind of attack?"

"Like maybe if they'd blend in a little more."

"Be more discreet?"

"Yeah. That."

And then they interviewed Sam Singer.

"These charges that my tenants deserve to be assaulted is complete and utter bullsh*t." Sam got beeped out. "This was nothing more than a dignified gathering for the reopening of a very important desert nightclub. It isn't a gay restaurant, or a Jewish restaurant, or an Italian restaurant, or a Mexie restaurant."

"Mexie?" the reporter queried cautiously.

In the background Kenny and Nick cringed as they watched him.

"I mean that with the greatest of affection. You ask anybody who knows me. I don't have a prejudiced bone in my body, see? I rent to all kinds of people. Gays, Mexies, I mean Mexican-Americans, whites, you name it. This assault was more than juvenile delinquents out for a joyride. These kids were tipped off and paid to cause some trouble."

"What are you claiming?" the reporter pressed him. "This was a premeditated assault which some person or group paid for?"

"Well, yeah—sure. We planned a nice event. My wife was headlining—coming out of retirement, she's a great singer, a beautiful girl. We were packed with nice folks from all walks of life. Everybody had a good time. Then bingo, just as we were wrapping up, these kids drive up with their paint guns and dirty mouths. In Halloween masks! They shot an old lady and a little girl! Oh, someone picked up the tab, you bet they did."

"Who, sir? Do you have any suspicions?"

"I know exactly who's behind it, and so does he. It's no secret my property is valuable, see? How can they redevelop downtown Cathedral City with my property square in the center of it?"

"Have you had offers to buy you out?"

"Insulting offers. Only two months ago I was threatened if I refused to sell. And I can promise whoever was behind this that I'll *never* sell. They'll have to kill me first."

"Anything you'd like to say to the perpetrators of this crime?"

"Yeah. Come back. Next time I'll be waiting."

"What do you say to the charges that this was a result of inappropriate behavior by some of the gay patrons of the bar."

"There has never been any dirty goings on in or behind the bar. It isn't a gay bar, can't you get that into your heads? It's a neighborhood bar! Got it?"

"I got it," the newswoman smiled, turning back to the camera.

In the moonlight the red paint splotches looked like the ghastly remnants of some bloody gangland massacre. Kenny's eyes glistened as he remembered seeing Anita Quintero being rushed to the hospital in an ambulance while Inez wailed and Ruthie and her daughter Soila tried to console her. Even in the horror of the moment, Kenny had been struck by how thin and dissipated Inez was. He'd had no idea that she was ill. Now he was filled with shame.

Tonight after it quieted down, after the police reports, the TV interviews, when everyone who wanted to reconvened in the lounge, Nick went around the bar and poured himself a drink.

Marcella had been especially shaken. Convulsing silently into a napkin until a dubious patron offered to drive her home. Shortly thereafter, Sam and Ruthie left, Ruthie filled with such sadness she couldn't be consoled.

"You'll be back tomorrow," Nick cajoled her. "You were great tonight. Nothing changes that."

In a moment Sam and Ruthie drove away.

Finally it was Kenny, Maria, and Nick sitting alone in the bar.

Maria's face was ashen and betrayed her discomfort about intruding on them. She hung off to the side while Kenny tried to keep Nick calm, but the bottle was out, Nick was on a bender, and Kenny decided it would be better to take Maria home.

"Come with us," he said to Nick. "You can drink at home."

"I want to stay *here!*"

"It isn't safe here."

"It isn't safe at home *either,*" Nick affirmed, shooting a bitter glance at Maria.

"I'll take her home and be right back."

"You don't need to come back."

"I'm coming back," Kenny said, and then to Maria, "Wait in the kitchen, okay?"

A stricken Maria lingered. "Nick, I never meant to cause trouble in your house. You've been so wonderful. I love you."

Nick looked dolefully into his glass. "I know you do, dear," he said gently.

She disappeared into the kitchen.

"I'll be right back." Kenny patted his shoulder.

"Yeah."

When Kenny came into the kitchen, Maria was hanging by the door to the alley. She looked up guiltily.

"I don't need to go to your house, Kenny. I can stay somewhere else!"

"No, you can't. Tonight you'll stay in your own room like last night and the night before."

"I don't sleep in my room, Kenny," she said softly, tacitly reminding him of their nightly sleeping ritual.

"Maria," he said pleadingly. "Tonight I need to know you're safe at home. I don't want you to go anywhere else. I want you home. I want Nick home and I want to go home. Everything is so confusing. So horrible. Please let me take you home and then I have to come back. I need to be with Nick now."

"I understand, Kenny," and a huge tear formed and fell down her cheek to the ground.

When Kenny came back, Nick was gone, the door to the restaurant was unlocked, and Kenny was surprised to see Father Gene sitting in the darkened lounge. Only the green neon light from a beer logo illuminated the room. He was dressed in street clothing. He looked like any fit older man, sitting in the bar having a cocktail.

"The door was unlocked. I just let myself in."

"You mean, 'back in.' "

"You saw me earlier."

"Yes."

"I remember Mrs. Singer. I wanted to be part of it. It felt like the old Cathedral City in here tonight."

"Hmm . . ." Kenny shrugged. "I'm looking for Nick. His car's in the back but he isn't."

"That would be because I took his keys." Father Gene held up Nick's key ring. He pushed them to the center of his table. "He was too drunk to drive. I offered to drive him but he thought it was a nice night for a walk. Said he had to think a few things over."

"I'll bet."

Father Gene swiveled around on his bar stool to address Kenny.

"Listen, son, I've been thinking about my previous admonishment to you. In light of recent events, I want to invite you back to the church as you are, to worship with us—"

Kenny started to laugh.

Father Gene felt ridiculous.

"No offense, Father, but I only borrow your building to pray."

Father Gene decided to try a different tack. "What happened all those years ago? Were you a seminary student? Is that it? Conflicted about your sexual orientation? That's so common, I know many young men who consider the priesthood thinking it's an honorable escape from desires they don't understand, or fear recrimination for—"

"You think I was studying to be a *priest?*" Kenny was incredulous.

"I assumed as much. I was guessing perhaps you met Nick as a theologian—"

"And he seduced me away from the church?"

"Well," Father Gene hypothesized, "to put it more gently, helped you come to terms with your sexuality."

"So you have this image of me wearing a cassock with theology books under my arm, and one day Nick comes into the sanctuary to light a candle, and bingo, he's giving me a blow job in the confessional?" Kenny roared with laughter.

"I guess I was wrong."

"That might be your story, but it sure isn't mine."

Father Gene stood up. Stung. This wasn't the sensitive, erudite young man he supposed Kenny to be. Now he was mocking and crude.

"We weren't talking about me," Father Gene chided him gently.

"Maybe we should. You're on my turf now. This is my church. Would you like to see my altar? I keep it in the kitchen and we light candles all day." Kenny marched to the door to the kitchen and threw it open. Behind him Father Gene could see a candle illuminated in the darkened room.

"We pray for safety in the alley. Pray for peace with our neighbors. Pray not to forget the ones we love who are gone. We pray *a lot* for forgiveness. Pray for clarity. No curve balls today, Heavenly

Father, *please*. But you know," Kenny observed cynically. "Mostly we don't ask for anything. We're just glad to be alive and know God but we're too disgusting to come to church."

Kenny allowed the door to swing closed. It swung back and forth until it settled uneasily on its hinges. He walked over to Father Gene's spot at the bar. Passion fired in his eyes. He looked magnificent in a terrible, frightened sort of way.

"Tell you what? I'll make you a sandwich if you'll confess all your demons. Deny those you love. You can come to this church anytime you want for sustenance, if you'll *just follow my rules*. You can listen to cabaret music. Have a drink. You can enjoy the company of other men like you. It's not such a stretch so far, is it, Father Gene?" He raised an angry finger to Father Gene's face. "Just turn your back on the man you love."

Father Gene finished his drink. He fumbled in his pocket for a few dollar bills. He was so rattled his hands were shaking.

"Forget it. It's on me." Kenny's eyes flickered with shame. He put his hand on the wrist of the priest. Father Gene looked up at him wildly. Kenny released him.

"I retire at the end of the year. I thought maybe I'd get off scott-free. You've changed all that."

"I have that effect on people. It's been quite a curse."

Father Gene nodded and moved toward the open door. "You know where to find me, son." He disappeared into the dark alley behind the bar.

Later Maria lay in her bed, alone in Nick and Kenny's house. The last twenty-four hours held more violence than she ever could have imagined in a thousand different lifetimes. It was windy, a hot Santa Ana wind blowing in from the west, and the air in her room felt parched and dirty.

That night she dreamed about her mother, who assured her that everything was progressing according to God's plan. She urged her to continue to say her rosary, go to Mass, and confess her sins to the priest. In time her anguish would diminish, her confusion fade. She must always remember that they were watching her, and although they could not alter the future, they could safely assure her that she indeed would survive.

Later she heard the front door open and knew by the polite precautions being taken not to disturb her that Kenny had come home without Nick. He turned on a light in the living room which flooded gently under the door to her room.

Moments later soft classical music began to play. She wanted to get up, go sit with him, but now she didn't know if he wanted her company.

She heard the sound of the living room sliding glass door, which opened onto the patio out by the pool area. She knew he would go out and smoke a cigarette, maybe sit with his jeans rolled up, his feet soaking in the shallow end of the swimming pool. And then he would study the lights of the desert cities, far off in the distance, as brilliant and lovely as a thousand new ideas, a thousand fresh starts.

And soon she was getting out of bed, pulling on her robe, thrusting her feet into thongs, and wandering hungrily down the hall. Sure enough, one old lamp with a green lamp shade was illuminated in the corner by his workbench.

The lights from the CD player flickered as she passed it, and cello music echoed her footsteps after she lingered momentarily at the open terrace door. She knew he sensed her presence. His shoulders tightened under his T-shirt, his head dropped to his hands, and he began to massage his temples with his callused fingertips.

Maria had had ample time to study his hands and fingers while they'd worked side by side over the grill, where cuts and burns were commonplace—and then later as she watched him carve and paint his dolls.

Now he dropped his hands from his head to his lap. He turned.

"I woke you."

"No, Kenny, I couldn't sleep."

"I don't blame you."

"Is Nick all right?"

"He's punishing me. Come and sit next to me."

She moved hesitantly across the patio floor and kicked off her sandals. Then she hiked up her robe to her knees and stepped into the water next to him. When she sank down to sit next to him, she modestly left several inches between them. He reached over and took her arm, pulling her next to him, close against his body.

She looked at him wonderingly but didn't resist.

For a moment they sat without saying anything and meditated on the sound of the pool pump, the noise of the water lapping against tiled pool walls. Then Kenny put his arm around her, at first stiff and uncomfortable, and then his grasp relaxed. After several moments he turned slowly to look at her, his gaze searching her face with hesitation, then without wavering.

"On the news they were saying we asked for it. But for as long as I can remember, Nick was always getting beaten up. When I met him, he was more discreet. You know the word? Discreet?"

Maria shook her head.

"Uh, lemme see, it means downplayed. Quiet. Reserved."

"Like you?"

Kenny smiled. "Maybe. More like you."

"Nick was like me?"

"No," he laughed. "He was never like you. But later he got a whole lot more exaggerated. As the drinking kicked in. When he got afraid of getting older. He felt it all slipping away. So he dressed more eccentrically. Maybe not to him. He was just wearing his old clothes. Sixties clothing in the eighties. People didn't get it. I got it. Some of the customers got it. But the local kids—they didn't get it at all. They were afraid of it. Hated it. Hated him because he was different."

"And you?"

"I always thought he was the best. If you needed five dollars, Nicky would give you ten. I can't tell you how many people borrowed money and never had to pay it back. Last year when we were really broke, no one would even call him back. We wouldn't have made it this long if it wasn't for Sam and Ruthie. Tonight was supposed to be a second chance. Sam'll sell for sure now."

"Sell?"

"The restaurant."

"I thought you owned the restaurant."

"We own the business. He owns the property. We rent from him."

"Oh," Maria said, adding plaintively, "You must feel so bad, Kenny. Nick must feel so bad. Maybe we should go get him."

"I tried to find him."

"I can help."

"No you can't. And you know what? You know what makes me really sad?" Kenny's eyes glistened. "I can't help him either."

The following morning Kenny woke up alone on the living room couch to the sound of a ringing telephone. The clock on the mantel read 8:37.

"Hello . . ."

"Kenny?"

"Nicky? Where are you?"

"I've checked into Betty Ford."

Kenny sat in his shorts on the stoop of the patio. He cradled the phone in the crook of his neck and began to pound his head. "What do you think you're doing?"

"I'm *trying* to get well. Nothing else matters."

"Nothing else?" Kenny's voice grew shrill and he tried to calm down. "I don't matter? The bar? The people who work for us? We all don't matter?"

"My counselor told me you'd try to make me feel guilty and it won't work. Not this time."

Kenny held the phone away from his ear and bit his lip to keep from screaming. "Okay, okay. Let's start over. Number one, are you physically okay?"

"I got arrested last night. For *drunk and disorderly* conduct. I was walking home. Cops stopped me two blocks from home for peeing in a cactus. They took me to Indio. Said if I checked into rehab, they'd get the charges forgotten. So I'm *here.*"

"In Betty Ford."

"It's an *amazing* program."

"How much is it going to cost?"

"It's taken care of."

"Wait. How?"

"They told me you'd put a *damper* on it. They *warned* me—"

"Hey—no. Don't you do this to me! Not after last night. Not after what we have to face today! We have no money. Those hospital programs cost at least ten thousand dollars and I know our insurance won't cover it. What did you sign?"

"I—"

"What did they make you sign? Did you put up the house?"

"I need to get sober."

"Did you put up our *house?* The house now, too? I have to cosign! They can't put a lien if I don't cosign. You put 'em on! You put them on!" Now Kenny was screaming and Maria ran from her bedroom down the hall into the entry hall.

"I'm in here," Nick said firmly. "I'm staying here for the whole duration of the program and I will make payments when I get out."

"How much is it?"

"Twelve thousand dollars a month. I'm committing to a ninety-day program." Nick hesitated while Kenny gasped. "I'm dying, Kenny," his voice broke. "I can't do AA."

"What do you think Betty Ford *is?* You're paying thirty-six thousand dollars for a Big Book. Lemme talk to someone."

Nick held the phone away from his mouth and said, "It isn't going well. He wants to talk to you. This is Betty. She gave me a ride over."

"Hello?" A gentle female voice came on the line.

"Who is this?" Kenny demanded.

"It's Betty . . ."

Kenny stared at the receiver. "You mean, *the* Betty? Betty *Ford?* Is this some kind of a joke? "

"No, I'm not Betty Ford. My name is Betty *B."*

"Betty *Bee?* What kind of last name is Bee?"

"I don't give my last name. AA is a program of anonymity. Now what seems to be your concern?"

"My concern is that he can't afford it. He's put up our house as collateral, half of which belongs to me. My concern is that our business is failing and that without him it most certainly finally will!"

"Your friend is quite ill. I think he's trying to save his life."

"Put him back on."

She covered the phone and whispered to Nick. Then he came back on the line.

"I'm not coming out for ninety days." Nick said flatly. "Family visitations are on Sundays at one. I'll put you on the list. Come if you *want."*

And he hung up.

Kenny looked at Maria, tried to speak, shook his head, and threw up his hands. "I have to get ready for work."

"I'll get ready too," she nodded.

When Kenny and Maria arrived, Sam Singer was supervising several neighborhood boys whom he'd hired to paint out the damage from last night. They were working furiously while he sat in his air-conditioned car, listening to the radio with cigar smoke floating in clouds above his head.

When Kenny and Maria pulled up in the open-air truck, Sam unlocked his door and got out.

"You're late," he said, chewing on his cigar.

"You're lucky I'm here at all."

Sam scrutinized Kenny as if estimating his mettle. He hitched up his trousers. He dragged on his cigar. "You throwin' in the towel here?"

"I wanna know what to expect, Sam. You gonna sell me out? If you are, I'm throwing in the towel. If you're gonna stand up for us, I'll stay. I'll work as hard as I have to if I can count on you. But I want a lease. None of this thirty-day-notice bullshit. And another thing. Nick's out of the picture. He signed himself into Betty Ford and that's where he's staying. So don't count on him. And another thing," he said for the benefit of the Latino painting crew who all lived in houses opposite the bar. "I want a town meeting. I want everybody who lives in the alley to agree to watch out for each other. If they won't, if we're gonna have more fighting, more name calling—then it's just as well if you sell the whole damn parcel out."

As Kenny's voice rose, neighbors began to peer over their fences, wondering what all the ruckus was about.

"It's nothing but fighting and yelling here lately," said a young kid, opening his gate and peering warily into the alley.

"You have anything against me?" Kenny demanded of him.

"No, you hired my cousin."

"That's right. Your cousin Hector. He was our dishwasher when no one else would hire him. He was a good worker after all. He made enough money to go back to help his family in El Salvador."

Kenny looked around. More faces popped up over their fences. He stepped back to his truck and reached inside, blasting the horn three times.

"Now what are you doin' here?" Sam demanded. "That's my signal to collect rents. They're gonna think something's wrong."

"Something is wrong." Kenny defied him and blasted his horn three more times.

Sam glowered as he watched representatives from each of his houses begin to open their gates.

"*Que tal?*" they asked.

"What's he want now?" they wondered.

Kenny turned back to Sam Singer. "You gotta tell them you aren't selling their houses, Sam. You can't commit to me if you don't commit to them. They're worried. I hear it up at the church. They see their friends being displaced and wonder if it's going to happen to them. So let's have it. Are you selling us out or not?"

"Aw, this ain't fair."

"None of us think it's fair either."

"He told my father he'd sell him his house," said Soila Quintero, who was listening from behind her fence but was afraid to come out. This caused tenants from the other houses to begin to murmur.

"Now this has gotten way outa hand. I don't have to stand for this."

"We all just want to know, Sam. If you'd been up front, last night would never have happened. They wouldn't have tried to force your hand."

"I'll tell you when I'm good and ready!" Sam blustered. Then under his breath, *Goddamned cocksucker. Fucking Spics."*

"We'll be here waiting." Kenny folded his arms. Maria climbed out of the truck and came over to stand by him. Sam trudged over to the Mark IV, opened the door, and climbed in. He was trembling so badly when he went to lit his cigar, he forgot he already had one in his mouth.

During the homily of his Mass the following Sunday, Father Gene elected to appeal to the community spirit of the members of his congregation.

"Some of you think it's the customers who patronize Nick's who attracted the trouble which came to Cathedral City. That's wrong! The patrons of Nick's were just an easy target because they're perceived as different. Because they won't hide in the shadows. Just like many of you have always been easy targets."

Many in the crowd began to nod and whisper.

"Many of you, or your parents or grandparents, came across the border, worked hard, paid taxes, wanted a better life. Some of you were only coming back to the land of your ancestors when California belonged to Mexico!

"Now politicians call *you* parasites. In California! They even want to build a big wall to keep you in Mexico. They don't think your children deserve health care. Or schools. They think you don't contribute to the economy. They don't know what it's like to be sick and not be able to see a doctor. What do you do first when your kids are sick? Look at your green cards? They think you expect everything for free. Are they right?"

They all looked at him, stupefied.

Finally a few began to shake their heads.

"Now they want to take the houses and the businesses which share the alley and tear it down. They want to build a big shopping center. With movie theaters, ice-skating rinks, and stores. That sounds real nice, but they don't want you to shop there. It's for them! They don't care what happens to the less affluent Latino residents of Cathedral City. Or the gay ones who only frequent bars and restaurants in Cathedral City, which were built here originally because it used to be they weren't allowed inside the Palm Springs city limits.

"And they like to see you all fighting. Bringing each other down. It makes it easier for them. They can just stand by and wait. Which is the main point of my message to you today. We all have more in common than you think. It's okay to say *anything* against an undocumented Hispanic, and they think all of you *are,* by the way—just like it's okay to beat up gay men and women, call them derogatory names—deny them constitutional protection.

"Did you ever think you had so much in common with another minority group? I'm talking about basic human rights. What if I told you that you were so repulsive to God by your very nature that you weren't welcome to take Holy Communion. I told a gay man that very thing only a while back and I'm very ashamed of myself now.

"All of us are neighbors in Cathedral City.

"And it seems to me that if we promise to try to be better neighbors, we deserve the same thing in return. If they come again and we stand together, they won't come back. If we don't stand together, they won't need to come back. We'll already be gone."

The crowd ruminated over what he had to say. Finally, Soila Quintero stood up. She was seated alone in the back pew of the church.

"But what if Mr. Sam wants to sell?" Soila asked from her chair. "It's his property, no?"

"Mr. Sam doesn't like to be told what to do," said Father Gene. "Nobody does. But I think if you tell him you like where you live, that you don't want to move, that you love Cathedral City—I think he might understand how you feel. Now all of us have to go to work. Help clean up the mess. Start over if we can. The owners aren't here, but I know them. I know they'd want me to convey that you're welcome at their club. That's why we call it a neighborhood bar."

He paused, surveying the sea of brown faces. "This is the Word of the Lord.

"The Word of the Lord stands forever."

PART THREE

The Inheritors

20

Nicky

Pablo lingered outside the kitchen door. He had just been to visit Inez and wanted to say hello to Maria. He didn't want to run into Kenny. He still felt embarrassed to see him, but sure enough, Kenny was alone in the kitchen.

"Hey." Pablo nodded through the screen.

Kenny nodded back. He went to the door and opened it for him, ushering him in.

"So how's things?"

Kenny laughed. How could he begin? He was glad to see Pablo. "How about with you?"

"I want my old job back. I want another chance." Then Pablo laughed. "That's not what I was planning to say. Sorry, I don't know what I can be thinking. I'll take off."

"You can have your job back."

Pablo studied him. "Yeah?"

"Start tonight if you want to. I need your help. In case you haven't heard, Nick is out for a while. I'm running the whole show. I could use an experienced waiter."

Maria appeared behind Kenny in the door. She was lugging a crate of lettuce. Kenny moved to take it from her, but she resisted him and put it on the cutting board next to the sink. She looked up and noticed Pablo.

"Hey! You came back!" She moved to kiss him on the cheek.

"You know each other?" Kenny asked.

"He was my boy friend in Mexico."

"*What?*"

"I'm joking, Kenny. Can't we tell a joke around here? Does it always have to be so sad and serious?" She was trying to be light but she had a point to make.

"I suppose not." Kenny shrugged. "He starts tonight."

In the months that Nick was absent, Kenny and Maria ran the restaurant. To the great umbrage of Kenny's kitchen crew, particularly Carmen, Kenny placed Maria in charge of the kitchen. Gabriel, usually happy-go-lucky, was nevertheless bitter that the years of his hard work standing next to Kenny at the grill could be dismissed in favor of a young woman with so little experience.

"With Nick gone, I'm going to have to work up front." Kenny explained to his crew. Then he dropped a bombshell. "Gabriel. Tonight I want Maria to work the grill."

Gabriel looked from Kenny to Maria. Maria's expression was passive. "Okay. I'll teach her."

"I've been teaching her at home. She knows what to do."

Miguel whistled involuntarily on Gabriel's reaction.

"But Kenny. Where am I gonna work?"

"Santiago called in sick today." Santiago was the busboy and the dishwasher. "Why don't you wash dishes?"

"But why does he have to wash dishes?" Carmen asserted. "He works next to you."

"Because I want Maria to learn as much as she can about the kitchen."

"We all start by washing dishes," Gabriel pointed out. "She never washed dishes."

"No," Carmen agreed. "Never."

"I can wash dishes, Kenny," Maria volunteered. She touched Kenny's hand. "It's better."

"No," Kenny said firmly. "I want you to work the grill." He contemplated Gabriel. Hurt, Gabriel complied. Shamefaced he moved to the sinks.

Carmen studied Maria with daggers in her eyes. Stalwartly Maria took her position.

"Good, it's settled." Kenny moved to the door to the dining room. He was dressed in a polo shirt and a pair of khakis. He peered through the porthole to the dining room. He looked back at Maria for encouragement. Greeting the public was the last thing he felt prepared to do.

She smiled. Kenny stepped into the dining room.

When he was gone, Maria glanced around the kitchen to take a poll of her coworkers. Her trepidation about assuming authority vanished as the door swung back and settled in the closed position where it creaked slightly on its hinges and came to a rest.

"Turn on the radio," Maria told Carmen.

Carmen shook her head. "You don't tell me what to do."

"Yes, I do." Maria glared at her defiantly. Shrugging like she wanted to listen to music anyway, Carmen reached up and Spanish music played softly overhead.

"*Mojada . . .*" Carmen muttered.

"You *what?*" Marcella had just snorted a line of cocaine and thought she must be tweaking. Her drug use had increased since the debacle of the alley, because it was the only way she could mask her guilt. Now Kenny was standing at the doorway from the kitchen dressed like some golf pro for Christ's sake. "You hate people. You don't know the first thing about making people feel comfortable."

Pablo was setting tables with the help of his new busboy, Gabriel. "This coming from the rudest bartender in the desert," he observed.

"I am *not* rude," Marcella said. "I'm efficient. There's a difference."

"Never-the-less," said Kenny, "I'll be watching the door while Nick's out."

"Watching the door do *what?* Have you looked around? I don't exactly see any customers and it's nearly five o'clock. I can't live on these tips."

"Then you can live on what you've stolen for a while," Kenny observed.

"Now *look!*" she began. "If Nick were here, he would *never—*" but before she could continue, the door swung open and a few young guys wandered into the lounge.

They stood still while their eyes adjusted to the light. "You open?"

"Sure," Kenny said. "Drinks or dinner?"

"Just drinks for now." The older one sized Kenny up. He obviously found him attractive. His friend snickered and led him to the bar. They ordered two Bud Lights. Shortly thereafter another car pulled into the parking lot. More young men came in.

They stood at the entry near the bar and looked around.

"This the place where they had all the trouble last month?"

"Yeah." Kenny shrugged.

"We read about it in the *Advocate*. They photocopied the article and plastered it all over the hotels in Palm Springs. We came to show our support."

"Thanks," Kenny said.

Marcella and Pablo exchanged a look of amazement.

"You Nick?" one of them asked.

"*No,*" said Marcella sarcastically from the bar. "He can never be Nick."

They studied Kenny questioningly.

"I'm Kenny. I'm Nick's partner. Nick's out sick."

"If he's your partner, why'd you let him name it Nick's?"

Pablo chortled good-naturedly behind Kenny. He clapped him on the shoulder. Kenny stiffened, uncomfortable with the banter.

"Kenny's always been more of a *silent* partner," said Marcella.

"Yeah, but that's beginning to change," Kenny asserted. "You guys want a drink?"

The two men smiled affably. "Sure. Can we buy you one?"

Kenny shifted. He didn't know what to do.

"Tell 'em yes," Pablo whispered.

"Yes," said Kenny. He wandered nervously over to the curve in the bar and motioned for them to sit down, which they did. Then he sat down, missing his stool. Marcella guffawed from behind the bar. Pablo and the two customers all scrambled to help him up.

Red-faced, he pulled himself to his feet. They dusted him off. Pablo offered him a stool and Kenny sat down. He looked with longing toward the kitchen door. The two customers nudged each other good-naturedly.

"You seem a little nervous," one of them observed.

"We won't bite," allowed his friend, the one who had initially admired Kenny. "Unless you ask us to." Then everybody laughed. Pablo watched from a distance in case Kenny got into more trouble. Marcella was as nervous as a rat in a coffee can. Nothing could be worse than Kenny working the front of the restaurant. For starters, he didn't drink much. Curiosity might get the better of him. He'd want to know more about liquor inventories, how you make drinks. He'd start to watch her pour, and count the number of bottles behind the bar. He'd figure out she'd been stealing, which he suspected already, but never had been sophisticated enough to prove.

The two men each ordered vodka stingers. After she'd served them, Marcella stood insolently in front of Kenny. "I don't think I ever saw you drink. What'll you have?"

"I'll have a whiskey." Kenny smiled at her. He'd never had a scotch before and he'd always wondered what it was like.

"A whiskey and *what*," Marcella asked him.

He looked at her blankly.

"Neat, rocks, with water, soda? How do you want it, baby? You gotta know these things if you think you can manage a bar."

"How do I want my whiskey?" he asked Pablo.

"Marcella takes hers with a splash of sour grapes," Pablo smirked at Marcella.

The regulars, frightened away by the fear of violence, were quickly replaced by younger locals and tourists who wanted to send a message and support the bar. Not only gays, but hipper straights who'd heard about the historical background of Nick's and wanted to time-trip and hear stories about the past.

Lastly, old fans of Ruthie's, wealthy retired snowbirds from Canada and back East who heard she was singing at the old location in Cathedral City came in expecting a worse-for-wear old lounge singer and found instead a beautiful vibrant woman with a mellowed and still exceptional voice.

While Ruthie sang, Sam worked the bar, reintroducing himself, shaking hands, reminiscing about the olden days, all under Kenny's watchful eye. Then later in the evening he moved to the alley, sat in the Mark IV which he parked in a shadowy alcove near the dumpsters, smoked his cigar, and waited for the kids to return.

Kenny was a man whose manner had changed. Nick's absence allowed his own personality to flourish. He became animated, personable, funny, and warm. Gone was the old uniform of T-shirts and jeans. Now he wore handsome short-sleeved shirts, pressed linen trousers which clung to his thighs, and Italian sandals on his big muscular feet.

Maria was now firmly in charge of the kitchen. Food costs went down because she was constantly watching for any signs of waste and theft. The crew came to appreciate her because the quality of the food improved, more customers came, and hence they were always paid. If they failed to wholeheartedly accept her meteoric rise, they did what they were told and that was good enough for Maria.

Maria was constantly in a state of prayer, and candles were lit on a daily basis for her parents, for Concha, and finally for Nick, a sweet gesture which Kenny discovered one evening when he came back to the kitchen to help her close.

"You lit a candle for Nick," he commented.

"So he'll get better," she said from the walk-in, where she was holding a clipboard and counting steaks for her ordering tomorrow.

"Do you want him to come back?"

She didn't reply. Then she stepped solemnly from the walk-in and closed the door with a clank. "Of course I want him to come back."

Kenny smiled at her.

"Do you, Kenny? Do you want him to come back?"

He sighed. He sank to a stool by the grill.

"His name is on the sign."

"How will things be?"

"I think they'll be very different. But how, I don't know . . ."

Only Marcella kept watching and wondering and hoping for the day Nick came back and saw what was going on. The only person making less money than before was she, because Kenny kept such a close eye on her register and conducted surprise inventories every few days.

She hadn't heard from Ralph Zola. The authorities were searching for the kids, asking questions at the high schools. Sam Singer even posted a five-thousand-dollar reward for information leading to their arrest. The more notoriety about the attack, the better business the bar was doing.

Nobody must have been more surprised than Ralph.

She knew they suspected Zola but luckily no one connected him to her. Later she heard he'd been fired from his position because he'd failed to deliver on his promise to make a deal with Sam Singer.

A news reporter, following up on the aftermath of the attack, asked Sam if he'd ever consider selling.

"Over my dead body," was all he kept saying. "Over my dead body!"

"Stop saying that," Ruthie had interjected. "Or I'm sure it can be arranged."

When Kenny attended family day at Betty Ford, he was turned away by the guard.

"I was told my name would be left on a list."

The guard scanned his clipboard. "Lemme see here. No. But there's a note for you." He handed Kenny a small envelope with his name written on it. "If you could pull around, I need to let people through."

Kenny took the envelope and proceeded through the gate. He steered the truck under a tree facing the street. He was surprised to see that his hands were shaking as he tore open Nick's note.

Kenny, I'm sorry about the wasted trip, but after some soul searching I think it best if we didn't see each other while I'm in here. If you think about it, we've never been out of each other's sight in eighteen years. Not a night away. Please respect my need to do this. I know it seems extravagant but I'm ashamed about what I've become. I'm sorry for all that I've put you through.

> *I love you,*
> *Nick*

Nick's personality had changed significantly from the time he arrived and began his therapy. He'd been so busted by his "class" for his grandiosity he fell silent and would only speak when called upon.

"Why do you always have to be the center of attention?" a fat, hostile woman named June had accused him. "Why can't you shut up and listen, just once for one entire meeting. You're always yapping, flapping your goddamn jaw. Who cares about your past? It would be one thing if you talked about your feelings, but I'd rather know why you think all this name dropping makes you the slightest bit more important. It's pathetic really. You must bore the crap out of people at that bar."

Hurt, Nick looked around the circle to see if what she was saying was true. Some stared at him with open hostility. Others looked away, embarrassed for him.

"I think Nick's stories are very interesting," Betty, the volunteer counselor, observed. She was walking around the outer perimeter of the group and stopped to place her hands on Nick's shoulders. "To be fair, we all suffer from grandiosity. It's a common defense mechanism for an alcoholic. I hope you didn't intend to be cruel, June. It would be a shame if a very good point was lost because of it."

June's jaw tightened. She gave every indication that she indeed intended to be cruel.

"An alcoholic often overcompensates for low self-esteem by overreaching. Once they obtain their goal, they often sabotage themselves because they don't think they deserve success. For today's exercise, I think I'd like you to write about the relationship between grandiosity and low self-esteem. Many of us can't get sober because we can't reconcile these powerful characteristics in our personalities. Let's break now. Tomorrow I'd like some of you to share what you've written."

And that evening during his quiet time, Nick recalled his early childhood in an orphanage, most of the memories which he had long since blocked.

I was considered unadoptable, he wrote, and then he began to shake from the pain and truth of the words.

The next day Betty called upon him to read his essay.

As a child I was given to an orphanage when I was eight. I remember my mother very well. One day she dressed me up, and took me to a movie. We were very poor, and I think it was probably the third movie I'd ever been taken to that I could re-member. I think we saw All About Eve. *All through the movie she continued to cry, and I tried my best to make her feel better but she couldn't stop.*

After the movie she took me to buy an ice cream cone but she couldn't stop crying. My earliest recollection of my mother was that she often needed consoling. I never knew my father and she didn't like to talk about him. I remember that she was pretty and used to cry that she couldn't afford to keep herself looking nice.

The day before she took me to the movies she come home and announced she'd been fired at her job in a department store. The boss's wife had it out for her. Accused her of flirting with the customers. That night she cried and cried. I tried my best to make her feel better. I told her jokes because I was a good storyteller. I sang. I think I even danced, because she always laughed when I danced. That night I couldn't get her to even smile.

The next morning I woke up and she was stroking my face, lying fully dressed in bed beside me.

"Nicky," she said. "Tell you what. How 'bout we see a movie? Maybe get an ice cream. How 'bout that?"

"Can we afford it?" I asked her.

"Sure. Now get up and take a bath. I want you to look your best for me today."

And I remember her hanging around, washing my back, tow-

*eling me dry, helping me get dressed—combing my hair. She
kept telling me she loved me and to always remember that. Will
you remember, Nicky? Your Mommy loved you?*

"Loved?"

"'Loves' I said. Loves you."

*Later at the ice cream shop we had finished our ice cream
and I began to wonder why we weren't going home. My mother
was getting more and more nervous, crying to herself, looking
at the clock.*

"Why aren't we going home?" I asked.

*"We're waiting for someone," she explained. "Someone
nice."*

"A man?"

*"A man and woman. They said they'd be here a half hour
ago."*

"Who are they? Are they friends?"

*And she looked at me real seriously. "Nicky—" but she didn't
finish because a couple came rushing in, real worried, very
apologetic about being late. They were nice looking, I remember. And they looked real hard at me. And introductions were
made, but I don't recall much except that suddenly my mother
was hugging me real hard, crying hysterically and telling me to
be a good boy, to mind them, to make her proud of me. And all
of the sudden she went running out.*

*I stood up to go after her, but the man said, "Hey, sport.
Why don't we go look for her later?"*

*The woman nodded in agreement. "Your mother has things
to get worked out, and asked us to look after you. There are
other children where we live. Lots of food and warm beds."*

"Can't she come too?" I asked.

*"No, Nick," he explained. "The place we live is only for
children."*

And it struck me I was being taken to an orphanage.

*A night lasted a day lasted a week lasted a month lasted six
months lasted a year and she never came back. I never got a
visit, or a letter or an explanation. Finally they explained that I
was too old to stay at the orphanage and needed to be placed in
a foster home. After a series of interviews, a few overnight visits, I was always rejected or returned. The men felt I was too
effeminate.*

"What's effeminate?" I asked.

"Queer," said the custodian before the matron could explain it to me.

And then I understood everything. And the more they tried to coach me to act more subdued, the more I was compelled to sing and dance around. At thirteen I was the oldest remaining child in the orphanage. I had grown used to the idea that I would never be adopted. I had grown used to the beatings when I acted up during my interviews.

And then to my amazement, and their amazement, an older single woman wanting to adopt a child came in, a retired seamstress with a background in theater and thought I was the funniest goddamned kid she ever saw. Her name was Lynn and she wanted me to leave with her that very minute.

My bag was packed and I was off for New York with the kindest woman in the world. She encouraged every bit of my outrageous behavior and gave me all the lessons in life a young gay man could want.

She raised me till I was seventeen and then she died of a stroke. Although I never called her my mother, she gave me the first unconditional love I ever knew. We were family, and all I've wanted as an adult was my own family to love.

"How can *you* have a family?" asked June.

"I do have a family. I've lived with my lover Kenny for two decades," Nick shot back.

"Look where it got you," June hissed.

And then Betty intervened, saying, "Anybody who's staying sober is doing all right with me. I think that's enough for today."

When Kenny told Ruthie Nick refused to see him, she sent a note asking if she could attend family day. Nick found himself somewhat relieved. Ruthie was radiant and many of the other residents noted her with interest, wondering who his glamorous friend was. At first she didn't recognize him. He came out wearing a pair of jeans and a sweatshirt. On his feet were a pair of plain lace-up shoes. He even sported horn-rimmed glasses.

"What did they do with Nicky?" she asked.

"I lost one of my contacts," he explained. "They were cosmetic and somebody said they liked the true color of my eyes." Instead of bright green they were a gentle gray.

"I like 'em too, Nicky."

"So where is he today?"

"Tonight's charity event for the Desert AIDS Project. He has to make appetizers for three hundred people."

"When did he book that?"

"I think it came up short notice." Ruthie avoided his eyes. "Some other club had to cancel." She looked at him in amazement. "I can't believe the difference."

"You mean my weight?" He tugged at his shirt. "I've gained twelve pounds."

"That's good, Nicky. You never ate anything."

"No," he said. "Unless it was an olive, an onion, or a stalk of celery. How's Sam?" Nick asked.

"Sam's Sam. But since the attack, he's gotten kind of emotional."

"Sam's always had a bad temper."

"No. I mean sentimental. I think he's afraid of dying. He even went to temple. I don't think Sam's been to temple in all the years we were married."

"Sam's always thought the way to know God was by acting like God."

Ruthie laughed.

"He didn't give up on the bar. I'll hand him that. I sing five nights a week. He drives me. Works the room. Guards the alley. Then we go home."

"Five nights? Are we that busy?"

"*Packed.* The negative publicity had the opposite affect. Brought 'em in. Didn't Kenny tell you?"

"We haven't spoken since I came in here."

Ruthie smiled sadly. "He's under a lot of pressure, Nicky."

"You don't need to explain for him. I asked him to stay away." Nick pulled out a cigarette. He lit it and smiled at her. "I'm glad it's going well. It's going well for me, too. This was the best thing I've ever done. I have a lot of work to do when I get out. Lots of amends. Looking forward to it."

"You don't owe anybody a damn thing, Nicky."

"Yes I do. I owe you and Sam. All the rent you fronted—"

"Sam's been watching the cash register. I'm sure he's stolen back everything he thinks he's deserved. Kenny's a terrific host—"

Nick was caught short.

"Kenny's working the front?"

"Yes. I thought you knew."

"I guess I thought Sam—or Marcella—"

"No. Kenny. You wouldn't believe it. He's really good with names. Jokes around."

The look on Nick's face caused her to catch her breath.

"Who's running the kitchen?"

"Maria."

"Maria?"

"You just got a great review. Frankly I think Kenny's a little jealous. So when do you get out of here?" Ruthie asked him.

"Next week."

"I'm proud of you, Nicky. I've always loved you, just how you were. You know that, don't you?"

"I hope so," he said, somewhat mystified.

"It'll be good to have you back. It isn't the same without you."

And he knew she had come to prepare him.

21

Frank Sinatra

It was Monday night, Nick's was closed, and they were hanging around the house with nothing special to do. Kenny asked Maria if she'd like to go to El Gallito. "Maybe get a hamburger, have a beer or two. Listen to some music."

Maria nodded.

When they entered the bar, many of the tables were full and salsa music played from the jukebox. They walked to a table in the corner.

When Maria passed, many men whistled, nodding with respectful approval at Kenny for being lucky to have such a beautiful girl friend. Maria smiled while he pulled out her chair.

On a tiny linoleum dance floor, several couples clung to each other in sexual desperation, the women draped into the contours of the men. Maria looked around and grinned.

"You look very handsome," she teased. "The best-looking man in the room."

A waitress approached. "What can I bring you?"

"How about two draft beers?" Kenny suggested, touching Maria's hand.

"Right away," said the waitress and she drifted back to the bar. She returned shortly and Kenny paid her, tipping her generously enough to make a good impression.

"My name is Ruby, and if you need anything tonight, just call me and I'll take care of you."

Kenny lifted his beer to Maria. "Okay if we drink to Concha?" he asked.

"That would make her very happy."

And they clicked their glasses to her grandmother and drank.

"And to you." Kenny raised his glass:

"No, to you."

"To us."

"To us." They laughed and drank.

And moments later, warmed by the alcohol, Kenny asked Maria to dance. It was a favorite ballad, a mournful love song by Soraya and Kenny clumsily guided her to the dance floor. There among six or seven couples they danced. Kenny grew increasingly intoxicated by the smell of her hair and soft skin of her forehead as it rested in the crook of his neck.

Four ballads later they stopped.

He smiled down into her eyes, leaned down, and gently kissed her.

She looked up at him in surprise.

"I'm sorry." He stepped back. "Too much beer. Maybe we'd better go home."

Later that night Maria woke to find Kenny gone from his usual spot on the sofa and the door open to the patio. Outside the pool glowed with candlelight. All the candles were lit and floating on the warm blue surface of the water.

Kenny lay floating on the raft, and when she stepped onto the terrace, she could see that he was naked. He didn't move when she approached the water and for a moment he seemed to be sleeping. Palm trees shimmered in the distance, silhouetted against the backdrop of the moonlit desert.

She hesitated at the water's edge, removed her robe, and dived under the surface of the water. When she broke the surface, many of the floating candles had pitched, hissing angrily but righting themselves and bursting up with self-righteous flame. She surveyed the raft which she saw had been overturned. Had she thrown him into the water?

Frantically she searched the surface of the pool, and not finding him, dove deep underwater. He was waiting for her, dancing on the pool floor, and she swam to him and together they burst to the surface. They huddled together along the wall of the pool, heads barely above the surface. Kenny grasped her hands and guided her up to the tops of his feet so her chin could clear the lapping blue water.

To steady her stance, he supported her at the small of her back. Her waist was tiny as he pressed her against him, her breasts swelling up against his chest. With his other hand he smoothed her hair back, cupping her jaw in the palm of his hand. They studied each other solemnly. For the first time since they met, neither of them looked away.

Kenny teased her cheek with his lips, grazing over it till he found the corner of her mouth, which he'd always found so beautiful. Brushing his lips over hers, lightly, barely touching them, over and over till he heard her sigh, Kenny kissed her passionately.

He pulled her along the wall to the shallow end of the pool, in a dark corner with underwater steps leading up to the terrace. He sat, legs splayed open on the middle step, and pulled Maria inside the circle of his body. There he gently began to examine her, to kiss her neck and her shoulders. Fearful of her resistance and his growing excitement, he began to test gently the limits she would allow him to go. He kissed the globe of her breast, gently at first, but when her head fell back, he pressed his face into them, greedily tasting her nipples.

Maria, too, began to test Kenny, kissing his neck, tracing her tongue up to the lobe of his ear. He reacted, groaning deeply. She extended her reach around his sturdy back. His lateral muscles were expanded and tight. Maria had always loved Kenny's back. She ran her hands down to his waist, lightly tracing the outer cleft of his buttocks with her fingers.

"Kenny," she whispered.

And he lifted her up out of the pool and they made love.

As Kenny rocked himself gently inside of her, Maria's thoughts began to whirl. Kenny had briefly entered the house and returned with a condom, a responsible act which shocked her momentarily. She wasn't a virgin, but no man before ever showed such consideration. She remembered Kenny, barely hanging on to the edge of the flooding arroyo after pushing Concha to safety, lingering before her as he began to give up. He'd uttered a word she couldn't decipher.

She was angry at herself, in this moment of passion, as her body floated with Kenny in her arms, to be thinking about something so far away, so out of context with these moments. She loved Kenny. The logistics of his situation didn't matter at this moment. What had he called out? He'd said it so wistfully, with so much love.

Kenny and Maria began to climax simultaneously. Just as they finished, she remembered.

Nicky.

*   *   *

They both lay back on the towel, their legs and arms intertwining. To Kenny, Maria's body seemed luminous; her almond eyes half-closed in ecstasy. He kissed her and winced. They had kissed each other with such force, his lips were bruised, in part, for Kenny because it had been so long.

He had hungered to touch every fold of her skin, every curve of her body. He lost himself as he traced the long line of her neck, first with his callused fingers, then with tongue and lips. There they elected to lie still for a moment, lie still cheek to cheek, listening to the breeze rustling the palm trees overhead, the water lapping in the pool; the sound of one body breathing, heart beating.

In the aftermath of making love they discovered the condom had ruptured. He'd been initially embarrassed by the revelation that he'd actually made plans to have sexual intercourse by purchasing the prophylactics. Now graver possibilities presented themselves, posed with the discovery of the broken rubber.

"I don't want you to think I assumed this would happen," he told her seriously. "That I was lying in wait for you. That I assumed I could seduce you."

"I'd rather believe you were hoping to seduce me and not someone else." She laughed and traced his smiling lips.

He grew serious in reaction to her playfulness.

"But M'ja, this is very important, something that you have to know." He sat up earnestly. "I also recently got tested for HIV. I'm completely negative. I knew I would be. But you may wonder later . . ." He stroked her hair away from her eyes. "Because of who I am."

"I know who you are," Maria whispered to him. "Don't say it as if I should think of you as incomplete or unfinished, Kenny. I know who you are . . . I love that man. That whole, complex man . . . The condoms you bought were too small," she teased him. She crawled up along his naked body, her long wet hair swathing his glistening skin.

"Still, what if you get pregnant?"

"What if I do?" she whispered, biting his ear. "I'd have a very lucky baby. I'd name her Concha. She'd have black hair and blue eyes. Like her papa. But what am I saying? This is only a daydream." She sat up suddenly, and reached for her robe. She wrapped herself up in it, drawing her chin to her knees. He sat up on one elbow and stroked her back gently.

"It's a beautiful daydream," Kenny whispered. "Beautiful. Can we live there?" he asked her. "Can we live in such a daydream?" A chagrined Kenny studied the broken condom. "We aren't very good Catholics," he murmured, lying back on the large bath towel they used by the pool.

In their ardor, all the pool candles had extinguished but one. It drifted, flicking in a circulating motion, circulating like a drifting, random thought, waiting for an opportunity to attach itself, make it more important. She didn't turn to answer him. After a moment she lay back next to him. They slept all night in each other's arms.

The memory of the night was so personal Kenny couldn't even speak of it with Maria. Nick would return in hours. Kenny would be leaving shortly to go pick him up. In his years with Nick, he'd never once been unfaithful. He marveled that he didn't emotionally equate making love to her as infidelity at all, but intellectually he knew he was a hypocrite.

They had breakfast this morning as usual. They were affectionate, even holding hands as they ate. No promises were made. No talk of the future. No jealousies. No furtive plans. Tacitly, in silence, they agreed to wait. She escorted him to the front door and lingered as he walked away.

He turned to smile at her before climbing up into his truck. She waited till he pulled away before retreating, before closing the door.

Early that morning, Nick stood naked in the bathroom mirror and studied himself critically. His normal, at-ease position was as follows: One hand usually rested on a slightly cocked hip, the other dangling down his side and flaring up at the fingertips. He contemplated the placement of his feet. One foot followed the line of his straight leg and pointed forward, the foot usually hanging back and dancing out a bit.

The first thing to correct was his posture. He stood up straight, instead of rocking cockily back on his hips. Then he dropped his shoulders, which caused his chest to protrude. Although slender, Nick was always blessed with a nice physique. He had wide shoulders and a narrow waist, unlike Kenny, who was muscular but wider in the waist and hips.

Now he relaxed his arms, hands falling to his sides, with no mannered flair-ups to interrupt the line of his forearm and wrist. All he had to do now was to pivot his wayward foot so it ran parallel with its straightforward mate.

Then he took a deep breath and relaxed.

This is a how a man stood, he reflected. How he used to stand. Calmly, without exaggeration.

The next morning Nick waited outside of Betty Ford for Kenny to pick him up, ninety days sober, subdued, fragile, and anxious about staying sober in the life he knew was waiting for him. Members of his class were hugging and kissing each other, promising to stay in touch, as family members arrived to carry them back to the real world. Nick stood off to one side, nervously scanning the driveway for Kenny's truck.

"You look like you're glad to be leaving," Betty observed. "I've gotta say, I don't remember anybody changing as radically as you have." The amount of pretense which had fallen away from Nick in the three months since the start of his treatment was the subject of much discussion among the counselors at Betty Ford. Never had they seen so much social debris, or "drag," fall off a client, almost as if he had entered in period costume and exited without a stitch of clothing.

"For the better, I hope."

"Different. I liked the old Nick. He told good stories, liked to laugh, knew how to make people feel comfortable—but I don't think I could ever get close to that Nick. I won't have as much time to be around the new one."

"The new one is scared to death." Nick winked.

"You have your whole life ahead of you. I think you'll do great."

"I have a big mess to clean up."

"You don't have to face it alone."

In the distance Nick could see Kenny's truck approaching.

"Tell that to my lover. He may have other ideas."

The truck pulled to a halt and they watched Kenny scan the crowd for Nick.

"He doesn't recognize me."

"How long have you lived together?"

"Eighteen years in May."

"Just remember. You owe him eighteen years of sobriety."

"Like I say, he may have other ideas. Thank you for everything."

"Good luck, Nick. I admire your courage." And she watched him walk nervously over to the truck.

"Oh God, please get out." Betty prayed silently to the strained-looking man who's eyes widened with surprise as he apparently recognized Nick. Betty could predict which marriages would fail by the way the mate greeted the clinic graduate on the day they came to pick them up.

And just as Nick was about to open the door to the truck, the younger man hopped down from the driver's side, came around the front of it, and the two of them embraced like strangers.

On the drive home Kenny kept glancing nervously over at Nick as if he didn't recognize him. The alcohol which had once bloated his cheeks and reddened his nose was gone and his complexion was healthy and clear. His eyes sparkled when he looked at Kenny, but any attempts at conversation were shy and somewhat stilted.

"Things are different between us, Kenny," Nick said after a long silence.

"I know."

"What should we do?"

"Wait till we get used to each other again."

Kenny had been stunned by the change in Nick's appearance. It wasn't Nicky anymore at all, in appearance or personality. Kenny had grown so used to shutting him out, ignoring the magpie chatter. Now Nick's silence was unnerving. He used words sparingly. His demeanor was shy. He acted like a visitor. Sometimes Kenny would catch himself staring, and Nick, feeling it, would look up and smile brilliantly, but quickly look away.

Nick spoke more freely with Maria. They chatted about the menu, or a new painting she was working on. She was very kind to him, very gentle. He confided to her that he missed the rehab center, his friends at Betty Ford. If anything, Nick and Maria were more comfortable with each other than either of them were with Kenny. Guilt was eating him up. Sometimes, sensing it, Maria would touch him gently as she passed.

One afternoon, Maria asked Nick to trim her hair. They sat out by the pool as Kenny watched from inside, huddled in the corner of the kitchen, doubled over with a knotting stomach. They were laughing and chatting. Nick looked younger and more handsome than anytime Kenny could remember. He looked new. Watching them together, Kenny began to cry.

Nick's return to the bar was greeted dubiously by his new clientele and enthusiastically by his old one as they gradually heard he was back. But when they came to see him, he wasn't the same old

Nick. He was quiet, reserved, and somewhat nervous. When patrons came in asking for Kenny, Nick would wander back to the kitchen and urge him to come up front.

"Some guys are here. They're asking for you."

And Kenny would reluctantly leave the safety of the kitchen, go to the bar, say a quick hello, and flee back to where he belonged.

The strain between Kenny and Nick did not go unnoticed by Ruthie and Sam. Ruthie had gamely continued to perform, but Sam virtually had to drag her out of bed to show up. The attack on the alley had been so distressful she stayed locked in her room for a week.

She usually sang two sets a night, forty-five minutes each. Each set was packed. The clientele was as disparate as could be imagined. Wealthy retirees from Rancho Mirage and Smoke Tree Ranch, gay tourists from Denver and Kansas City, a smattering of local Latinos who nursed single beers—all convening peacefully at Nick's in Cathedral City to hear Ruthie sing.

And every night Sam would guard the alley, holed up in the Mark IV, smoking his cigar with his pistol at the ready and praying for the day those bastard kids would return. Most nights he dozed off, cigar hanging from his mouth till the hot ashes dropped to his trousers, started to smolder, and woke him up.

A chagrined, withdrawn, and reticent Nick reclaimed his position at the door and shuddered at the number of reservations. Instead of red shoes he wore loafers. Instead of Campari he drank Coke. When customers came in he didn't recognize, asking for Kenny, asking to be served their regular drinks by a now completely unrecognizable Marcella, Nick thought he was going insane.

Only Sam and Ruthie's arrival gave him some semblance of comfort because both of them knew exactly what he was going through.

"Maybe you'll sing a few numbers," she offered sweetly. "Get your feet wet, huh?"

All Sam wanted to know was if Nick thought he could stay off the sauce.

As Nick surveyed the changes, he was reminded of what he'd been taught in the last three months. Sobriety changes everything and not necessarily for the better. Sometimes you just get *different*. As Nick surveyed the bar which bore his name, he knew he no longer belonged, and unless he drank, it would only be a matter of time before it all came crashing down.

He decided instead to make a call.

*   *   *

"It's a phase," was all Sam said. He sat opposite Nick, thumbs hooked in his trousers, puffing his cigar, leaning back in his chair. They were sitting at Michael's. It was late in the afternoon and they had the place all to themselves. Sam peered across the table at Nick.

"If a man could ever use a drink, it's you. What'd they do to you in there, anyway? You got no color. No spunk left." Sam shook his head in annoyance.

"Did you ever go through a phase?" Nick asked plaintively, ignoring Sam on his other comments.

"Yeah," Sam muttered through his cigar. "Plenty of 'em." His gaze wandered through the window to the bulldozers lined up across the street in front of Judy's. "Jesus," he said. "They're really goin' through with it. Remember how she did everything herself? Took your order, fried your food, served it up, and cleared your dishes? If you spoke profanity, she threw you out."

"Sam," Nick chided him. "We were talking about me."

"We're always talking about you," Sam retorted. "Lemme tell you about a night I had over at Judy's. I can see her now, the diner packed. It's one o'clock in the morning. We're talkin' the winter of 1962. Ruthie and I was only married a couple of months.

"So one night we had a beef. She wanted to discuss having kids. The only reason she gave up her career was to have kids. My kids in particular. She told me that up front. And I loved Ruthie enough to give up my freedom. She was a beautiful young girl. Remember what a beauty she was? And she had a set of pipes. I ain't exaggeratin' here. She had it a hundred percent.

"Wasn't a red-blooded man in the desert who wasn't hot for her and she picked me. Sweetest girl in the world. Wants my kids and I lied to her. I knew I could never give her children. My plumbing was shot, but in those days, a man wasn't comfortable giving out that kind of info. See I thought we'd get married and go through the hoops, have fun trying but when push came to shove, she'd forget about it. I thought sell the club, travel a little, have kicks—hell, I had the money. I was willing to spend every dime on her, too, but she wasn't that kind of a woman. She was decent. She wanted a home for her children. She wanted me to give her children.

"So I leveled with her. She gets hysterical. We'll just keep trying, she told me. Maybe the doctors were wrong about me. To look at us, any idiot would know we was capable of having a hundred babies. Go look in the mirror if you don't believe me. But she pushes the issue. Makes a halfhearted threat. So what do I do? I walk out on her. Left her crying. Headed out to Cathedral City. I lied to her so she'd marry me."

Sam's eyes dimmed with memory.

"So I had a dozen girls I coulda called who would have loved to spend a couple hours with me, but I didn't feel like it, see? And I didn't feel like hitting the sauce because my stomach was uneasy— like I was hungry but I wasn't really hungry. The only place I could think to go at that hour was maybe to Judy's for a plate of eggs.

"Judy had this cool kinda quality about her, like she disapproved of her customers or somethin' but it kinda made you feel safe to go to her place. Of all the places in the world I coulda gone that night, only Judy's fit the bill. And remember it was across the street from my old place, your place now, and I had awful good memories of Cathedral City in those days. Still do, I suppose, but I remember less and less.

"So in I walk, head held low 'cause I'm in no mood at all to make small talk. The place was pretty full and the only stool left was in the back. Judy brought my coffee and biscuits, like she always had at the ready, and just as she was about to take my order, she heard something which took her attention. So did the rest of the room, except for me, and all of the sudden she's caterwauling her head off and takes off for a table in front.

" 'I don't care how famous you are, you can't talk dirty and eat in here. Get out."

" 'Aw, Judy," someone tried to sweet-talk her.

" 'Out!" she said again, "Or I won't serve one more breakfast."

" 'He was just telling a joke, Judy. Give the guy a break."

" 'Not one more breakfast! Out. Everybody out! I'm closing up! You bring that kinda talk in my café you'll probably take it home, too. I pity your wives and girl friends. Now get out the lot of you."

" 'Hold on, hold on," said the guy who told the dirty joke. "I'll go, I'll go."

" 'What's goin' on?" I said to the guy sitting next to me.

" 'It's Frank Sinatra and Judy is eighty-sixing him!"

" 'No kidding. Is he leaving?"

" 'See for yourself, and he's sitting with Sammy Davis and Dean Martin."

" 'And sure enough he was right. The three of 'em were all having breakfast and Sinatra was pulling on his coat.

" 'Nobody can accuse me of disrespecting a decent woman,'

Sinatra said to the crowd. 'I apologize, Judy. I stand corrected and I go!'"

"And out he went. The whole room was howling with laughter. Martin and Davis, they just kept eating while Sinatra mugged at 'em though the window. Judy ignored him, got back to business, and everything was running like clockwork.

"Then it all unraveled, because across the street a blue Packard pulled up, and I recognized it and got sick to my stomach. It was Ruthie out looking for me and out she stepped and then the whole restaurant started cat-calling. Luckily one look from Judy shut 'em all up, but I never saw her look sadder or more beautiful than she did when she crossed that street.

" 'Check out the redhead." The guy next to me nudged me.

" 'Does she see him yet?" somebody else asked.

" 'Look at him—look at him." The guy nudged me again. "Frank Sinatra is about to hit on her and she hasn't recognized him yet.'

" 'And I looked up and saw Ruthie crossing the street, and when she came into the light, I could see she'd been crying and all she wanted to do was see if I was in there, which I was but I was hidden in the back. And he came up to her, and bowed real low, and she tried to ignore him, and wasn't even looking at him till he got a little closer and she was face to face with Frank Sinatra.

"Now even Judy stopped what she was doing, because everybody in there wanted to see how she'd handle it, and the room went dead—everybody watching as Sinatra handed my wife his handkerchief.

" 'Whichever one of you louses is married to her,' Judy called out, 'you won't be married to her long if you don't drop what you're doing and hightail it back to your house. She's apparently had her feelings hurt plenty by one of you and this is God's way of evening the score. Even God, my friends, can be small.' "

"What did she do, Sam?" Nick asked.

"I didn't stay to find out. I left the way I came. Through the back door."

"Did she come home?"

"Eventually," Sam admitted. "But that's what I deserved for taking her for granted."

"Did you ever ask her—"

"She's a lady."

"You think I take Kenny for granted?"

"I think you're like me. An attention-grabbing pain in the ass."

"That's pretty direct."
"You still thirsty?"
Nick shook his head and smiled.

Kenny and Maria never spoke about the night in the pool, the night before Nick came home, but he often woke up in the middle of the night after dreaming they were making love.

Since Nick came back, he'd returned to their bed instead of the nightly ritual of the dolls. If Maria listened in her room for the sound of his footfall, she never gave any indication the change distressed her.

Although they were sleeping together again, Nick and Kenny remained celibate. Since Nick was alcohol-free, he slept quieter, more soundly, and didn't dream so violently, and Kenny was finally able to sleep through the night. He no longer perspired so heavily, and the air wasn't permeated with the sweet sickly smell of booze. He didn't get up in the middle of the night to vomit, either into the toilet or missing it all together. Kenny's nights on the sofa were over for now.

Nick, who'd never had sex without the benefit of alcohol or grass, was too intimidated to initiate sex with Kenny. For Kenny the act would have been indefensible. Not with Maria only a wall away. Kenny fell to wondering what purgatory he'd entered. What was he now? Was he gay or straight? He always hated those labels. *Bisexual?* Revolting. For the whole history of his sexual life, Kenny had always felt like an experimental adolescent. It was that he didn't have desires. He'd masturbated twice a day since he was eleven. But now to what images? Was he incapable of intimacy? Had he blamed too much on Nick's drinking? Where was his responsibility?

As for Maria, she began to attend Mass every morning, rising at six, taking a shower, and walking the seven blocks over to the church. Sometimes Kenny would go with her, and little more than small talk might be spoken between them. Father Gene was always happy to see Kenny.

What a strange pair they were—solemn, beautiful, clearly in love. Maria had already confessed in an emotional meeting with the priest shortly after it happened.

"Bless me, Father, for I have sinned."
"And what transgression have you committed?"
A quiet sob erupted from her confessional.
"I'm guilty of the sin of adultery," she stammered.
"I don't think I understand. When? With who?"

"You know who," Maria whispered.

The priest found himself filled with bitter envy.

"Oh . . ." he uttered involuntarily. "That's terrible."

"Yes, Father, I know."

He tried to collect himself. He suddenly felt very flushed, like he was going to pass out.

"Father?" she asked. "What is my penance?"

"Ten Hail Marys and sin no more."

"Only ten?" she asked meekly.

"I think you acted out of confusion. Because you've suffered so greatly. Perhaps we should arrange to meet. Discuss this all in more detail. I'm afraid I'm not feeling well now. Perhaps you'll come back another time."

And he rushed from the confessional and up the sloping ramp to the parish exit. Later that night he advised the sisters that he was commencing a fast and would not require a meal for twenty-four hours.

22

The Heart of a Bar

One afternoon as Maria was prepping the kitchen, she heard a knock on the kitchen door and turned to see Sam Singer standing at the screen. Although they had met only briefly, Maria recognized him as Ruthie's husband; Kenny and Nick's landlord.

The door was kept locked since the night of the assault, and Maria moved to unhook it.

"Kenny isn't here," Maria offered.

"That's okay, dear, it'll give us time to talk."

"I'm just chopping vegetables for my soup . . ." She wiped her eye with a towel. "Onions."

"Onions never bothered me. Let me help. I was a bachelor for many years." And Sam assumed a position at the cutting board. Over the locker where the crew stored their belongings, Sam noticed the little altar Kenny had made last year. A candle was burning in front of a small *retablo*.

"What's that?" Sam asked her.

"To remember my grandmother."

"It's beautiful . . ." Sam stood on his toes to examine it. It pictured a woman drowning in a river with an angel flying down to rescue her. In the clouds above, a translucent image of a man and woman were feeding golden rope to the angel who in turn was dropping it to the old woman in the river. "So they're all together now. Is that what you believe?"

"It's what I hope," Maria said.

"Then I'm sure it must be true. I envy you people your faith. I confess I'm a quart low myself." He took an onion and peeled back the layers of brown skin. Then he quartered it and vigorously began to dice. "So how long have you been here, Maria?"

"Close to a year."

"You've changed. It's quite remarkable." He scraped a pile of chopped onions into the bowl. "But so have we all. I don't recognize Nick at all. The only person who's stayed the same is Kenny. You don't teach an old dog new tricks."

He was clearly here to tell her something. Something about Kenny.

"How long have you been married, señor?"

"Let's see, thirty years. Ruthie's seventeen years younger than me. I was forty-two when I married her."

"You waited a long time."

"Oh," Sam shrugged. "She didn't really want to be married. She wanted to be a nightclub singer. I wanted us to settle down."

"What changed her mind?" Maria filled a huge caldron with a large pitcher of cold water. She turned on the gas and set it to boil. Then she began scraping Sam's chopped onions into the brew.

"Actually, I knew she'd never be able to marry the man she wanted so I stepped in, picked up the slack."

Maria hesitated.

"Why couldn't she marry who she wanted?"

"He wasn't available, dear." Sam shrugged. "He worked here as a bartender when I owned the club. He was much younger than me. Her age. You never saw a more handsome man. Now don't get me wrong, I wasn't hard on the eyes. I had lots of girl friends. But this man was a movie star. Blond hair. Tall, slender, well built. Always tan. Everybody loved him."

"Nick?"

"That's right."

"Him and Ruthie were great pals. She tried to make it something more, but that's all it could ever be between them. He knew that. So did Ruthie. And I loved her from the wings."

"But how could you love her if she loved him?"

"I thought she was confused. I thought if I impressed her enough, I could make her love me. That's why I handed my club over to Nick. To please her. This used to be my place, see. My pride and joy."

He glanced around. He was clearly disappointed by what it had become.

"I made one big mistake. I thought I knew human nature, but I was wrong. Ruthie didn't love me. She respected me. But this thing for Nicky had its own power. Luckily I didn't walk out, make a fool of all of us. I think Nick would have married her if I had. Am I being too frank with you, dear? I know you're Catholic, but the story's got a point." Sam smiled.

"Please," Maria said softly. "Go on."

"So Ruthie was getting pretty antsy. Nick was confused. I was putting a lot of pressure on her. She started talking about finding a gig in L.A. Maybe even try her hand in New York. But something else was bothering her too. She was an only child and my parents were both dead. She was aimless. Had no family to speak of. She forced Nick's hand.

"She didn't want a husband but a kid, that was something else again. She'd have a kid to keep her company. But times were different then. You had to be respectable. She and Nick could get married. Ruthie could keep singing. Have her baby. They'd have an understanding, you know? But Nicky was too honest. Didn't want to pretend he was something he wasn't. By then it was too late."

"What happened to this baby?" Maria's voice trailed off.

"Ruthie took matters into her own hands without discussing it with anybody. Mexicali. Had complications from the procedure. That's how she came to find you. Sometimes she . . . lives in the past. Goes looking for her little girl."

Maria slumped against the wall of the kitchen.

"We were all glad when Nick met Kenny. They were happy for many years till the bottle got the best of Nick. Kenny's pretty sensitive. He's been lonely for a long time. A lot of people told him he should walk out. That's the vogue these days. Save yourself. People told me I should walk out on Ruthie but I'll never give up."

Sam lit his cigar.

"When Nick and Kenny came to Cathedral City, I leased 'em the bar. I gave Nicky instructions. 'Don't drink all the profits. Be fair with your partner. It's no business to operate alone. Oh, and always pay your rent on time. Never be late with the rent.'

"We were all great friends. You should have been here then. We had so many laughs. Kenny never knew about Ruthie and Nick. There wasn't any reason to drudge it up. Not till now."

As Sam watched her, Maria continued to add ingredients to her soup. Chopped carrots, cilantro, cubes of potatoes. Overhead, above the lockers, the flickering candle occasionally caught her eye.

Sam studied her for a moment. Framed in the kitchen screen door was the bright alley. Small children ran by laughing. A few older boys, hanging on the fences, teased them. One of them started crying and a mother quickly reacted, shouting in Spanish till she drove the offending boys away.

"Do you miss home?"

"I don't have a home, *señor.*"

"But you have a home with Nick and Kenny . . ."

"It's their home. Not mine, not really. I think I want to go back to Mexico."

"Why?"

"Because here I have no face."

"No face?"

"Without papers, I'm nothing. I can't do anything."

"I could help you get papers."

"It's not so easy now. Before, maybe. Too many new laws. I'm here illegally. I'll stay illegal. I've looked into it. I'm not *necessary.* It's my fault. I'm nobody. I have nothing. I'm of no use."

"That isn't true!"

"It's true. Besides, you and your wife have helped me enough," Maria said firmly.

"Maybe you'll get married. There's no reason you can't have a family of your own one day." Sam contemplated Maria working on her soup, her beautiful long hair tied back with merely a string. Her cheeks were flushed with the steam of the whirling water. Behind her somber eyes were whirling thoughts.

Sam moved to unhook the screen door. "I want you to know that I understand how you feel and I'll do anything I can to help you, but if you pursue this thing, it'll end badly for everybody. I know it feels exciting now. But he can't ultimately change for you. Even as much as he loves you. If you love him, cut him loose now."

It was time to go. For a moment Sam thought nothing had registered with her. But she leaned up to kiss his cheek goodbye.

"Yes, *señor.* I understand everything."

Kenny glanced up from his worktable.

"Where's Maria?"

"I heard the shower," Nick said.

"You okay?" Kenny studied him. "You seem nervous."

Nick paused. "Does my sobriety make you happy?"

"If it makes you happy."

"I'm doing it for both of us."

But Kenny's attention diverted to Maria, emerging from her

room, dressed up as if ready to go out. With downcast eyes she entered the living room. Nick and Kenny stared at her, but both for different reasons.

"You look very pretty tonight," Nick offered cheerfully.

"Thank you." Maria sank to the chair in the entry hall.

Kenny didn't say anything. He was too busy wondering why she was acting so skittish.

"Shall we order a pizza tonight?" Kenny finally suggested.

"Sounds good to me," Nick said overcheerfully from the sofa.

"I won't be home for dinner," Maria said softly.

Kenny looked up in surprise. He composed himself.

"No?" he asked her.

"Where are you going?" Nick asked.

"I have a date." Her answer was barely audible.

Nick shot a glance at Kenny to gauge his reaction. Kenny's face was ashen. Suddenly Nick felt like he should offer to excuse himself, to allow them to discuss this turn of events.

"With who?" Kenny asked.

"A friend of Carmen's . . ." Maria explained.

"Do you know him? Or is it a blind date?"

"Blind?" Maria glanced up, as if worrying he was being completely literal, as if her date might arrive with a white cane.

"Someone she's fixed you up with. Someone you haven't met."

"Yes," Maria explained. "That."

"Well, isn't *that* terrific!" Nick remarked, all smiles. "Kenny? Isn't that great? She won't have to be all cooped up with us tonight. She has the night *off!*"

But by the look in Kenny's eyes, Nick and Maria could both tell that he didn't think it was so great at all. If anything, he looked so worried and pale that Maria thought she had made him physically ill.

"Who is it? Did she say?"

"Just a boy, Kenny. Someone who saw me and wanted to go out."

"But you didn't meet? You don't know what he looks like?"

"What's with the third degree?" Nick demanded. "She going on a blind date. You're acting like her mother. You gonna give her a dime for a phone call? Is she expected to be home at a certain hour?"

Kenny shot a look of annoyance at Nick which was so rebuking Nick fell instantly silent.

"Are you going alone?" Kenny asked. "Or with Carmen?"

"With Carmen and her husband. Maybe a few others. We're going to Indio. To the Date Palm Festival."

"When did you make these plans?"

"Yesterday."

"Yesterday," Kenny replied almost accusingly. He was mixing a small tube of paint which he began to smear with quick, angry brushstrokes.

"Are they picking you up?" Nick asked, and wondered why he felt bad for her. Kenny's reaction was obviously making her terribly guilty.

"Yes."

Kenny didn't say anything. He wouldn't even look at her. Maria gazed with pleading eyes at Nick.

"Well, I hope you have a nice evening. You look very beautiful," Nick offered.

Outside a car pulled up with loud Spanish music playing. A horn honked, startling Maria. She stood to go.

"Good night," she said. She looked again in Kenny's direction but he didn't respond.

"Good night," Nick replied, winking at her sympathetically.

After a long moment, Kenny finally muttered good night.

She slipped through the front door. From inside the curtains Nick could see her being greeted by Carmen, who was motioning for her to climb into the backseat of Gabriel's older two-door sedan. Carmen climbed in behind her, slamming the passenger door with finality. Then the car turned and roared down the block, the music lingering in the air, then growing softer.

Inside Kenny continued to work on the doll.

"Shall I order a pizza?" Nick asked. "Or do you want me to call for a private detective?"

"Nick? Tonight I don't want to talk, okay?"

"But—"

"Not one word. Please."

Maria had been nervous about accepting Carmen's invitation. Nervous for not discussing it with Kenny. Nervous because the kitchen crew was jealous of her, for reasons she understood, but Kenny's devotion made it difficult to make overtures to them. She was lonely for peers. She hadn't gossiped with a girl friend for over a year. Tonight she hoped would be a new beginning. Her talk with Sam had opened her eyes.

As old and conservative as she sensed Sam was, she didn't think he was totally looking out for her interests with his remarks in the kitchen that day. Nor did she believe he was as mercenary as he'd like everyone to think. She knew he liked Kenny and Nick as a couple, and not just for the sake of the business. Even as an ignorant world would cheer her on for coming between two gay men and showing one of them the righteous path to a heterosexual lifestyle, Sam was rooting for Nick and Kenny. Perhaps because Nick had once threatened his relationship with Ruthie and maybe she'd get ideas if Kenny left Nick for Maria.

But no, Marie reflected. Sam loved Kenny and Nick together as a couple because he believed in marriage. So, in fact, did she. So she decided to get beyond Kenny and start her life over. She agreed to Carmen's blind date.

Once in the car, she knew she'd made a terrible mistake. After shyly greeting Carmen and Gabriel with downcast eyes, Maria climbed into the cramped backseat and found herself sitting next to Alex Quintero.

On her stunned expression, Gabriel spoke to her through the rearview mirror. "He asked to go out with you. He says he likes you."

"Let me out!" she demanded.

"He's over that thing in the alley. He understood we had to do what we had to do. You know, for Kenny."

"He's sorry," grinned Carmen menacingly from the front seat, happy to see Maria so uncomfortable.

"Yeah, you can relax," said Alex. "Relax and enjoy." He tried to put his arm around her but she elbowed him so fiercely he recoiled. All she had to do was wait till they let her out. She knew enough about being trapped not to expend her energy till she could maneuver.

So he tried again, and this time she relented, staring angrily out the window while the car headed south for Indio. When she thought about Kenny, her disappointment dissolved into private, angry tears. This is exactly what she deserved, she thought. She had enjoyed his jealousy. His hurt. Now she missed him. Now she just felt frightened and guilty. As soon as they got to the festival, she would call Kenny and ask him to come and get her.

The Indio Date Palm Festival attracted thousands of visitors from Southern California. Five bands were scheduled to play, and as they walked, Gabriel passed a flask filled with tequila. Carmen took a big gulp. Then Alex. Now it was Maria's turn. They looked at her with contempt.

Would she join them or run crying back to the gringos? They knew by the look on her face how uncomfortable she felt. Alex dangled the flask in front of her. What would she do? Call Kenny and cause more trouble between him and Nick? What did she want? For Kenny to abandon Nick and the two of them to run away with each other? After Nick had taken her into his house?

No. It was all ridiculous. Loving Kenny would lead to unhappiness—even tragedy. All the prayers in the world wouldn't change facts.

Maria took a bold sip from the flask. The burning tequila took her by surprise. She coughed as her companions laughed. Not to be ridiculed, she took another gulp and this time managed to keep it down to the delight of Alex and Carmen.

Gabriel was dubious about this unfolding evening. "Hey, take it easy," he admonished her. "I can't take you back drunk."

"He's afraid of Kenny," Carmen observed.

"He doesn't need to be afraid of Kenny," Maria interjected. She took another gulp, shuddered, and wiped her mouth with her hand.

They began to stroll through the festival. Many men noticed Maria, causing Alex to feel proud and jealous at the same time. Maria herself became intoxicated with the crowd, enjoying the community of Latinos, the smells from the food carts, the happy families strolling with their children, the parents drinking foamy beer from plastic cups.

When offered the flask, Maria continued to indulge. Alex shot a look at Carmen. They exchanged private grins. She was clearly loosening up. Although she refused to hold his hand, she allowed him to guide her through the crowd, his hand resting lightly at the small of her back. Her cheeks were flushed with the warmth of the evening, the pleasant burn from the alcohol. The air was sultry and sensual. She felt like she was home in Mexico.

Alex purposely slowed down, hoping to lose the others. Ahead of them Gabriel and Carmen greeted several cousins with their small children. Soon he and Maria were wandering along the periphery of the festival grounds, where lovers had immigrated to escape the harsh stadium lighting of the festival. Softly, Alex began to nuzzle her.

"No," she shook him off, giggling.

"Please. Let me kiss you just once."

"No," she said again. Her head was beginning to spin. Alex sensed her instability and tried to soothe her by stroking her cheek. She knocked his hand away.

"Leave me alone!" she ordered. "I want to go back with the others."

"They're gone," he shrugged. "They went home."

"How will we get back?" She looked around wildly. They were enveloped in shadows. Several lovers moaned nearby.

"I have a lotta friends here. Don't worry about nothing. We'll get a ride when we're ready." After a long pause he smiled at her drunkenly. "I really wanna kiss you."

"*What?*"

He pressed himself against her body and kissed her, tightening his grip on her wrists. She wrenched free and slapped him. Someone watching from the shadows whistled softly. "She don't want you, man," he laughed.

Alex's eyes darkened to onyx bullets. "Don't you ever hit me."

"I'm *going*," she defied him and he stunned her by punching her in the shoulder and knocking her to the ground. Several onlookers saw this happen but nobody made a move to help her. Alex dropped like a panther to the ground and held her down.

"No!" she cried, thrashing beneath him. She was strong but he was stronger. "*No!*" He pinned her shoulders down with his knees and covered her mouth with his hand. Then he began grabbing at her breasts with his other one. He eased the weight of his body on top of her, sliding down and blanketing her with his superior weight.

"*Shut up or I'll fucking kill you,*" he hissed. "*I'll fucking kill you, you wetback bitch.*"

"Stop," she whimpered and he reached down inside her jeans. "*Please, no!*"

"*You fucking hit my mother and called her names? Wait till you see what I do to you!*" As she struggled under his grasp, he managed to unzip her pants and peel them away from her waist. When he pulled at her panties, she wrenched violently under him, freeing her knee which she brought up hard into his groin. Then she managed to scream.

He slapped her across the mouth. "*I'll fucking kill you if you scream. I'll fucking smash your face in.*"

"No! Please no!"

"*Stop fighting me,*" he warned her, raising his fist, and when a strange flicker of calm entered her eyes, he felt her body relent, and quickly he arched his back, scrambled to unzip his jeans, and in seconds he was ejaculating inside of her.

A moment later, ass-naked, Alex Quintero found himself being dragged to his feet and flung face forward into the ground like a rag doll. A rescuer was on him, pummeling away on the back of his head, boxing his ears and slugging his kidneys. Soon Alex felt the ghastly sensation of blood draining into his throat and found himself gagging for air.

He could hear Maria scramble to her feet, pulling up her jeans and adjusting her blouse. "Somebody's coming," she warned his assailant, thus finally ending the assault.

"Let's go," her rescuer urged her in Spanish in a resonant, cultivated youthful voice.

"Who are you?" she protested. "I don't know you."

"Yes you do," he replied authoritatively. "It's me. Pablo." And they disappeared into the shadows with Alex bleeding and beaten in the dirt.

With the wind whipping around the windshield of the Jeep, Pablo had to shout to communicate with her.

"We need to take you to a hospital," he declared. "And file a police report."

"No," she whimpered. "I'll be deported."

"You need medical attention! And that bastard needs to be arrested."

"I just want to go home."

"Are you on birth control?"

She looked at him, astonished that he would ask so personal a question. The possibility of pregnancy was more than she could cognate. All she wanted to do was get home. Take a bath. Curl up in her bed with a doll. Her shoulders were hunched inward, her hair whipping wildly in her face as they drove. Even in the dark, Pablo could see tears flooding down her face. He reached over to touch her hand. She pulled away.

"I'm sorry," he shouted over the noise of the engine. "But we have to take you to a doctor. We can go to a free clinic. We won't have to give your real name."

"*No!* I want to go home. To Kenny!"

"Okay, okay! Maybe he'll know what to do!"

"*We can't tell him anything!*"

"Why not? He'll want to help."

"*No!* He'll kill that boy!"

"He deserves to be killed!"

"Kenny must never know!" and her body wrenched. She began to vomit, and Pablo quickly veered to the side of the road. Maria dropped to the ground and threw up. Pablo jumped down and went to help her.

"You need to get help." He touched her shoulders, kneeling in front of her.

"Then take me to the priest at St. Louis. Take me to the church."

The priest.

Pablo shook his head. He could sense her growing hysteria. He stepped on the gas and roared up the highway toward Cathedral City.

The priest was surprised to find Pablo standing in the dark, pounding on the door of the rectory. He was also certainly alarmed. What could the boy want at this hour?

"The girl in my Jeep. She says you know her."

Father Gene saw Maria sitting slumped in the front seat of the Jeep.

"Yes, I know her."

"She's been raped," Pablo said, choking on the word. "And she won't let me take her to the hospital."

"Let me wake one of the sisters." He shook his head. "Bring her inside." He disappeared into the rectory. By the time Pablo was helping Maria up the sidewalk to the rectory door, a nun rushed out to assist him. Then the hastily dressed Father Gene returned, holding the door and ushering the small group to a guest room opposite the rectory kitchen.

"Leave us alone," ordered the nun, a small older woman with strong expressive features. She pushed Pablo and the priest into the hallway and firmly closed the door. Pablo and Father Gene hesitated in embarrassed silence.

"I'll make some coffee," the priest offered lamely. "Come into the kitchen." When he noticed Pablo staring miserably at the door separating him from Maria and the nun, he patted his shoulder kindly. "Sister Agnes has extensive crisis training. She was a trauma nurse in Central America."

"She wouldn't go to the hospital. She's afraid of being deported."

"Did she know her attacker?" Father Gene reached for the coffeepot and filled it with cold water. Then he opened a canister and measured out ten scoops of fragrant coffee.

"Yeah."

"She tell you who he was?"

"I broke it up. I recognized him. He lives in the house behind the bar where I work. The Quintero kid."

"Inez Quintero's son?" The priest shook his head. He switched on the coffeemaker. "I know that one."

"She won't press charges."

"No," said Father Gene. "I suppose she's afraid. You'd be amazed how they all chew each other up when they know someone's undocumented. I hear stories of betrayal in the confessional you wouldn't believe." The coffeemaker began chugging steadily, the sound of it comforting the two of them. Pablo sank to a chair and stared uncomfortably up at the priest. He covered his hands with his face and ran his fingers through his hair as if hoping this might revive him.

"When did this happen?"

"Date Festival."

"What were *you* doing at the Date Festival?"

"Trying to fit in," Pablo smiled. "I got it in my head that I missed Mexico."

"Did it work?" Father Gene interrupted the dripping coffeemaker to pour Pablo a cup of coffee. He passed it over to him.

"No." Pablo shook his head. "It made me realize I feel like I don't fit in anywhere."

"You probably saved her life," said Father Gene. "Do you think he . . ."

"Yes," Pablo said. "Yes I do."

The priest shook his head and crossed himself again.

"Is your nun equipped to . . . interfere?"

"With God's will? She'll stabilize her and nothing more."

"Oh." Pablo sat back in his chair. "You're a priest. I forgot where I was."

They waited for several more moments in silence. Then the door to Maria's room opened. The little nun appeared. She came into the kitchen.

"Bruises. No bones broken."

"Just her heart," Pablo offered.

"God will heal her heart," the nun fired back with a scathing look of rebuke.

"Will she report it?" asked Father Gene, but he already knew the answer.

"She's adamant. She wants to be taken home. Is that something you can handle, young man?"

"Yes, sister," he nodded.

In a moment the door to the bedroom opened and Maria emerged having just taken a shower. Her clothing had been stitched where Alex had torn it. She looked at Pablo gravely.

"Thank you all for everything," she said. And she walked toward the exit with Pablo following.

As Father Gene locked the door, he turned to see that the nun wanted to tell him something but was hesitating.

"What?" he said wearily.

"She was already pregnant," the nun sighed.

"Oh. I wondered. Good night, sister."

When Pablo's Jeep pulled up in front of Nick and Kenny's house, the porch light was on and Maria could see Kenny inside, sitting hunched over at his workbench. A sob erupted from her throat at the sight of him. She covered her mouth with her hand. Shame overwhelmed her, shame and sorrow, because he looked so lonely through the windows of his house and she knew how surprised and hurt he'd felt about her going somewhere without him.

"I'll go in with you," Pablo offered. "I'll just say we ran into each other at the festival and you asked me to give you a ride home."

"He'll know anyway." Her shoulders sagged.

"How will he know?"

"He knows me," she explained. "He just will."

Kenny appeared in the frame of the front door looking questioningly out to the street. Pablo got out on his side of the Jeep and ran around to her side to help her down.

"What's wrong?" Kenny called from the porch. "What happened?" and he ran down the steps where he met them halfway.

"Where's Carmen and Miguel?" Kenny demanded, pulling Maria away from Pablo and under the comfort of his arm.

"They got separated at the festival and I found her wandering alone."

"Did they leave you?" Kenny asked angrily.

"I . . ."

"They were riding the Ferris wheel while she went to the bathroom—when she came back they must have gone looking for her and got swallowed up by the crowd."

Kenny searched Maria's face for corroboration. Her eyes were empty. "What about your date? Where was he?"

"I told him to leave," Maria said.

"Who was he? Why did you tell him to leave?"

"She's real tired," Pablo intervened.

"I want to know what happened."

"He . . . insulted her," Pablo explained.

"Who was he?"

"Alex Quintero," Pablo said.

"Alex Quintero!" Kenny looked at her in astonishment. "They set you up with Alex Quintero?" Kenny's mouth contorted. "Why'd you have to tell him to go away?"

"Probably because—" Pablo ventured.

"I'm asking *her.*"

"Kenny, I'm tired and I don't want to talk about it," she said wearily.

"Fine." He searched Pablo's face for more information. "Thanks for getting her home."

"Precious cargo. I know what she means to you." Pablo grinned. He and Maria exchanged a knowing glance and Kenny led Maria up to the porch. As Pablo turned, he heard Maria whisper plaintively, "I missed you tonight."

"I missed you too, *Novia,*" Kenny murmured, and they stepped inside and closed the door behind them.

Pablo stood on the walk and studied the house with longing.

It was close to sunrise when Alex Quintero returned home. He could hear his mother coughing when his buddies helped him up the steps to his front door. When the door opened, he saw his father stretched out on the sofa trying to catch up on lost sleep before he went to work. Many nights Thomas couldn't sleep because of his wife's discomfort.

Alex nodded good night to his friends and closed the door. Behind him he heard his father swear. Alex turned. Thomas could see that his lip was swollen, and blood was caked on his shirt and jeans.

"They beat me up, Pop," Alex winced.

"Who did this to you?" Thomas shouted, jumping up.

"One of the guys from the bar in the alley. A waiter."

"Which bar?" Thomas demanded.

"Nick's, Pop."

"One of the chicos?" Thomas called Kenny and Nick "the boys."

"No, Pop. The Mexican. The waiter. You've seen him."

Thomas guided his son to the kitchen, where he plopped him in a chair and began to examine his wounds. He reached for a dish towel and soaked it in tap water, wringing it out and moving to clean the blood off Alex's face. Soila and Anita appeared, rubbing their eyes and wondering what all the commotion was about.

"He was attacked!" Thomas proclaimed, waking the old aunt, who was sleeping in her customary place on the pad under the kitchen table. She scrambled to her feet and started wailing at the sight of Alex. Finally Inez appeared. She trudged wearily into the kitchen.

"Mommy, go back to bed," urged Soila.

"What's going on?" Inez asked. "What's happened?"

"Your son was attacked by the bastards from the bar!" Thomas exclaimed.

"They beat me up, Ma," Alex affirmed.

"Who?" It didn't sound right. "Which one?"

"The Mexican waiter. Your friend."

"No," Inez protested. If it was true, she knew her son well enough to realize he had provoked whatever had befallen him.

"What friend?" Thomas demanded.

"Mommy doesn't have any friends from over there," Soila assured him. She took the washrag from Thomas's hands and began vigorously cleaning blood from her brother's face, pleading with him silently not to say anything else.

"Maybe I was wrong, Pop. But he definitely works there. I've seen him."

"Where were your friends?" Thomas wanted to know. "Didn't they help you?"

"I was with the girl. We were alone and the bastard attacked me!"

"What girl?" Inez asked. She was so weak she had to steady herself by holding on to a chair.

"The girl who works in the kitchen at Nick's. The illegal one."

"*La Mojada?*" Inez wheezed.

"*Lo mismo,* Mommy."

"What were you doing with her?"

"Gabriel and Carmen fixed me up. They told me she liked me. And I wanted to get even for what she did to Mommy," he added darkly. "And the guy came out of nowhere and started beating me up." A hush fell over the room. Soila and Anita looked at each other fearfully. Thomas took the rag from Soila's hands and continued to clean the blood from Alex's face and hands.

"And did you?" Thomas asked solemnly. "Did you get even?"

"Yes, Pop," Alex grinned, wincing from the bruises on his cheeks. "In spades."

"How?" Inez asked. She looked at her daughters. "Go outside!" They hesitated, wanting to hear the whole story, but Inez clapped her hands. Soila whisked her little sister out of the kitchen. Inez sank to a chair.

Alex could only continue to smile. Thomas and Inez understood his meaning. Thomas winced with shame.

"Did anybody see you?"

"Only the waiter. And her."

"The girl's illegal," Thomas began to reason. "She won't make trouble."

"And the boy?"

"Inez knows the boy," the old aunt observed.

"How do you know this boy?" Thomas exploded.

"How, Mommy?"

"He used to work at the motel. Nothing more . . ." Inez explained, glaring scathingly at the old aunt, who shrank meekly into the background. "He won't make trouble. She won't let him if she's illegal."

"And Kenny? What if she tells him?" Thomas wondered. He didn't want trouble with Kenny and Nick. He knew about their friendship with Sam Singer.

"She's in love with him," Inez observed, provoking Alex to laugh sharply. "She won't want him to know."

Alex continued to laugh mirthfully.

"What's funny?" Thomas asked.

"She was a good piece of ass."

Thomas reached out and slapped him off his chair.

"Today you'll go to the priest and ask forgiveness," Inez declared.

"Ma!"

"Shut up, you idiot! Your father didn't give up Mexico to be disgraced by you. You'll go to the priest or you'll leave this house!" And then she began to wheeze for air.

"Soila!" Thomas cried with disdain. "Help your mother!"

And Soila rushed from where she and Anita were eavesdropping on the conversation. She helped her mother to the tiny bedroom at the front of the house and sat with her until she could catch her wind.

The following day Kenny bitterly confronted Carmen and Gabriel about arranging the date with Alex Quintero. Gabriel had been contrite, but Carmen strangely blustery.

"She wanted to go," Carmen asserted.

"C'mon, she had no idea you set her up with Alex Quintero."

"She wanted to go out," Carmen explained again, her solemn eyes wide with umbrage. "He likes her. He ask. I arrange."

"He ditched her, did you know that?"

"This never happen." Carmen shook her head. "She wanted to go. She left him," Carmen gestured. "We went looking for them and she was gone. Alex was alone. She left with some other guy, he said. Just left him," she shrugged.

"Are you saying she's lying to me, Carmen?"

He challenged her in a tone none of them had ever heard before. A tone which had never been necessary, or for that matter, deserved.

"Might be, Kenny. Am I lying to you? After all this time?" Carmen shook her head sadly. "This is very bad, very bad thing. Kenny. I not lie." She shook her head again. Gabriel stood mutely guilty behind her. It was possible, Kenny considered, that he knew more than Carmen. He searched both of their faces. Now he was angry and they were sullen.

"I don't know how to tell you this, but she means a lot to me. To me and Nick," he corrected himself. "No more blind dates unless I okay 'em. Understood?"

"You don't *own* us, Kenny," she admonished him. "Even if you did help us."

"No problem, Kenny," Gabriel offered behind her. He was eager for this confrontation to conclude. He reached for his apron and started working. Carmen stood her ground until Kenny walked away, resentment and embarrassment flushing in her cheeks.

A recorded message from the Department of Immigration and Naturalization Hot Line:

If you are calling to report criminal alien activity, or persons thought to be in the country illegally, please contact your local INS office.

"What did you say to her? *What did you say to her!*"

Nick opened his eyes. "What is it? What's wrong?"

"She's gone! What did you say to her?"

"Who's gone?" Nick sat up and yawned.

Kenny held a note in his hand. His face was ashen, as if the most horrible reality in the world had presented itself to him. "It's Maria. She left! Her room is empty. She wrote this note! What did you say to her?"

"I didn't say a word to her." Nick became cold. He stood up and pushed past Kenny to the bathroom. Kenny followed him, flailing his hands. "Where could she go? What will she do?"

"She'll survive, Kenny. She's a survivor." And Nick closed the door in Kenny's face. He emerged several minutes later to find Kenny shouting on the telephone. Nick gathered he was talking to Ruthie. Then apparently Sam came on the line and closed the conversation. Kenny slammed the receiver down so hard it broke.

"Sam offered her money but she wouldn't take it. No one could know where she was going. Even Ruthie doesn't know."

"You think she's telling the truth?" Nick asked Kenny calmly.

"Yeah." Kenny's voice broke "She was crying."

"What's she say in the note?"

"She said to tell you she loves you. And thank you . . ."

"And . . ."

"She's asking me to let her go."

When Nick saw the anguish in Kenny's face, his victory was hollow, but he couldn't hide his own relief. Now perhaps they had a chance. He'd make it up to Kenny. He'd seduce him again. Maria had become a ghost in their lives. Without her, he could make up for all the lost time. He owed him eighteen years of sobriety. That's what his counselor had told him at Betty Ford. He could finally start making his amends. He began to get animated. When Kenny noticed, he checked it.

"I'm sorry, Kenny. I know how you must feel."

"How can you know how I feel?" Kenny demanded.

"Trust me," Nick said like ice. "I do."

"I was planning to ask her to marry me. To protect her."

"Marry you. You're already *married.*"

Kenny stared at the note. "I thought we'd all continue living together. I thought we could remain a family."

"You and me and Maria," Nick said, only calmly and quietly. His head was spinning. "Who sleeps where?"

"Nothing would change between us."

"Or maybe the two of you would sleep in the living room, you on the couch, her on the floor, and me in the bedroom. Does that make sense to you?"

"We'd all have each other! Don't you see?"

"No! I don't see at all! Maria and I have nothing to do with each other. You can't have it both ways, Kenny. You want to know why she really left?"

"Why?"

"You treated her like one of your dolls. She was a fantasy you created. And so am I."

The wall of unfinished dolls in his workshop stared at Kenny in blank judgment.

"You're right," Kenny said, and bowed his head.

Nick was relieved by his reaction. Maybe he was coming to his senses. "What do you think we should do, Kenny?"

"I think I should live alone for a while."

Nick took this in. He stared at Kenny blankly, as if he'd just been shot.

"No," Nick protested softly. "No." He sat hard on the sofa and began to moan. Kenny watched as Nick's body contorted. He began to fidget in nervous jerky motions. His leg began to twitch. Both hands knotted into fists, which he brought to his temples, tapping them lightly, and then more forcefully.

"Nicky." Kenny knelt in front of him. "We'll always be in each other's lives. Everything in our relationship now can be accommodated by friendship."

"I don't need any friends. I need my family."

"We'll always be family."

"No, Kenny. No, we won't. Who do you think you're trying to kid? They'll say anything, just to get out the door. Promise *anything*." He began to moan again.

"This isn't the same thing as your childhood."

"No." Nick shook his head, covering his face with his hands. "It's different because I'm older and I know how bad I'll feel tomorrow."

Kenny took a small apartment over a garage in Desert Hot Springs which contained the following items: a twin bed, a table, and a chair. In the kitchen he had one cup, one plate, one place settting of silverware; a pot for cooking and one for frying. He owned two pairs of jeans, four T-shirts, one pair of work boots, one pair of sneakers, a sweater if he ever got chilly, and a beat-up old leather jacket if he ever got cold.

Desert Hot Springs was a small town across the desert from Palm Springs and Cathedral City. A little city of hot spring spa motels, some grand, some small—lost in time from the forties and fifties. Known for high crime and high winds, Desert Hot Springs' dubious claim was also the highest witness protection program population per capita in the United States.

Rumbling through late-night Desert Hot Springs streets were roving gangs of teenagers making it as surreal urban as downtown Los Angeles or New York City.

Often as Kenny sat at his table under the naked light of a single hundred-watt lightbulb hanging from an overhead socket, painting the faces of his dolls, he heard the staccato burst of semiautomatic gunfire, somewhere outside on the dusty streets of Desert Hot Springs.

Kenny continued to work at the restaurant, arriving at dawn to set up and staying till ten when the kitchen closed. He never set foot in the dining room and Nick never came back to the kitchen. They weren't uncivil, only sad and restrained, and each did his part to avoid unnecessary confrontation.

Ruthie sang Thursdays through Saturdays, and other than the obvious toll their breakup was taking on Nick, Sam's friendship with Kenny proved to be a major casualty. Kenny couldn't bring himself even to speak to him, and Sam knew he'd never be forgiven for intervening in Kenny's relationship with Maria.

Sam kept watch on the alley, waiting in the Mark IV, which he hid in the shadows, and still prayed for the day the kids would return to face his wrath. Ruthie didn't interfere in the dynamics between the boys and Sam. She knew Sam was devastated by Kenny's coldness, and she herself had been surprised, even for Sam, that he would take it upon himself to interfere.

As for progress, it was springing up all around them. The entire parcel opposite the bar had been torn down, and a huge shopping complex was being built. The little houses above Sam Singer's quadrant were being torn down and hauled away at the rate of four a day. With exception of the row of businesses including Nick's, which fronted the highway, and the block of houses across the alley, old

Cathedral City was being erased and every day Sam's parcel looked more and more like an old-fashioned movie set surrounded by concrete sound stages.

Harry consistently refused every insulting offer the developers offered him and instead hired a private detective to investigate the assault on the alley. As for Nick's, the business, it was never more popular, two hundred dinners every night, the bar ten deep with curiosity seekers, and Ruthie getting great reviews as far as Los Angeles, San Francisco, and San Diego.

Trouble was, Sam thought, they were all unhappy.

Nick wasn't the same without Kenny or the bottle. Not funny or warm or friendly, but it didn't matter because all the regulars stopped coming. The tourists either scared them away, or their houses had been torn down.

One way or another the heart of the bar was gone.

23

The Test

When Thomas got an official-looking notice from the Riverside County Department of Health in Indio, he immediately took it to his boss Andy to request that he interpret it for him. Andy scanned the first sentences carelessly, expecting it to be a form letter looking for a donation. Instead he read:

DEAR <u>MR</u>/MS. *Thomas Quintero:*

YOU MAY HAVE BEEN EXPOSED TO A SEXUALLY TRANSMITTED DISEASE. WE ARE REQUIRED BY LAW TO NOTIFY YOU. IT IS IMPERATIVE FOR YOUR SAFETY THAT YOU COME TO OUR CLINIC FOR TESTING. YOU MAY BE AT RISK TO THE HEALTH OF YOUR SEXUAL PARTNERS.

THE RIVERSIDE COUNTY
DEPARTMENT OF HEALTH

"What, Mister Andy?"

"It's somewhat serious, Thomas." Andy struggled to explain. "Someone has given your name to a local clinic. A hospital. This says you have to go in for tests."

Thomas blinked. He didn't understand. "Who gave my name?"

"It doesn't say who listed you. Just that you have to come."

"What kind of test? Like a driving test? Citizenship test?"

"No." Andy shook his head. "A blood test. To examine your blood for diseases."

"Why my blood have diseases?" Thomas asked in amazement. He sank to a chair in front of Andy's desk.

"Someone who had sex with you probably tested positive for a communicable disease. Look, this is pretty personal stuff," Andy said, stuffing the letter back in the envelope. "Can I be frank with you, Thomas?"

Thomas shrugged. "Please."

"Are you having sex outside of your marriage?"

Thomas's face reddened. Andy had his answer.

"If you are, then that person probably gave your name to the clinic. Not wanting to tell you face to face. If they find something, you'll have to tell Inez. So she can be tested. It's very complicated. Very awful. But you have to be tested."

"I'd have to tell my *wife?*" This seemed too unreasonable. Thomas shook his head in amazement.

"Absolutely. For her protection. I want you to go to Indio this very minute. I'll close the shop and go with you if you need me to."

"No, Mister Andy. I'll go alone."

"You may not have been infected with anything so don't panic. You just have to get tested. I get tested every six months. It's very simple."

Thomas took the envelope back from Andy and folded it carefully.

Once outside, he paused to look up at the sky. He got into his pickup and started his own long, long journey to Indio but halfway there he turned around. Instead he would go to Ruby's.

The exchange was brief and passionate. Thomas waved the paper in her face and threatened to kill her if she didn't name her other lovers. Why had she placed him in such a position? Thomas was attracted to Ruby for qualities Inez didn't possess. So instead of responding with angry, obdurate silence, as Inez would have done, or immediately begin reciting her rosary to block out his imperial outrage, as Inez would have done, Ruby instead slapped the face off Thomas's head.

Then she spat at him and ordered him *out of the house, out of her life,* and although she was quick to point out she had no other lovers, she would immediately begin amassing them by scores of ten and whisper *every* detail of their lovemaking to poor Thomas Quintero as he passed on the street with his *dry, shriveled, ugly little crone* he called a wife!

Thomas responded predictably by falling to his knees while she dealt her blows, begging her forgiveness and swearing to avenge the cruel prankster who gave his name to these authorities because they were jealous of his new status as an American citizen, jealous of his raise at work, jealous that he was buying his own house, and lastly, clearly jealous of his beautiful *novia,* his future wife, the future Mrs. Ruby Quintero.

Mrs. Ruby Quintero. This was the first time any discussion of marriage had passed between the lovers. They were both, after all, practicing Catholics. The marriage to Inez would have to be annulled; there were ways, there was cause . . . Ruby was a fierce competitor. A priest could always be *convinced* with the right reasoning.

The paper from the Riverside County Department of Health fluttered to the floor and was soon drenched in the perspiration of their make-up sex. It literally began to rip apart under their writhing, shredding to so many tiny pieces, into so many fine, now disjointed chards of paper that it finally dissolved into opaque droplets of viscous liquid and soon absorbed into the hungry pores of their exposed skin.

It was in this way Thomas finally managed to infect Ruby with HIV. By ignoring the facts on the paper. By putting out of his mind that Inez more than once had caught him in the alley fucking butterflies.

After leaving Ruby, Thomas found himself still aroused, so he took the long way home and headed for the date palm groves behind the gay hotels back off the highway in Cathedral City.

Since moving to the United States, his macho sense of entitlement became so engorged that Thomas Quintero soon found himself hard for everything on two legs. He truthfully didn't know what had come over him. He had a wife at home, a *novia* on the side, and he still found it necessary after leaving Ruby to get himself serviced by *los putos* in the date palm groves between the gay hotels.

He had two rules.

He always closed his eyes and would never allow them to place his fingers around their *vergas, or worse* certainly never allow them to guide their *vergas* in his mouth. It was an abomination, and more than once, if pressed to do such things, he found himself flailing out with drunken fists, (that is, if he'd been gratified already) because he, Thomas Quintero was no *maricon,* he was not a homosexual like those sick perverts of the night. He was a man with a wife and a steady *novia;* and these quick, simple releases escaped the notice of God.

In Mexico, Thomas remembered, homosexuals were easily identified as transvestites or effeminate young men who for pesos would guarantee ecstasy . . . The same man who might savage a *maricon* in broad daylight for no apparent reason might seek sexual gratification from the same effete, lip-bruised butterfly that night.

In Cathedral City the image of *los maricones* was much different, which Thomas didn't mind, because here they were most likely rippling with hard muscular shoulders, had thick wavy hair, and were mostly clad only in tight shorts and hiking boots. And what was more, they didn't seem to want any money. They just wanted to please him!

Because Thomas was so handsome, they didn't seem to mind his own lack of generosity, and if they were lucky and so inclined, a very drunk Thomas Quintero could be coaxed into fucking their assholes. His only condition was his refusal to wear a condom, because a condom compromised his potency, his manhood, and was clearly an insult to God. Only a homosexual wore condoms because, in Thomas's mind, only a homosexual, because of God's will, could ever possibly contract AIDS.

Inez's health improved because Pablo insisted that she take her pills. He patiently sorted all her various medications into daily packets, each containing over eighteen tablets, which she took three times a day on a very precise schedule. He filed her application for an MISP: Medically Indigent Services Program. All her pills were provided free of charge.

"I want you to attend a meeting with me. At the Desert AIDS Project."

"Never."

"It isn't just gay men."

"There's nothing wrong with gay men," she observed. "I never said there was."

Pablo looked at her in astonishment and laughed.

"You could meet other people with HIV. They'd assign you a case worker who can help you with paperwork. Get you assistance."

"You help me all I need."

"But I may not always be around."

She looked up. Sadness flickered in her eyes. "Where will you be?"

"Well," Pablo stammered. "I may go back to Mexico. To school. Or I might meet somebody."

"Who?"

"A boy friend, perhaps."

She grew very silent. For the very first time in her life, Inez Quintero wanted to control her temper. She contemplated the handsome, compassionate boy in front of her and was struck suddenly by how dependent she had become on him. How much she loved him. She even wanted his happiness. But to that kind of life?

She hardened. "Go now."

"I'm not going anywhere now."

"I don't need you," she started up.

"Yes," he insisted. "You do need me. But you also have to respect me!"

"I have my daughter." She folded her arms. "And Señora Singer." Ruthie visited her on a regular basis. Her lawyer was handling Inez's INS problems. Under strict orders from Inez, no one could know details about her health. Not even Ruthie.

"Then I'll go." He shook his head miserably. "I've always let you speak your mind. I've tolerated your prejudices because deep down I thought you were really above them."

"I don't have prejudices!"

"Yes. You do. And it must be difficult for you, knowing that the only person who's shown you any respect is a gay man. *Un maricon.*" He became angry and moved to leave. "We've all had to learn some hard lessons this year," he shouted. "I've been there for you. You have to"—he struggled for his words—"you have to stop being so mean! You're mean. At first I thought it was funny, but not anymore. You hurt me! You want me to be alone all my life?"

Inez's jaw began to quiver. "You'll have me."

"And you'll have me! But you don't have to be an invalid. You aren't dying! You'd see that if you came to the meetings. You need to be more independent."

"Maybe you should go." She waved her hand, dismissing him. "You don't have to come back."

"Oh," he cajoled her, "I'm coming back," Pablo adjusted her blankets and patted her leg. He leaned over and kissed her. "Once the infection clears up, you'll feel good as new. People are *living* with HIV." He smiled into her eyes. "I love you, Inez."

"I love you too, Pablito," she whispered emotionally.

That night Pablo left Inez's house and walked down the alley toward Nick's. His Jeep was parked in the parking lot so Thomas Quintero wouldn't be suspicious. He'd asked Inez if she'd ever planned to tell her husband. She shrugged, her mouth an inverted crescent moon, and advised Pablo that her family found her so unpleasant she was surprised they hadn't dropped her off in the desert long before this.

"But he'll take care of you, right?"

"My husband is hardworking and very proud and my value to him was the money I made. I worked very hard, cleaning two houses per day and supervising my crews at the motel. He wants to buy a house, and now we can't because I'll be too sick to work. He'll find a new wife to be his partner. I'm not needed anymore, and what's worse, I'm a burden. He should get rid of me."

She was apparently in complete agreement with Thomas's logic.

Thomas Quintero rarely drank and was regarded in Sam Singer's alley community as straitlaced and teetotaling and, like Inez, devoid of humor. But tonight Thomas had been to El Gallito and returned late under a cloud-covered moon.

Staggering across the highway, he cut through Nick's parking lot to get home.

Tonight Pablo had stayed late with Inez, taking the risk largely because he knew he was her only company. The old aunt was their ally because Pablo did her errands; the younger children were sworn to secrecy; Alex was usually gone. When Pablo left, he distributed candy to Anita and books for Soila after he kissed Inez goodbye. Then he exited through the kitchen, letting himself out of the gate to the alley.

Since the last assault, a large number of loiterers hung off the fences and the feeling was very sinister. As Pablo walked, the loiterers mocked him, hey *puto, maricon* . . . you want me to fuck you, and Pablo knew not to demonstrate fear. He scowled and swaggered, puffing up like a python, and was so distracted he failed to see a big drunken man looming out at him from the shadows, and although he hadn't met him, he was certain this must be Thomas Quintero.

Pablo stopped, because Thomas was only steps from the entrance to Nick's. He reasoned that a confrontation might result in easier access to Inez, if he could explain that he was only trying to help her, that his affection for her extended to Thomas and his children and this could all be made more civil with conversation.

"What are you doing with my wife? I know you visit her when I'm working."

"I—"

"Are you fucking her? Why does she go off with a *pincha maricon?* Where do you go? A hotel? She's so ugly you have to hide her?" Behind him Pablo could hear snickers, and the soft thud of bodies dropping from fences, wanting to watch the fun.

"Señor Quintero—"

"Did you give her *la SIDA?*"

"You *know?*" Have you been to the clinic? It's very important that you go to be tested."

Thomas's huge hand flew up and clipped Pablo across the jaw, knocking him backward into the dirt. He tasted blood.

Pablo found himself surrounded by *pachucos,* who held him while Thomas moved in to finish him off. Pablo struggled and managed to hold them back, but his physical strength was no match for the men of this alley, and again they managed to pin back his arms.

Thomas slugged him again, Pablo kicking and shouting obscenities, and soon the others were incited to join in. "*Pincha puto, pincha maricon,*" they taunted, a kick to his groin dropping him to his knees. Pablo thought they intended to kill him.

The old aunt suddenly emerged from the gate and was astonished to see her staid nephew leading the attack on Inez's caregiver. She retreated behind the wall, and soon Inez appeared with Soila helping her.

"Leave him alone!" she cried. Thomas looked at her in horror. She looked emaciated from her illness.

"What's wrong with her?" someone cried. Pablo's attackers looked from her to the bloodied Pablo and frantically wiped their hands of his blood. Pablo lay bleeding in a heap in the dirt, and the attackers suddenly began to disburse.

"*I don't have it!*" Thomas began swearing. "She didn't get it from me!"

Thomas staggered toward his wife, swearing at her in Spanish and pushing past her, leaving the old aunt to hold her up and keep her from collapsing.

"What has happened?" the old aunt cried to the alley, but all but a few had disappeared. Soila emerged and rushed to her mother, helping the two of them inside.

"What about the boy?" Inez whimpered, and Soila and the old aunt could only shrug and push her into the gate toward the house.

Pablo lay alone like a pile of bloodied old rags.

In a moment a figure rushed up to him from the shadows with a damp rag, and quickly wiped the blood from his mouth and nose. Pablo moaned as he tended to him, cradling his head in his lap. Pablo's face was bruised and one eye was beginning to blacken shut. Pablo tried to get up but a hand held him in place.

"Drink this," the stranger told him and Pablo took a sip of water which he barely managed to swallow. He sputtered and sat up. His good eye fluttered open and focused on his rescuer, and for the first few moments he thought he was suffering delusions.

"Nick?"

"Welcome to the club," Nick smiled wryly. "We need to get you cleaned up. I'll drive you home."

"No," Pablo protested. "I live too far away."

"Then come back to the house with me."

Pablo felt strange alone in the house with Nick. For one thing, since Nick had stopped drinking, his personality was much more subdued. Dressed in a short-sleeve shirt and a pair of jeans, he looked so normal, a trim, nice-looking, middle-aged man. Pablo noticed that a few strands of gray were beginning to dust the blond tendrils of his temples.

He sat Pablo on a stool in the master bathroom while he riffled around for first-aid supplies. He found an ancient box of cotton balls and a bottle of hydrogen peroxide and began dabbing at the abrasions on Pablo's body. Pablo had been wearing shorts that day, and both knees were skinned from the struggle.

"Take off your shirt." Nick asked him. "You're bleeding on your left shoulder blade." Pablo peeled off his shirt. Nick studied him clinically, but Pablo heard his heart racing. Nick clearly felt uncomfortable and wanted to excuse himself. "It's nothing. Must have been Quintero's blood. If you take a shower, you'll be good as new. I'll find you a fresh T-shirt. Kenny didn't take all of his clothes." He moved to leave.

When he came back, Pablo was already in the shower, the glass door partially left open. Nick could see the water cascading down Pablo's naked body. Pablo's eyes were closed. Nick could see that he shaved his body with the exception of a tiny triangle of pubic hair, framing the shaft of his penis.

When he looked up, he saw that Pablo's eyes were open. Staring through the cascading water at Nick. He reached for the shower door, but instead of closing it, he opened it wider, as if in invitation.

Astonished, Nick turned away

When Pablo came out of the bathroom, he found Nick sitting on the edge of his bed, quivering.

"Nick? What is it?"

"I haven't had sex in so long," he said. "And I definitely never had sex when I was sober."

"But what about you and Kenny?"

Nick looked up at him. "It's been at least five years."

Pablo didn't know what to do. Sex to him had always been so simple. He marveled at how it complicated so many other people's hearts. "I only offered because I like you. I'll go if it makes you more comfortable."

"Would you do one thing for me?"

"Yeah."

"Do you think you could kiss me?" He was trembling so hard when Pablo reached him that Pablo circled his arms around him as if to warm him. Gently Pablo kissed the side of Nick's face. Then he grazed his lips over his forehead and kissed the other side. Nick couldn't look at him.

Then Pablo kissed him on the lips.

He sat back.

"Thank you," said Nick. He looked up at him. Pablo leaned down to kiss him again. This time Nick accepted him hungrily.

Later they were seated on the edge of the bed, both coincidentally wearing identical boxer shorts, flies buckling at the groins. They had just spent the last hour locked in one passionate kiss.

Nick could see Pablo's cock protruding. He trembled so hard his teeth were chattering.

"I feel like I'm molesting you," Pablo whispered, tracing the contours of Nick's face with his finger. "You're afraid. We haven't done anything to be afraid of. I promise we won't. Maybe this is all we should do. It was wrong of me to insist on sex after our first date."

He started to get up, but Nick pushed him back.

"Are you sure you want me to stay?"

"Yes."

"Then close your eyes."

Pablo sat back on the bed and climbed under the sheet. He scrambled out of his boxers.

"Let me show you everything is okay."

Nick opened his eyes. Pablo undulated under the sheet. Nick could see his enormous erection, arching over his stomach, swathed in cotton like some bridge cloaked in a white cloud. He moved onto the bed and studied him.

Nick's long period of celibacy was over. Pablo helped him ease out of his shorts. Straddling Nick, Pablo smiled down at him, his thick mane of black hair toppling into his eyes. Nick gazed up at him in awe. Pablo took his hands and, after kissing his inner palms, guided them up to his chest.

"You're very beautiful," Pablo told Nick. "Anybody ever tell you that?" He leaned down to kiss him again. At first Nick resisted, then relented. Pablo lowered himself on top of Nick's body. Even after years of hard living, Nick's body was still lean and well made. He'd managed to regain his tan after his month at Betty Ford, but now he didn't augment it with fake tanning creams. His gray eyes gazed frankly into Pablo's as Pablo worked his way down to the blond hairs of Nick's stomach, trailing below his belly button to his groin.

"Do you have a condom, baby?" Pablo asked.

"No." Nick shook his head. "Do we need one?"

"You're single now," Pablo explained quietly but with purpose. "You need to be prepared."

The light in Nick's eyes dimmed. A reminder that he was alone. That times were different. Nick sat up, extricating himself from Pablo's embrace.

"No, no, don't go out of the mood."

"There are new rules." Nick shook his head again. "I don't know if I'm ready. I don't know if I'm gonna like this new life."

"Then let's just hold each other. Or you can watch me. I can be fun to watch . . ." His voice trailed away as he saw Nick wince in reaction.

"You aren't a whore." Nick reached for his glasses.

"No. Not anymore." Pablo reached for his shorts. "I don't know if I'm ready either. I don't know if I'm gonna like this new life."

Nick smiled at him. "We'll both have to do the best we can."

"Could I still spend the night? In here, with you? I haven't slept with anyone for so long."

Nick reached for his shorts and pulled them on. He climbed into bed and reached for his book. Pablo reclined behind him, stroking his back till he fell asleep.

The next morning Nick lingered in the doorway of the bedroom and watched Pablo sleeping. Pablo lay curled into the tightest ball, the white sheet pulled around him, outlining his body like fine powder. Then he woke up and saw Nick watching him.

Pablo knew that look. "You miss him, don't you?"

"He's my mate," Nick explained.

"For life?" Pablo asked in hushed amazement.

"For life."

"Think I'll ever mate for life?"

"If you're lucky. If you're patient."

"This one hurts." Pablo smiled in dazed amazement.

Moments later he was driving alone across the desert to Sky Valley.

Inez awoke to the sight of her husband looming over their bed. His eyes were dead with fear and disappointment. He studied her suspiciously. Then without warning he scooped her swiftly up in his arms.

"What are you doing?" Inez asked him wearily. The previous evening's events had profoundly distressed her.

"Quiet," Thomas growled.

He carried her into the living room, where the old aunt was sleeping on the sofa. Soila and Alex heard the commotion. They both appeared from their respective rooms and gathered behind Thomas holding their tiny mother aloft in the darkness.

"What are you doing with her, Pop?" asked Alex.

Thomas kicked at the sofa. The old aunt stirred. "Move," he said. She leapt to her feet like an overeager old dog. Thomas placed Inez on the sofa.

"Papa, what are you doing?" Soila asked him again.

"She's leaving this house in the morning!"

Inez looked up at him incredulously. Soila moved to comfort her.

"Where will I sleep?" the old aunt began to weep.

"On the floor mat in the kitchen. What do I care!"

He turned, the shocked eyes of his family trained on him like cowering animals. Alex started to say something but Thomas held one finger up and he fell silent. Grimacing, Thomas disappeared into the dark hallway and slammed the door to his bedroom behind him.

The next morning Soila arose to find her mother at the end of the sidewalk, sitting on a suitcase and holding in her lap a few belongings from her childhood.

"*Mamita!*" she screamed, rushing out to the street.

"Quiet, *Hija,*" Inez shushed her. "Be good now when Ruby comes to live with you."

"*Ruby?*"

"Of course. Your father could never survive without a wife. She's young and pretty. She'll work hard. If you act sweetly and flatter her, I'm sure she'll be pleasant to you," Inez observed.

"What about Anita?"

"Anita will forget quickly."

"Mommy, where do you think you're going?"

"I'm going back to Mexico. When I get my wind, I'll walk to the corner. After I rest for a while, down to the highway. I want to go home, *niña,* home to Mexico. This was your father's dream, not mine."

"Mommy." Soila stroked her mother's hair. "Come inside now. He didn't mean anything."

"It doesn't matter what he meant," Inez observed. "I want to go home and that's where I'm going. Be a good girl, try to forget me and go to Mass every day." Inez struggled to stand. She grasped her daughter's shoulder and teetered slightly, but finally caught her balance.

"Mommy, no! I'll go get him, you'll see he didn't mean anything."

"He won't come, Soila. And I don't want him to come. I don't approve of him or your brother. Anita will be pretty so she has a chance. The only one I really love is you, Soila. Don't make leaving you any harder. Kiss me goodbye and go back inside." And she reached out and stroked her daughter's face, tracing her birthmark tenderly and touching her lips with her fingers.

"Look how beautiful the desert is this morning."

They both gazed out over the pink and lavender dawn. "Sometimes I must admit, the light is spectacular!" Then she pursed her lips and declared, "But only rarely and not enough to justify staying."

And slowly she eased herself down the walk. Several steps and then a rest. Then several more. And more. And finally she rounded the corner, happy her term in Cathedral City was coming to a meaningful end.

At Cathedral Canyon Drive and Highway 111, Inez's plans were thwarted when Pablo pulled up in his Jeep after a frantic call from Soila and a high-speed drive across the desert.

"Where do you think you're going?"

"Home."

"Where's home?"

"Mexico."

"How are you going to get there?"

"I'll call *La Migra*."

"They'll just keep you in jail."

"I'm not a citizen! They have to send me back."

"Don't you have any other relatives?" he stammered.

"No!"

"Then you must feel very lonely. You'll live with me."

This sentiment caught her completely off guard. She began to cry and allowed him to hug her. Her body felt as frail as a bag of raked leaves.

Inez collected herself. "If you want to help me, take me to Mexico."

"Okay. Get in." He opened the door to his Jeep. He picked her up and she allowed herself to collapse into the bucket seat.

Inez struggled in her seat. She wanted to search her purse, which lay next to her satchel on the ground next to the Jeep. Pablo reached for her bags and handed them to her.

"Do you have your pills?"

"I don't want to take my pills. They make me feel sick."

"Do you want to die?" he said incredulously.

"If I die, my family will accept it."

"But you don't need to die," he lamented. "They should have warned you about the risks."

"What was I to them?" Inez whispered. "A peasant. A maid."

"We don't have peasants in this country."

Unexpectedly, a laugh rattled from Inez's throat.

Inez slept as Pablo drove across the desert to Sky Valley. When she opened her eyes and saw his little trailer, tucked up against the rocky hillside with the funny little garden and the long view south of the unpopulated desert, Inez assumed in her cheery delirium he had driven her into Mexico.

"It's good to be back home!" she remarked as he helped her down. "Do we have any chickens? I feel like an egg . . ."

But when he opened the door of the little trailer, she looked inside and quickly proclaimed:

"Surely I'm in hell!"

Maria stood up to greet her.

24

The View of the River

Late in the afternoon, Nick came and took a seat at the bar. Marcella looked up.

"What's wrong?"

"I'm not doing so good."

"No?" she asked calmly. "Why not?"

"Everything's gone to hell since Kenny moved out. I miss him."

"He's back in the kitchen," she said. "Go talk to him."

"You know what I mean."

"Yeah," Marcella grunted.

"What's the use?" He got up.

"Wait a minute. I'm sorry. I'm sorry, baby. You want company? I'm here. I owe you that."

Nick reconsidered. He plopped back down on the stool.

"You want anything? Diet Coke? Evian?"

Nick studied the bottles of alcohol, lining the shelf behind her. "Yeah. A Bombay martini."

"I'll make you one," she said brightly.

"I was joking."

"Remember how you used to be able to tell the difference between all gins by smelling the bottles? Nobody could do that better than you." She laughed gaily.

"One night you bet me your whole tip jar and you lost!" Nick grinned. His eyes fell to the bottles of gin. *Bombay, Boodles, Tanqueray, Gilbeys . . .*

"And you took it," she said, her voice a little sharp.

"I've gotta use the john." Nick stood up. "Save my seat."

When he came back, four shots of gin were lined up on the bar.
"What's this?"

"I want a rematch."

"That's ridiculous," he said. "This is a waste of inventory."

"I already paid for 'em." She motioned to the register. "Let's see your stuff."

He studied the glasses intently. Then he sat up. "No."

"A week's pay."

"You should get Sam Singer in here. He's the gambler. Not me."

"No? I disagree. I think you're a big gambler. You don't have to drink 'em. Just smell. How 'bout it?"

"Week's pay?" Business was good but he and Kenny had mutually agreed to pay off their investors. Spending money was tight.

"Yeah. Wait a minute. Now I gotta use the can."

Jauntily she stepped around the side of the bar. Inside the women's restroom she took a moment to snort some coke.

When she came out, all the shot glasses were empty. Her face flooded with happy victory.

"You're fired, Marcella."

Nick was standing behind her. Sober as a judge.

"What?"

"You're fired, Marcella. Get out of my bar."

"You're crazy, " she said. "Here, let me fix you a drink."

"I don't want you to fix me a drink. Just get out of my bar."

"You can't fire me."

"If you don't get out of here, I'll throw you out myself."

"I'd like to see you try, you fucking faggot."

"Marcella. Get out."

They turned. Kenny stood standing in the swinging doors. He walked up behind Nick and placed his hand on his shoulder.

"I'll fuckin' turn all of you in. I'll fuckin' call the INS. You'll fuckin' pay for this!"

She ripped off her apron and threw it in Nick's face. "This is a bar. I'm a bartender! We serve liquor here!" Then she stomped from around the bar and out the front door.

"*Fucking faggots!*" she screamed on the street outside.

"That word is always waiting somewhere," Kenny observed.

Nick slumped in his bar stool and shook.

After Marcella got fired, she figured it would all blow over and Nick would call to apologize the next time he got drunk. She planned in advance to be a hard-ass, to swear at him, to hang up and really make him beg for it before she finally, of course, would relent.

But Nick wasn't calling, and she'd asked around and it seemed that he was staying sober. Pablo was now the bartender. Had Marcella been there, she'd spike a Coke, just to get the old taste buds fired up again. Ralph Zola wouldn't return her calls after the screwup with the kids from Palm Springs. This was perfectly fine with her, and secretly she felt happy Sam was winning his war. Still, she wished she could have her old job back, have things the way they were before.

On her bad days she plotted revenge but decided it wouldn't get her anywhere. She even tried calling the INS, but they no longer took reports over the telephone. She thought it would be easy as changing her voice, whisper the names of a few Mexicans, and they'd be all over Kenny like a bad rash.

And then a stunning thing happened at home, up in Whitewater Canyon, after which she decided to pay Father Gene a visit and confess everything. Her whole life history.

It was early in the morning, and Marcella had wandered up to leave her rent in Mrs. Ridley's mailbox, which hung to the right of her front door up on the porch.

The door was closed and the house felt quiet, so Marcella assumed she was still sleeping and this gave her license to help herself to a climbing rose, which clung to the trellis on the side of the porch. Just as she snapped a young bud from the vine, she sensed someone behind her and whirled around.

"Hello, dear," said Mrs. Ridley, seated on the swing, ankles crossed, perspiring under an afghan.

"Mrs. Ridley!" Marcella noticed immediately that she wasn't well. The pallor of her skin was ivory and she was breathing quite heavily. At her feet was a small pool of vomit, nearly dry.

"What's wrong?"

"Nothing . . . nothing at all."

"But you've thrown up."

"Doesn't matter . . . My arm was hurting, and I just got a little nauseous. It'll go away."

"Which arm is hurting?"

"The left one, but it's nearly stopped."

"And you were sick to your stomach?"

"I'm afraid so. I had terrible gas."

"I think you've had a heart attack."

"No, no, I'll be okay. Would you mind staying with me?"

"But I need to call an ambulance." Marcella was surprised by a wave of guilt.

"I don't want you to do that, dear."

"But this is serious!"

"It's very serious, which is why an ambulance is the last thing I need right now. I'd love your company much more than that. I'd like you to sit right here with me and just hold my hand."

"I don't think I can do that," Marcella protested, absolutely repulsed. She hated physical pain and here Mrs. Ridley was saturated with it.

"Yes. Yes, you can. I'm asking you to do something very special. I'm asking you to witness the power of God's will. God and I are extremely close right now. This is an experience not to be missed."

"Look, I have to call an ambulance."

"I won't permit it. I won't go." Her face suddenly convulsed with pain. "If you can't help me, then I understand," she whispered through gritted teeth. "Leave me be."

To her own amazement, Marcella began to whimper softly, hopping from one foot to another as though the porch boards were scorching her feet. Then she slid onto the swing next to Mrs. Ridley, touching her hand tentatively at first, and then gripping it firmly.

"I always wanted a daughter," Mrs. Ridley sighed. "I always thought this would be pleasant and it is." She closed her eyes, and Marcella could see how translucent her eyelids were. She could almost make out the blue eyes underneath.

Marcella's thoughts began to race. She thought of her mother and her own childhood. Her own mother had been so cynical, with cause, Marcella knew, but the end result was a mean-streaked daughter incapable of spontaneity. It was difficult to love when you live by agenda, and the control and manipulation of others was Marcella's legacy from her mother.

"Mrs. Ridley, I've made some mistakes. I've done some bad things."

"You're perfect, Marcella. Just as you are. God loves you, Marcella. You're one hundred percent perfection in his eyes."

"Really bad things."

"You'll do more before you're through, but it doesn't matter." After a moment she added, "Not that you shouldn't attempt to do better. You should always try to be loving, Marcella . . ."

"I don't know how to be loving," Marcella sobbed.

"That isn't true for you, Marcella," Mrs. Ridley said softly, "God would never have picked you out to live here if you weren't capable of love."

Marcella was silent.

"I know you all make fun of me . . . Don't give it a second thought. I have a past, Marcella. But I've forgiven myself for everything. I had to in order to proceed."

Although she talked easily, her breathing became erratic and Marcella was growing increasingly frightened. It was starting to get hot, and Mrs. Ridley grew very, very pale and began to perspire heavily.

"Maybe we should move you inside . . ."

"And miss my lovely view of the river?"

"The riverbed has been dry for a month, Mrs. Ridley."

"We'll have floods in August. God is my life." Suddenly she gasped, lurching forward. Marcella leaned forward to ease her back to an upright position, but when her hands seized the old woman's shoulders, she knew Mrs. Ridley's body was dead and a flash of light in the trees caused Marcella to look heavenward.

"What should I do?" she asked Father Gene. He'd been listening to her for two hours. He decided he should make a rule about hearing confessions from non-Catholic petitioners.

"Are you asking me practically or spiritually?"

"Both."

"Confess. Get on with your life."

"You think I should call the police?"

"What are they going to do? Why don't you call Sam Singer? Let him make the choice.

Pablo, Maria, and Inez all lived together happily in the little trailer overlooking the desert in Sky Valley. To the mail carrier or any traveler exploring the back roads of the desert foothills, they looked like a young couple caring for an elderly parent. Inez now understood that instead of Mexico she was only seven miles across the desert from Cathedral City. It was arranged for Soila to pay visits to her mother, once they were certain she wouldn't reveal the whereabouts of Maria or Inez.

Inez liked to sit outside in the sun, and often Maria would keep her company on the long dusky days Pablo worked in Cathedral

City, as a bartender at Nick's. She didn't ask about Kenny and Pablo didn't volunteer anything, including the fact that Kenny only lived miles away in nearby Desert Hot Springs.

Maria clearly enjoyed taking care of Inez. She reminded her very much of Concha as she had probably been when she was younger. Feisty, passionate, brittle, and kind.

As for Pablo, he liked being *el patron*. He liked to pretend that Maria was his wife and Inez his cantankerous mother-in-law. An occasional dalliance in the date palm groves could be forgiven such a wonderful provider.

One evening Inez and Pablo were sitting outside, in chairs around a small campfire Pablo had built, watching the sun set in the western sky. Maria stepped from the trailer with a glass of water and Inez's nightly regimen of medication.

"You didn't take your pills, little monkey."

"I haven't come here to be insulted. I can be insulted by my husband in Cathedral City."

Maria rattled the small paper cup filled with pills. "Take them and be grateful. In Mexico poor women with HIV stand in line with bags on their heads to collect their medication because they're made to feel ashamed."

They received *POZ Magazine* in Spanish every month, and Maria read it to Pablo and Inez, cover to cover.

"I take twenty pills a day, and I am not ashamed," Inez admonished them gravely.

"Twenty more and you'll have enough for a rosary," Pablo cracked.

Inez smiled at him. "I am grateful. For many gifts." She patted Pablo's hand and took the pills. She swallowed them, her face registering her distaste. Maria watched her patiently. Then her own face suddenly blanched. She ran around the side of the trailer. Pablo stood up. He could hear her throwing up. He started to go after her.

"Leave her alone . . . She's pregnant."

"I'm not sorry. I'm happy," Maria said, coming up behind her.

"Are you going to tell the father?" Pablo asked her.

Maria wavered.

"He's a priest," Inez said. "He has too much on his mind. Better wait till later. We'll help with the baby." She patted Maria's hand. "She can have it here, in the trailer."

Maria and Pablo looked at each other skeptically.

"Maybe other arrangements can be made," Pablo observed.

Inez surveyed the faces of her friends. "I was thinking I might attend one of those support meetings at the clinic."

Pablo and Maria smirked at her. Inez frowned at them.

"I've overcome many of my prejudices. And I'm thinking, there might be other women like me."

"Women who might help you?" Pablo queried.

"No, silly," Maria observed. "Someone *she* could help."

"*Muneca,*" Pablo was saying. "I've done something you may hate me for." They both slept in the foldout cots in the small living area of Pablo's trailer so Inez could have the back bedroom to herself.

"What?" she whispered back. "There's nothing you could do to make me hate you but one thing." The moonlight illuminated the small sheer curtains she had made for the porthole windows of the little trailer. Pablo lay shirtless under his blanket as he studied her.

"You could never even hate me for that," he sang to her teasingly. He was smiling, but she could see how troubled he was.

"Kenny—" he began.

"You *told* him!" she shouted.

From the back, Inez woke up from a nightmare. She began to convulse. Pablo and Maria both jumped up, struggling to maneuver through the tight galley kitchen to get to her. Maria angrily elbowed her way past Pablo. Then when he backed out of her way, she slugged him again for good measure. Inside her tiny sleeping quarters, Inez was gasping for air.

"*Ayyy, Mamita,*" Maria called out. "I'm sorry we woke you."

"We're sorry," Pablo called after her.

"*Where's her oxygen tank!*" Maria demanded angrily. "I left it right here!"

"It's next to her bed."

Inez was now sitting up, eyes ablaze with panic, getting enough air on her own but needing the tank for security. Pablo pushed into the room and retrieved the small portable tank which the Desert AIDS Project had supplied free of charge for Inez. He sat next to her on the bed and stroked her back soothingly while deftly unwinding the tangled oxygen tube. Finally he managed to place the tube over her head and under her nostrils. The oxygen started to flow.

"There, Mamita," he whispered to her, kissing her gently on her cheek and the moist coiled tendrils of her thinning hair. "We can all breathe easier now . . ."

Inez clearly loved his touch and began to calm down immediately.

Maria sank to her other side and took her hand, patting and kissing it tenderly, the three of them sitting at the edge of the bed, all in a row.

"Why was I so blessed?" Inez whispered. "To have children such as these."

Maria stole a glance at Pablo, his own eyes closed as he rocked Inez in the hollow of his chin and neck. A small growth of beard was beginning to darken his cheek. As she patted Inez's hand, she caught sight of the tableaux of the three of them, reflected from a tiny mirror which Inez kept at her bedside.

The room was littered with Catholic artifacts. Statues of the Virgin Mary, plates with paintings of the baby Jesus, a crucifix over her bed which her husband Thomas had carved by hand when they were married. Her only treasure from that life. A small votive candle. A *retablo* painted for her by Maria.

When Maria glanced back in the direction of Inez and Pablo, she could see that Inez was now sleeping and Pablo was studying Maria with remorseful eyes.

"I'm sorry," he mouthed to her.

"What did he say?" she whispered.

"He wants to see you. I wouldn't tell him where you are. He's begging you. He loves you."

Several days later it was decided that Maria would drive Soila home while Pablo remained home with Inez. This was her first trip back to Cathedral City, and Pablo knew why Maria insisted on making the trip.

"He won't be there," Pablo reminded her.

"I just want to see it," Maria shrugged, and he handed her the keys to his Jeep.

"Are you going to tell him about his baby?"

Maria ignored him and drove away.

Maria and Soila arrived at sunset, and Maria was moved to see how much construction surrounded the little quadrant of Nick's and Sam's houses. She parked the Jeep in the alley, several houses away from the old kitchen door, having let a tearful but grateful Soila off a block away so no one would trace her to Pablo and Inez.

It all looked the same albeit more weatherworn. The colors Kenny had so proudly chosen were already fading from the hot desert sun. Maria decided to leave the Jeep and allow herself a modest stroll past the entrance to the bar. She was surprised to hear music softly playing, and as she came closer, she could see that the kitchen door was open.

She stopped, frozen in her tracks. Her heart began to pound at the prospect of seeing Kenny. She had been true to her word. Had honored her commitment to him in her letter, written with such sadness and pain. She promised never to bother him again and she hadn't, not wanting to cause any more confusion or grief.

Now she needed to summon every bit of strength she had left to reverse her direction, return to Pablo's Jeep, and go back across the desert. She used Inez as her incentive. Inez was restless if Maria wasn't close by. She knew she soothed Inez and this gave Maria the strength to turn away.

The alley had two exits, three counting Nick's parking lot, which opened out to the highway. As Maria turned away, she heard the screen door opening to Kenny's kitchen, and couldn't resist turning to see who was emerging. To her great chagrin, it wasn't Kenny, but Carmen and Gabriel.

They looked at her and she looked at them. No one moved. Then things began happening very quickly when a gray sedan roared into Nick's parking lot followed closely by a large green and white government van. Then, behind Carmen and Gabriel, at the throat of the alley opening onto Van Fleet, Maria could see another Border Patrol van squeal around the corner and halt abruptly, rocking violently until it came to a standstill.

Behind her more squealing of tires. Without looking, she knew that the last exit had been blocked and then came the predictable running of feet.

"La Migra!" someone shouted, and suddenly the alley was awash with activity, with frightened illegals leaping over fences, thinking they were escaping the assault no doubt being launched on the street at the front of the houses.

Unwittingly they were being herded into the alley where a dozen immigration officers stood waiting, guns drawn, and with all exits blocked, no chance for escape. Soon the alley filled with crying and pleading, begging the officers for mercy.

"I have my papers at my house, lemme just go and get them."

"I have children in school! What will they do when they come home and I'm not here?"

"My mother's sick. I can't leave her!"

All the usual lame excuses.

Since Maria didn't move, but merely relaxed into her spot, no one immediately took notice of her. A young immigration officer even passed her to accost Carmen and Gabriel, but Carmen was already grinning gleefully at the door to Kenny's kitchen.

"You want papers? I'll show you papers!" and she reached inside her purse for her papers. She waved her certificate of naturalization in his face. "I'm an American citizen!" she crowed. "And so is my cousin." And the officer held up her card and scrutinized it. Reluctantly he handed it back to her.

And soon everybody accosted had been processed, arrested, or freed with the exception of Maria, who still lingered nonchalantly against the wall in the shade near the Jeep. She couldn't believe that they didn't see her. Her look must have registered her amazement, which Carmen noted after she and Gabriel were safely free to go.

Gabriel nodded to her briefly, a complicit gesture which seemed to encourage her not to make any sudden movements. As the last person was being handcuffed, and the van in Nick's parking lot was loaded and ready to drive away, Maria found herself able to start edging her way toward Pablo's Jeep.

And then Soila Quintero, who had already been rousted at her own front door, pushed open her gate to inspect the goings on in the alley. A voice rang out:

"What about her? You didn't check her! She's not legal!" And Soila saw that it was Carmen alerting an INS officer to the pretty pregnant woman standing in the alley near a Jeep.

The officer obliged Carmen by glancing in Maria's direction. He called to a fellow officer. The two of them approached her.

Aghast, Gabriel slumped against the wall of the bar.

Maria wasted no time on any reproach of Carmen. She wanted to invest her opportunity with Soila. "Tell them I love them," she whispered to Soila, and she turned to face down her captors.

South this time. Noise allowed. Another crowded van. Misery. Inconsolable weeping. Begging. Many nationalities. Korean. Mexican.

"My children! What will they do tonight without me!"

"My wife and I had a big fight this morning. I threatened to leave her. Now she'll think I did! She won't know how to look for me!"

"I have no money! What am I gonna do in Mexicali with no money?"

"All my groceries are gonna rot! I just went to the Von's this morning!"

And in some faces. Like in Maria's.

Resolve.

Weariness.

Loneliness.

A young woman comforted her tearful older mother. Maria smiled sympathetically. A few boys laughed and nudged each other.

"Hey. Lighten up. We've done this ten times. It won't be a problem. We'll all be back in a week. *Tops.* Who needs a little cash?"

The INS van rattled down Highway 86 toward El Centro and the INS Detention and Deportation Center. Fancy word for jail. The guards talked and laughed with each other. One of them passed back a canteen filled with water. Business as usual. Unlike the *coyotes,* they weren't paid by the head. No ax to grind.

Just past the Salton Sea, Maria recognized the terrain where Ruthie had rescued her on the highway. The riverbed was empty. Dry. She scanned it for her grandmother's bones.

Concha.

Whatever happens, *keep going.*

After Maria was processed at the Calexico Border Station and shoved through the turnstile back onto Mexican soil, an agent stepped forward and intercepted her.

"I have someone who wishes to meet you," he advised her.

He ushered her over to a huge Mercedes, parked by the curb. An elegant woman, beautifully dressed, her hair pulled back into a high tight bun, emerged from the car and graciously extended her hand.

"Hello." The woman smiled, seemingly delighted to see her. "My name is Elena Seladon. I'm *Pablito's* mother. He's told me all about you. I have strict orders to look after you!"

"Your son is a wonderful, wonderful boy," Maria advised her solemnly.

"You'll never know," Mrs. Scladon cried softly, taking Maria's hands and kissing them gratefully, "how *happy* it makes me that you think so!"

25

Pietà

In his final months as a priest, Father Gene was both mystified but somewhat honored to minister to the troubled residents of Cathedral City yet never felt more amazed when a sister informed him that Sam Singer wanted to speak to him. It was midafternoon, and Father Gene was taking a nap. Ordinarily the surly little nun would never disturb her parish priest from a nap, but she indicated that Mr. Singer, who looked a little Jewish, seemed particularly distraught, even though gruff in manner.

When Father Gene entered his office, Sam was sitting in the same leather chair where Kenny had sat nearly a year before. Where had the time gone? Behind Sam, through the window, Father Gene now had a clear view to the highway. Only obstructed by a small group of houses and the bar.

Father Gene remembered Sam from the night Ruthie came out of retirement, but he also remembered him from years ago, when the bar was called Sam's, and the parish priest of St. Louis prayed for that set of regulars as fervently as Father Gene prayed for the present-day patrons of Nick's.

If Inez Quintero thought her confessions scandalized the priest, she had nothing on the stories which rattled the confessionals in Sam Singer's prime.

They contemplated each other like two wise, battle-scarred old soldiers. One a father confessor, the other a self-appointed Don, a godfather of a small hamlet whose days were numbered.

"It's good to see you again, Sam."

"Likewise, Padre."

"For a desert rat, you've aged quite well. Keeping busy, Sam?"

Sam pulled a cigar from his pocket. He offered it to Father Gene. Father Gene stood up and took it. Then he moved to close the door to the rectory hall. "If she smells cigar smoke, I'll be sleeping on the couch," he grinned. Sam smiled at his joke. He pulled out another cigar and, after lighting Father Gene's, lit his own.

They puffed in comfortable silence.

"No secret that I'm having a little difficulty, Padre. Had nowhere else to go."

"Why not go to a rabbi?"

Sam contemplated the big gold ring on his finger. It was studded with diamond chips. He always loved the ring. He was wearing it the day he met Ruthie. She'd pretended to admire it, but told Nick later that she thought it was too gaudy. She hadn't wanted to hurt his feelings.

"I'm having trouble with my girl. With Ruthie, Padre."

"I saw what happened opening night."

"You were there?"

"I wouldn't have missed it, Sam. Not for the world."

"Best-laid plans." Sam coughed.

"A terrible tragedy for all concerned. No winners that night."

"Only the cash register. I must be getting old. In the past, that'd be enough. All that mattered. Now, everybody's unhappy. My wife. My tenants."

"You?" Father Gene studied him gently.

"Me," Sam said, and his voice choked. Father Gene reached in his desk and pulled out a packet of tissues. He offered it over to Sam. Sam took several, crushing them as he dabbed at his eyes. Then he unceremoniously blew his nose.

"I'm really confused," he admitted. "I always thought I knew the right thing to do, but now . . . I don't know what's right. I came to you because of the little black girl . . ."

Father Gene nodded. Marcella.

"She did a terrible thing. Unforgivable."

"She's asked for forgiveness. God has forgiven her."

"What about all the rest of us? Don't we count?"

"What *counts* is her relationship with God, Sam. So in answer to your question, no. Where her spiritual growth is concerned, nothing else matters. Of course, I'd say the same thing to her about you, or your wife. Or Kenny and Nick."

"Kenny and Nick! Who brought them up?"

"I did. Not to mention Inez Quintero and her family. Not to mention Maria, the young woman who saved your wife's life."

"You got that wrong. My wife saved her."

"Whatever." Father Gene smiled. He folded his hands in his lap. "So what brings you here? Have you purchased the church? Are you going to evict me too?"

His eyes twinkled. Sam knew he was joking but he didn't really appreciate it.

"I'm here because my wife won't get out of bed. I'm here because I've made promises I can't keep if I wanted to."

"Why can't you keep them?"

"Two words."

"What two words?"

Sam reached in his pocket and unfolded a careworn piece of paper. On closer inspection, it looked like an official document. He handed it over to the priest.

"Eminent Domain," he said simply.

"They're forcing you to sell?"

"By order of the governor . . ." Sam grew pale. He wiped his brow with the tissues. "How am I ever going to prove that I never really intended to sell, Padre? They won't believe me. My wife, the boys, the Quinteros—"

"Show them the letter!"

"You don't understand," Sam began to really weep. "I fix letters like this all the time. They come to me with their problems and I make a call, pay someone off. I fix problems like this all day, but this one I can't."

"How do you know you can't?"

"Because I been tryin' for a year. Arncha hearing me? Look at the date of the letter!"

Father Gene scanned the letterhead. Sam was right. In several days the letter would be one year old. He looked up at Sam in amazement.

"I threw everything I had at them. Would'a worked if it hadn't been for those bastard kids. I never reckoned on them. Bastard kids. Goddamned little bartender."

"They were coming anyway, Sam," Father Gene chided him gently. "She isn't entirely at fault and neither is Mr. Zola. They were coming whether invited to or paid to or not. Hatred, I find, is entirely free of charge."

"The only thing I have left up my sleeve is my request for historical status for my bar . . . I filed over a year ago."

"Won't that stop them?"

"It may slow 'em down, but my houses behind it aren't protected." Sam pondered his hands. "And when I'm gone, they'll get the bar before the day is done."

"But surely they have to pay you a fair price."

"You don't understand, Padre. I don't *need* the money. I *need* Cathedral City like I remembered it. So does Ruthie, see? Are ya' following me here, Padre?"

Father Gene sat completely still. After a long moment, he nodded that yes, indeed, he understood. He understood why they all needed Cathedral City. It was the subject of a homily he'd been formulating in his subconscious for years.

The mother had a baby and two older toddlers. She and Ruthie were in the pharmacy department, off the beaten path and out of view from the long, long aisles of food and staples one normally sees in a supermarket.

The pharmacy was closed. They were alone—Ruthie and the young, distracted mother and her baby, gurgling in the shopping cart. The toddlers ranged in age from three to five; she must have given birth one after another, Ruthie decided. She must be exhausted, poor thing. Exhausted but very blessed.

She was slight, maybe twenty-five, and far too young to have three kids. Ruthie had noted her earlier on the other side of the store. She might have once been pretty, but now her hair was stringy, her skin freckled, and the older children were especially high-strung. Not the baby, though, the baby was beautiful, calm, serene, and smiling, smiling at Ruthie as she passed.

Ruthie felt a kinship immediately, much in the same way scouts for the next Dalai Lama must feel when they blunder onto the perfect child, a prophet for a new generation. She was rounding the corner, looking for corn pads for Sam of all things, and then saw the baby in the basket. Behind her she heard something crash, like a stack of cans. A child wailed and the young woman wanted to go inspect. She didn't know what to do about her baby. Ruthie knew the young mother was sizing her up.

"Kids," the woman muttered.

"If it'll help, I'll wait with the baby."

"Thanks, you're a doll. I wonder what this is gonna cost me." She shooed a kid in front of her. They disappeared around the corner.

In an instant, Ruthie snatched up the baby, abandoning her cart and rushing away with him smiling in her arms. Out of the corner of her eye she could see the young mother consoling her five-year-old as a very irate store manager lectured her to never let her kids out of her sight for a second. They would be all afternoon putting the display back together. The child could have been hurt trying to climb it.

Ruthie was one aisle over when she heard her name. She knew the voice, not well, but she knew it just the same. "Ruthie!"

She kept going.

"Ruthie! Stop." The voice was calm, not angry but convincing. Wild-eyed, she turned. Sam was standing behind her.

"What?" she said, her eyes tearing up.

"You have to give the baby back. I saw everything. Don't take it this far." Then sotto. "She doesn't know it's gone yet. Just say you went to find her and you ran into me."

"No, it's my baby. Mine and Nick's."

"No, Ruthie. It isn't your baby. It belongs to someone else."

Ruthie stared at him blankly, pulling the happy baby closer to her. This was the most attention this baby had ever had. He knew how much Ruthie wanted him, and the feeling was mutual.

"Let's go," Sam said firmly. "Now. I'll cover for you but we have to go back." He took her elbow with one hand. She held tightly to the baby. Her eyes filled with agony. He steered Ruthie back to the pharmacy where the then hysterical woman stood with the manager. Her other kids were crying and she was demanding that he help her. Sam surveyed the scene from the distance.

"Is that the mother?" Sam said loudly. To Ruthie he whispered, "We're in luck. I know the manager."

The group looked up in Sam's direction. Their gaze traveled from him to the elegant woman holding the baby. They ran toward her.

"Yes, the very one!" Ruthie said merrily, but she perspired around the eyes. "We couldn't find you," she smiled. "Yes, honey, here's your mommy now." She passed the baby off to the young girl, holding on to it a second too long. "You must have been terrified."

"Where did you go?" the mother demanded, stepping back from her.

"She went looking for you, miss," Sam snarled, not liking the tone she was taking. "Hi, Karl," he said to the manager.

"Sam," the store manager nodded, a former customer at Nick's, one of the boys. "We had a scare."

"Guess it worked out okay. This is my wife, Ruthie."

"I'm sorry if you were frightened." Ruthie smiled beautifully at the relieved mother. "When you didn't come back, I went looking for you."

"I was only on the next aisle." The young woman regarded her mistrustfully. They locked eyes for a second, and Sam knew the girl was on to her.

"You're lucky someone nice found your baby, miss," Sam advised her.

"I was just warning her about leaving children unattended," offered the manager, admiring Ruthie's accessories. "You were lucky," he said to the mother.

The young woman yanked an unruly child to her side. Holding her baby tightly, she pushed past them, the remaining child in tow. Passing Ruthie, she said, "You can't just take a kid, lady. I know what you were doing and we're both just lucky he stopped you. Get help."

Outside in the parking lot, Sam held Ruthie while she cried. "I know everything, Ruthie. It's behind us now."

"I just don't want you to hold it against Nick. He didn't instigate anything. I would have gone on my own. I nearly bled to death. He probably saved my life."

"I'm sorry you felt you couldn't come to me. Times were different then."

"I know I could have come to you. That's why I feel so guilty. I know eventually you could have handled it. I didn't know it would be my last chance. I know you would have accepted my child."

Ruthie held her hands to her face and took several deep breaths. The sweet, sweet smell of the baby still lingered and comforted her.

On August 1, Sam Singer pulled his white Mark IV into the alley behind Nick's and blasted his horn three times. As usual, his tenants obediently lined up in 112-degree heat to pay him his rents. All the while Sam remained in his car, the air-conditioning blasting, opening and closing the power window to receive the cash. Occasionally Sam clipped a finger, causing the lessor to lose control of the bills, and for a moment it was as though Sam occupied one of those grab-all-the-cash wind bubble contraptions as money rained down around him.

Sam expected that, as usual, the only two tenants who paid by check would wait for Sam to come to them—Kenny and Thomas Quintero. Astonishingly both appeared outside his car almost simultaneously, though Thomas was accompanied by his daughter Soila.

But Kenny almost charged the car, causing Sam to rear back in his seat. *"I want to talk to you!* Don't leave without coming to see me!"

"What's eating you?"

Kenny waved the newspaper in front of Sam's windshield. "You know exactly what's eating me! You promised us, Sam!"

"Calm down, calm down. I'll be with you in a minute."

Kenny glared at him, turning and pushing past a startled Thomas Quintero. As he passed a trash can, he kicked it hard enough to send it toppling. Once Kenny was gone, Sam cautiously lowered his window to address Quintero. Thomas nudged Soila, handing her an envelope, bulging with cash.

"Mr. Sam?" Thomas said, nudging Soila impatiently.

"What can I do for ya, Quintero?" Sam lit his cigar. The air-conditioning continued to blast. Thomas and his little girl bent to his window like unlit melting candles.

"This is the down payment on the house." Soila held out the envelope. "Five thousand dollars!" Ruby's life savings.

Sam's eyes bulged. She waved the envelope in his face.

"It's all cash!"

"Look little girl . . ." Sam decided he better get out of the car, a gesture which caused Thomas's face to fill with hope. Sam mopped his brow.

"It's his dream," Soila added, her father's intercessor. "It's why he got legal. To own our house."

Thomas whispered something to her.

"He says he's sorry he called you names."

"Gee, it's awfully hot out here." Sam hesitated. In all of his life he never dreamed Quintero could come up with this kind of cash. "That's real sweet, honey." He nodded to her and then to Thomas. "But I can't accept this."

"But it's cash!" she said, her tone suggesting she thought cash was a word that fixed everything with Sam Singer. Then Thomas darkened, sensing something was going wrong. He demanded for her to translate.

She answered.

Thomas began shouting in Spanish. Then in English he said angrily, *"What's wrong with my money?"*

"Nothing," Sam stammered, and regretted getting out of his car. He backed toward it, but Thomas pressed toward him. Behind him faces were peering over their fences. Several younger men dropped to the ground with soft, sickening thuds.

"See, I'm selling your house with all the others. Together. Explain it to him, honey," he urged Soila. "I'm selling 'em all together. The whole block. See? I can't split 'em up."

"You're selling our house?" Soila was appalled. *"Why not to us? What's wrong with us?"*

Thomas was livid, and Soila rattled off Sam's answer in vivid Spanish. Sam quickly opened his door and slid into the driver's seat. Then he started his engine. Thomas Quintero's pale disappointment was presently converting to rage.

Behind him were all the neighbors he wanted to save face with. It had been Thomas's hope that purchasing the house would offset the disgrace Inez's being sick with AIDS had brought to him and his children. He was all ready to turn and announce to his neighbors that he, Thomas Quintero, had worked hard, become a U.S. citizen, and saved enough to buy his own little house. He could hear their cheers, or better, had actually savored their envy.

"I'm sorry." Sam shook his head and slowly began to drive away, and in his rearview mirror, all he could see were Thomas Quintero's angry eyes.

Passing Kenny's open kitchen door, he pressed down on his gas pedal, because if Quintero took it bad, Kenny's was a conversation he couldn't face right now.

"Sit down, Misty, you'll get hit by a plane." Misty was standing on the North Runway of the Palm Springs International Airport. Logan and Drew hung outside on the fence near Ramon Road.

"Misty—"

In the distance Drew could see a plane on approach. Misty saw it too, and she started to edge farther away from them, deeper down the runway.

"You'd think those assholes in the tower would send security or somethin'," Logan suggested.

"Or somethin'—" Drew pounded the chain link fence with the heel of his hand. "Misty!"

Misty twirled on the runway. The approaching jet was signaling the tower. Suddenly the runway was ablaze with flashing lights. Misty imagined she was on stage, maybe a rock star, maybe a dramatic actress.

"Misty, for God's sakes, come back here! Now! Christ, I've gotta go get her." Drew quickly scaled the fence, swearing as he cut himself on the barbed wire. Misty was retreating deeper into the runway, closer toward the terminals. Even in the darkness, Logan could see the landing gear of the 737, the wing flaps adjusting. Misty lingered in a spot then she sank to her knees.

Drew tackled her just as the belly of the plane roared overhead. He held her ears, and the din of the jet engines nearly burst his own. In the distance they could see flashing lights, and finally airport security was on its way. After yanking Misty to her feet, both of them ran sprinting for the fence. Both of them were cut and bleeding, but Misty seemed really invigorated.

"We have to get home," said Drew. "I'm bleeding like a stuck pig."

"I wanna go back to Cathedral City."

"It's a loser, Misty—"

But Misty knew she was wearing him down.

"She confessed the whole thing to me. On tape. About her, Zola, and the kids. The whole thing."

"So where's the tape?"

Sam didn't respond. They all knew who had the tape.

"This hasn't been easy on me either."

"I don't understand how two million bucks can be bad news to anyone," Kenny interrupted. Sam and Nick were seated in the lounge. It was late, and Kenny had just locked up.

"Let him *finish*," Nick said with irritation. Kenny sank heavily into the booth next to him. They looked across the table at Sam.

"Now, about Ruthie," Sam said quietly. He fidgeted with a cigar, rolling it back and forth in his fingers without lighting it. "I'm afraid my girl is in trouble. She's got bad, bad depression. Doctor thinks I've gotta put her in a hospital. Now it's none of my business, but she loves you both and I'd think more of you if you could put your troubles behind you now and give her a call."

"We'll visit her tomorrow," Nick said. Kenny nodded.

"This isn't gonna be easy to say, but it changes my feelings about hanging on to Cathedral City. Pressure's pretty high to sell. We've had some troubles. Fact is, I want out. You know about the offer. What you don't know is that it includes a pretty healthy share to you guys."

"What about the rest of your tenants?" Kenny erupted.

"When did you get to be such a hothead?" Sam responded. "Now lemme finish here. Under the circumstances, you're lucky I'm having this discussion at all. Fact is, they'll all be taken care of too. I'll pay 'em to move. Expenses and then some. They already know. A few of 'em are disappointed but I can't help that. I'm just saying Ruthie and I will be more than fair. Enough to relocate and get set up."

"I don't *want* to relocate, Sam," Kenny insisted. *"You stood right in the kitchen and promised me you wouldn't sell."*

"That was before." Sam replied evenly. "This is now. I've got no wiggle room. Read the letter yourself. We're all getting evicted. You can move up to Palm Springs. Lots of you guys are buying houses, starting businesses."

"I don't want to go where I wasn't *allowed* before, just because they want our money."

Sam looked at them and grinned good-naturedly. "It's the way of the world, kid. I'm kinda surprised you didn't know that."

"What are you fighting so hard for?" Nick exclaimed. "You won't be here anyway."

They fell silent. Sam looked up from his hands. "That so?"

"You haven't *told* him?"

"I haven't told anybody but you and Pablo," Kenny said.

"Who else do you know?" Nick retorted. He threw back his head and laughed.

"Good point, Nick." Kenny replied, gritting his teeth. "My thoughts exactly."

"Where's he going?" Sam demanded. Fear was rising up in his throat. The possibility that Nick and Kenny would not remain together filled him with cold regret. "Where's he going?"

Nick looked at Kenny. "Mexico."

"Mexico. On a trip? But you're going with him."

"No, Sam. He's going alone. For good."

Sam felt like all the air had been sucked out of the room. He felt like his mother had died. That Ruthie was leaving him. He felt that if Kenny and Nick couldn't make it, they were all in jeopardy. No marriage was safe.

Kenny and Nick looked at him in astonishment.

"You okay, Sam?"

"I gotta get going. I'll keep you apprised. I gotta guard the alley."

"Sam?"

Sam just sat with a sad look on his face, gazing around the bar. Kenny looked over at him expectantly. All Nick could do was smile and shrug.

"I'm gonna go out back and guard the alley." Sam stood up. "You take a day or two to come to your senses. You'll come around to my way of thinking. You'll agree it's for the best. Now remember to call Ruthie."

They both watched him trudge sadly through the door to the alley."

Nick and Kenny sat in silence for several minutes, Nick's head propped up by his hand, leaning on his elbow, Kenny facedown on folded arms.

Nick spoke first. "I want it to be over. I want out. We can split the money and go our separate ways, but I don't want to stay in Cathedral City any longer. Everything is different. I'm tired."

"I'm sorry," Kenny offered. "It's all my fault."

"No. Don't say that. But maybe you could do something for me."

"What?"

"Explain."

He looked over at Kenny and smiled. Kenny sat up. He started to speak but he couldn't. Then he tried again.

"I can't explain," he said simply. "I just started to feel feelings for her I never saw coming. No one was more surprised than I."

"Maybe I was."

"You probably were."

Nick stood up. He went behind the bar and searched through a stack of CDs. He found a favorite Frank Sinatra album. He selected a track, and quiet music filled the bar. He picked up a microphone and mimed "Put Your Dreams Away" to Kenny, imitating Sinatra to every hand gesture, every single note.

"Come here," Nick beckoned to Kenny. "It's all gone to hell. One dance."

Kenny pulled himself up to his feet. He moved over to Nick, who took his hand and pulled him close. They clung together clumsily while the song finished, not really dancing—just holding.

At the end of the song, Kenny gazed down to where Nick's head rested on his shoulder. Behind him in the mirror he saw how much confusion registered in his own face. But he also saw Nick's relieved expression and Kenny smiled. He had no conclusion to draw from the events of the previous year. No reasons or excuses. He could no more judge the mysteries of why any two people come together, remain together, or why they grow apart.

Regardless of the journey he was about to make, Kenny still believed that steadfastness was worthier than excitement. Nick had taught him that. Nick, in fact, had loved more in the dynamic of their life together, had martyred himself to Kenny's loneliness. Of the two of them, who had been the orphan after all?

Kenny pulled Nick close. In place of romantic love, devotion would have to do.

Several minutes later Kenny offered to drive with him up to the house.

"I'll follow you," Nick said. "I just want to sit here alone for a few more minutes."

When Kenny left through the alley, he saw Sam dozing in his car and decided not to wake him. The sky was black, a breeze was up, and he climbed in the Scout and drove away.

When Nick stepped into the alley and stood fumbling to lock the door, he turned around to find a beautiful young girl smiling at him.

"Hello." She grinned.

"Hello, young lady! It's a lovely night, isn't it?"

Behind her a white Blazer rolled into view. Several young men hopped stealthily to the ground and formed a semicircle behind her.

Nick took a deep breath. Across the street he was surprised to see the lights on at Judy's. Inside Judy was serving breakfast. They were all there. Dean Martin. Sammy Davis, Jr.

Frank Sinatra on the street mugging through the window to his buddies.

Then a car pulls up. Ruthie gets out. Mink coat. Hair up. Looking like a million bucks but crying. Standing across the street and searching the café for Sam. The men all ogle her but she ignores them. She crosses over.

A man approaches her. She tries to ignore him. Looks up.

Frank Sinatra.

Did she? Nick paused to study Sam, sleeping in the Lincoln in the shadows across the alley.

She was a lady.

Sinatra cajoles her and Ruthie does an abrupt about-face.

She runs back across the street to the parking lot of Nick's.

Nick the Sinatra imitator is waiting for her.

"We've made a terrible mistake," Ruthie cried. "I'm pregnant. The baby can't possibly be Sam's. It'll kill him. I've gotta find a doctor."

"Okay," he relented. "Okay. I've heard about a doctor in Mexicali."

When they finally found the right clinic, they signed in as man and wife. The whirling fan in the waiting room of Dr. Pena's offices reminded Nick of the fans over Sam's bar before they put in the central air. At the time, everybody smoked—the bartenders, the cocktail waitresses, and most of the clientele. The smoke collected on the ceiling, filtering the soft overhead light. To enter Sam's in those days felt mysterious and foreign. It took a while for your eyes to acclimate to the goings-on in the bar.

Sam never worked the door; that's why he hired Nicky. Sam always sat in a booth in the back, cigar gripped in his front choppers, his gold accessories glinting from the lights in the bar. This booth had the best view of the lounge, which was why Sam could always keep an eye on Ruthie. Not that he didn't trust her. He just didn't trust the desert rats and hoodlums who frequented the joint.

Nick and Ruthie became fast friends, which was a relief to Sam. He was good for her, made her laugh. And he was honest. Sam could keep one eye on the cash register, one eye on the bartender's pour, one eye on the front door, and one eye on Ruthie, all at the same time. Sam had the eyes of a fly.

The night they decided to elope, Ruthie had been down, and Sam couldn't figure out why. He figured she was burning out from the night life in the club. She sang two sets a night, six nights a week. This was no life for her. She claimed she wanted children, a home. Sam kept pressing her to get married but she kept putting him off. He couldn't figure out what was eating her.

Ruthie had big sad green eyes, and that night she was singing ballads and had the boozed-out audience eating out of the palm of her hand. People drank more then. It was socially acceptable, and at Sam's they drank till they cried. Sam was playing black jack with a few of his cronies. He'd asked her to elope that night, but he proposed once a month so it was nothing new.

In the middle of a song she abruptly stopped. It was late and nobody really cared, but Sam looked up and asked her what was wrong.

"I need some air," she shrugged. "I'm going for a walk."

"I'm ahead here," Sam shrugged. "Can you wait ten minutes?" He was surrounded by a mountain of poker chips. "If I leave now, it'd be unsportsmanlike."

"You don't have to come, Sammy. I just need five minutes. It's so close in here."

"Take Nicky with you. I don't want you walking in the desert alone."

Nick was chatting with a group of dapper-looking men at the end of the bar. He was telling a story, and they were roaring with laughter. The same small group came in every night, good-looking, well-dressed, clever-talking young men.

"Nick!" Sam barked. Nick glanced over. "Take my fiancée outside for a walk. She needs company."

"I don't need company."

Nick abruptly left his friends and moved to the piano. Together he and Ruthie disappeared through the back entrance to the bar.

The night was sultry, and pitch black. The air swathed with earthy perfume. Ruthie didn't say anything, just started walking. Nick followed, several steps behind.

"Sammy asked me to elope again."

"You should. He loves you."

"I'm thinking about going back inside to accept, but I wanted to talk to you first." She turned and held out her hand to him. "Let's take the car and go for a drive."

"He'll miss us."

"I'm about to give him my entire life. I'm owed a half hour."

"Okay." Nick smiled. He tossed his cigarette to the desert floor. "You drive. I'm too drunk."

They climbed into Sam's Caddy convertible. He always left the keys in the ignition, daring any fool to steal it. She started the engine and they roared off. She switched on the radio to her favorite jazz station. They drove north into the desert. The wind whipped their faces. Nicky edged next to her on the seat. He reached over and kissed the side of her cheek while she drove. They were affectionate like that. Nick loved to touch her and she let him.

Abruptly she turned off the main road and drove several hundred yards down a dirt road. They were surrounded by open desert. Stars everywhere.

"What's up?" he laughed.

"Nicky," she said, and began to cry.

Instead of saying anything, he put his arm around her and began to kiss her eyes, the side of her face. They both knew Sam would never give up. Was probably her best option. He loved her. Would treat her well. If she wasn't in love with him, what were her other options? In her world, the jazz nights didn't offer much else but different kinds of Sams or lowlife gigolos. Nice men didn't hang around in joints. Sam for all his coarseness was ultimately a nice man.

"Go with him." Nicky caressed her. "He loves you. It's better to be the one who's loved."

"You would know," she whispered.

He hesitated. "We know who I am, dear. Do you want that kind of life?"

"But can't you just—"

"No." He shook his head. "I can't. I want the same things you want."

"I want you to have them." She smiled simply. "I'll make you a deal. I'll go back and accept Sam's proposal. Just kiss me once."

"You promise?"

"I promise." She closed her eyes.

Nick pulled her close. The lovemaking was quick. Passionate. Careless. Twenty minutes later they were roaring back across the desert to Cathedral City.

Thirty minutes later Sam was announcing his engagement. They were driving to Vegas that night.

"Señor." A voice woke Nick out of his daydream. He opened his eyes. An attendant was shaking him awake. "Complications, *señor.*"

"What? What's wrong?"

"Come back with me." And Nick was rushed through the white door where he saw an anemic Ruthie laying on a gurney, the sheets crimson with her blood. Two Mexican doctors and three attendants were working furiously to stop her hemorrhaging.

"We need permission to give your wife a hysterectomy."

"Hysterectomy!"

"If we don't, she'll die."

When a dozing Sam Singer heard the scuffling, he woke up, and from his vantage point couldn't believe what he was seeing: four white teens, kicking at Nick, their Gap T-shirts and jeans covered in their blood.

He pulled out his gun, checking for the safety. *"You stop right there or I'll shoot you bastards!"* his voice rang out.

Misty was huddled gleefully over Nick's body, turned to see Sam advancing, her eyes glazing over. She raised her third finger and flipped him off. *"Fuck you!"* she shrieked. "You're fucking *next,* you old Jew!" Her words blew over him like hot, ugly wind. Logan fell back at the sight of Sam's gun.

Drew came up from nowhere, tackling Sam from behind. Sam was so solidly built that his sheer body weight surprised Drew, but the force caused Sam's prized pistol to fire, the bullet impaling Misty, her body flopping against the cool white skin of the Blazer.

"Jesus, he shot me, Drew!"

Logan began to hustle her into the Blazer, leaving Drew to deal with a stunned Sam Singer, who lay facedown on the pavement. Drew ran to the Blazer and shortly after they were roaring down the alley.

Sam tried to stand up, but couldn't because his arm and his chest felt like they were engulfed in flame. Nick lay bloodied and groaning in a heap several feet away. In a moment Sam heard footsteps, and looked up to see Soila Quintero standing in the alley looking at him curiously.

"Help me, little girl. He's bleeding. Call the police."

But instead of running back into the house, she approached him carefully as if he were a rare curiosity, something she didn't recognize at all.

Sam pulled himself to his knees. "Little girl, help us."

And she came even closer, staring at him impassively, as if she didn't understand plain English.

Sam was breathing heavily now, and light was firing in his eyes. When Soila didn't obey his command, he became angry and began to berate her.

"C'mon!" he roared. *"Cantcha see we're in trouble here?"*

She recoiled from his anger as if the words exuded a wretched odor.

"Call 911, doncha understand plain English? Call the police! Call 'em goddamn you! Fucking bitch! *Fucking Mexie!"*

And Soila began to back away as Sam sank slowly back to the ground.

She took a seat on a crate outside her gate. Sam looked up at her, pleading like a dying old mutt dog. "Aw c'mon, that's just my way of talkin'. Please, little girl, help us. Help us," Sam begged her, his voice little more than a whisper.

But Soila just sat and watched.

Finally Sam lurched up, summoning all the strength he had. For a moment he seemed held up by air, and fell back down like an ancient gnarled old tree and after that he didn't move.

One by one the tenants of his houses began opening their gates and filing into the alley to see what the commotion was all about and in the distance sirens could be heard.

Moments later Kenny's truck roared back down the alley just before the police cars arrived. In the distance he could see a body lying prone in the middle of the alley. Near him, a young girl with long dark hair, knelt on the ground, cradling a figure in her lap, her arms encircling him, gazing down into his face with a mixture of great love and sadness.

It was Soila Quintero. Cradling Nick's body in her arms.

"*What have they done?*" he cried out to the fences as he ran to them. "My God, what have they done? You have to tell me, they'll blame it on you!"

But no one came from their gates to tell him.

The mayor of Cathedral City was dead.

26

Communion

Cathedral City was thrown into turmoil with the murder of Sam Singer and the violent assault on Nick. Nick suffered injuries equivalent to a head-on automobile crash. They broke his nose and his cheekbones and shattered his jaw. He nearly choked on his own teeth. He suffered a broken collarbone, broken left arm and wrist, five broken ribs, and a punctured lung. They thought he'd probably sustained permanent brain damage and wouldn't be able to talk again. He proved them wrong within twenty-four hours.

Ruthie's mental health virtually collapsed. She returned to her bedroom the morning after and didn't really leave the house for six months. She stopped dying her hair, bathed only weekly, and slept most of the day on the old couch in the den.

She only had Kenny to look after her. When Nick recovered enough to be up and around, they'd take a daily drive up to Palm Springs, where a chronically depressed Ruthie and a badly diminished Nick would sit out on the cabana and mumble about old times in Cathedral City. Without telling her what she was taking, Kenny obtained a doctor's prescription and began to administer antidepressants. If the grieving didn't go away, at least it subsided and slowly Ruthie began to feel better.

Their talks cheered Nick, and although Kenny was advised he'd never be a hundred percent, often the old glint would come in his eye, a dream take hold, and Kenny knew Nick was scheming about the future.

The question of the sale of the property was forestalled because Sam was dead and Ruthie was incompetent to understand all its implications. Sam's parcel remained where it stood on the night he died, while all around it old Cathedral City had been leveled to make way for new construction.

Sam's tenants were still ensconced, but no landlord or agent on his behalf came at the first of the month to collect their agreed-upon rents. True to her vision, Ruby the waitress soon moved in with the Quinteros and assumed Inez's position as the matriarch of the family. They bought a new house out in north Cathedral City. Alex moved down to Indio with friends in a gang, Ruby spoiled Anita, ignored Soila, and turned the old aunt into her personal maid. Thomas continued his work at the Arte de Sonora without incident and lived his life as if Inez Quintero had never existed. He refused to get an HIV test and never told Ruby there might be a problem.

After the alphabet streets, the houses in the Cathedral Canyon cove started getting bigger and nicer, not glamorous by Palm Springs or Rancho Mirage standards, but some with unparalleled views. The owners of these homes suffered the short drive through the Cathedral City ghetto but many didn't like it, and would have been happy to see every shanty house torn down and replaced by a super shopping center.

Nick and Kenny lived on Las Tunas, a cul de sac off of Chuperosa. The house had fallen into disrepair, and the neighbors were not very happy about it.

"I thought homosexuals improved property," one of the neighbor ladies was heard to say.

"Well, something should be said about the way the lawn looks. It's bad enough that we drive through slums to get home."

"Maybe they need a hand," offered Buddy, the beefy next-door neighbor to the right of Kenny and Nick. "Maybe I'll just mow the lawn for 'em," and the ladies tittered how neighborly it was of him to suggest. Next to Kenny and Nick, Buddy was regarded as the next least desirable neighbor, largely because his kids were fat and he liked to work on old cars in the carport of his house.

That morning Buddy came by to mow the lawn. Nick saw him, peering through their curtains with slitted eyes. His beating had taken a terrible toll. His vision was stilled blurred, he'd lost most of his upper teeth, and now he was adjusting to his dentures. To his credit, he remained sober through it all.

Kenny stood behind to see what he was looking at. When they fell back asleep and woke up in the late afternoon, the sprinklers were on and the lawn glistened. Several hours later Buddy returned with a fertilizer cart. He waved to them jauntily when Kenny parted the curtain to see what he was going to do next.

"Did you hire him to take care of the lawn?"

"No." Nick thought for a moment. "Did you?"

"No." Kenny waved to Buddy and allowed the curtain to drop.

In the morning Kenny went out to survey the effort, and was invigorated to see the lawn looking neat and green. Standing at the end of the driveway he suddenly rubbed his eyes. Words seemed to be appearing in the grass, burning the lawn where Buddy had left them a special message in fertilizer: FAGOTS

Kenny could then hear laughter, Buddy's two fat sons, hysterical as they stood at the edge of the lawn. Kenny ran to turn on the sprinklers. When he reached the nozzle, he could see that the handle had been snapped off. There was no way to water the lawn. Swearing, he ran around the side of the house and returned with a hose. His first order of business was to water down the two fat neighbor kids.

The blast of cold water shocked them, and they retreated screaming from their posts back to the house, yelling for their dad.

Kenny began spraying the lawn, desperately trying to diffuse the scorching fertilizer, but he was too late. The epithets won, and so had good neighbor Buddy.

Nick strolled out to see what all the commotion was about.

"What's going on?"

"Can't you read?"

One of the neighbor ladies, unaware of the vulgarity emblazoned on the lawn, came out on her front porch to tell them how beautiful the lawn looked.

"Isn't that better?"

He ushered her over for a closer look. She ran back to her house.

All Kenny could do was to continue to water the lawn in vain. There wasn't any fight left in either one of them. The house was three months in foreclosure and the cars had bald tires.

He looked up at the sky. "Don't bother," he told Kenny. "It looks like rain."

Last night he dreamed they were getting married in the chapel at St. Louis in Cathedral City. Father Gene officiated. Maria wore a long white dress and looked so luminously beautiful Kenny thought he was the luckiest man in the world. Nick was his best man. Pablo a groomsman.

Ruthie was Maria's bridesmaid, and Sam gave her away. Little Anita was the flower girl, Inez and Soila, maids of honor. Concha smiled proudly from the front pew.

All the patrons of the bar attended. Ruthie sang "Oh Promise Me."

Today Kenny would finish packing the Scout with the last of twenty years of belongings. He was worried about the tires and prayed they wouldn't have a blowout because he had no spare and no money to pay for one if the need came up.

Ruthie continued to offer, but they both refused her. They needed to figure things out on their own. Money would justify staying on. They were finished with the desert.

He had ninety-two dollars of available credit on his MasterCard, and forty-three dollars in cash and change hidden in a sock. Nick lay dead to the world, snoring next to him, and for a moment Kenny allowed himself the mirage that all was well. The bed had been pushed under the open wooden-framed window overlooking the date palm grove, and as the sun warmed the damp desert floor, a subtle mist crept among the date palms, and the sky and the distant hills faded back and forth from lighter to darker shades of blue.

Now Kenny had one last thing to do.

Father Gene was surprised to see him kneeling in his usual spot. So surprised, in fact, that he was certain he was imagining him. It was midmorning, and they were alone in the sanctuary. Votive candlelight flickered under the statue of the Virgin Mary. Father Gene had only a week till he retired. Festivities were planned later that afternoon. The entire remaining congregation of Cathedral City was assembling to say goodbye to him.

Kenny sat back on the pew and leaned forward, resting his chin on his forearms.

"I came to say goodbye. And I'd like to confess, Father."

Emotion welled up in Father Gene's throat. Together he and Kenny knelt in prayer.

"Bless me, Father, for I have sinned. It has been twenty-one years since my last confession."

"How have you sinned, my son?"

"I'm guilty of the sin of confusion," Kenny began.

"Confusion . . . that's no sin."

"Then envy. Envy of everybody who lives a normal life."

"What's normal? I don't think I know what *normal* means."

"An ordinary family. A mom and dad. Sons who play football. Daughters who serve. Dad goes to work. Mom stays home. Dinner at six. Dad's stern but loving. Mom is gentle and funny. Keeps her figure—wears high heels to church. Teaches Sunday school." And he paused, adding pointedly, "They're welcome at church. They have the right demographics. The right credentials. No curve balls. That's my envy."

"Jesus wasn't so worried about them. Remember Mary Magdalene."

"I couldn't leave him behind." And Kenny began to cry. "I loved the church. I wonder if the lucky ones know what they have."

"The lucky ones?"

"The families who don't have a daughter who gets pregnant. A kid who kills. A son who's gay. They told me they'd drive me out with whips and chains."

"Who told you?"

"The Christians."

"Fanatics."

"I never had a problem with God. I need to express, Father Gene, how much it has hurt me to be reviled by the Catholic Church. Why, then, was I saved from the flood in Mexico?"

"Has it been worth it to give up your life for him?"

Kenny began to unravel right before the eyes of the old priest. He didn't seem to hear him. He was lost in his own grief. His regrets. "She sent me a letter. She told me she loved me. She told me that she and the baby are well looked after. She said under the circumstances that she would never forgive herself for taking me away from Nick. Not now. Nick needed me more than she did, she wrote. Staying with him only made her love me more! To leave him, she said, would be an affront to God."

Kenny fell to his knees and grasped the frayed hem of Father Gene's robe. Father Gene hesitated at first, but then began to stroke Kenny's hair, gently massaging his neck and shoulders, and Kenny buried his face in the drape of the old priest's cassock.

"You didn't answer my question, son. Has it been worth it to give up your life for him?"

For Nick or God, Kenny wondered.

"Yes," he finally answered. "I had no choice."

"I choose to look at your deliverance as a measure of *God's love for Nick.* You were called into service," he gently reminded him. "I commend you, son, for honoring your vows."

And then Father Gene led Kenny into the sanctuary to administer the Eucharist.

This the Lamb of God who takes away the sins of the world. Happy are those who are called to his supper.

Lord, *Kenny whispered,* I am not worthy to receive you but only say the word and I shall be healed.

The body of Christ.

Amen

The blood of Christ.

Amen.

Standing in the parking lot Father Gene noticed a bouquet of flowers on the St. Anthony statue donated by Frank Sinatra. He looked up questioningly at Kenny.

"Did something happen I don't know about?"

"He died today." Kenny shrugged. "I haven't had the heart to tell Nicky."

Ruthie came to say goodbye. She wasn't up to dying her hair again, but at least she was dressed in clean slacks and a blouse. Before they left, Nick cut her hair, but the nerve damage in his trembling hands caused her bangs to come out a little uneven. He got so exasperated he kept trimming. Kenny gently put a stop to it when they were an inch above her eyebrows.

"I wish you'd accept my help. I wish you'd stay! You can have the land under the bar. You can sell it and relocate in Palm Springs. Everything is so much better now. All the fun new businesses. The gay conventions. Houses are being snapped up right and left."

Nick's eyes brightened. He became animated. "Key West. Fire Island. Provincetown. Palm Springs!"

"No," said Kenny firmly. "I'd feel like a hypocrite. I refuse to spend *one dime* in that greedy, anti-Semitic, racist, homophobic whore of a town."

"You have to be patient. They're *trying,*" Ruthie insisted.

"It'll never be like Cathedral City. Not like it was. The weekend tourists don't want to hang out in Speedos all day just to pig out on pot roast and honey-glazed carrots before dancing the night away at the local dance halls. They want skinless chicken breasts and plain steamed broccoli zested with lemon rind." He studied Nick. "We've talked about this. We need to start over clean."

Nick relented, shaking his head. "Kenny's right. We're dinosaurs.

Cathedral City has driven us out. We'll do what Kenny wants to do for a change. We're gonna keep it simple."

"But how can you start over with nothing? You can't just drive off into the desert without a plan, without anyplace to go."

"That's funny advice, coming from *you,*" Nick observed wryly. "I've started over before and I can start over again."

"And I'll get a job as a fry cook," Kenny said. "Or work with my hands. I don't need all this stuff." He glanced around the living room, packed with boxes for the Good Will. He allowed Nick to keep a few of his favorite mementos. Kenny would take the remainder of his best dolls. Even after paring back, the back of the Scout would be overloaded with possessions.

The house had been sold for little more than the price of the first mortgage, a secured note payable to the Betty Ford Center, and three years of back taxes Nick had never bothered to pay. Whatever remained was given to Carmen, Gabriel, and Miguel, in gratitude, Kenny said, for all their years of loyalty.

Before they pulled away, Ruthie pulled out a small suitcase from the trunk of her car. "Just a few odds and ends I've been saving to give you. Sam would want you to have them."

Kenny acquiesced. He took the case. The only place to store it was up front, under Nick's feet.

It was already hot, and the sun burned any mist and cloud cover away. Nick took little gulps of air from the open window as he leaned heavily against the passenger door. Kenny reached around behind him to lock it.

"I guess we're about to have another adventure," Kenny observed, trying to sound bright.

"I wanna go home," Nick muttered.

"Home is you and me," Kenny said, patting his knee. His fingers danced away from skin and bone. For his trip across the desert, Nick wore white linen pants, a red belt, a white shirt, and red espadrilles. Natty to the bitter end. "Try to sleep."

"It's so hot . . ."

"The sun'll be down soon. Don't give up hope."

"Oh, we must never give up hope, dear. As long as we're together we'll be okay . . . I love you, Kenny," Nick whispered.

The old priest flashed through Kenny's mind. "Has it been worth it to give up your life for him?" Kenny smiled over at Nick, who was sleeping now, his head resting in the crook of the truck door where it joined the seat. When Nick slept now, he took tiny little breaths, snoring gently. He looked both childlike and wizened. His still handsome face was a road map of fading scars. If they bothered him, he never complained.

"I love you too, Nicky," Kenny said.

Later that night, as the truck crossed the Nevada border, and chugged up a short incline, the ropes holding the tarp tight over their loosely packed belongings gave way. The tarp snapped back like a wild sail and the truck veered, all of their things spilling out onto the freeway.

"God damn it!" Kenny struggled to keep the wheel straight. After holding it steady, he was able to pull it over to the side of the road. Swearing, he jumped down from the cab and surveyed a lifetime of possessions, scattered on the highway like junk.

"God damn it!" he shouted. "This too?" He shook his fists at the stars.

Fearful that another car would come along and have an accident, he spent an hour in the darkness dragging boxes and suitcases and miscellaneous pots and pans over to the side of the road. Clothing from four decades was scattered all over the road.

The blacktop was littered with dolls. Each item was a memory rushing at him, and he hurt so badly he began to hurl them back onto the truck. Finally Nick opened his door and hopped to the ground.

He rounded the other side of the truck and began tossing everything overboard.

"What the hell do you think you're doing?"

"I think our work is finished here." Nick suddenly looked very invigorated. "Have a little faith, Kenny."

And after thinking for a moment, Kenny stacked all their possessions neatly on the desert floor. After wrapping them in the tarp, he added a quickly scrawled note. *Free.*

Several moments later they drove across the Nevada state line, where Nick wanted to stop at the Good Luck Casino and insisted on feeding the last of their change into a slot machine while Kenny stood back and let him.

Long-suffering wasn't practical so close to the edge. It was time to bow to blind optimism. On the last quarter Nick won eight hundred bucks.

Back in the truck his feet got caught up in Ruthie's little suitcase. Kenny had stayed behind to use the bathroom.

"What's in here, anyway?" He muttered to himself. He popped it open. Inside, in stacks of hundreds, was Ruthie's mad money. Over a hundred thousand dollars. Kenny was coming. He quickly closed it up and put it back under his feet.

Kenny climbed in behind the wheel. He was jovial about Nick's luck in the casino. It appealed to his sense of humor. "We made it through our first day," he laughed. "See how God takes care of us? Where to now?"

"Let's just keep driving," Nick smiled. "I have a *good* feeling about Nevada."

Kenny stepped on the gas.

Behind them, California.

EPILOGUE

Kenny's Blessing

27

The Whitewater River

The Rand McNally map clearly details the Whitewater River extending from the northwestern edge of the Coachella Valley and spilling eastward across the desert cities of Whitewater, Palm Springs, Cathedral City, Rancho Mirage, Palm Desert, Bermuda Dunes, Indian Wells, La Quinta, Indio, Coachella, Thermal, and beyond.

A visitor unfamiliar with desert terrain might look at the map and expect exactly that, a cool river, and not an arid wash with rotted-out cactus, gila monsters, and big horn sheep, scuttling over sand and rock. The map makes it seem at times to be a wide, wide wash of river, which narrows erratically and then splays out again, not unlike the way water flung from a bucket hits a sidewalk.

Before the canals and bridges were built, a freak rain of furious intensity could dump six to eight inches on the mountain ranges flanking the Coachella Valley in a matter of minutes, and the resulting water would flash-flood the washes and slice the desert communities in half.

Hence, bridges started being built from the northeast—first over the freeway at the Palm Springs exit at 111, then over Indian Avenue, the highway connecting Desert Hot Springs to Palm Springs, and then Vista Chino, Ramon, but skipping Cathedral Canyon Drive.

When it rains, the storm channels flanking both sides of the Cathedral City cove fill with water, as does the wash a mile south of Highway 111. On stormy days, Cathedral City is an island unto itself, and in geological renderings it abstractly assumes the shape of a

Mexican peasant woman shielded under a serape, or a Madonna knelt in prayer.

In August the desert sky often whitens to an endless skein of condensation; purloined from swimming pools, irrigation ditches, public sprinkler systems, automobile radiators, purring swamp coolers, automatic misting systems at open-air cantinas; even human perspiration as die-hard retirees play early-morning golf on carefully groomed pastures of green.

Sometimes without warning the sky can change from blue to white to black in minutes, the heat so fierce that clouds explode like supernova water balloons, drenching the desert cities from Cabazon all way down to Indio without any warning at all. The rains pound the range of San Jacinto Mountains, washing onto the desert floor. Water floods streets and parking lots and date palm groves, cascading into the man-made washes till they, too, are overcome and spill over their banks.

A ghost river which rises and rages at will.

Ruthie popped a Prozac and stepped jauntily down the hall to her front door. The pills had the strangest effect on her. She didn't want to say anything for fear they'd take them away. She was in a hurry and had to get out to Cathedral City by ten-thirty. It was a beautiful Palm Springs morning but the weather forecast predicted rain for later that afternoon.

Most of the frame houses were torn down now, from Palm Canyon Drive to the Catholic church. The few remaining had been painted rich Mexican colors—Pepto Bismol pinks, radiant oranges, robin's egg blue—several even flew the Mexican flag.

Across the street, in the block which Judy had occupied, a huge parking lot was being paved, five acres of tar stretching to an enormous City Hall which obstructed the view of the desert floor and the distant purple hills.

But on her side of the street, the bar remained standing, in solitary complaint against the nature of progress. The developers intended to intimidate her, Ruthie knew, but she was resolved in her effort to re-open the bar. Shortly after Sam died, historical landmark status had been granted by the State of California.

Now they could never tear it down.

Ruthie parked in the shade behind the restaurant. When she got out of her car, she could see that the door to the kitchen was ajar, but unconcerned, she pushed her way inside. Ruthie looked around. The kitchen was immaculate, just the way Kenny had left it. An older man was placing a small new candle at the back of Kenny's old prayer box.

He turned to greet Ruthie.

"My name is Father Gene."

Before she could respond, she heard voices coming from the dining room.

"We forgot Holy Water," a younger woman complained.

"So we'll have to make do with this."

The door swung open and Pablo entered, holding it carefully for Maria, who followed him, in her arms a pretty baby girl with black hair and blue eyes.

"With *what?*" asked Father Gene.

Pablo held up a dusty bottle of Smirnoff.

"He wants to baptize my baby with vodka." Maria shook her head.

"To this kind of church vodka was Holy Water," Father Gene retorted.

The baby laughed and clapped her hands. Ruthie rushed forward to take her from Maria. "I brought a picture of Sam," she said. "It's in my bag."

"Here's Inez," Pablo offered up her photo. "She sends her love."

Inez now lived in Mexico with two of her brothers, who she discovered were both gay. She worked as a crisis counselor at a Guadalahara SIDA clinic for women. Pablo, Maria, and the baby were back in the United States with visas, courtesy of Pablo's mother and diplomat father.

"Kenny and Nick are already up there."

They assembled under the altar while Ruthie held the baby. Maria stepped forward and lit the candle, the light flickering on the images of Sam Singer, Inez Quintero, and lastly of Kenny and Nick. She kissed her fingers and touched each one, lingering on the image of Kenny.

Pablo poured a few drops of vodka on the back of her daughter's head.

"In the name of the Father, the Son, and the Holy Ghost."

They lowered their heads in prayer.

One evening, late that summer, Maria rounded the corner of the bar, now hers from Ruthie, holding the hand of her tiny daughter, Concha-Inez, only barely walking.

"Try always to look at the sky," she observed. "They can't touch the stars."

She referred to the monstrous shopping mall now erected across the street. As if on cue, directly opposite her restaurant, a garish Santa Fe mission-style bell tower rigged to change colors from blue, red, green, and yellow began to chime the strains of "Summer Wind."

Maria leaned down to pick up her little girl. Above them a new sign buzzed on. They looked up.

Cathedral City Café

Fine Cuisine From Mexico

A plaque in the corner of the newly refurbished restaurant stated: *This building has been designated as a State Historical Landmark.*

"Conchita!" Maria exclaimed to her daughter. "For Papa and Uncle Nick. So someday they can find us!" In the corner window of the lounge, a neon candle illuminated. Tomorrow the former governor of California would officiate at the grand opening of the Cathedral City City Hall and Entertainment Complex, touted as a climate-controlled environment for the entire family.

Maria could hear Ruthie singing. Holding Conchita, she rounded the side of the building and went inside. It was the tail end of Happy Hour. The lounge was packed. Ruthie stood at the microphone, hair slicked back, dressed in a man's suit and sporting a fedora on her head.

She was imitating Frank Sinatra.

From inside the bar, the music drifted lazily into the parking lot and scented the desert air with the past's perfume.